A Time to Disappear

Other books by Terrence Rundle West

Ripe for the Picking (2002)
Run of the Town (2006)
Not In My Father's Footsteps (2011)
The Methodist Man (2017)
A Time to Disappear (2023)

A Time to Disappear

A NORTHERN ONTARIO NOVEL

Terrence Rundle West

For my older brothers who answered the call
to fight fascist tyranny in WWII.

Harvey West who died on the beach
at Pourville (Dieppe) France, August 19, 1942

Howard West, who spent three and a half years of his youth
patrolling the icy North Atlantic on convoy duty, between
Halifax, Canada, and Londonderry, Northern Ireland.

Contents

PART FOUR
1950

PART FIVE
Northern Ontario, 1955

PART SIX
Hearst, Northern Ontario, 2022

Acknowledgements

I'm indebted to the people who provided information for this book, and to all those who rescued me from numerous blunders. Special heartfelt thanks to Peggy, the love of my life, who seldom failed to come up with the correct word when my mind had gone blank, advised caution on meandering secondary plots, worked tirelessly in the search of a fitting title, and who patiently edited the various drafts. Final touches to the book I attribute to Frank Pellow, Ernie Bies, Paivi Alto-Setala in Finland, my editor Susan Code McDougal who steered me onto a myriad of improvements, and to Magdalene Carson, who prepared the text and layout for printing, and who created a cover that is a work of art.

I also wish to acknowledge the help received from the late Mauno Jansson. Mauno shared his vivid recollections on two fronts—his vivid memory of those Finnish immigrants to Hearst who returned to their homeland to fight the invading Russians in 1939, as well as his experience working with German POWs employed by Newago Timber, in the 1943-45 period.

And I am grateful to my inveterate trapper friend, Tony Joanis, who set me straight on the ins and outs of trapping in the great boreal forests of Northern Ontario.

The genesis of *A Time to Disappear* goes back to the Finn adults of my youth, who aroused in me the deep respect for Finnish history and culture which I hope shines through this book. Namely:Johannes Hietala, Mauno Jansson, Ellen Niskanen, Vaino (Wayne) Halme, Henry and Ella Kurki, Tauno Suni, Albert and Allan Lähde, Helli Hietala, Anton Seabloom, Aero and Sivi Mäki, Jalo Kurki, Mr. Rantti, Ingrid Suutala, Martti Rasinpera, Elmi Saarikoski, Hilkka Leivo. Also my Finn classmates, in whose homes I played and always felt welcome as a child: Jackie Luoma, Toini Jansson, Mai, Miriam and Pentti Rasinpera, Aini Martin, Elizabeth Miller, Eila Aalto, Billy Koivisto, Veikko Koskinen, Allan Kurki, Doris and Helen Paasila.

A Time to Disappear

Preface

And into the forest I must go, to lose my mind
and find my soul."
— John Muir

Carve your name on hearts, not tombstones.
A legacy is what is etched into the minds of others,
and the stories they share about you.
— Shannon Adler

To every life there is a story. Most get told—family and friends see to that. And because they do, it becomes a link, sometimes even a legacy. But what of people who lead solitary lives—alone and adrift? When they pass on, does it follow that because no one comes forward to document their history there was never anything worth recording?

Raised over my parents' grocery store on the main corner of Hearst, Northern Ontario (1940–62), I encountered men who spent most of their lives hidden away in the bush—oddball-hermits, was how I thought of them then. They seldom came to town, and when they did it was because provisions were running low. I have a clear image of such men standing awkwardly off to the side, heads bent to avoid eye contact. Which suited clerks and customers alike, because these men often reeked—unwashed bodies, clothes, urine. They rarely spoke, and when they did it was often in foreign accents—Finn, Norwegian, Swede, Bulgarian, Belorussian.

Indelibly etched in my mind's eye is Mustafa, a Turk. When he died, my father, myself, the minister and the undertaker were the only ones at the funeral. Now, seven decades on, I ask myself: what was Mustafa's story? What drove him, and others like him, to seek the solitude of Northern Ontario's boreal forest? The assumption is that these men had been damaged. But why and how? What trauma, hazard, bad luck, or event had sent them scurrying to the bush. Each of them must have had a story—possibly an exciting and meaningful one.

A Time to Disappear, is a work of fiction, in which two men, one Finn and one German, find refuge deep in the bush. The inspiration comes from recollections of those mysterious, reclusive, bush-hermits of my youth. I've placed my characters in genuine historical events, and have tried to give them creditable stories—possibly ones not unlike that of the men I wish I'd taken the time to befriend and understand, so many years ago.

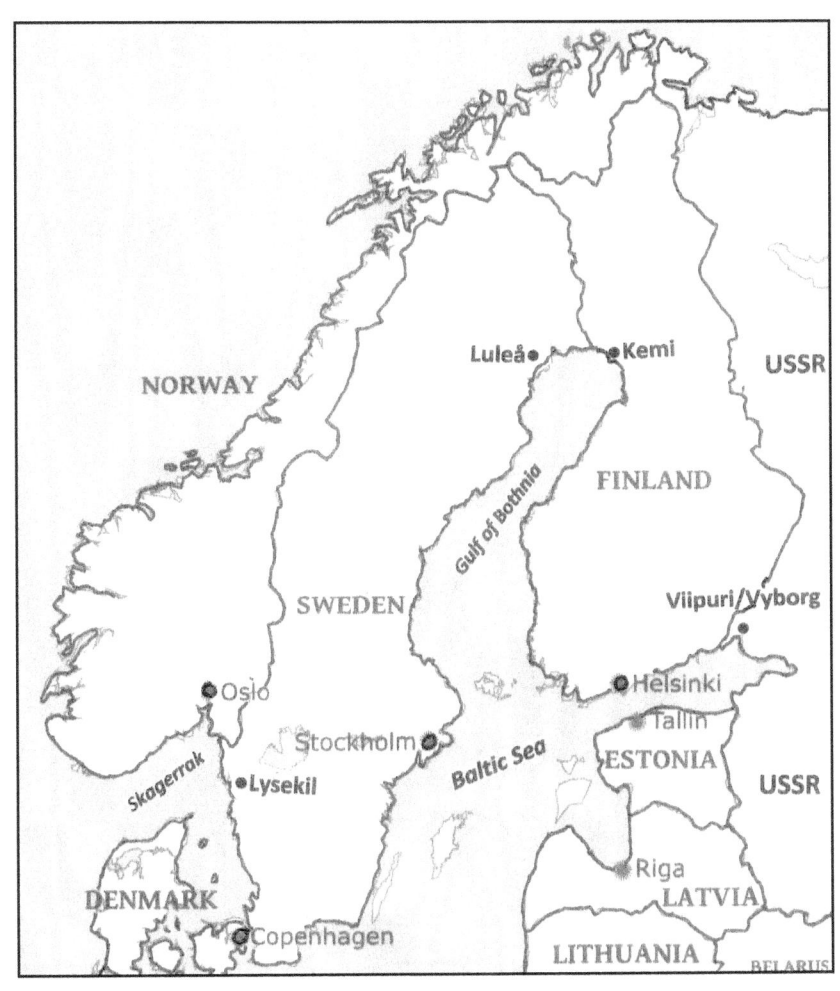

Map of Scandinavia

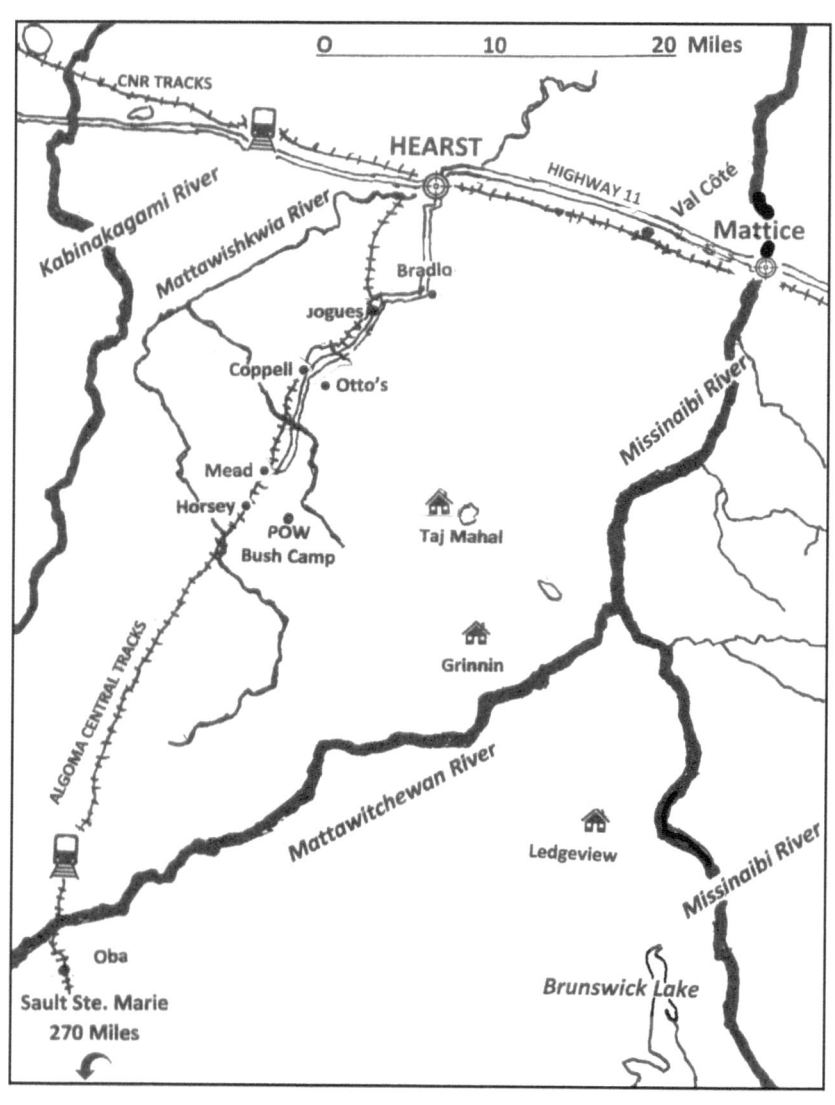

Map of Hearst Forest

PART ONE

Hearst,
Northern Ontario,
March 2022

1

The Photograph

Foyers des Pionniers,
Hearst, Northern Ontario,
March 2022

There's something mighty empowering about reaching old age and still being able to piss people off. Take the staff here at the home. One glimpse of me reaching for my parka of a cold January morning and they're all over me. Just last month the director marched into my room to read the Riot Act: "This roaming nonsense has got to stop, Mr. Martin," she said. "No more wandering around out there on your own. Our job is to keep you safe. Lose a toe to frostbite and heads will roll. Mine included. You wouldn't want to get me fired now, would you?"

I get it, but I have to occupy myself, somehow. Basket weaving and chair exercises just don't cut it. Not for me.

Fortunately, the doctor's on my side. God, how I love that young woman. Besides, when I sneak out, it's only to my little bush place on the river, upstream from the home, not a trek to Thunder House Falls on the Missinaibi. I've got a hidey-hole in a clump of black spruce up there that's become my special retreat. Sadly, none of the inmates here at the home seem keen on joining me. They're either too fond of their creature comforts, or too intimidated to break out. All of which makes it my own private moose yard.

Lately I've resorted to hiding my parka and boots in Sonny's closet. Sonny's my neighbour, four rooms down the hall. He's English, like me, which is probably why they put us close to each other. Frankly, I don't give a damn what his mother tongue happens to be, because we're not exactly bosom pals. What's important is that he's closer to the exit than me. From his room I can jump into my winter duds and be out of the building before you can say "Jack Robinson." By the time they discover me missing, I'm long gone. Worries me though that they're threatening to alarm the side doors in our wing. That would kill me.

The flaw in my arrangement with Sonny is that I have to see him so often. Not that he's that bad, or would ever blow the whistle on me. It's just that he's not my kind of person. He used to be, but old age has whittled his moods down to two—bitchy or melancholic. I never know which it'll be when I cross his doorstep. Of the two I'll take bitchy, a mood I can respond to with a few barbs of my own. Melancholy stirs up dark memories best left untouched. Too much of it leaves me ugly for days.

Yesterday they caught me on the way out the door. I kicked up a fuss, but mostly for show. Secretly I wasn't disappointed considering the blizzard that was brewing. Today the plan is to break out early while the girls on the floor are busy, and Sonny is still groggy from sleep. I'll be in and out of his room in a flash.

The instant I crossed his doorstep I knew I was in trouble. The old bugger was sitting there waiting. "Well, well," he said from his swivel chair next to the window, "look who just blew in." I tried to ignore him by heading straight to his closet. "Making a run for it early, are we?" he continued, all folksy-like.

Avoiding eye contact, I slid open the closet door and reached for the Habitant pea soup box where I hid my outdoor clothes. "Jesu Marie," I said, looking down. Not unexpectedly, Sonny's dirty underwear and socks lay atop the box; another one of his jokes that have long ceased to be humorous.

"Hoping to spot raven in the moose yard," I said. "This time of year, they shelter there overnight. Gotta get there early, though. No time to waste." Head down and tugging at the velcro on my boots, I didn't notice him get up from the chair. When I straightened, there he was, smack-dab in the middle of my getaway path clutching a photograph that someone had thought enough of to enlarge. He stood, legs splayed, holding it at eye level to be sure I couldn't miss it.

"See that LCBO box down there," he said, motioning with his chin to the box he'd pulled out from under the bed. I nodded. "Photographs. My niece's grandson brought them by yesterday. Figure you'd want to see them; especially, this one." He pumped the picture back and forth in front of me, like he was performing one of those calisthenic exercises they try to con us seniors into.

"Doubt that," I replied, ignoring the picture and fiddling with the zipper on my parka.

"Stop being so goddamned ornery, R.J."

"Come on, Sonny, don't do this. How many times do I have to spell it out? Photographs, old letters, souvenirs—none of that stuff works on me. Leaves me glum. Sometimes for days."

"Jesus, R.J., you are a cold one."

"Trying to keep looking forward, that's all. There's too much living in the past going on around here; like we're about to fall off our perches, or something. When are you gonna get it through that thick skull of yours that this boy isn't working on his obit." Immediately I regretted the tone; Sonny had lost his wife not that long back. Besides, he still had his faculties, unlike many in this place, and might be good company, if I could get him to live in the present. By himself, he was free to let his memories take him wherever. I just wasn't going down that road with him.

"For Christ's sake," he said. "Just take a peek. It's not gonna kill ya."

Short of pushing him aside it was unavoidable. I unzipped and pulled out my glasses, sure as hell I'd be gazing at the faces of long-gone friends. Guys I missed so much I'd stopped going to hangouts we'd once shared.

"Come on," he insisted, wobbling the picture at me. "Just give me the name of the pretty girl in the front row—the one wearing the CGIT uniform. Being older than me I thought you'd recognize her."

I followed his finger to the girl in question. I knew her alright; I'd even dated her. Now, looking at her face seventy years on, I realized just how pretty she was. "Hilka Rasinpera," I said, a pang reverberating through my gut.

But it wasn't only Hilka's face that had my pulse racing. It was the picture itself. I figured it to be circa 1950, and in it a crowd was gathered in a small clearing beside a lake. They're holding song books, which fits, because it's probably one of the grade-eight school picnics they used to have every spring. In the foreground is a dock with a rock to the right and a weed bed to the left. No sand beach here—this is Northern Ontario, muskeg territory. Higher up in the background are a cabin and a shed, both log. Behind that, a thick, dark wall of boreal forest.

If I were to guess, I'd say the photo was taken with one of those three-dollar, Brownie Hawkeye cameras. Cheap device or not, this snap is so sharp that not only do I recognize each and every face, but also the expressions on them. Faces so familiar they're almost family. Which is astounding, because if you showed me a picture of the nursing staff here at the residence, I'd be hard pressed to come up with more than a handful of names. But this photograph, seven decades old, has me looking at them in virtual real time. Suddenly, I'm Einstein, with names, loves, hates, friends, enemies, and idiosyncrasies scrolling across my mind, like formulae on the physicist's blackboard. From the kids sitting cross-legged in the front, past the parents, to the old folks in the back, I could recite chapter and verse on the real person behind each face—flirters, lusters, no-nonsensers, drinkers, gamblers, liberals, conservatives, war-damaged. Gossip and intrigue were coming at me so fast I could even distinguish the voices.

I'm not sure how long I stared at the picture, but when I finally raised my head, it was to the gotcha grin on Sonny's beaming face. "Told you this was a grabber," he said.

More than a grabber, I thought, but wasn't about to admit it, lest he take it for weakness. Instinct told me to run, and I might have, if not for the faces of four, strange men standing at the back of the crowd. Decked out in suits, ties, and broad-brimmed fedoras, they looked like they'd taken a wrong turn en route to a funeral and wound up at a school picnic. As to age, I'd put one in his early twenties, two mid-thirties, and the last, close to seventy. To a man, the leathered faces and world-weary eyes, spoke of lives that had not been easy. They're trying to smile but the lips won't turn up, as if out of practice. They're too well dressed to be town drunks invited to the school picnic by the well-meaning church minister who's also there. "My God!," I said, "it's them."

I'd never intended for Sonny to hear this. But with the shock of seeing the four strangers together in a picture, the words had just slipped out. He stared at me, all questions.

"Them who?" he asked.

"Who took this picture?" I replied, in an attempt to deflect.

Sonny shrugged. "No idea. It was just one of many in the box."

My mind was racing. I'd been told that there was a picture of these four guys, but after years of searching I'd never uncovered a copy. I'd ask, and people would hunt through old snapshots, then come up empty—as if by some mysterious force the photograph had been culled from the family collection.

"When you say, 'them,'" Sonny pressed, "who're you talking about? There's gotta be forty people in the picture."

Reluctantly, I pointed to the four strangers. "Those guys," I said.

Sonny frowned. "What about 'em. DPs if you ask me."

"Don't call them that!" I snapped.

Sonny took a step back. "Why not? That's what they probably were. I mean, look at 'em, talk about out of place."

"Maybe, but you make it sound like they were trash. You know nothing about them, or what they might have lived through. Back then, there were lots of men like this around—single guys with history, but no family, or friends, to pass on their stories."

"Stories! Ha! Come on, R.J., half of them were rubbydubs who wound up hanging themselves down at the bridge. These four, what did they do that's got you so worked up?" I shrugged and tugged at the zipper on my parka, but Sonny wasn't about to quit. "Shit-a-Goddamn, R.J., you got my curiosity up. Don't you dare clam up on me now." He must have noticed my hesitation because he took a step closer.

"It's complicated," I said. "Best keep it in the box, so to speak."

"My God, that's weak. Since when has R.J. Martin, ex-reporter for the *Timmins Daily Press*, ever kept his mouth shut about anything?"

I took a deep breath. Once again, I was letting my impatience with Sonny get the best of me. Which wasn't fair, because all he'd done was parrot the, "dirty DP," attitude prevalent back in the day—one I'd shared myself, until I got to know several bush-bound mavericks while working in my dad's store. For the main, they were lost souls—trappers, prospectors—hiding out in the bush and barely scraping by. I'd talk to them. Occasionally they talked back. They never divulged much, but here and there I detected hints of experiences past, sometimes hair-raising ones. I never got more, because when they died, their stories died with them. Once gone, the lasting memory most folk carried was of scruffy, stinky, nebulous figures, who showed up briefly, only to slink back to their hidey holes in the bush on the first train out of town.

I plunked myself down on a chair, debating how much to tell him. "When I was a kid," I finally began, "about the same time this picture was taken, something very hush-hush took place."

Sonny leaned forward with a grin. "Yeah? What?"

"Never quite sure, until decades on. Oh, at the time, I dug hard to get to the bottom of it, but the adults, Mom and Dad included, took pains never to discuss it in the presence of, 'the little guy with the big ears.' All I ever got were hushed voices and the odd word. I recall, sitting in the chair at Joe Charles' barber shop, with the usual gaggle of men chattering away. On this occasion they're casting furtive glances in my direction and talking in whispers, but not low enough for me to miss words like 'DP', and 'police', and 'murder.'"

"And?" Sonny asked, rolling his hand in encouragement.

"And nothing. That's it. After a while I gave up and forgot about it. It wasn't until forty years on while sifting through some of Dad's papers that it all came flooding back. There it was, a file entitled, 'Affidavit on the Sami Aalto Case, by O. Schneider, witnessed by Harvey Martin.' Turns out, Otto Schneider—he's the older one of the four guys in the photograph—left a hand-written document for Dad to witness and keep in his safe."

"So, you finally got your answer?"

"Christ, if only. Oh, I found out what took place, alright—names, timelines, how the men happened to come together, details on their final days—but not what counted most."

Sonny frowned. "Jeez, RJ, sounds to me like you got chapter and verse. What could possibly be missing?"

"The important part, that's what—the why of it. Sure, I knew who did what to whom, but not why. For that I had to dig. It bugged me so much I couldn't stop picking at it. And, yes, I admit, as a reporter, I saw a good story in it. Spent years piecing it all together, and when I finally did, I walked away. Gotten too close to it. They'd become family. You don't go writing up secret stuff on family."

"If that's the case, why are you so gobsmacked by this one picture?"

I picked it up and pointed to the four men. "See the guy next to Otto, the one that looks like he just got pulled through a knot-hole backwards?"

Sonny examined the picture. "If you ask me, they all look the same—like they'd just been freed from one of those concentration camps."

"That's Sami Aalto. Until today, I'd never seen his picture, but I know it's him. The others I recognize from photos their families shared with me."

Sonny took the photograph and examined it closely. "So, who are these guys?

"Two Finns, one German, and one German-Canadian."

"All, dare I say, DPs?"

"Nope. Otto had his papers. He lived in a log cabin south of Jogues and about a mile east of the Algoma Central tracks." I looked at Sonny, expecting him to gloat for being correct about the other three being DPs, but he didn't. Perhaps, with his curiosity running high, he didn't want to risk not getting the whole story. I looked out the window. The moose yard beckoned, but with heavy snow falling, and with the wind slamming it against the window, I found myself settling in. "How's your history?" I asked.

"Try me."

"The Winter War and the Continuation War? Mean anything?"

Sonny shrugged. "*Nada.*"

"Finland. World War II. That's where it begins. But it ends right here in Hearst."

Sonny went to the cupboard and came back with an enormous box of cookies.

"You sure you want to hear this?" I asked. "It's kinda convoluted."

"I got the cookies out, didn't I?"

PART TWO

Finland,
1944

2

Viipuri/Vyborg in Flames

Viipuri, Finland,
January 1944

Were you shitting me when you said you had grandparents in this hellhole of a burg?" Tuomas Korpi snapped. The Russian army had just occupied Viipuri in Eastern Finland. The Finns and Germans were retreating.

Alvar winced as he inhaled the heavy, damp smoke and glanced up and down the street. He was trying to orient himself midst the snow-covered rubble that days earlier had been homes. Surprisingly, some of those still standing had smoke coming from the chimneys, signs that not everyone had fled the Russian bombardment. He guessed that the people remaining were either too old or too dazed by the speed of the attack to evacuate. Why some homes had merely suffered structural damage while others had burned to the ground, was probably related to which households had doused the flames in their stoves at the start of the shelling.

"Viipuri's no hellhole," Alvar said. "Far from it. Normally, it's a beautiful city. If only you'd seen it before we pulverized it. At least beautiful is the way I remember it. Anyway, to answer your question, why would I lie about my grandparents living here?"

"You tell me," Korpi replied, with a shrug. "Sometimes I think there's not much goin' on up there in that head of yours. Like right now. You even sure you know what street they live on?"

Alvar knew the street name, but it had been a long time, and he wasn't sure he could recognize the house—even if it was still standing. There was only one thing he was certain of these days and that was how he hated the man beside him, and how he regretted letting it slip that his grandparents lived in Viipuri. It had happened in the early hours of the offensive, when at last they had the Finns and Germans on the run. In a fit of euphoria, he'd commented that at the rate of their advance, and the direction their division was headed, it wouldn't be long before he'd be sipping coffee with his mother's parents.

From that moment, Korpi, the regimental commissar and bully, had been on him like a vulture on dead meat. What he was hoping for eluded Alvar, but one thing was clear, the odds were stacked against it being pleasant. It occurred to him that it might be safer for all involved—him, his grandparents, and his own parents back in Soviet Russian Karelia—if he'd just pick a stack of rubble, claim it was the remains of the house and give up the search. Korpi wouldn't be happy, but then when was he ever.

There must have been food spattered in the rubble because a murder of black and grey hoodie crows screeched and swooped from the tall sticks that had once been trees. Alvar hesitated and pointed right. "Could be this street," he said, "but with so many signs gone, and half the houses obliterated, it's hard to tell. Maybe we should just give up."

"No! Jesus, man, I'm looking for some hot food. Christ, they're your grandparents. They gotta be around here someplace. You said you used to visit them."

"That was before my parents relocated us to the Soviet side. I was just a kid. After they shut the border, we were never allowed back into Finland."

"Tell me something, Alvar, were you lying when you said your grandparents were Red?"

"Goddamn right they're Red. That's how I remember it, though *Äiti* and *Isä* never said much about it to us kids growing up."

Korpi chuckled, but there was no mirth in it. "They better be. Because, if not, your *mummo* and *isoisä* are goin' be shittin' their pants when they spot their grandson marching up their walkway in Russian uniform."

"Do me a favour when we get there, will ya?" Alvar asked. "Refer to the city as Viipuri and not Vyborg. That's the Finn name for it. Calling it Vyborg is what we Russians call it, and it kinda rubs Finns the wrong way. Alright?"

"Depends how they treat this boy," Korpi responded. "Real food and a hot bath and I'll call it anything they want. Oh, and a good piece of tail would go down nice, too." He looked around at the smoldering devastation. "There's gotta be some half-decent-looking women hiding somewhere in these ruins."

Bile churned up in Alvar's stomach. He'd seen this side of Korpi and longed to be rid of him. But his comrade-in-arms had smelled opportunity, and one did not say no to Tuomas Korpi.

Halfway down the block an old man was sifting through the remains of his home. Alvar approached. "Would you happen to know Aino and Helli Lampi?" he asked.

The man snarled at the uniforms and went back to his digging. Alvar turned to move on, but Tuomas was having none of it. In three strides he was on the man with a swift boot to the rear, knocking him to the ground. "I didn't come through hell to be sneered at by some ignorant Finnish peasant," he hollered. "My comrade asked you a question. Do you or do you not know the Lampis?"

The old man struggled to his feet, palms bleeding from the debris he'd landed on. His arm came up. "Third standing house on the right," he pointed.

The soldiers moved on. "Jesus, Tuomas, did you have to do that? The guy's an old man who just lost his home. Who knows what else."

"Fuck you! Why should any of these people get off Scot-free? Three days ago on the other side of town that guy's sons were killing us. There's gonna be a lotta changes around here, so they better get used to it. You, too, if you know what's good for you."

Ahead of them a wounded dog dragged her shrapnel-impregnated backside across the road. A small puppy whimpered along behind. Korpi picked up his pace and shot the bitch, the gunshot reverberating up and down the street, bringing all activity to a halt. Korpi smirked at the reaction, picked up the puppy, and placed him gently inside his parka.

Only when they were on top of it did Alvar recognize the house. Shrapnel had marked the wooden siding, and the tree was gone where he used to swing as a child, but this was indeed the home his mother had been raised in; a place that would have been a regular feature in his life had his devoted communist father not dragged them off to Russian Karelia. Having lost the Civil War, and in an attempt to escape the wrathful vengeance of the victorious White Finns, thousands of loyal Red Finns had done the same and fled to Russia. For a second Alvar stood still, savouring the warm sensation crawling up his spine.

"Well?" Korpi said, "you just gonna stand there gawking, or what?"

"Wait here, Tuomas, will you?"

"Why?"

"Just give me a few minutes alone with them. Please?"

The curtains were pulled shut, but the smoke in the chimney, the snow banked against the base of the house, and the shoveled walkway, showed that the house was occupied. Alvar prayed it would be family. He knocked gently. No one came. He tried again, a tad more forcibly this time. Still no response.

"Oh, for Christ sake," Tuomas said, pushing past him and banging hard.

"Who is it?" a voice said.

Alvar opened his mouth to respond but Korpi beat him to it. "Your grandson, Alvar Sorsakoski. And a friend," he shouted.

The door opened and two heads peered out searching for Alvar's face. But the smile that had begun to form quickly evaporated at the sight of the Russian uniforms. The door began to close. "Russians are not welcome here," his grandmother said.

"*Mummo*? It's me. We've opened the border. It's safe to visit now." No reaction. Terrified with how Korpi might react to the hesitation behind the closed door he struggled for something to say. "*Äiti* and *Isä* would never forgive me if I didn't look you up. They're fine, last I heard."

Muffled voices came from behind the door. "Helli!" Alvar heard his grandfather say, in a voice barely louder than a stage whisper. "Be reasonable. It's Anna-Leena's boy. He's alive. He'll have news. We can't turn him away. Just give him a few minutes."

"He's turned Russian?"

The instant Alvar walked into the parlour, memories began exploding in his head—aroma, furniture, wallpaper, braided rugs, all just as he had imagined. Even the framed tapestry on the wall, depicting a sauna bath and spruce trees beside a lake with mist rising from the water, was exactly as he remembered. Only the portraits on the piano had been updated. His eyes locked onto them. Foremost were those of four handsome young men. All soldiers. All in Finnish uniform. He hoped this might escape Korpi, but it hadn't. His comrade glared at them, but mercifully kept his mouth shut.

His grandmother followed his gaze. "Your cousins," she said in an acid tone. "Two dead, one missing."

Alvar felt his stomach lurch. "I'm sorry," he managed to get out. "Wish . . . I'd . . . had a chance to know them." He swallowed, searching for words. Korpi stood beside him, gently patting the puppy head protruding from the top of his parka. Pointing to his comrade Alvar said, "This is Tuomas Korpi." Only when it was out did it strike him that he had not referred to Korpi as buddy, or friend, or even fellow Karelian Finn. It was a mistake for which he was sure to pay. When and how would be determined.

The silence was awkward. No handshakes took place. The impasse was broken by Alvar's grandfather who motioned for them to sit. "We don't have much to offer," he said, "but I've got a bit of vodka stashed away waiting for a spec . . ." *Mummo's* withering look stopped him in mid-sentence.

"Vodka would be wonderful," Korpi said. "And a little food, too, perhaps?" Alvar slumped.

Mummo had hardly budged from the front door, as if toying with the idea of reopening it and asking them to leave. She stood, fists clenched, ready to take on Stalin's army. Only under her husband's glare, and head jerks in the direction of the kitchen, did she finally come to life. "There's not much here that would please our conquerors," she responded in a monotone. "A few eggs, potatoes, the *korvike* that passes for coffee these days, and cabbage, cabbage, cabbage."

"It'll do," Korpi replied, rubbing his hands and following her into the kitchen. "Can't be worse than the slop we get at the Front."

For Alvar, setting foot in the home his mother had sobbed over every Christmas for as far back as he could remember, this was not the reunion of his dreams. He'd been under no illusion that explaining away the uniform would be easy, but he hadn't anticipated the depth of *Mummo's* hostility. She wasn't budging and, if he was reading it correctly, *Isoisä's* slightly more welcoming response was mostly a reaction to Korpi, than filial loyalty. Food arrived, but not conversation. Alvar stared at his plate, pushing his food around and listening to Korpi slurping and smacking, the puppy at his feet. Alvar and his grandparents sipped their vodka. Korpi knocked back a glass with each bite until the bottle was empty. Finally, done, he burped, rose, and, weaving his way to the door declared: "A little stroll after dinner, good for the digestion. I'll be back. Take care of my dog." The last directed at Alvar.

Alvar winced, full in the knowledge that for his comrade the word stroll was code for troll, with the victim the first unfortunate woman who strayed across his path.

Korpi slammed the door behind him, and for a moment silence reigned at the table. An intense sadness settled in, the three of them deep in their own thoughts. "Everybody in the platoon hates him," Alvar finally said. "Some call him 'rat face' behind his back, but you've got to be careful."

"It's bad enough to watch a man probe his nose with a finger," *Mummo* said, "but does he really have to examine the results?"

"He's an animal," Alvar said. "And he's not my friend. He forced me to come here and bring him with me."

"Will he be back?" *Mummo* asked.

Alvar nodded. "Soon as he's satisfied himself with a woman. Are there any young girls in the neighbourhood we should warn?"

"All gone," his grandfather replied. "The only people left are old, like us. Your Russian reputation preceded you."

Alvar assessed the predicament he was in and considered his options. That no photographs were going to be pulled out, nor family tales exchanged, was clear. Nothing would please him more than to hear little gems about his mom in her youth, but this was not the time. It weighed on him, but he pushed his thoughts on to a more pressing problem—how to get his grandparents out of the dangerous position he'd put them in by showing up with Korpi in tow.

His grandmother turned to her husband. "Aino, they must go. Both of them. Our neighbours have lost everything—families, homes, businesses. What'll they be thinking seeing Russian uniforms moving in and out of our place?"

"But this one has a right to be here," Aino protested, pointing to Alvar. "And we've lost, too; three grandsons we've given."

"*Mummo's* right, *Isoisä*. We have to get out of here, but getting Korpi away won't be easy."

"Would more vodka help?" Aino asked.

Alvar looked at him, a grin tugging at the corner of his mouth. "You have more?"

Aino nodded. "Hidden in the root cellar."

"Perfect. If he doesn't find a woman he'll be back soon, and in a rage. Quick, fetch two bottles. If you have a wheelbarrow, put it at the back door. I'll use it to haul him away when he passes out."

Aino came back with the vodka, which he placed on the table in full view of the front door. "Maybe your friend will get himself lost in the rubble out there," *Mummo* said.

Alvar shook his head. "Not drunk enough, and it won't be dark for another hour. And *Mummo*, please, he's not my friend. We're in the same platoon, that's all. He found out I had relatives here and stuck to me."

"That doesn't explain why you're here, or why you're part of the army that killed your cousins?"

"Helli," Aino, pleaded. "Be reasonable. Don't go there. We don't have long with him."

"It's alright, *Isoisä*. I understand. It bothers me too. But please don't think I wear this uniform willingly. It was either join up or be shot. All Finn-Karelian men in Russia were given the same choice."

"And what about Korpi?" Mummo pressed. "By his accent he's obviously Karelian Finn. Same with him?"

"He's an exception. A dangerous one. As a well-known athlete, he's become a Karelian poster boy to the Russians. They treat him well, setting him up as the communist commissar in our platoon. It's his job to listen and report on everything we say or do. Which puts me in an impossible position. For some reason he doubts my commitment to the cause. It's severe treatment if I don't jump when he hollers. I could take it, but any lapse on my part and the folks back home will pay.

Before I was drafted, Karelian boys started defecting. That stopped the instant the authorities began murdering their families."

"Have you ever considered defecting?"

Alvar shook his head. "Every day, but I love my family too much."

Aino nodded several times as he grasped the dilemma. "Do the other Karelians in your outfit feel the same?"

"There aren't any. That's the other thing the army did; split us up by moving us into units from more patriotic parts of the country. Me and Korpi are the only Karelians in our platoon. With him monitoring me I don't dare display the slightest lapse in communist fervour. It's a sham and it stinks."

"They've got you in a vise," Helli said. "What a sick world we brought you children into. How do you manage to keep going?"

A warmth had crept into her voice. Alvar caught it, and turned to see her fishing for the blue and white polka-dot handkerchief tucked up her sleeve. A recollection flashed through his mind. In it, *Mummo* is performing this same act to wipe away his tears. He clamped his teeth onto his lower lip, lest they return. "By keeping my ears open, head down, and nose clean," he said. "I've also worked hard at making myself the worst shot in the platoon. Only when I sight on a German am I accurate. I swear, I have not knowingly killed a single Finn."

"Can you get away with that?" she continued.

"Korpi's suspicious. Lately, he's been hinting at something he claims will test my loyalty. Says it's a job tailor-made for the two of us."

"Any idea what it could be?"

Alvar had an inkling, but could not bring himself to divulge it to his grandparents. "None whatsoever," he answered. To fend off any more probing he changed the subject. "I assured Korpi that you two were good communists. That still true?"

Aino and Helli looked at each other. "We were," Aino replied, "and maybe still are, but we're Finn first, and sure as hell not anything close to the perverted Russian brand. After we lost the Civil War to the western Finns in 1920, we chose to stay, but a lot of our neighbours followed your *Äiti* and *Isä* to Soviet Karelia."

"To be treated like dogs," Alvar said. "*Äiti* and *Isä* would have come back in a heartbeat if they hadn't sealed the border. They'll be able to see you again, though, now that Viipuri's to be part of Russia once more."

"God help us," *Mummo* said.

The conversation stopped with the sound of feet crunching snow. "He's back," Aino said.

Alvar leaned forward, talking rapidly. "Whatever he asks, just go along. And keep filling his glass with vodka. I'll have a few myself, just to make sure he doesn't suspect I'm setting him up. Our unit moves out tomorrow. Once I get him away from here, we won't be back. Promise. You'll be safe."

"Whatever it takes," Aino said, "get yourself clear of that man, son. He's evil."

Mummo reached over and squeezed his hand. "God bless you, boy."

The door opened and the puppy raced to greet Korpi, tail going a mile a minute.

3

The Russian-Finn Front

February 1944

"**P**erkele," Mika Saarinen screamed, between eardrum-shattering explosions. "Don't those goddamn Russians ever run out of shells?"

They were huddled in a shallow foxhole with pieces of frozen earth, tree fragments and the odd body part raining down on them. Jari Hoivuniemi waited for an interruption in the pommeling before yelling his answer. "Keltamaki claims that with the Germans on the run in Poland, the Russians have begun shipping munitions up to our Front."

The shelling had been going on for so many weeks you could set your watch by it—air raid followed by artillery barrage, followed by infantry attack. The results were equally predictive: the outnumbered, out-supplied Finn army would be forced to retreat to new lines where they would regroup, only to have the scene play out all over again. It didn't matter that the Russians, or Ivans as the Finn soldiers referred to them, fell by the hundreds in the process, because each attack brought them closer to Helsinki and victory. The Finns and Germans were getting licked, and they knew it.

Right on cue the shelling ceased, and the Russian infantry came swarming at them. This time it was quick. Realizing that they could hold them off no longer, Command ordered Jari and Mika, along with their whole platoon, onto their skis and back to a new position. The army called it repositioning, but it didn't take a genius to see that with the city of Viipuri gone, it wouldn't be long before the Russians were at Helsinki's gates. Finnish hero, Field Marshal Mannerheim, the military genius who'd humiliated the Russians in the 1939 Winter war, was running out of rabbits.

"You shoulda gone back to Canada right after the Winter War," Mika said, when they'd settled in to their new position. "Before the second war had a chance to get started."

"Would have," Jari answered, "if not for the way Mannerheim caved in, back in 1940; his truce with the Russians pissed me off so much I stayed on for another crack at them. We all knew it had to happen sooner or later. Thanks to Hitler, we got a chance."

"Right, and how you feeling about that now?"

Jari didn't look at him, concentrating on the half-frozen piece of food he'd pulled out of his pocket. "Don't give me that shit, Mika. You and everyone else in this country thought joining the Germans was a good idea. Our mistake was not stopping once we'd pushed the Ivans out of the territory they stole from us in 1940. If we'd halted at the old border and made peace, maybe we'd be out of this."

"We could still turn this around."

"Not this time," Jari said. "The Germans are finished here, and we can't do it alone. From the looks of it, I'd say they're getting ready to hightail it for home to protect their own borders. Best we can hope for now is another truce, and I don't think I could stomach that again. Two in a lifetime is two too many."

"You don't really think the Germans will up and quit on us, do ya?"

"Wake up, Mika. All the signs are there. With the Russians hounding them in Poland, what option to they have?"

"But they wouldn't just leave us high and dry."

"They don't give a shit about us."

"We're not licked, Jari."

"Dream on. Christ, we killed 130,000 Ivans in the 1939 Winter War and still lost. How you figure we'd do better this time? Especially, now with the Brits and Yanks giving the Russians everything they need, and the Germans giving us sweet fuck-all."

"Goddamn it, if you feel that strong why don't you just quit and be done with it?"

"Go AWOL? Don't think it hasn't crossed my mind, because . . ."

"Cut it!" Mika interrupted. "Here comes Keltamaki." Jari turned to see their sergeant bearing down on them. He was a respected soldier and leader. Tolerant, too. But one topic you did not discuss in his presence was the possibility of defeat.

The new position turned out to be no different from the last one—
same snow, same trees, same sleepless nights, same empty bellies,
same artillery shells raining down. The only thing that changed was
the length of the barrage; this time it was shorter. "Probably a sign of
Russian confidence," Jari moaned to Mika. Surprisingly, the instant
the shelling stopped, whistles did not begin blowing on the Russian
side, nor did their soldiers begin pouring out from the trees to streak
across the clearing. Nevertheless, the Finns crawled in their winter
whites to prearranged positions. For Jari and Mika, it was behind a log.

Mika glanced back at the fallen balsam under which he and Jari
had cached their skis. "I put on the wrong wax," he said, "I'm going
back to redo them."

"No time," Jari said. His eyes were focused on the trees across the
large field some Finn-Karelian farmer had carved from the boreal forest generations earlier. Like so many of the clearings they'd retreated
over, it was peppered with snow-capped boulders too large for any
farmer to move. Sitting like tiny, isolated islands, they offered protection points for the attacking soldiers. Jari estimated the distance of
each, making a note to adjust his sights accordingly, as the inevitable
attack progressed.

"Nobody fires until I give the order," sergeant Keltamaki advised
in his cool, calming voice. "Train your sights on the boulders, that's
where they'll cluster."

They waited. Nothing. The air was still, save for a couple of ravens
who came gronking out of the trees. Jari's thoughts flew in two over-
lapping directions. Food was one; the kitchen sleigh hadn't made it
through in four days. They'd been surviving on biscuits, frozen bits of
horse flesh and scraps the Lotta paramilitary women were able to get
to them. Second thought went to the Russian attack, as in, when was
it going to start? The bombardment had stopped over an hour ago,
but nothing was happening. If the Ivans didn't come soon, it would
be artillery again, and if shelling resumed, the kitchen sleigh would
not get through. Another blow to their already devastated morale.

After two hours in the snow, with the cold working its way through
parkas and sweaters into the fibers of their thick, scratchy, woolen
underwear, Keltamaki finally ordered half of them back to their holes.

Fires were forbidden for obvious reasons, but with movement came a semblance of heat. Jari and Mika were among those who went back, where they joined the others jumping about and windmilling their arms, like boys at soccer practice. No sooner had the blood begun to flow to their limbs than they were sent back to their forward positions to give the rest of the platoon a chance to get their inner heaters going.

The light was fading behind them when Jari leaned into Mika. "What are the Ivans up to? This isn't their way. How come all that shelling and no attack?"

"Looks like we're not the only ones bamboozled by this," Mika replied. Behind them at the edge of the trees a group of officers stood huddled in debate. Food arrived and the platoon was summoned back. Keltamaki let them eat before passing on the news.

"Apparently, the big guys have no more clue about what's going on than we do. You know what that means? Patrols." He pulled out a map, spreading it open on the remains of a pulverized tree. They huddled around him in the fading light. "We're to find out what they're up to on the far side of that field," he said, pointing to the east. "Quickest way is to split the platoon in two. I'll take half around to the right of it," his finger moved along the map to a river. "Korpi will take the rest of you around the other side in the direction of Syskyjärvi."

"Shit!" Jari groaned, into Mica's ear. "Korpi." For two years the Finns had harassed Russian supply lines into Leningrad with minimal push-back. But this new, unrelenting Russian offensive had decimated the platoon. Although they still numbered eighteen, only seven, counting Keltamaki, were originals. The rest were either raw recruits or trans-plants from the remnants of shattered Finn IV Army Corps units.

In the chaos, vetting replacements was all but non-existent. Show up in a Finn uniform and you were in. Understandable, but the two latest additions, Tuomas Korpi and Alvar Sorsakoski, gave Jari the jit-ters. One pitch-black night, the platoon had been skiing back to a new defense line when these two showed up out of nowhere; just popped out of the bush and slipped into the line, like they belonged. Only with the morning light did Jari finally get a close look at them. No hollow eyes or gaunt cheeks on these two. Fresh as waxwings. There was something cockeyed about it, but they had a credible story, and with the army in disarray they got to stay. Regardless, Jari and Mika had been keeping their heads up.

"Jesus!" Mika whispered, "Korpi *and* Sorsakoski. I was afraid this might happen. You should have been firmer with Keltamaki about your suspicions."

"I did my goddamn best! Told him that Korpi was the spitting image of a communist asshole I'd run into in Canada, in 1937. Explained how he and his gang of Red Finns saw to it that non-communist Whites got beaten up and fired from their jobs in the Sudbury mine, or fell down shafts, or had their legs run over by ore cars."

"How come you didn't put a stop to it back in Canada?"

"Too many Reds, not enough Whites. Those guys were hellbent that only Red Finns were to make a go of it in Canada. Got so bad one guy hung himself. And when he did, Korpi and his ilk were all sympathetic, going on and on to the police about how lonely and depressed the poor boy must have been, and how he feared this might happen. All the time the bastard was waging the Civil War all over again—right up there in Northern Ontario. If it's the same guy, and I'm sure it is, he must have had a helluva change of heart to wind up on our side."

"What're you saying, Jari?"

"Been a lot of stories about Karelian Finns from the Russian side slipping over the line."

"What about Sorsakoski?"

Jari shrugged. "Seems to do what he's told, doesn't he? The two of them stick pretty close, but Korpi's definitely the leader."

"And Keltamaki doesn't buy any of what you said?"

"Claimed his hands were tied. Said, 'So the guy's a communist. Finland's full of them. What do you think the Civil War in 1918 was all about?'"

"And you let it go at that?"

"Christ, I pushed as hard as I could. We're desperate for men. You know that."

"But why would Keltamaki pick Korpi to lead the patrol?"

"No choice. Korpi outranks us."

"Shit!" Mika said. "Now that prick is taking us behind enemy lines in the pitch black. We better be on our toes."

"My encounter with him, if it's the same guy, was seven years ago. That, and the fact that he and his thugs were so busy beating up Whites, probably explains why he doesn't remember me. Once I cottoned on to what he was doing, I got out of Sudbury and found a job cutting pulp up near Hearst."

For two days, between the last retreat and the announcement that they were to go out on patrol, the regiment had not moved. In that time, Jari and Mika had managed to scrape out a foxhole and line it with spruce bows. They'd even liberated a thick blanket from a prisoner. But in the hours leading up to the patrol, even all that relative comfort couldn't buy them sleep. Patrols were always perilous, but neither of them had ever felt this vulnerable before. It was one thing to fret about the enemy ahead, quite another to fear what might be coming at you from within your own ranks. They couldn't shake the possibility that this patrol could be their last. Finally, they gave up on sleep and set to hashing out their options—all of which, they decided, were abominably bleak.

"Up shit's creek," Jari said, "that's where we are. Refuse to go out on this patrol risks a Finnish bullet; going out, a Russian one."

"It's possible we've got it wrong, Jari. I mean, look around. We got Whites and Reds right here in our own platoon. Our Reds want to keep Russia out of Finland as much as we do. Maybe it's the same with Korpi and Sorsakoski."

"Nice thought. But if that's the same Korpi I encountered back in Sudbury, he didn't give a damn about Finland back then, and I doubt he does now. He's communist to the bone, and a friggin' psychopath to boot. You and me are gonna hang back on this patrol. Keep our eyes open."

The skiing conditions were perfect when Keltamaki finally gave the order to move out. Earlier, the full moon had made the platoon edgy, but delaying departure had paid off. A thin cloud had since moved in, along with a light dusting that made for perfect patrol conditions— enough new snow to muffle the sound of skis sliding over a firm crust and enough light to see the guy ahead, but not enough to be spotted from a distance. Waiting for better conditions hadn't pleased the major but, once again, Keltamaki's caution had paid off. To Jari, he was undoubtedly the best sergeant in the army. How crappy that he'd be leading the other half of the platoon on this patrol.

Progress was quiet and fast. They zipped along in a line, Korpi in the lead, Sorsakoski the sweeper, bringing up the rear. Jari and Mika found themselves midsection, skiing so close that Jari's skis were in constant danger of tapping on Mika's. The sound of wood striking wood in the dark night would be a dead giveaway to trained ears. But by running this close they could converse, albeit it hushed tones. "They got us boxed in," Jari mumbled. Mika didn't respond. Either he hadn't heard or was too terrified by prospects ahead to answer.

Thirty minutes had them scooting around the edge of a clearing onto an abandoned logging road. Jari took a deep breath to calm his raging pulse. That the last three turns had been to the right had set alarm bells ringing in his head. "Time to take a leak," he whispered to Mika.

"What? Already? But I don't have . . ."

"For chrissakes just pull out!"

They edged out of the line and stopped. The Vatanen brothers, Teemu and Kimi, whizzed by, followed by Sorsakoski, who stopped. "What's going on?" he said.

"Tea," Jari replied. "Drank too much before we left. A quick piss and we'll catch up."

Sorsakoski hesitated, checked his watch, then moved off. "Make it fast," he said, double poling to catch the others.

"What's wrong?" Mika asked, unbuttoning his fly.

"Have you noticed all the right turns we've been taking?"

"Left ones, too."

"Half as many. I figure one more right turn has us heading south, smack-dab into the whole goddamn Russian Seventh Army. We're supposed to be prodding around, looking for Ivans, but Korpi's turning this into some Karelian, cross-country ski loppett. It's as if he's taking us somewhere."

"You're seeing a trap?"

"It fits, Mika. The speed at which we descended that steep ravine back there was suicide in this darkness. Only a man who knows the territory would take it that fast."

"What're you saying?"

"That Korpi's got better intelligence on the area than Keltamaki seemed to have."

"How you figure that?"

"Ask yourself, how come he never stops to check his compass, or listen, or make decisions? He just plows right on, like he knows where he's headed. The guy's up to no good. I feel it. Jesus, this patrol's not going to have a happy ending."

The two men shook themselves off and pushed snow over the pee holes with their poles. "What do we do, Jari? Can't just go back and say we had a bad feeling so quit the patrol. Get shot for that."

"No, but we can catch up and hang back," Jari said, buttoning up. "See what happens. If there's trouble, and it turns out he's doing the right thing, we'll close up and pitch in. If not, we'll just have to take it from there."

After ten minutes they still hadn't caught up to the rest of the patrol. In the process they'd made another turn, once again to the right. This time off the logging road and onto a narrow trail. Neither Jari nor Mika spoke. Instinctively, they slowed down as they scanned the trees. Moving cautiously, they rounded a bend and were about to descend into a ravine when Jari caught the faint sound of voices. Mika heard it too. Herring-boning in slow, deliberate steps, they inched their way down the hill, until close enough to make out what was happening. A group of Ivans had surrounded the column, but it was Korpi doing the talking. And in Russian. A figure that Jari guessed had to be Sorsakoski moved out of the line and joined him. A machine gun came to life. Four soldiers fell. The last two in the column, the Vatanen boys, turned to make a break, but only got a few yards, before they fell. Jari and Mika moved off the trail into the bush and waited.

Mika raised his gun but Jari pushed it down. "No!" he said. "Suicide. We can't take them all out, and it's stupid to die now."

The Russian soldiers skied off, Korpi and Sorsakoski among them. Someone laughed. "Korpi," Mika said.

4

Convalescence

Helsinki, Finland,
March 1944

He'd seen the smoke. Another train had come in. Any second now the main doors at Helsinki Central Station would burst open, and the pigeons would be lifting to avoid the tramping feet. Jari had decisions to make, and he found this a restful place. With his flesh wounds all but healed, he'd been released from Eria Hospital and Medical Centre and placed in a convalescent home. Once his hearing returned—soon the doctors assured him—he would be sent back to his unit at the Front. Convalescence had benefits over the hospital; he could roam, provided it involved only minimal exertion.

After three years of combat, just sitting and watching ordinary folk go about their business was a balm to the soul. There was always the chance, too, of running into a familiar face. He especially loved it when the plaza was filled with beaming adults and squealing children, come to greet soldiers home from the Front. Now and then, he would arrive to find Station Square awash in nurses and orderlies rushing wounded men from evacuation trains to ambulances. On those occasions he turned away. Even on good days, just having to share the space with newly injured soldiers could be tough. Some were up to conversation, some just stared into space. Jari wondered how many were like him, last survivors of their platoons. He wondered, too, but would never ask, how many shared his belief that they were locked in a hopeless cause. In only one way did he envy them: their war was over, his was not. The instant the doctors declared there was no longer anything wrong with his hearing, he was going back.

Or was he? Why continue killing with the final outcome now so clear? Why not just slip away? If the war ended today, his combat record would mark him as a loyal patriot. But quit now, even if only days before the nation officially capitulated, he risked being branded a traitor. Shot, too, if arrested. But returning to his platoon placed him right back in the kill-or-be-killed trap. At this point in the war, the odds of survival favoured the deserter.

On this afternoon, the guy sharing Jari's bench struck him as one of the catatonic vets. Which was why he was jolted out of his own reverie when the man actually spoke up. "Helsinki's no longer the happy place of my youth," he said. "At least here at the station you get the odd smile. Come here often?"

Jari cupped an ear to catch the words. The man spoke louder. Jari nodded, praying that if the soldier insisted on talking, it would not be about the war. "Most days," he replied. "Not much else to do. Got discharged from the hospital to a convalescent home. Seems that soon's you're able to walk and feed yourself, they push you out. Gotta clear the beds for the incoming. Never ends, does it?"

"We can't complain," the man said. "At least we're alive and have all our parts."

"Yeah," was all Jari could muster in reply. He wasn't going to tell him that he was the lone survivor in his platoon; that the last bombardment had killed his best friend, Mika, along with sergeant Keltamaki; that he had walked away with nothing more than pierced ear drums, and some minor injuries; that six of his group had been murdered by Russian-Finn infiltrators; that he was sick of the whole goddamn business; that they would be sending him back, once they discovered he could hear again.

Jari wished the soldier would get off the war; especially when he began straying into territory barely discussed with friends, let alone a stranger. "We'd be out of it already if not for the Germans. Stupid buggers don't know when to quit. They're still dreaming of miracle weapons. Beats me how we ever got suckered into this mess."

Jari had an answer, but shrugged, as if it was all a mystery. What was mysterious, was how quickly people forget their history: almost to a person Finns had wanted to join the Germans in order to get back the land the Russians had stolen in 1939. General Mannerheim had been a hero for attempting just that.

"Now we stand to lose everything," the soldier continued. "Soon we'll be a Russian province all over again. Just like before 1919."

A group of men with briefcases walked by. Jari waited for them to pass before answering. "An arrangement with the Russians might be the answer," he ventured.

"Sue for peace?"

"Worked in 1939, after our licking in the Winter War. Might work again, what with Russians appearing anxious to finish the Germans off in Poland."

The man shook his head. "Look around the square. We're infested with Germans." Jari lifted his head to see a half-dozen Wehrmacht soldiers coming towards them. The stranger tipped his chin in their direction. "Think they're gonna let that happen? Hell, no, they're prepared to fight to the last Finn."

"You don't seem confident in Mannerheim pulling something out?"

"Sure," the man replied, "he'll try, and we'll wind up fighting the Russians, plus the Germans."

"What if the Germans just up and left?" Jari said. "Moved all their troops to Poland? Maybe that would force the Russians to do the same, and we'd be able to . . ." He didn't finish the sentence.

The soldier waited a few seconds before interrupting. "Everything okay?" he asked. "You look sick. Can I help?"

Jari heard none of this. His eyes were fixed on the first familiar face he'd seen in weeks. Of all the people he knew in Finland, Sweden, or even Canada, this was the last person he ever expected to encounter. His heart raced. He broke into a sweat, got to his feet and drifted off in pursuit. Ahead of him, strolling bold as brass out of the station, was Tuomas Korpi, the man whose image flickered daily in his head, like a Pathé newsreel. Collar up, shoulders back, the traitor moved with all the lithe confidence of a champion athlete heading to the podium. Jari shook his head. Was he imagining things? Could this really be Korpi? What was he up to in Helsinki? For several blocks he held back, lest his prey turn and recognize him. Finally, without ever having looked around, the traitor entered a small hotel. Through the window, Jari watched him approach the desk and joke with the clerk. Only at that point did he turn enough for Jari to get a clear view. There was no disputing it, it was definitely his former "comrade," Korpi.

Watching Korpi collect his room key and disappear, Jari was overwhelmed with the urge to enter and ask the desk clerk what name the traitor was travelling under. Better sense prevailed. He hovered in the shadows across the street, wracking his brain for a plan. Expose him or kill him seemed to be his options. Denouncing him to the army was sure to see Korpi executed. But it would also put the spotlight on himself, and kill any prospect of disappearing.

Time passed. Darkness fell. People made their way home. The streets emptied. Clearly, Korpi was in for the night. Which suited Jari, because he'd worked out a third option, one that would take care of the traitor, and leave his hands clean. The weakness in the plan would be in the arranging. It would require persuasion, an art that he had never fully mastered.

It was approaching midnight by the time he found the building and apartment number. He knocked gently, but when that failed to rouse the occupants, he was forced to bang harder. After several minutes, he heard footsteps, followed by a voice behind the door. "Who is it? What do you want?"

"Mr. Vatanen," Jari replied, "sorry to bother you this late. My name is Jari Hoivuniemi. I served with your boys in the army. They were my dear friends. I'm sorry for your loss. Can we talk?"

"Are you drunk?"

"No! Haven't had a drink in days."

"Why are you in Helsinki, and not at the Front?"

"Convalescing, sir," Jari replied.

"What were my boys' names?"

"Teemu and Kimi, sir. We were together from the beginning of the Winter War."

"Oh my God! You really knew them." The door opened. "Come in. Come in. Please."

Inside, Jari found himself facing a square-jawed, broad-shouldered man who once must have been a force. But time and mourning had sapped him of his strength. Jari sighed inwardly. It was a disturbing first impression of the man he'd hoped would solve his Korpi dilemma. And it got worse. When the lamp was switched on in the parlour, he was shocked by the man's appearance—the rheumy eyes clouded with a white film, and uncontrollable tremors, were those of a person who had descended into his own personal hell.

"I'll call Aila, my wife," he rasped.

Jari placed a hand gently on the sleeve of Mr. Vatanen's pajamas. "Can we talk first," he said. "For now, what I have to say should remain between the two of us men."

Mr. Vatanen stiffened before pointing to the sofa. His wife Aila came to the bedroom door, nervously clutching her nightgown tightly at her throat. "It's alright, Aila," he said, approaching her. They whispered for a second before she stepped back into the bedroom and closed the door.

Mr. Vatanen pulled a chair in close. "Tell me. Please. Where you there? How did it happen? Was it quick? Did they suffer?"

"What's the army telling you?" Jari responded.

"Not much, so far. Telegram. That Teemu and Kimi were missing-in-action and presumed dead. Further details to follow."

Jari glanced at the bedroom door and lowered his voice. "There won't be further details, Mr. Vatanen, and if there are, they'll be lies. What I'm about to tell you is the truth. It's up to you whether you tell your wife or not."

"She's strong."

"They were good soldiers, your boys. You can be proud of them. Resourceful and dependable and reliable. We worked as a team to do our job, and keep each other alive. It wasn't carelessness that brought them down. They died in an ambush. One set by two Karelian infiltrators in Finn uniform."

Mr. Vatanen's face paled. "Traitors! You're sure of this? You can prove it?"

"Saw it with my own eyes. We were on a night patrol. My friend Mika and I had stopped to take a pee. We hadn't caught up to the others when guns started going off ahead. When we got there your boys, plus four other comrades, lay dead in the snow. Only the traitors had survived, and they were blabbering in Russian as they skied off alongside a dozen enemy soldiers."

"What's the army doing about it?"

"Mika and I reported it," Jari said, with a shrug, "and word went out to all units to be on the lookout, but that was the end of it. Nothing more. We swore to avenge our comrades, even if it took a lifetime, but two weeks later Mika, and everyone else in our platoon, died in an artillery attack. I was the only survivor."

Mr. Vatanen's hand reached out to a cigarette package on the end table. With shaking hands he managed to light one, then inhaled deeply. "So, even if they turned up, it would be your one voice to their two," he said, the smoke swirling above his head. "Meaning, there'll be no justice. Ever."

Jari glanced at the bedroom door and lowered his voice even more. "That's what I thought, too, until early this evening. Which is the other reason I'm here."

Mr. Vatanen leaned in, the smoke from his cigarette creating a protective smog.

"I've been convalescing from damage to my hearing. To pass the time, I often go to Rautatientori Square at the railway station. A few hours ago, one of the traitors walked out of the station, plain as day. I followed him to the Hotel Kämp on Pohjoisesplanadi and waited. He never came out. He's still there."

Mr. Vatanen grabbed Jari's wrist, his grip now surprisingly strong. "Tell me you're going to kill him. Please."

"You're their father," Jari answered, carefully. "I thought maybe you would want that honour."

Mr. Vatanen took a deep breath. "Yes, yes, of course. Avenge my two sons. I still have my pistol from the Civil War." He stood up, stiffly. "Can you take me to the Hotel Kämp? What's this man's name?"

"Korpi is the only name I know him by, but he probably has a new one by now."

"We can go to his hotel. Ask at the desk."

Suddenly, they became aware of another presence in the room. "Don't be ridiculous, Eero," Mrs. Vatanen said from the bedroom door.

"Give the soldier your pistol. He can do it. If they trace the gun back, it will be registered as yours and we can take the blame, not this fine young patriot. That's the way Teemu and Kimi would want it."

"Go back to bed, Aila," her husband admonished, as she approached.

"Eero means well," she continued. "But have you noticed his eyes? My Eero can hardly see anymore. If he attempts this someone will die, but it won't be this Mr. Korpi. It'll be my husband, and the traitor will go free."

"With a little direction I can do it," Mr. Vatanen persisted. "And I won't be squeamish about it. I don't know your politics, Mr. Hoivuniemi, but I'm not ashamed to say that in the Civil War I took up arms against the Whites. I fought for the Red cause, because I love Finland. I did it because I wanted to live under communism, but never again under Russian rule."

"Lots of our boys at the Front feel the same, sir, but in the end, we're all Finns. Right now, however, ridding us of this traitor might be tricky. We can't just blunder in. We'd be caught and probably shot ourselves."

"I've got nothing to lose."

"And if you fail," Mrs. Vatanen said, her voice rising, "what would we have accomplished? You shot and me a widow. Please, Eero, fetch your pistol and give it to this man." She took a deep breath, in an effort to calm herself.

Mr. Vatanen sighed, then left the room and returned with the weapon. His wife put her arms around him and held him tight.

Jari checked the gun, surprised to see that it was fully loaded. "Sorry to drag you into this," he said. "I vow to you, as I vowed to my comrades, to avenge this treachery. When it's done, I'll throw your gun into the harbour. And I'll take your names to the grave, however soon or long that may be."

At the door, Mrs. Vatanen hugged him. "What will you do when this is finished?" she asked.

"I'm supposed to return to the Front."

"Supposed to?" she pressed.

Jari shrugged, but didn't answer.

She nodded and patted his shoulder. "As a mother, I would understand if you made . . . other arrangements."

Jari caught the insinuation and nodded.

"Just a minute," Mr. Vatanen said. He turned back into the apartment and returned with a knife. "This was my grandfather's *puukko*. It's been in the family for three generations, and was supposed to go to one of the boys. I still have a daughter. Some day she will understand why her great-grandfather's *puukko* went to a stranger. Please, take it. Use it on Korpi if necessary. If not, it's yours to keep."

Jari turned it over in his hands, feeling the balance and admiring the artwork on the scabbard. He extracted the knife from its sheath. Like so many good Finn knives, the steel bore the "Rovaniemi" imprint. "I am honoured to accept this," he said. "My father also fought in the Civil War, but for the Whites. When he was killed somewhere near Tampere, my grandfather's *puukko* was lost along with him."

5

Pursuit

Helsinki, Finland,
April 1944

Why he and Korpi had been sent to Helsinki as a team then separated, was a mystery to Alvar. But then much of life had become a puzzle. Not a pleasant one at that. The only constant he could count on these days was his revulsion for the crimes he was forced to commit, and his hatred for the man who'd blackmailed him into perpetrating them. What had begun as normal reconnaissance missions behind enemy lines had morphed into ambushes and murder. Now the two of them were in Helsinki on a mission yet to be divulged by whomever was pulling the strings. "Handlers," Korpi called them, which was appropriate, in as much as he could feel their dirty paws all over him. Regardless, whatever this mission turned out to be, Alvar was certain of one thing—Korpi would revel in it.

Locating to Helsinki had one benefit. They had been separated, and ordered not to contact one another. This "holiday" from Korpi had given Alvar an opportunity to explore the city he had heard so much about, but as a Karelian Finn trapped inside Russia had never had a chance to visit. For days he'd played tourist. Even with the city dressed for war, with sandbags piled around strategic buildings, windows taped, and fountains turned off, he couldn't help but marvel at the architecture, boulevards, parks, and public amenities.

This all came to an abrupt halt with the arrival of a note at the front desk of his hotel. Right out of a Joseph Conrad novel it instructed him to take a noon-hour stroll down Esplanadi Boulevard to the Havis Amanda Fountain, circle it twice, then stop to admire the nude sculpture. Emphasis was put on dress—civvies, green tie, brown cap.

Having examined the nude, he was to sit on the steps circling the fountain and eat a sandwich. His contact would approach and say, "With the war on, good bread is hard to get these days." To which he was to reply, "Some bakers have their own sources." But if no one approached, his instructions were to repeat the process day after day until someone did. It all sounded embarrassingly foolish, but Alvar feared the consequences if he didn't follow instructions to the letter.

He was at the fountain, and into his third bite, when he noticed an older man approaching to his left. Wearing horn-rimmed glasses, and a black fedora in desperate need of blocking, he appeared to pay no attention to Alvar as he sat down and extracted a sandwich from his briefcase. He took a bite, chewed for a moment, then cleared his throat. "With the war on," he muttered, "good bread is hard to get these days."

Alvar was so shocked it took him a minute to come to his senses and give the arranged response. The man in the fedora nodded, and took another bite. "Were you followed?" he asked, barely moving his lips.

"Followed?" Alvar responded, cranking his head around to scan the office workers pouring out of the buildings for lunch. Most were women and older men.

"For God's sake, stop looking around," the man admonished. "You'll draw attention."

Alvar swallowed. Although he was no stranger to fear, at the Front he always knew who the enemy was. Here, he had no idea what to expect, let alone where the danger lay. "Followed by who? Military police? You think they're on to Korpi and me?"

"Possibly, which is why this conversation will be short." He reached into his bag and extracted a piece of cheese. "Korpi? Have you been talking to him?"

"No! We were instructed not to communicate. Isn't that why we were put up in different locations?"

"And you're sure you haven't seen him?" Alvar shook his head. "Know anyone who might have?"

"Little chance of that. Neither of us know a soul here. Why?"

"He seems to have disappeared, and you were the last to see him."

"Yeah, but that was three weeks ago." From the corner of his eye,

Alvar saw the man take a bite of cheese, as if waiting for further explanation. "Look, Korpi likes women. Helsinki's full of them, with few men around to keep them happy. My guess is he's shacked up somewhere, and has lost track of time. He'll show. Always does."

"So, you don't know anyone who might have had it in for him?"

Alvar could think of a raft of people who fit the bill, but wasn't about to tell this guy. Didn't these people know how vile Korpi was? Then again, maybe they did. "No personal enemies here in Helsinki to my knowledge," he answered.

Two young ladies approached, walking arm in arm, and giggling. Alvar allowed his eyes to linger on one of them, a tall brunette. She caught his gaze and smiled. He felt a slight flip in his stomach. Beside him the man began gathering up the remains of his lunch. "Find out," he muttered.

"Find out what?"

"What happened to Korpi," he said, crumpling up the paper bag his sandwich had come in, and sliding it surreptitiously behind him. "Korpi's Helsinki address is written on the inside of the bag. When you find him, make sure he knows the trouble he's in."

"What if he's not there? What do I do then?"

The man bent down to tighten his laces. "Use your goddamn imagination, Sorsakoski. We had Korpi in a hotel until a week ago when we ordered him to relocate. He did, to a rooming house near the coal docks. Your orders are to do the same: find a place close to Korpi's, then make contact. Safer that way."

"Move? I'm happy where I am."

"Happy! Jesus Christ, this isn't a goddamned holiday. You're a member of the Red Army and you've just been given an order."

"But finding a new place is not going to be easy. Surely, you can see that? What, with Karelian refugees pouring in, and all the bombed out neighbourhoods, there's hardly anything available."

"Korpi managed to find something," he grunted. "But then, maybe he's smarter than you."

Alvar shrugged off the insult. He knew exactly where his comrade's talents lay, and it wasn't in the grey-matter department.

"Meet me back here in three days," the man said. "With intel on Korpi."

The man rose to his feet, and without a side-wise glance walked away, like he was just another office worker heading back to work. Alvar noted a slight limp, and wondered if it might be a war wound. If so, he was too old for it to have been either of the Winter or Continuation Wars. That left the Civil War, twenty-four years earlier. Helsinki Reds had been pulverized by the Whites in that conflict, as well as in the concentration camps that followed. Memories like that don't disappear. Ever.

To Alvar's relief, finding Korpi's rooming house proved an easy task. It sat between a bombed out building and a warehouse one block from the pier. Down the street, coal was being shovelled onto a conveyor belt that transferred it to an ever-growing pyramid. Plumes of black dust picked up by the onshore wind drifted lazily into the neighbourhood, coating everything in a thick layer of soot. With hours of light left in the day, Alvar opted to watch. Finally, with evening approaching, and no sign of Korpi, he crossed the street and knocked on the door. The knock went unanswered. He tried again, louder. Eventually, a squat woman in a soiled house dress, and hand-knit slippers, opened with a dismissive expression on her face. "I'm looking for my friend, Tuomas Korpi. He's expecting me," he blurted out.

"Good luck there. I'm looking for him, too," she snorted, as she began to close the door. "He's been gone a week, and his rent's past due."

Alvar stuck his foot out to prevent the door closing and reached for his wallet. "Perhaps I could pay his arrears. Maybe, stay in the room until he shows up." He could see she was interested. Her jaw moved up and down, as she contemplated the offer. "I could throw in a little extra. Just to cover the inconvenience."

That sealed the deal. She motioned him in, and wrote down his name. "Upstairs," she said, "second door to the right. No noise, no vodka, and no women. *Ymmärsi?*"

The rooming house, like the war-battered city, went to bed early, but Alvar was too agitated to get much rest. The contact had made it clear: "Mess this up and you pay dearly." Strangely, however, it was the thought of Korpi showing up in the middle of the night that had him most on edge. Then there was the woman with the two kids in the next room. He'd learned that her husband was missing at the Front. She cried non-stop. He'd also managed to chat up other roomers—one old man, two drunks, a veteran with a missing arm, and an exhausted coal shoveller—none of them were able to shed any light on Korpi. Even casual queries at the café down the block had drawn blanks.

With only one day left before the rendezvous at the fountain, and with nothing to report, desperation began to set in. Alvar considered disappearing altogether, but where would he go? The Russians would be looking for him, and it wouldn't be long before some Finn busybody challenged him for not being in uniform. Best to find Korpi and stay the course, he ruefully decided. But how? He wished he had the nerve to go to the police and ask for assistance in finding a missing friend. But if Korpi had been caught carrying bogus papers, they would pounce on him. He looked at his watch. Fourteen hours to the rendezvous. It was going to be a long night.

Alvar awoke at dawn to the sound of car doors slamming. Running to the window, he saw two policeman, one short with high cheek bones and grey hair, the other tall, broad-shouldered, and blond. *One Finn, one Swede,* he said to himself. Quickly, he stepped into the hallway to listen as they banged on the door. The landlady, wrapped in a faded housecoat, cursed as she shuffled to let them in. "I'm sergeant Eriksson, and this is corporal Raikkonen," said the taller of the two.

"I know who you are. What do you want?"

"You have a Mr. Tuomas Korpi, staying here, I believe," Eriksson said.

"Maybe."

"Don't be coy, Mrs. Kovalainen."

"Not coy, officer," she shot back, "honest. The room's listed in his name, but Mr. Korpi hasn't been around for days. There's another guy staying there now. What's Korpi done?"

"You don't look surprised, Mrs. Kovalainen. Why would that be?"

Peeking over the railing at the top of stairs, Alvar saw her straighten up as she took a deep breath. "All I do is collect the rent and ask no questions. That's my motto."

If the old lady thought that would satisfy Eriksson she was wrong. "With the war, and who knows how many aliens about, I was expecting better from you, Mrs. Kovalainen. Perhaps, you'd feel more comfortable talking to us down at the police station?"

Mrs. Kovalainen rolled her eyes. "I'll tell you this much. Korpi showed up a week ago looking for a room. Having nothing available, I turned him down. He left in a huff. Next thing you know one of my roomers, a war amputee with a pension, gets beaten to an inch of his life, and up and leaves. Before I got the room cleaned Korpi's back, asking about the room and refusing to take no for an answer."

"Know where this war vet might have gone?"

"No idea."

"Do you see him as the type to get even."

"Really, officer? I told you the guy's an amputee."

"Might he have had friends capable of revenge?"

"*Jumalauta*! I was his landlady not his auntie. How would I know?"

There was a shuffling of feet, and Alvar feared the policemen would leave without even a hint as to why they were after Korpi. "*Come on Mrs. Kovalainen,*" Alvar said under his breath, "*keep the conversation going.*" He leaned over the railing for a better view. Landlady and policeman were locked in a staring contest.

Eriksson spoke first. "If Korpi walked into the room right now, would you recognize him?"

"Stupid question. Of course I would."

"Good, then you're coming down to the morgue with us to identify a body."

"Not on your life. I hardly knew the guy. Why not ask his friend upstairs?" She glanced up, catching sight of Alvar. "That's him there," she said, pointing. "Get him to go."

The policemen bounded up the stairs. Alvar stood his ground, thinking fast. "I caught the tail end of that," he yawned. "Heard the name Korpi. Came out to check. We're old army buddies."

"Then what are you doing in Helsinki? All leaves have been cancelled," Raikkonen snapped.

"We're here to check on new equipment and supplies coming in from Germany," Alvar countered.

"What kind of equipment?"

"Really, officer, you know better than to ask. Spilling that could get me shot. What I can do, though, is identify the body."

Alvar's brain was in high gear as they made their way to the morgue. Eriksson was acting friendly, but not enough to hide his suspicion. From all appearances he seemed a thorough type, which was terrifying, in as much as he was bound to have Alvar's credentials examined closely. If the body turned out to be Korpi, what kind of questions would that provoke? How would he account for the past three weeks in Helsinki? All Eriksson had to do was contact the Finn army unit he claimed to belong to and he'd be summarily marched to the wall. On the other hand, if Korpi had died in a bombing raid, there'd be no further questions. In that case, all they'd want from Alvar would be a possible identification. He'd fake a bit of sadness, and be on his way. With this possibility lodged in his mind he began to relax, until it hit him that Eriksson would know the difference between a bombing victim and a homicide.

Given Helsinki's compact centre town, and lack of vehicular traffic because of the war, it should have been a short trip. It wasn't. Craters and rubble from bombed out buildings had them proceeding carefully, which gave Alvar enough time to come up with a cover story. It was now almost 08:20—four hours until the rendezvous at the fountain. If he could talk his way out of this police thing, all he had to do was keep low for the morning, report on Korpi, and demand to be sent back to the Seventh Russian Army, where he belonged. Four hours and a bit of luck was all he needed to put Korpi, and this mess, behind him.

The instant the coroner pulled the sheet down past the cadaver's nose, Alvar knew he was in trouble. Aware that all eyes were trained on him for a reaction, he tried his best to play the co-operative, dedicated citizen. It was not a strong performance. The problem wasn't that it was unmistakably Korpi. The danger lay in the way he'd died. Alvar had seen it often at the Front: bullet enters eye, travels through brain, exits the back of the skull. Only in this case, with half the back of the head missing, and burn marks on the face, the bullet had clearly been fired from close range.

"Well?" Eriksson asked. "This your friend?"

Alvar nodded. "Korpi, alright," he replied.

"You don't seem too upset, Private Sorsakoski."

"What do you expect?" Alvar responded, turning to meet the policeman's gaze straight on. "You think this is new to me? I'm a soldier, I see this sort of thing all the time. And would you stop calling him my friend. Just because we were in the same unit didn't make us bosom pals."

"So, are you saying that Korpi wasn't a likeable guy?"

"I'm saying we weren't close. Nothing more."

"It's possible then that he could have had enemies in his unit?" He waited for a nod before continuing. "You among them perhaps? Maybe enough to kill him yourself?"

"That's ridiculous. I've hardly stepped out of the rooming house in three days."

Eriksson glanced down at Korpi's chart. "According to the coroner's report, your friend has been dead for anywhere from four to seven days. That leaves you with a minimum of ninety-six unaccounted hours."

"Look here, sergeant Eriksson, does it make sense that I'd kill him, and then move into his room?"

Eriksson reached down to pull the sheet back up. "Maybe you were expecting something. A delivery, say, or someone showing up."

"Why are you so anxious to put this on me?"

Eriksson stepped closer. "Let's just say because something smells fishy here. We speak Swedish in my house so variations in Finnish dialect escape me. Corporal Raikkonen, on the other hand, is a Finn's Finn, and he tells me you're Karelian."

"And proud of it. What's that got to do with anything? Helsinki's full of Karelian refugees these days."

"True, but he's also detected a hint of Russian phraseology in your speech. Makes one wonder, doesn't it? Especially, with talk of Russian soldiers . . . well let's not go there for the time being. Right now, how about you fill me in on those missing days, starting with where you were staying before the rooming house."

Alvar still had a few cards to play, but he could feel the odds turning against him. How ironic to be facing his demise over an outcome that pleased him, but one that he had nothing to do with. "I was booked in at the Polytechnic Student Centre on Lönnrotinkatu," he said, flatly.

"Wow! Pretty fancy. Must have had a powerful reason to give that up for Korpi's dump." Alvar let it go. The sergeant pressed. "Booked in there until four days ago, or booked in still?"

"Still."

"Why pay for a room you're not using? Rather strange, wouldn't you say?"

"It wasn't intentional. When I got to Korpi's I stayed on, waiting for him, that's all; one day led to three."

Eriksson stepped in closer to Raikkonen. Following a whispered conversation, they seemed to reach an agreement. "Listen carefully," Eriksson announced, "here's what's going to happen. First, we go to the Student Centre to verify your story, then it's off to the police station to get you settled into your new accommodations. You'll be safe there. Nobody can get to you."

Raikkonen's seemed to find this funny, but kept quiet.

"You can't do that. You've got nothing to . . ."

"There's a war on!" Eriksson snapped. "I can do whatever I think necessary. Got it? Right now I want you close while I make a few inquiries, and check out your documents. After that, we'll see. Who knows, maybe the army will shed some light on this, 'special equipment' coming in from Germany, you've been hinting at."

"I'll do the talking," Eriksson said as they approached the front desk at the student centre. The clerk recognized Alvar with a nod. "Key for room 6," the sergeant demanded. "Oh, any messages for Alvar Sorsa-koski?" The clerk shook his head as he handed over the key.

Alvar's panic dissipated on hearing the 'no messages' message. Perhaps, the anonymous men controlling his life were not so stupid after all. Perhaps, he might even get out of this alive. He checked the clock on the lobby wall—09:10—three hours to the rendezvous. He'd have to come up with something.

Located in the heart of the city, the Polytechnic Student Centre couldn't have been more different from Korpi's rooming house. Built in 1903 to resemble a medieval castle, it boasted towers, Karelian gables, granite walls, and archways. In all respects striking. But this was not where Alvar was quartered. The student dorms were located in the annex at the back, with access through a connecting passageway. Alvar's dorm was on the third floor. Two other guests were in the eight-bed room when they entered. They gasped at the police presence. Alvar moved quickly to the trunk at the end of his bed, unlocked it, and stood back. Eriksson motioned with his head for Raikkonen to rummage through the belongings.

"Nothing more than socks, underwear, couple of shirts, and a sweater, sir," he reported.

Eriksson pulled the blankets down, turned over the mattress, and glanced under the bed. Finally, with a hint of disappointment on his face, he turned back to Alvar who was clutching his stomach. "What's your problem?" he snapped.

"I haven't had my morning shit, that's what."

"Then take one, for Christ's sake. Raikkonen will go in with you." The deputy made a face.

"For crying out loud," Alvar responded, "it's not as if you're dealing with a desperate criminal here. Grant me the decency of a moment of privacy."

Eriksson seemed to reflect on this, as if unwilling to let Alvar slip out of sight even for a second. "Alright," he said, finally, "you've got two minutes. If you're not done by then we'll break down the door."

Unlike the main building, the annex had been constructed with lumber, calling for stricter fire regulations. The ideal would have been an external fire escape, but the institution went for the cheaper option—an anchored rope under the window in every room, including the toilet. In an instant, Alvar had the door locked, the window open, and the fire rope in his hand. Had it been deep winter, frost would have welded the window shut, but with the warm April weather it slid open with barely a squeak. Dropping the rope, he saw that it reached down to a shed in the alley. He had just touched down on the roof when he heard the ruckus above. Eriksson's face appeared then vanished from the window. Raikkonen grabbed the rope, but the deputy did not share either Alvar's dexterity nor his soldier's conditioning. The last thing Alvar heard as he bounded down the alley was a heavy plop on the roof, followed by a sharp scream.

If Alvar had answered Eriksson's question honestly, as to his activities during those unaccounted days in Helsinki, he would have said exploring the city. Which was why he knew which back alleys to take, and which to avoid. With two hours to kill before the rendezvous, he was considering going back to the coal docks when he picked up the sound of aircraft in the distance. Not one, but dozens. The noise grew louder. He burst into a run. That the Russian air force was bold enough to bomb Helsinki in daylight spoke volumes about the current state of Finn air defences. For Alvar, the impending raid was about to make walking in the open extremely hazardous. On the other hand, with everyone scurrying for shelter, who would take note of one, harried-looking man running at their side?

Alvar did not wait for the "all clear" sirens, before leaving the basement shelter for the Havis Amanda fountain. Back on the street he walked quickly, covering his face, so as not to inhale the dust, heavy smoke, and the sharp smell of cordite from the explosions, that hit the nostrils like fresh nail polish. A fire engine raced by, bells clanging. By the time he got to the Esplanadi, people were beginning to come up from the shelters. Still, as he closed in on the Fountain, it was clear that no one was there waiting for him. He had a moment of panic, then checked his watch to see that it was only 11:25. Half-way down the Esplanadi people were frantically clearing debris from a damaged building. A wall looked about to collapse at any minute, but with muffled sounds coming from the inside, the impromptu rescue team laboured on. Alvar joined them, trying his best to keep his head down and face hidden.

At five minutes to twelve, an elderly woman was pulled from the rubble to cheers. Hands were shaken, backs slapped. To Alvar's amazement the mood of the crowd was one of resolve more than anger, even though it was obvious that Finland's days were numbered. He was bent over brushing at the dust on his clothes when a woman with a child rewarded him with a peck on the cheek. Straightening to acknowledge he caught a glimpse of the fountain where a lone person was seated. His contact.

"You look like a chimney sweep," the man said, taking in Alvar's soot-stained attire.

Sitting a few feet away Alvar, took another futile swipe at his clothes. "Korpi is dead. I saw the body at the morgue. The police are looking for me. You have to get me out of here."

The contact pulled out a book and pretended to read. "Kaivopuisto Park," he said. "Eight o'clock tonight. Go to the observatory, and keep circling back to it every fifteen minutes until you're approached."

"Are you setting me up? That'll look suspicious."

"I am not setting you up and, no, that will not look suspicious. Not there. If approached and asked, 'Looking for company, soldier?'— those exact words—you'll know it's our man. You reply, 'Only if they're clean and friendly.'" Alvar had a ton of questions, but before he got a chance to blurt them out, the contact was on his feet, and walking away.

Watching him disappear in the crowd, Alvar realized that he had to get off the Esplanadi, and fast. The three hours he'd managed to elude capture before the meeting had seemed an eternity. Now he was facing eight more. Where to go? Where to hide? The coal docks offered the greatest potential, but it was a long walk, and much of it out in the open. Kaivopuisto Park, on the other hand, was supposedly closer, and might offer something. Decision made, he struck out, moving south down Fabianinkatu Street. Instinct screamed run, but common sense had him walking at a steady pace. He came close to panicking when two policemen rounded a corner heading straight towards him, but he managed to stay calm, and avoid eye contact. They passed by, barely noticing him.

When Fabianinkatu Street came to an abrupt end at a wooded park, Alvar couldn't believe his luck in hitting his destination so quickly. Now, all he had to do was find the observatory, but after wandering up and down over the treed hill, with no sign of it, he began to wonder if the handler had purposely misguided him. Twice he tried, and twice he found himself back at the bottom of Fabianinkatu Street. Realizing the futility of aimless wandering, he decided to risk asking for directions. The middle-aged woman he approached appeared only too happy to assist.

Fifteen minutes later, Alvar found himself walking into a second park that backed onto the harbour entrance. *Kaivopuisto Park for sure*, he said to himself, glancing around. To his right was a long hill, and atop it a tiny, domed structure that had to be the observatory. Barren of trees and exposed, the hilltop location might have made sense to astronomers, but not to a fugitive in search of a place to hide. He would have to leave, but at least he had his bearings. Foremost on his mind was shelter. Walking briskly, he headed west.

With the sun finally down, it felt good to crawl out of his hiding place and move again. He'd spent the day under a tarp in a stinky boat, listening to his growling stomach. By mid-afternoon, when the pressure to relieve himself had grown too intense to ignore, he'd fumbled about and found a bailing can. Now, re-entering Kaivopuisto Park, he was surprised by how many men and women were there. From the appraising glances cast his way, it didn't take long to realize what was up. That, and the hushed whispers and occasional moan coming from the bushes, told the story. Yes, people were pairing up, but not always male and female. The passwords he was to exchange with his new contact suddenly took on new meaning.

Approaching the observatory, he realized he was late. Not by much, but by now it was clear that his handlers were methodical, as well as ruthless. He slowed his pace. No one approached. Fifteen minutes later, he walked by again. Still no contact. On the third go around, just as he was beginning to wonder if he should clear off, a voice from behind proffered the "looking for company soldier?" question. When Alvar replied accordingly, the contact took him by the hand and led him, not to the bushes, but to a waiting taxi.

Not a word was spoken as they drove north through the inky darkness onto unfamiliar streets. Fifteen minutes later, the taxi turned into what appeared to be an elegant neighbourhood of wide boulevards, treed parks, and row upon row of two-storied, timbered, homes; each identical to the neighbour on either side. They entered one, where he was taken into a back room and left. Alone.

Confused, he tried to come to grips with what was happening, but exhaustion and hunger had his head in a muddle. Why had they brought him to Helsinki? Who killed Korpi? If the Finns were responsible, it had to be because they knew what they had been up to at the Front. That would bring his usefulness to the Russians to a crashing halt, and they'd want him out of the way. But if so, why taxi him all the way up to this house, when they could just as easily have shot him, and dumped him in the harbour? The harder he tried to put sense to it, the milkier it got.

He considered making a run for it, but no sooner had it crossed his mind than the door opened, and two burly men entered. "What's happening?" he demanded.

"Your clothes; take them off," one of the men ordered. "Off!" he repeated, when Alvar hesitated. Naked, they led him to a sauna at the back of the house. Clean clothes hung on a hook behind the door. Bath completed he was ushered into a dining room, where a single plate of hot food lay waiting on the table. The escorts left without a word. Alvar eyed the food and hesitated, until hunger trumped caution and he dug in. Alone in the room, and with the food gone except for a plate of buns, he stewed over the possibility that this might have been his last meal. His eyes were at the point of closing when the French doors opened, and a matronly woman stepped in. She sat down opposite him and smiled.

"Well now, Sami," she said, "feeling better, are we?"

Alvar frowned. He didn't have to look around to know that there were only two people in the room, and neither of them was a Sami. "Beg your pardon," he responded, "but I think you're mistaking me for someone else."

She chuckled and leaned towards him. "Mistakes are not allowed in this organization. We've seen fit to change your name, that's all. You see, in our business, yours and mine, name changes are common. You'll get used to it. That is, if you show aptitude and meet our standards."

Alvar straightened. "In all due respect, I'd prefer to be sent back to my unit at the Front. Soldiering I understand."

She reached for a bun. "You want to be useful to Mother Russia, don't you?" Alvar nodded. "And you do know that it's the sworn policy of the Comintern to promote communism around the globe?"

On this Alvar hesitated. "Didn't I read somewhere that they'd changed that policy?"

She flushed slightly, but didn't let go of the smile. "Let's just say that we need you to be a different kind of soldier now." She slid a large manila envelop across the table. "It's official; these documents are proof that you are now Sami Aalto."

Alvar looked at the envelope then back at the woman, trying to imagine what else might be in there. He suspected that whatever it was, it wouldn't be good. Was he to kill somebody? If so, he'd have to protest because that was Korpi, not him. But, based on what he'd done behind Finn Army lines, maybe that's how they saw him. "May I speak freely?" he asked. She nodded. "Why me? There must be lots of people far better qualified to do whatever it is you've got in mind."

The smile vanished. "I think we both know the answer," she replied. "In this war, we need people who know how to take care of business when asked. Such people are rare. You show signs of possibly being one of them." He blanched. They really did see him as just another Korpi.

She opened the folder she'd brought in. "Says here that you speak four languages: Finnish, Russian, Swedish, English. That true, Sami?"

He nodded. "Swedish and English not so good."

"And how is it you come to know those two languages, Sami?"

He grimaced inwardly at her persistence in calling him Sami, but tried not to show annoyance. She still hadn't identified herself, but she had his dossier, as well as the command of all the subservient goons he'd encountered since the initial rendezvous at the fountain, three days earlier. "My father and his parents lived in the United States for several years after the Civil War. I learned it from them as a kid."

"Perfect, that's what it says here," she said, with a nod. "What about your mother's parents in Vyborg? They speak any foreign languages?"

Alvar felt a chill shoot through him as he recalled Korpi's threat to harm his grandparents if they failed to co-operate. Was this well-spoken, cultured lady merely reinforcing the threat, but in a more sophisticated manner? "I really can't say," he responded. "Other than a few minutes with them after we liberated Viipuri—Vyborg," he hastily corrected, "I haven't seen them since I was a toddler. Does it matter?"

"Depends," she said, briskly. "Now then, shall we get down to business?"

"If I may?" he interrupted, hoping still to find a way out of this situation. "You're looking at nothing more than a regular grunt from the Seventh Army with no special skills. If I don't get back to my unit soon, it'll be a firing squad for desertion."

"Already taken care of," she smiled. Then changing the subject, "on that special assignment you and Korpi undertook at the Front, any idea who you were working for?"

"The Seventh Army, I thought."

"Right, but which branch?"

Alvar shrugged. "No idea. Korpi took care of that stuff."

"And he never told you?"

"Told me what, exactly?"

"That you were under direct orders from the NKVD."

"Who?"

"NKVD—the military intelligence branch of the Soviet Army. Korpi was a junior officer with them; not a bright one as it turns out," she added. "He got himself killed while you kept your head, and worked your way out of an extremely tight spot. That, *Sami*, makes you potentially valuable. It doesn't guarantee that you've got the right stuff, but who knows, with training you could turn out to be more than, 'just a grunt.'"

"Does this put me back with the NKVD then?" She whooped so loud that he wondered what could possibly be so funny.

"Not on your life. They wrote you off with Korpi. Which just might turn out to be their loss and our gain."

"I'm confused. And you are?"

"GRU," she answered, watching for a response that never came. "There's a bit of similarity between us and the NKVD, in as much as we're both into intelligence gathering. But unlike them, we're looking beyond the war. Way beyond."

Alvar realized he was sitting on his hands, something he hadn't done since high school when he trembled at the prospect of the chemistry teacher calling on him to rhyme off formulas in front of the class. The picture was becoming clear. Because he'd been lucky enough to give the Helsinki police the slip, she figured he had the smarts to do undercover stuff; a notion he was going to squelch right now. "Do I have an option?" he asked.

"One does not refuse the Soviet secret police."

He took a deep breath, and stared at the photo of Stalin on the wall behind the woman. "Tell me if I have this right," he said, looking at her directly. "If I don't co-operate, you'll turn me over to the army with instructions to shoot me for desertion. If I do sign on, you'll post me to some place with zero chance of survival."

She shrugged. "Crude, but not completely off the mark."

He sighed and looked away, wondering if GRU personnel ever gave straight answers. "Why wouldn't I just say no, and get it over with? It's not that I've got anything to go back to—last month my parents and family died in a German air raid."

"There's still your grandparents?"

He caught the implication and gasped. "You wouldn't?" he said. "Not them. They're old."

"It would give me no pleasure, but, surely, as a soldier you understand that sometimes, for the greater good, we're called upon to do unpleasant things." She gave him a minute before adding, "Your decision, 'Sami.' What's it going to be?"

He shrugged, cognizant of the vice she had him in. "GRU, I guess."

"Wise choice," she said. "Good to get that cleared up." She handed him a document and took him through it, pointing out where to sign along the way.

"So does this make me GRU?" he asked.

"Not yet. An apprentice, says it best. You have to prove yourself to a lot of people first."

"If I do, they'll have me shooting more Finnish soldiers in the back, I assume?"

"Heavens, there's no longer much need for that. The German-Finn offensive is collapsing. Our Intelligence has it that they're getting ready to pull their troops out to Norway, via Rovaniemi."

"So, where do I fit in?"

"A six-month training course in Moscow to begin with. Do well there, and who knows. These are promising times for young communists like you, Sami. Russia is coming out of this war as a world power. Our job is to make certain we never get pushed around again, and to do that we need people on the ground in a host of countries. Soon, all of Europe will be communist. Why not the New World, too? There are lots of communist-leaning Finns in the United States and Canada, longing for just that. All they need is a little assistance in realizing their dream."

6

On the Run

Kemi, Finland,
(near the Swedish border),
May 1944

Moving cautiously in the darkness, Jari worked his way down the side of the house, careful lest he stumble on something and awaken the neighbours. It had taken him three weeks to get from Helsinki to his aunt and uncle's place in Kemi, on the northern tip of the Gulf of Bothnia, close to the Swedish border. Mostly, he'd been travelling by night—a combination of walking and hopping freight trains. Considering the roadblocks, and the ongoing national crisis, exposing himself in daylight was out of the question—patriotic citizens were prone to challenging men not in uniform. Daylight hours he'd spent under bridges, or holing up in wooded areas.

Reaching the backyard he halted in his tracks, certain that the nebulous form looking up at him from the ground was an animal, ready to pounce. For a minute there was no movement on either side, until swallowing his fear, he inched forward. Only when directly upon the object did he recognize it for what it was—an overturned wheel barrow. Mind going to beat the band, he sat down on it to catch his breath. The instant he did, he began to have second thoughts. Maybe coming here was a mistake. Never expecting to get this far, he hadn't considered the reception that might be awaiting. Aunt Toini would be her usual welcoming self; ex-Civil War officer, Uncle Pentti, would be anything but. Who could blame him? Jari's mere presence was a danger to both of them. A more considerate nephew would never put aging relatives in this position—something Uncle Pentti would not hesitate to draw to his attention. But they were all the family he had, and he was in desperate need of help.

Picking what he remembered to be their bedroom window, he tapped lightly. After a few tries, the curtains moved slightly, and a familiar face appeared at the window. "Uncle Pentti, it's me, Jari," he said, in a voice barely louder than a whisper.

Jari's heart sank. The stern stare glaring back at him told the story. He should never have come. The authorities must have been around asking about him. It was going to be a short visit. After a long pause, Uncle Pentti came to life. "Back door," he mouthed, pointing a finger.

Even with the door open Uncle Pentti hung back, scanning the shadows and neighbouring houses before motioning Jari in. Only when they'd entered the kitchen, and the curtains had been pulled tight, did he turn the lights on and speak. "Jari, what the hell are you up to?"

Aunt Toini moved towards him, a look of anguish on her face, but her arms wide open. The bear hug that followed was too much for Jari. He tried to swallow the sobs, but they refused to be stifled. She pulled him in closer, rocking him in her arms and patting his back. "There, there, all's good. You're safe with us."

Jari closed his eyes, conjuring up a hazy image of his mother, and the security of her embrace. Although eleven years younger than her, Toini was the spitting image of his mom, as he remembered her before the sickness had set in. He would have continued clinging to her if not for Pentti clearing his throat. When she released him, he swiped his eyes with the back of his hand, and turned to face his uncle. For a moment the two men stood mute, staring at each other like boxers studying an opponent in the opposite corner.

Uncle led with the first jab. "You got a lot of explaining to do, young man. And it better be good. What kind of Finn would . . . ?"

"Pentti!" Auntie snapped. "Later! First, we get food into the boy. Look how gaunt he is. Goodness knows when he last ate."

Uncle Pentti plunked down at the table, and motioned for Jari to do the same. Auntie hustled to the larder. When she was out of hearing range, Pentti got right back into it. "You're not in uniform? They came looking for you," he said, lowering his voice.

Jari rubbed his hands together and straightened his shoulders. "My uniform days have come to an end," he replied. Pentti waited, rolling his hand for a fuller explanation. Jari continued. "Wish I could say it's because I've been discharged, or that the war's over, but that would be lying. Oh, I've been injured alright, but my kind of wound gets no sympathy from the army."

"*Perkele*! You've gone AWOL! That what you're saying?"

Jari took a deep breath and leaned forward. A noise came from the larder—Toini shifting pots. "You may not want to hear this, Uncle Pentti, but the war's lost. Just a matter of time before Finland surrenders. We're *kaput*, as the Germans say. We backed the wrong horse."

"Finns don't quit. Germans neither."

"Fuck the Germans! They suckered us with promises of getting back what we lost in the Winter War. Then, when we recovered what rightfully belonged to us, they forced us to keep going deep into Russia. Soon as we did that, we lost the moral high ground. Now that the Russians have their act together they've got us on the run, and won't stop until they take Helsinki."

"Nonsense!"

"It's a total cock-up, Uncle Pentti. And you're wrong about the Germans not quitting. Wait and see. They're getting ready to drop us for their own homeland."

"*Perkele*! Such shit! What's gotten into you? After the Winter War four years ago, when you could have gone back to Canada, you didn't. Why? Because you were all gung-ho for another crack at the Russians. Claimed Mannerheim had caved early."

"Yeah, well, that was then, wasn't it? Two wars and two losses has put paid to that. I've had my fill of war and killing. And what the hell do you know about it anyway? Sitting up here in Kemi, hundreds of kilometres from the Front, you haven't a clue about what's really going on."

"Now you come crawling back here with your tail between your legs. You're a disgrace to the family. I'm just glad my surname's not Hoivuniemi."

"Wake up, Uncle Pentti. This isn't you're Civil War, where the good guys are White and the bad guys Red. This is screwed up, convoluted and dirty—Russians, Germans, Finns, Karelian-Russian infiltrators, Nazis killing Jews, SS torturing Russians, daily bombing raids on Helsinki civilians. Look, I've no more use for the Ivans than the next guy, but what the Germans do to them is inhuman—made me ashamed to soldier in the same cause."

"Bullshit! All I'm hearing is a weak excuse for saving your own ass—a cop out. And whatever the SS gets up to is none of our doing. That's something the Germans are going to have to wear."

"Yeah, but we've turned a blind eye. Shoulda told them to stuff it two years ago. Now we're about to pay, and it's not going to be pretty."

"And the solution is to run? You don't see it, do you? The more resistance we put up now, the greater likelihood of the Russians agreeing to an armistice. Just like in the Winter War. So, do your duty like a good Finn and get your ass back to the Front."

Jari shook his head. "To late for that. I've been liberated."

"What are you talking about, liberated? By whose authority?"

"The only one that counts, my own. Like it or not, I've declared Jari Hoivuniemi a decommissioned soldier."

"Coward is more like it. Makes me sick."

Jari jumped to his feet. "Fine, I'll get out of your hair! Wouldn't want to upset old, hard-ass Uncle Pentti" He picked up his rucksack. "What the hell was I thinking, coming here?"

"Stop fighting! Both of you!" They turned to see Aunt Toini in the doorway. "Sit down, Jari! And you, Pentti Peltonen, keep your mouth shut! I don't know what to think about this any more than you do, but the nephew we scrubbed, raised, and sent off to repel the nation's enemies has come back. Crawling, maybe, but we owe him a listen. He's not leaving this house until he's eaten, rested, steadied his nerves, and, maybe even gotten his senses under control. I don't care how long it takes we're not sending him away in this condition."

Pentii raised his hands. "Then he's your responsibility," he replied, "and he better not stick his face one inch outside our door. No way do I want the neighbours seeing a deserter moping around my place."

Jari sank back into the chair, his eyes on the floor. Taking the door was the logical solution, but in his exhausted state how long could he last on his own? All his efforts in the past weeks had been geared to reaching the Swedish frontier. But that was as far as his planning had gone. Now that he was close, he had no idea how to go about crossing over. He couldn't do it alone.

It was well into the afternoon the next day when Jari wandered into the kitchen. Pentti was sitting at the table in a haze of smoke, an overflowing ashtray and a cup of spruce tea in front of him. Toini was on the back stoop, hanging out a washing. Some of it Jari's.

"Not too late to change your mind," Pentti grunted.

Jari sighed and sat down. "For God sake's, Uncle, give me a chance to wake up, will ya?"

"I've been thinking. If the army's as desperate as you say, they'll overlook this little lapse in judgement. What's important is that you get to them first, before they come back here looking for you. I could go with you. Speak on your behalf. I'm respected in these parts."

"They'll have me shot."

"Not if you approach them the right way." Pentti went to the gramophone and put on a record. Up came the opening notes of Sibelius', *Finlandia*.

"Good God, Uncle. I suppose you think that's subtle. Turn it off." Jari grabbed the salt shaker and began sliding it back and forth from hand to hand.

Pentti lowered the volume and sat down. He'd seen the look on Jari's face and knew the music was having an effect. "You have a good military record," he said, in a low voice. "Three years at the Front. Only member of your platoon to survive. Nerves shot up a bit. They'll respect all that."

"Normally, yes, but everything's changed. These days the army has no time for my kind of crap."

"Well, supposing I approach them, by myself? Just to sound them out. I wouldn't have to give away your whereabouts, or anything like that. I could just . . ."

Toini came back in and glared at her husband. "Good heavens, Pentti," she said, "could you not at least have got the boy something to eat?" She disappeared for several minutes, returning with a mug of steaming tea, jam, and homemade biscuits that he could smell long before they made it to the table.

He ate in silence, while Auntie prattled on about nothing, and Uncle puffed away. "Damn roll-your-owns," Pentti muttered "You gotta keep dragging on them or they go out."

When Jari finished eating, Toini rose to clear away the dishes, but he motioned her down. "You two are good people," he said. "It's important that I come clean. I owe you that."

Pentti rubbed his face. "Christ! There's more?"

"Are you sure you want to do this," Toini said. "Whatever it is, maybe, it should wait."

"I want to get everything out before they come looking for me." Jari took a deep breath and continued. "They may be after me for more than desertion."

Uncle stared at him. "What could be worse?"

"Three weeks ago, I killed a man."

Pentti looked puzzled. "So? You're a soldier and this is war. That's what you're supposed to do."

"It was in Helsinki, Uncle. Not at the Front. And the man was wearing a Finn uniform."

Toini covered her ears with her hands. "*Herran tähden*" she said, "Jari, Jari, what have you done?"

"It's not what you think, Auntie. And I'm not sorry. Uncle would have done the same."

Pentti had his eyes closed and was rubbing his temples. "Are you telling us the police are after you as well as the army?"

"Not sure," Jari said, with a shrug. "Only thing I know for certain is that I can't stay here long. Just long enough to rest up, figure out how to get to Sweden, and move on."

Auntie cleared her throat. "Whatever you did, I'm sure you had no choice. Best we don't know the details."

"But I want to tell you. If the police are actually onto me they'll be sure to have all the details. What they won't have is the why. It's important to me that you understand before word gets out."

Uncle was on his feet, getting ready to pace. Toini glared at him. "Sit down, Pentti," she said. "He's right. Best we get it from him." She turned to Jari. "Talk, then, if that's what you want. We'll hear you out.

After that we can decide what's to be done."

"I'm not looking to drag you into this, Auntie."

"Go ahead. We're listening."

Jari's mind was in a muddle. He fidgeted uncomfortably. All the way up to Kemi he had rehearsed how best to explain. Now he found his carefully concocted speech collapsing in a jumble of disconnected words. "You fought the Reds in the Civil war, Uncle. You know how they can be." Pentti nodded, but didn't speak. "Thousands of them went to live in Russia after it was over, because they couldn't stomach the idea of living under a government that wasn't communist. Well, some went to Canada, too."

"What's that got to do with this killing?" Pentti said.

"God, will you just let him talk, Pentti?"

"By the time I got to Canada, in the '30s, they were pretty well established up in Northern Ontario—Sudbury, Timmins, Port Arthur, even Hearst, where I finally found work. Seems they were determined to drive any Finn who wasn't Red out of the country. Got pretty tense between the two factions. But when the Winter War started, a lot of us, Reds and Whites alike, came home to fight—most on the side of Finland, but apparently not all."

"What are you suggesting?" Pentti said.

"I'm not suggesting anything. I'm telling you what I saw with my own eyes—Red Finns from the Russian side infiltrating our units at the Front. Surely, you must have heard about this?"

Pentti took a second to answer. "Rumours," he said.

"So, you were aware then?"

"I guess so. Vaguely. But we know how to deal with those types," he replied, tapping his temple with a finger. "We're not going to forget. When the war is over, those bastards will pay. What's this got to do with you?"

"A few months ago, two guys showed up in our unit. One of them I recognized from Canada; a cruel bastard named Korpi, who beat White Finns to an inch of their death. Then, one night on ski patrol, they ambushed my platoon, killing all but my friend Mika and me."

"And you killed the traitors on the spot," Pentti said. "So, what's the fuss? That deserves a medal. It sure as hell isn't murder."

Jari shook his head. "What I did happened in Helsinki, not at the Front. I wouldn't be alive if I'd tried it there; there were two of us and a gang of them. No, we skied back and reported the ambush, then waited for them to return to the platoon. But those two never showed up again. A warning was issued to be on the lookout, but in the chaos there wasn't much more the army could do. Me and Mika and the remainder of the platoon, though, including sergeant Keltamaki, swore to shoot those two on sight, should they ever cross our paths."

"Outnumbered or not, I can't believe you didn't at least try . . ."

Toini cut him off. "You weren't there, Pentti. Let him finish."

"Two weeks later, what's left of my platoon was wiped out and I found myself in a Helsinki hospital with nothing to do but think about how sick I was of war and death. When they finally let me out on day passes, I took to going to the railway station, just to be around normal civilians." Jari tipped his head to the ceiling as if unsure how to proceed.

"And?" Pentti said. "You can't stop now."

"That's where I saw him."

"Saw who?" Toini whispered.

"Korpi, walking out of Helsinki Central Station, bold as brass. My head spun. What to do? Couldn't turn him in, not if I was about to desert, but couldn't walk away either. All I could think of was Mika and the Vatanen boys and my dead comrades. In the end, I let the killer in me take over and got hold of a gun and . . ."

"And what?" Pentti pressed. "Spit it out."

"You get the picture," Jari said."

"But . . . ?"

"Let it be, Pentti," Toini cut in. "He doesn't want to go into it any further." She turned to Jari, patting him on the hand. "That's fine. We understand how difficult this must be for you. That's a good sign."

Pentti was on his feet. For the first time since his arrival Jari saw the uncle he respected most. "You did exactly what I would have done," Pentti declared. "A soldier's oath to his brothers-in-arms is sacred. The army will understand."

Jari shook his head. "They'll think I'm making it up. If they don't shoot me, the Helsinki police will. All I want now is to get to Sweden.

Is that even possible?"

Aunt and Uncle exchanged glances. "He's earned that," Toini said. "Your nephew in Sweden—the one who makes a living fishing with a bit of smuggling on the side. Could something be arranged with him?"

"Possibly," Pentti said. "Got a passport?"

Jari shook his head. "Army took it away when I enlisted."

Pentti continued pacing. "There may be a way to fix that," he said, after a few minutes. "This is a border town. Lot's of phony papers being arranged these days. Getting to Sweden won't be easy, but not impossible. You could stay there, and when the war's over, go wherever you want."

"I can't wait that long. War or no war, it has to be Canada. And right now."

Uncle shook his head. "Not going to happen, Jari. Be reasonable. You'd have to get to England first, and that's impossible. Swedish ships are only allowed to sail to Nazi-held ports. Try anything else and they get shot out of the water. You're trapped. Why not just settle for northern Sweden. Lots of Finns there. You'd blend in."

"Lots of Germans there, too," Jari responded. "Sweden may be neutral, but the Wehrmacht move troops back and forth from Norway to Finland like they own the place. Can't stomach any more Germans. Probably scores of Finn deserters there as well, and I don't particularly relish being around them, either. I just want to make a clean break. Get my life back. Start afresh."

Pentti shrugged. "Have it your way. Dream of England. Dream of Canada. But neither is going to happen until the war ends. You'll see. I say forget it."

For several days, Uncle Pentti hustled about Kemi, making contacts and calling in favours. Jari didn't dare set foot outdoors. He wondered if the neighbours were getting suspicious with the curtains drawn night and day, but no one came to the door nosing about. The time alone with Aunt Toini, gave them a chance to talk. She stuffed him with food. Colour began to return to his cheeks.

On the fifth day, Uncle Pentti came home with an announcement: "I've had a productive morning. A friend put me onto somebody. The guy seems reliable and the wheels are in motion for a passport."

"How much?"

"Doesn't concern you," Toini answered, from the counter. "We've got this."

"Here's what's being arranged," Pentti began. "The name on your passport will be Olaf Anderson, a Swede from Lysekil. It's a port town on the southwest coast, about 100 km up from Göteborg."

"That puts it close to England then," Jari said.

"Yup, about as close as Sweden has to offer, but escaping from there by water is as dangerous as it gets. Any ship heading for the open sea has to run the gauntlet down the Skagerrak."

Aunt Toini frowned. "Why more dangerous there, Pentti?"

"Because with the Germans occupying both Norway seventy-five kilometres to the north, and Denmark seventy-five to the south, they've been able to put radar on both coasts."

Jari shrugged. "Radar is not infallible."

"Maybe,"Pentti continued, "but they've also got the Skagerrak mined, spotter planes in the air, and gun boats on the water. And, even if by some miracle a Swedish freighter managed to break out, they'd run smack dab into the Royal Navy, which shoots first and asks questions later. Between the Germans and the Brits, Sweden's ports are completely blockaded."

"So, even though Sweden's a neutral country, it only gets to trade with Germany," Toini said.

Pentti nodded. "Hitler's got them where he wants them."

"What about fishing boats?" Jari asked. "Some of them must get out. Once in Lysekil I could nose around."

"I expect the Royal Navy has them bottled up, too."

Aunt Toini looked up from the dough she was kneading. "Change your plans, Jari," she pleaded. "Stay in northern Sweden. It wouldn't be for long. The war will be over soon. You say so yourself."

"I just want to get home, Auntie."

Toini hesitated before replying. "Aren't you home here? Or is that Canada, now?"

Jari nodded. "Nobody's shooting over there."

"Which," Pentti said, "is bound to make it hard for you to fit in."

"What's that supposed to mean?" Toini asked.

"Well . . . just that he's . . . used to solving problems in a different way. A man with his experience, might . . . lapse. I mean, killing Korpi might be forgivable on this side of the ocean, but over there? Well."

To Jari's surprise Aunt Toini wasn't scolding her husband on this point. Instead, they were both staring at him with concern, and waiting for a reaction. "So, you're saying you don't trust me to control myself should push come to shove over there. That it?"

Toini reached out and touched his hand. "We'd like to think you can," she answered, "and given time, we're certain that would be the case. But, Jari, you're not there . . . yet. You've always been headstrong and quick to action. That's just the way you are." He opened his mouth to speak, but she held up her hand and kept going. "You said there were two soldiers responsible for that ambush, Korpi and . . ."

"Sorsakoski. Alvar Sorsakoski."

"Right. What if you ran into him somewhere? What then?"

"Come on, Auntie, that's nigh on impossible."

"You can't be sure. You're still responding to situations like a soldier at the Front. Didn't you prove that in Helsinki? Until you get beyond that, well . . . who knows? Wherever you go there's bound to be aggravation and challenge. How you handle it is sure to affect your future. Look, all Pentti and I are saying is, stay close to people who love you, at least until you're on . . . how shall I put it? . . . thicker ice."

Jari hoped it didn't show on his face, but Auntie's words were cutting deep. What made it so troubling was that she was dead right. "So, you're convinced I need more time?" he said.

"Time, and maybe even help," she replied. "Face it. You've got a lot to work out." Jari's head dropped. "Please don't be angry with us, Jari. You told us what led up to the murder, and why you did it, but you couldn't bring yourself to go into the details."

"Because I didn't want to burden you."

"Or, was it because there's something you're not yet ready to face? Look, unless you can get it all out, you'll never be able to put that part of your life behind you. I'm no fancy doctor, but if you ask me, at this moment, you're a walking time bomb waiting for a spark to set you off."

There it was, on the table. Heavy stuff. For a long moment, the three of them sat with the only sound coming from the clock ticking on the wall. It was Jari who finally broke the silence. "Alright," he began, staring past the others and out the window, "here goes; promise you won't hate me."

"Take your time," Toini said.

"Truth is, it's not what I've done that haunts me, it's that I'm not troubled by it. It came so easily. I mean, only a psychopath kills then goes out to get something to eat. Which is exactly what I did in Helsinki. The whole murder thing was as natural to me as returning a book to the library. Only the danger I'd put myself in, and not the act, had me fretting. How sick is that? What does that make me?"

"Troubled," Toini responded, "but fixable, like many soldiers coming home from war. Every vet returns with demons. But demons can be overcome. Is there anyone you're comfortable enough with to talk about this?"

"You," he replied, turning to face her straight on.

"I was meaning the place you're so determined to return to—Canada."

Jari nodded. "There is someone. And she'd listen; if I could ever bring myself to get it all out."

"Ah, a woman," Toini said. "Good, good. But Jari, be reasonable, Canada might as well be the moon these days. And even if you did manage to make it back to this special person, what are the chances she'll be waiting, let alone willing to help?"

"No idea. I left five years ago promising to return. Last we exchanged letters was in 1942. You'd like her, Aunt Toini, her name is Kerttu, Kerttu Nurmi."

"Nurmi, like the runner," Pentti said.

"Like the runner," Jari repeated.

Aunt Toini placed a hand on his arm. "Word of caution, Jari," she said. "When and if you get back, best not rush it."

"What are you saying? I'm thirty-three years old. I can't wait around forever. She's the one I'm willing to risk my neck to get back to. I thought you'd be delighted."

"I am. Don't get me wrong. It's just that you're not the person you were five years ago. Wouldn't want you showing up out of the blue and scaring her off, that's all."

"Meaning?"

"That it might be wise to take time to work out some of the problems you're carrying; kinda take the edge off them."

Jari straightened. "I should wait a bit? That what you're saying?" Aunt Toini nodded "What if she's just like you, happy to help me get back on track?"

"In that case, God bless her. But if it turns out she isn't, or has already moved on with somebody else, we're always here. Don't you forget that."

7

Blockade Runner

Sweden,
May 1944

Let me get this straight," Jari said. He and the captain were standing in the wheelhouse of the fishing boat, as it headed out into the Gulf of Bothnia. "You leave Kemi with a crew of five, drop me off, and return with four. How do you get that past the harbour patrol on return?"

The captain grinned. "I could tell them you fell overboard."

"No, seriously."

"Not your problem," the captain said.

"What if we're boarded for inspection? One glimpse of my wobbly sea legs and they'll know in a flash that I'm no fisherman."

"Been taken care of."

"Super, but how on earth . . . ?"

"Hey!" the captain interrupted, "no more questions. The less you know the better. For everybody, you included. Got it?"

Jari had no idea how many Suomen markkas his escape from Finland was costing Pentti and Toini, but it couldn't have been cheap. Up to this point his getaway had gone smoothly; to the point where he was beginning to suspect that something might be amiss. This was supposed to be a fishing voyage, but so far he'd seen no evidence of nets about to be dropped, and the captain wasn't answering questions.

He stewed. Eight hours later, and half-way across the Baltic Sea, his fear intensified with the appearance of another boat. It approached and came along side. Only when it turned out to be another fishing vessel, with a passenger preparing to be zip-lined to theirs, did he begin to relax. No sooner was the harness off the new arrival than it was put on Jari. One man in, one man out. He wondered if the newcomer had paid the same tariff, or if he knew any more about fishing than he did.

Once his new boat neared the Swedish coastline, he was put in a rowboat, taken ashore, and dumped. Alone, and ignorant of his location, he was contemplating his next move when a man approached from the treeline. The stranger stopped several metres away, eyes focused on the pukko knife in Jari's hand. "Who's your uncle?" he asked.

"Pentti Peltonen."

The man nodded and smiled. "Good soldier. I served under him in the Civil War." With that he came closer and handed Jari a thermos of hot tea.

"And your name would be?" Jari asked.

"Oskar will be enough. My instructions are to brief you on how to get to Lysekil."

"Do I detect a slight Karelian accent?" Jari asked. "How'd you and Uncle Pentti get to know each other?"

"Please, no questions," Oskar replied. "Here are your train tickets. I'm to accompany you as far as the railway station in Luleå. After that, you're on your own. You change trains in Stockholm, and again in Göteborg. There'll be police checks, but your Swedish passport should get you through, although why you would want to go to Lysekil is beyond me."

"What's wrong with Lysekil."

"Too small," Oskar continued, "and your papers have you born there, which is dumb because you know nothing about the place. You'll be challenged, so you'd better have a believable story prepared."

"How about, my parents moved to Kiruna when I was a baby?"

"Good start, but if they're suspicious, they'll check the hospital records and then you're screwed. Your biggest concern will be the Swedish navy. The government, plus nine-tenths of us Swedes, hate the Germans, but the navy brass seems to love them. You'd think they were a branch of Hitler's Kriegsmarine, the way they police the harbours for suspicious activity. It's enough to make you puke."

"I have to get to England," Jari said, with more conviction than he felt.

"Ha! Fat chance."

"So people keep telling me. Surely some boats make it out of the harbour?"

"Only those bound for German-held territory. The British tried to fight their way in a couple of times, but got blown out of the water."

"What do you suggest I do?"

"Go somewhere else and wait out the war. There's lots of work to be had in this country."

Oskar turned out to be right on all counts—jobs were plentiful, the Swedish navy patrolled diligently, Lysekil harbour was under tight control. Making sure to keep a low profile, Jari landed work as a stevedore loading goods destined for Nazi Europe. The hours were long and the work hard, but it suited him. With eight to a room the accommodation at the Seaman's Hostel wasn't the best, but the intel on the comings and goings in Lysekil harbour was fresh, and accurate. Two weeks on the job had him one of the gang. A month had him just another hired hand. Jari latched onto the card players in the dorm because when they played, they talked. They were also astonishingly free about sharing their origins and past. No secrets here, except for one person.

The odd man out was a Dane by the name of Carl Freiss. Everything about him led Jari to suspect a war record similar to his own. Several times he attempted to chat him up, but to no avail. Two weeks after his arrival, they still hadn't exchanged more than curt greetings. Some might have put Freiss down for a dozy lightweight, but Jari saw through that. On the docks he seemed to come to life, with outbound ships and their cargo getting his full attention. To Jari, this confirmed that there was more here than just another strong back. Something consequential was going on. Jari burned to find out what.

The Seaman Hostel's communal bath consisted of a large shower area with six open stalls, where banter flowed back and forth in a mix of friendly jibes, and cutting remarks. Carl Freiss avoided this by showering only when the others were done, even though the hot water would usually have run out by then. Either he was partial to cold showers, unnaturally shy, or up to something so important he dared not draw attention to himself. Jari had a hunch it was the latter, and was determined to find out the evening he followed him into the shower area.

"Fuck off, Anderson," Freiss snapped, when he caught Jari staring at his naked body.

Hurriedly, and with apologies, Jari left. But he had seen what he had come for. Freiss had turned away, but not before Jari had seen the gnarled balls of white, dough-like flesh that scarred the Danes midriff.

When Freiss came out of the shower wrapped in a towel, Jari was waiting for him. "Those scars on your stomach?" he said. "I'm guessing machine gun, possibly shrapnel."

Freiss looked at him coldly, ducked into a changing stall, and pulled the curtain.

It was still dark the next morning when the Dane left the hostel for the docks. Jari had been waiting and fell in beside him. "Why do I have this feeling that you and I can help each other, Carl?"

Carl's face screwed into a frown. "Absolutely no idea," he said, after several steps. "Runaway imagination, is my guess. Probably because you're like those younger guys in the dorm who, starved for excitement, somehow see me as a mystery man."

Jari groaned. "Believe me, I've had enough excitement to last me a lifetime. But let's talk about what I saw last night: I've been around long enough to know a war wound when I see one."

"And that makes you an expert, does it? Think you've got me all figured out, do you? Well, you're way off the mark, so piss off and leave me alone."

"Look, Carl," Jari pressed. "I don't know where you got that wound; could be fighting the Germans after they invaded Denmark, or volunteering in the Finn Winter War like a lot Danes, but it sure wasn't from some tricycle spill as a kid. As far as I'm concerned though, that's your business."

"You've had your eye on me for weeks, Anderson. What is it you're after?"

Jari swallowed. If he was wrong about this, his next few words could land him in prison. "Because deep down I think you're working for the British and could help get me out of here."

Freiss let loose a harsh laugh, but when Jari showed no sign of backing off, he stopped and turned to face him. "You better be careful what you say, my friend. You just as much told me you're hiding something the authorities in these parts would be happy to hear about. I'm thinking the smart thing for me right now is to report this."

It was Jari's turn to smile. He'd hit the mark. "I don't think you'd do that, Carl. Because, if you did, I wouldn't be the only one under the spotlight, would I? The Swedish government may be cool on Germany, but this is a navy town, and they're about as pro Hitler as Göring and Goebbels."

Carl resumed walking, with Jari hot on his heels. "How do you know I'm not working for them, too?"

"Because I saw your reaction when the Germans shot up that foreign cargo ship trying to make it up the Skagerrak. You had something riding on that, didn't you? The *Svenska marinen* brass pranced around the docks happy as hell, which thoroughly pissed you off. Since then, you've been sizing things up in the port and looking out to sea, as if waiting for something. Or, are you trying to get some cargo out and need a way to do it?"

"You gotta be desperate, Anderson. Think about it: if I did have something going with the Brits, what do you think your chances of seeing another sunrise would be right now? I'd have you snuffed out," he snapped his fingers, "just like that. Accidents take place on these docks all the time."

"I've considered that, Carl, but you're looking at a Finn who's been staring down death for so long it no longer fazes him. Truth is, I promised myself I'd never kill again. Not even a Russian. That's how sick I am of this whole fucking war. I just want it to end."

"If that's the case then go home and . . ." Carl paused at Jari's look of puzzlement. "Or haven't you heard?"

"Heard what?"

"The Finns signed a cease-fire with the Russians last night. They've turned on the Germans. As we speak, they're killing each other in Rovaniemi. They could use your help."

It took a second for Jari to absorb this. "Too late. That bridge has already been burned."

They continued walking, with Freiss getting more anxious as they neared the docks. To Jari, this was clear indication that the Dane wasn't working alone. His hopes rose when Carl made one last attempt to get rid of him. "Listen, Anderson, I'm no spy. You're looking at nothing more than a Danish Jew who's lost his family, and is trying to survive. So, just forget we had this conversation. Respect my privacy, and leave me alone."

Jari had no intention of jeopardizing whatever Freiss and company had going. Not if it might present a chance of getting away. He was about to say so, when they began to pick up the sound of excited voices. Upping the pace, they saw people running towards a pier on the other side of a German freighter. Something was happening, but the freighter blocked their view. By the time they got there, a large crowd had gathered, with Swedish navy personal attempting to push them back. Freiss pressed to get a better view. Jari right behind him.

But even when they drew closer, with the object of attention in full view, Jari had no idea what he was looking at. Before him was a ship of sorts, but unlike anything he'd ever encountered. Sleek, narrow, and built low to the water, it appeared to be a cross between a gunboat and a mini-destroyer. That it had run the Skagerrak was evidenced by the badly chewed up bridge, bullet marks in the wooden frame, and blood splashed across the deck. Wounded men were being taken off and loaded into ambulances. "What the hell is that?" Jari said. To his surprise, Freiss responded.

"Viking Class, motor gunboat," he said. "Greyhound of the sea. Fifty-two metres long with three of the fastest Paxman diesel engines ever made. It's a British Merchant Marine vessel." He stopped abruptly, as if spilling the ship's specifics was a lapse in judgement.

Jari smiled and slowly turned to question him further, but all he got was a glimpse of Carl's back, as the Dane pushed his way back through the crowd. *Catch up with him at work*, he thought. Two hours later Carl still hadn't punched in. At noon, the stevedores toted their lunch boxes over to check on the boat they now knew to be, the *Gay Viking*. Jari found himself standing beside an older man who chortled in amusement as he sucked on his pipe. "What's happening?" Jari asked, when he saw the bickering going on between a group of navy officers and civilians in suits.

"The navy want the boat impounded," the man responded. "But the local judge and town officials are telling them they don't have the legal right to do that. The seaman in the middle is the English captain. He's been waving a bill of sale saying the goods he's come to fetch have been paid for, and as a neutral country, Sweden can't keep him from collecting. The navy's having none of it. It's now in government hands. They're waiting for word from Stockholm."

"Any idea what the cargo might be?"

"No secret there," the man said, pointing in the direction of a warehouse across the water from the pier. "Those trucks belong to SKF, makers of the finest ball bearings in the world. Most of them go to Germany. Seems the Brits want their share. Apparently, they've bought and paid for them, and are here to pick them up. Should be interesting."

Back at work, Jari kept an eye open for Freiss, but the Dane didn't show. Shift over, he rushed back to the hostel. No sign of him there, either. When the lights went out at the customary 9:30 p.m., one bed remained unoccupied. He wondered if Carl might slip in during the night, but when the men began to rise at 5:30 a.m., his bed had not been touched. He'd vanished, and along with him Jari's hopes for deliverance. He wondered if the pressure he'd put on Carl had somehow compromised his plan. If so, would there be retribution?

The answer came late in the day on his way home from work, when a cold, deep voice addressed him from behind. "Don't turn around. I'm armed. Don't open your mouth, either. Just keep walking and follow instructions." That was the only exchange until they reached Rosvikstorg Street, several minutes later. "Turn right, and keep going until we come to an alley just past the Gastro Box Restaurant. Take it down to the large warehouse."

According to the sign on the building, the warehouse was actually a garage, but the instant the door opened Jari was certain more interesting things were taking place. The smell of burning wire, combined with the whine of drills and hammering of steel, was a dead giveaway.

He counted fifteen men hard at work on items that had nothing to do with automobiles. At the back of the garage he spotted a mount for a machine gun.

Mixed in with the odour of welding came the familiar aroma of pipe smoke. Four men approached, one carrying a pistol. Of the other three, one was Carl Freiss, who stared solemnly at Jari, but said nothing. The second man was the pipe smoker from the dock. He wasn't smiling either. "I'll make this fast," the pipe smoker began. "Pestering Carl was a mistake. We've had you checked out."

"Waste of time," Jari said. "Not much to uncover. My name is Olaf Anderson, bred and born right here in Lysekil. Coulda told you that."

"Not what you told Carl yesterday, so shut up and listen. We checked. Your name is Jari Hoivuniemi, and you're AWOL from the Finnish army. Question is, what to do with you?"

"You're mistaken . . ."

The senior man raised his hand. Jari closed his mouth. "I see three options here: drown you in the harbour—simplest; turn you over to the Finn legation in Göteborg—time consuming; sign you up—risky. I have my preference, but I've been out-voted. Carl suspects you might know your way around machine guns. That true?" Jari nodded. "In that case tell, me what the machinists are working on over there."

Jari turned his head in the direction of the pointed finger. "I see one mount completed and a second in the works, each seemingly designed to house a Vickers .303 machine gun."

"Could be a wild guess. Why pick that gun in particular?"

"Because," Jari said, pointing, "the stripped-down weapon being cleaned on that bench over there is a Vickers .303."

"Can you put it back together?"

"In a flash," Jari responded, approaching the bench and beginning the task.

The four men looked at each other. "He'll have to do," the pipe said. "Brief him, Carl."

The others peeled off, leaving only Freiss. "I told them you might know machine guns Hoivuniemi, and it better be true. It's a bullet to your head if I'm wrong. Here's what's happening. The government's decision came down this afternoon; the *Gay Viking* was given forty-eight hours to be out of Swedish waters. If they fail to comply it'll be impounded."

Jari made a quick calculation. "Meaning it has to be gone by 7:00 a.m. tomorrow morning."

"Wrong! Ten o'clock tonight. Darkness is our only hope of making it through the Skagerrak. The Germans will know the instant we cast off, and will throw everything they have at us. They're out their licking their chops, waiting for us to enter international waters. They've got bombers and destroyers on their side. We'll have a few small arms, and the fastest blockade runner in the world."

"Sounds like even odds to me."

"Not quite. Problem is, the forty tons of ball bearings delivered to the *Gay Viking* will slow us down. Our three Paxman engines may be the world's fastest, but they're like thoroughbred horses: work them too hard and they come up lame."

"What about the Royal Navy?"

"Waiting for us in the North Sea alright, but unable to risk coming in close to help. Nothing for us but to run the gauntlet on our own."

"I'm guessing you're offering me a job?"

Carl smirked. "Offering? I suppose you could put it that way. You can take your chances on a venture that's certain to fail and probably see you dead, or die in the next ten minutes. You're decision."

Jari answered without pause. "What have you got in mind?"

"Replace the machine gunner killed on the run in. Handle one of those Vickers."

Jari nodded. "I'm good with that. He held out his hand."

Carl looked at it, but didn't take it. "Jesus Christ! We're not friends! Up to now I was the Danish resistance man in Lysekil, but you all but outed me in public. A full year's work up in smoke, and now I'm going to get killed trying to flee to England. Most of the crew are trawler men with no military training. You're only here because you claim to be able to handle a machine gun. Otherwise, you'd be at the bottom of the harbour." He looked at his watch. "We leave in less than four hours. I've got work to do. There's food and cots in the back room. I suggest you eat and get some sleep."

The instant the *Gay Viking* slipped its moorings, Jari got to work. With international waters but a few minutes away, time was not on their side. Cross that line, and hell was sure to be unleashed. Darkness made progress difficult, but working frantically, he set to opening ammunition boxes, and showing the crew member assigned to him how to feed the gun. Satisfied, he asked for and got clearance to test. Considering the haste in which the mounts had been fastened to the deck, he'd worried it might jerk about. It didn't. To his surprise, the gun fired and rotated smoothly. That done, he huddled on his backside behind the gun, tightened his shoulder harness to keep him from being washed overboard, breathed in the diesel-fumed salty air, and scanned the darkness ahead.

They weren't far out when the wind hit them like a sledge hammer. With it came plummeting temperatures and high, rolling, seas. He and his partner crouched behind the gun, water spraying over the rails and sloshing around them and down the deck.

"Is it usually this rough and cold?" he shouted to his gun mate.

The sailor gave him a bewildered look. "This is nothing. You want rough and freezing, sign up for the Murmansk run. Don't worry, things will be heating up soon as we hit international waters."

"Shouldn't we be there by now?"

"Soon, I'm guessing. The captain has us running northwest inside Swedish territorial limits. That way the Germans can only guess where we might choose to make our dash across the line. Gives us a bit of an advantage."

Thirty-five minutes later the *Gay Viking* gave the horn a toot, warning them that they were about to pass into the danger zone. Jari stared even harder into the blackness, the rhythm of the blood coursing past his ears matching that of the Paxman diesel engines. Nothing. Regardless, expecting to see a phalanx of German ships bearing down at any moment, he flicked the gun off safety.

"No need for that, yet," his gun mate yelled.

"How come?"

"Because the Germans haven't pinpointed us yet. The Skagerrak's 150 kilometres across at this point, and they don't have enough ships to cover every inch of it."

"But they've got radar. They must be tracking us."

"Trying like hell, I'd say, but the seas are high, and we're low in the water. Radar has its limits; especially, up against a wooden frame vessel. Going to be different come daybreak. That's why we have to risk running these temperamental motors so hard. Best hope is to get out of range of their airplanes before dawn. Make it, and the Royal Navy will be there waiting to escort us into Hull. In the meantime, we hang on and pray."

8

Moscow Recruit

Moscow,
May 1944

lvar Sorsakoski's initial reaction on learning that he was being transferred from Helsinki to Moscow, was one of relief. The woman who'd interrogated him in Helsinki after his escape from the police, the one so motherly looking with her hair done up in a bun and all, turned out to be anything but. She was outraged by his insistence that he had no idea who had killed Korpi, even accusing him of doing it himself. The more he denied the charge, the more frustrated she became. For three days she fired questions at him, all the while calling him Sami Aalto. On the fourth day, she threw up her hands, and turned him over to two guards. Their job was to get him to Moscow for, "further discussion," as she put it. Once there, he feared it would be torture until he told them whatever it was they wanted to hear.

It took five days for the guards to get him through the Front lines to Viipuri. This time there was no visit to his grandparents. He kept his mouth shut about them, lest they get Korpi-like ideas. From there the three of them piled into a rickety truck packed with wounded soldiers, bound for Leningrad. There they boarded a train for Moscow. Thanks to layovers for troop trains, supply trains, and who knows what trains, it took forty hours to complete the 700 kilometre final leg to the capital.

However tedious and uncomfortable the trip may have been, it had left him ample time to assess his future. He concluded that it was anything but bright. Never once did the guards smile, take their eyes off him, or communicate with him, except to bark orders. After three miserable years in the army, life was about to get worse. He'd been snared in a tiny box with Korpi, and now found himself caught up in an even bigger one. From where he sat, there were only two escape hatches—vodka or suicide.

His spirits rose slightly when he caught a glimpse of the Kremlin as they drove through Red Square. He craned his neck to take in as much as possible, only to find the golden copulas and majestic towers all but hidden behind sand bags and war cladding. Even St Basil's Cathedral, so magnificent that Czar Ivan the Terrible had ordered the architect's eyes plucked out to prevent him from ever replicating such a glorious structure, was obstructed. Minutes later, the car stopped at 19 Bolshoi Znamensky Lane, a dull two-storey building close to the Kremlin. Inside, he was led to an office and ordered to wait.

The high ceiling, grey walls, and sparse furnishings, screamed peril. The unopened dossier on the desk that bore his name did little to put him at ease. He was toying with the idea of sneaking a peek, when a middle-aged officer sporting a Stalin-like moustache entered the room. Heart racing, Alvar jumped to his feet and saluted. The officer, a full colonel, sat down and opened the file.

After scanning several pages, he steepled his fingers and turned his gaze on Alvar, studying him like he might a sculpture at the Hermitage. "Sit," he ordered. "My name is Colonel Yan Karlovich Topoloff, Chief of the Main Intelligence Directorate, and former director of the Fourth Department of the General Staff of the Worker Peasants Red Army." He paused, letting this sink in. "That's more detail than I normally need to provide, but our agent in Helsinki seems to find you ignorant in these affairs. That true?"

"My focus has always been on soldiering," Alvar replied.

"Hmm," the colonel responded, as he scanned Alvar's dossier again. "Apparently, our agent in Helsinki found your inability to provide information on the killing of this man . . ." he searched for the reference, "Tuomas Korpi, extremely disappointing." Alvar swallowed, but held his tongue. The Colonel continued. "But she also thought you to be, 'intelligent, resourceful, composed, and cannily capable of hiding your emotions. That what you're doing now? Concealing your emotions?"

Surprised by this favourable assessment from such a detestable woman, Alvar's heart rate turned down a notch. "Trying my best, sir," he replied.

"I see," the colonel said, raising his eyebrows, "why might that be? Does my rank intimidate you, or is it something else?"

"Yes, your rank intimidates me, sir, and, yes I'm hiding something."

The colonel sat back in his chair, a smile tugging at the corners of his mouth. "Intriguing. What might that be?"

Alvar had in mind to say, Figure it out yourself, you over-bearing, pompous ass, but self preservation prevailed. "Ignorance as to why I'm here, and worry that, whatever it is, I'll mess it up," he replied.

"If you're the patriot and communist you claim to be, you've no reason to be nervous. I'm not going to eat you."

Alvar was uncertain how to respond. Was this man genuine, or a trained con artist setting a trap? "True, but at my rank I'm powerless. It's been my experience that superiors tend to place me in precarious situations."

"Touché," the Colonel chuckled, "our orders can sometimes be puzzling to people forced to carry them out. However, those who comply down to the letter generally do alright, wouldn't you say?" Alvar raised his eyebrows. "You've got a problem with that, I see."

Alvar had dealt with officers before, but never had he encountered one quite like this. Here was a full colonel who actually seemed interested in a soldier's opinion. "Begging your pardon, Colonel Topoloff, but can't blind obedience sometimes be counterproductive?"

Topoloff crossed his arms. "Explain."

"I'm only a private, but it's my experience that, in the field, orders often fall apart, leaving soldiers unsure what to do."

"So, as a private, you think you could handle battle chaos better than the generals? Is that it?"

"No, sir, but on those occasions where plans go off the rails, if field officers allowed lower ranks to improvise, objectives might be reached with fewer casualties. That's all I'm saying, sir."

Topoloff smoothed his moustache, and smiled. "When you were operating behind enemy lines, weren't you and Comrade Korpi given the freedom to improvise as you saw fit? And wasn't it your own initiative that brought you so much success?"

"Kind of, I guess."

"Says here that not only did you provide good intelligence, but you captured and killed scores of enemy soldiers." Alvar responded with a slight nod. "You should be proud of that. Helped shorten the war. Saved lives. As an officer of the Red Army, I congratulate you."

Alvar took a deep breath. Aside from superiors who'd debriefed him on his escapades behind enemy lines, he'd never spoken to anyone about this. It was too painful. Too repulsive. Yet, here for the first time, he was not only being lauded for his actions, but forced to see them through new eyes. He felt lighter. "Thank you, Colonel Topoloff."

Topoloff looked at his watch. "Enough idle chat. The GRU thinks you have possibilities. Before we consider if you could be of any use to us, is there anything you'd like to ask me?"

A myriad of questions leapt to mind, but Alvar stuck to what he thought least likely to get him into trouble. "This GRU, what is it they do, exactly?"

"Gathers military intelligence. Surely, you knew that. Who do you think you were working for behind Finnish lines?"

"Never questioned it. Just obeying orders. Korpi was the one who . . ."

"Well, those orders were coming from the NKVD which was the forerunner to the GRU. Apparently, they/we, liked what we saw in you. We are always on the lookout for new talent. With eyes set for after the war, our organization has been given a bigger, more sophisticated mandate—one that goes far beyond the battlefield. It's possible there might be a place for you in our plans. Interested?"

Alvar had no idea what this might entail, but prudence suggested it was worth a nod. "I think so," he said.

"Even with the war over, Russia will still have enemies. Capitalists around the globe hate communism. Hate us. We need good people in the field to help us stay ahead of them."

Alvar was still baffled, but tried not to show it. While it would be a relief to be done with skulking around behind enemy lines, what exactly did this new stuff entail? He opened his mouth to ask, but thought better of it.

"If you pass our tests, and they are demanding, you'll be posted to a foreign country. Your task would be to observe, report, and possibly undertake periodic, covert missions to promote the communist cause."

Alarm bells began going off in Alvar's head. Observe, encourage and report, sounded innocent enough, but covert missions? "Where do you think I would be assigned?" he asked.

"Well, since Finn's your native tongue, and you also speak English, a couple of possibilities come to mind. The United States for one, and Canada for another. Both have a lot of Finnish immigrants who may have backed the losing side in their Civil War, but still carry a deep devotion to communism. It's possible you'd be working with them."

"Spying on them?"

"That's a rather crude way of putting it," the colonel responded. "Try to see it more as guiding them along the right path; a little encouragement here, a firm push there, and sometimes helping them remove obstacles in their way. It would be an act of patriotism on behalf of your country" He waited a second before continuing. "You look perplexed."

"No! Overwhelmed. Worried, too. I wouldn't know how to go about it, get started, that sort of thing. But, yes, it's a rare opportunity. Thank you."

"Wonderful. Let's proceed then." Topoloff scribbled something on a piece of paper and slid it across the desk, pointing to where Alvar should sign. "I'm recommending you for a six-month course at our training centre for operatives at Borobyevo. It's in the Lenin Hills outside of Moscow. It comes with a promotion to officer rank, probably captain, and a raise in salary."

Alvar knew better than to read the full text of what he was signing, but from the little bit he could see he wouldn't have understood it anyway. With more confidence than he felt, he signed his name and passed it back.

Topoloff stood. "I should warn you," he said. "What you just agreed to gets you in the door, nothing more. From here on it's up to you.

If you make it through the course, you'll be asked to sign an oath of loyalty to the GRU. With that, you become part of a family that, no matter where on earth, or whatever the circumstance, looks after its own. Conversely, apostates who betray their oath are hunted down and taken care of—eliminated."

Alvar walked to the door, turned, and saluted. The colonel returned the salute, along with one last piece of advice. "You are now Sami Aalto. Repeat it over and over in your head, until your old name and your old life, fade away. No one, and I mean no one, must know your true identity. Understood?"

9

Spy School

Moscow,
September 1944

What about you, Sami?" Dietrich asked. "Got a girl back home? Maybe one you might have considered marrying someday?"

The two men were roommates at Borobyevo Spy Academy, and after five months of intensive training, had been granted a twelve-hour pass to visit Moscow. Unless they wanted to get drunk, which neither of them found appealing, there wasn't a lot to do. At the moment, they were wandering through Gum, Moscow's famous glass-roofed department store.

Sami shrugged. "Yeah, there's someone. But the agency seems so anxious to get us placed in the field I doubt they'd ever let me go back and ask her."

"Makes sense on their part. Family and postings don't mix."

"How can you say that? You're married with kids, and you're here."

"Doesn't make it easy. Each time they send me somewhere, like on this course, I become a stranger all over again, especially with the kids. Helga gets it, but that doesn't make it any easier. Stay single is my recommendation. You'll sleep better at nights."

To glance at them, the two men seemed unlikely friends. Certainly, the difference in age and marital status had made it difficult in the early weeks. But they had found common ground, and came to trust one another, to the point of straying onto forbidden topics, such as postings, past experiences, and opinions. In the process, Alvar Sorsa-koski had disappeared into the past. He was a new man, with a new name, and a new future.

Slight in build and balding, Dietrich was a committed communist from Berlin, who'd gone toe-to-toe with the Nazis, been beaten and left for dead by Hitler's Brownshirts, and had fought fascism in the Spanish Civil War. Currently he was working for the communist cause in China. Every day of his life as an agent had been filled with adventure, daring-do, and peril.

"Tell me, Dietrich," Sami said, "would you ever consider giving up spying for a quiet family life? Be honest."

Dietrich smirked. "Never crossed my mind. Not allowed. The GRU is for life. And don't you forget it."

"But, say, if it was permitted. Would you?"

"Only if I was crippled or something; otherwise, I could never bring myself to cut my ties with the agency."

"I admire that," Sami said, "but really? The agency over family? How's that possible?"

"We get our orders, then we use our wits to carry them out. What could possibly be more intoxicating? Don't get me wrong, I love my wife and kids, but the thought of a Monday to Saturday job gives me the willies."

"You make it sound romantic."

"Wouldn't go that far, although must admit, cheating death, relying on your wits, calling upon every verbal, physical, and psychological skill you possess, is pretty heady stuff. You can be on a high for days— no vodka required. Of course every day's not like that. There can be long periods of earth-shattering boredom."

"Ever wonder about some of the others on the course? What their experiences have been? I mean, there are eighty of us, men and women, and from all over—France, England, America, Poland, Spain, Italy, you name it. Gotta be some wild stories."

"Don't know and would never ask. It's forbidden. But, between you and me, my guess is that this bunch of battle-scarred pros probably feel just like me."

"You think?"

"It's in their eyes. They've been to the brink and back, which explains their gratitude for the advanced skills they're learning here. You and I may not need arms training, or sabotage techniques, but most of them do. And all that stuff about Morse code, camouflage, drop sites, brush contacts etc, is invaluable."

Sami wasn't sure why he found words like these so comforting from Dietrich, but distressing from anybody else. For a few minutes, they strolled in silence. The shop windows from Gum Department store were basically empty, which was why they picked up the pace when they spied a line beginning to form up ahead. When they drew alongside, it was to see two elderly women making a window display out of tins of fish. They moved on.

"All that talent on our course," Sami said, as they continued their walk, "makes me wonder what the GRU sees in me."

"Each one of us was picked for a reason. You, too."

"Yeah, and from the emphasis on Canadian and American culture, plus English grammar, it's pretty clear what they've got in mind for me. Seems that the Finns over there are ripe for revolution. Which won't be easy. Take Canada, all those strikers getting gunned down in the streets."

Dietrich frowned. "You sure about that?"

"Yeah. Remember? We were shown pictures of police firing on picketers in Winnipeg, Ontario, and Regina, and men being forced into gulags in the bush, run by the Canadian army. All it needs is a good spark and . . . boom!"

"And you think the GRU has picked you to be that spark?"

"Well, perhaps not just me. I've no intention of setting the world on fire. Just let me be a loyal cog in the wheel and I'll be happy. But, yeah, I think they've got me pegged for America. Being Finn, communist, and able to speak English kinda makes me a natural."

"Don't count on it," Dietrich replied. "Bureaucracy can be a stupid beast. I speak four languages, none of them Chinese, yet where do you think they've placed me?"

Sami shrugged. "I'll take whatever they give me with no complaints. I've signed my oath and I'm ready. And I'll do what I'm told, too. One wrong step with the agency and it's,"—he drew a finger across his throat and chuckled. "Correct?"

Dietrich stopped, and waited for a middle-aged man with a limp to pass them by. "You see me as a veteran of the field, right?" Sami nodded. "Then take some advice: Sure, you might get to work with a few Finns, but mostly they'll have you gathering, stealing, and buying military secrets. Nod to whatever Borobyevo tells you as if you're swallowing it all, but wait until you're in the field before drawing conclusions."

"What are you saying?"

"Just that you'll find there's often a gap between what Moscow says and reality. And Sami, please, don't get married. Find yourself a mistress, use prostitutes, whatever it takes, but for the love of God don't burden some woman with marriage to an agent in the field. She'll only grow to hate you. The kids, too. Lastly, keep your nose clean, don't proffer too much, and be sure to document everything. Agents can be a hero one day and a zero the next."

Sami was uncertain how to interpret advice so contrary to everything received in five months at Borobyevo. He thought of his pledge of allegiance to the GRU. To a soldier nothing was more sacred than keeping an oath made to comrades. The GRU had made it clear that those who failed to live up to their vows would be hunted down and eliminated. And he agreed. But Dietrich's advice left him troubled. Were there limits? Might his friend be prepared to forsake his oath in certain circumstances? He was certain that in his case it would never come to that.

PART THREE

Boreal Forest, South of Hearst, 1944-46

10

Bush Asylum

Northern Ontario,
September 1944

Pulling out of Detroit Jari hadn't given a second thought to the large number of American soldiers on board the train. Questionable, after several hours, was why they hadn't gotten off? Where were they going? Could it be to the Canadian border? And if so, would they be crossing, too? Had there been some military development up there that he didn't know about? He'd been counting on a sleepy customs office when he picked Sault Ste. Marie to cross into Canada. Now he wasn't sure how diligent the customs agents might turn out to be. He prayed his bogus credentials would work one more time.

"Excuse me," he said to the officer across the aisle from him, "is something happening up north? I mean, why so many of you heading for the border? Last I checked, the war was overseas."

"Baffles me, too," the GI replied, "but going there beats getting your you know whats shot off in the Pacific, or France. Seems Uncle Sam has decided that the locks at Sault Ste. Marie are critical to the war effort, and need special protection. They say more tonnage passes through there than the Suez and Panama canals combined."

"Like what?"

"Mostly iron ore going to the eastern steel mills to keep us in tanks, planes, and, you name it. Stuff Uncle Sam's gotta protect."

"From who?"

The soldier shrugged. "Good question. Japs and Germans, I guess." They both laughed at the remoteness of the possibility of the Sault locks ever being attacked.

"Saboteurs, maybe?" Jari asked, nonchalantly. "That what they're worried about?"

"Most likely air attack," the GI replied. "Case they ever got aircraft carriers into Hudson Bay."

"Slim chance of that I'd say," Jari responded. The two men smiled at each other, and turned away.

Jari switched his focus to the approaching border. He'd successfully entered British and American territory with his phony passport, so was feeling pretty confident of it getting him through customs one more time. Still, you never knew. Most concerning was the bogus employment letter he hoped to get by the border agent. Having a destination, and a job to go to, was a government requirement. Unfortunately, his letter had been done in haste, and on cheap paper by a New Jersey hotel clerk. Just in from England, and having jumped ship, the clerk had guessed he was in a hurry, and had charged him an arm and a leg for a very unsatisfactory forgery. Even to an untrained eye, it was an amateur job. An astute customs officer was sure to spot it in a flash. Should that happen, a few phone calls was all it would take to have him behind bars. Still, having come this far, he was willing to risk it.

Obviously nervous, and looking like she was just out of high school, the customs agent studied Jari's passport. "Lysekil, Sweden," she said, "never heard of it."

"Few have," Jari replied. "It's a small town on the coast, close to the Norwegian border.""How does one get from there to here in the middle of a war?"

Jari tried to remain calm. If she pressed, he'd be in trouble. "Long story," he said, looking over his shoulder to take in the line of impatient travellers behind. "Believe it or not, some boats actually make it out. In my case . . ." He stopped. Clearly perplexed by the direction of the conversation, the agent had turned to look at the older gentleman at the desk behind her. When the man refused to acknowledge her, she shrugged and turned back to Jari. Behind them, people murmured their discontent at the slowdown. With no help coming, the agent cleared her throat and straightened. "What brings you to Canada,

Mr. Anderson?" she asked.

"Job offer with Haavaldshrud Timber in Hornepayne," he said, handing her the forged letter.

The woman read it, then examined him closely. "Company sounds Swedish. Fellow countryman?"

"Old school friend of my dad's. We Swedes stick together."

With that she nodded. "Always helps to know someone, doesn't it? Welcome to Canada," she said, stamping his passport.

The name Haavaldshrud had come to him from out of the blue, one remembered from his Hearst days. He wasn't exactly sure where Hornepayne was, and with bigger problems on his mind, had no intention of finding out. Now that he'd successfully crossed the border, he had to decide if, when, and how to approach Kerttu. If there was an answer, it kept eluding him.

After spending the night at a hotel near the station in the Sault, he boarded the Algoma Central train, carefully selecting a seat far from the other passengers. For most of the day, he sat by himself in a cloud of smoke wrestling with his dilemma. Even the spectacular Agawa Canyon wasn't enough to deflect his thoughts. The cigarette thing was a renewed habit. He'd given up on smoking years before, but had relapsed in England, where they handed them out like life jackets on a storm-tossed sea. In the Sault, he'd picked up a carton of Buckingham's, promising himself he'd quit when they were gone. It wouldn't be long, the way he was puffing his way through them.

Hawk Junction and Franz came and went. So did Oba. Still no decision on how to approach Kerttu. All the years he'd dreamt of reuniting with her, and now there she was just a few miles up the line, and getting closer. But Aunt Toini's words kept ringing in his head. "Don't rush into making contact," she'd advised, "best shed some of the war baggage first."

Back in Kemi, these words had sounded unreasonable. They'd hurt, too, prompting him to boast that, with all the good food and rest under her roof, he'd pretty well vanquished his demons. "Sleeping like a baby," he'd said. Looking back, maybe she'd been right, because not long after that he found himself happily manning a machine gun on the *Gay Viking*, ready to kill Germans. Then there were the night-mares. Turns out he couldn't wish them away either.

Auntie was far from dumb. He hated the advice she'd given, but was she right in suggesting that barging in on Kerttu in his current state might be burning his bridges? And what if she was stepping out with someone else? Or possibly even married. Who could blame her. He'd been gone a long, long time.

He couldn't decide whether it was wisdom, or cold feet, that finally brought about a decision, but somewhere between Jogues and Hearst a plan had finally fallen into place. He would go into the bush for some needed R and R. Not forever, just long enough to get his feet back on the ground. Solitary living might do the trick. He remembered hear-ing about two American trappers, the Smith brothers, who'd aban-doned a string of cabins somewhere between the ACR tracks and the Missinaibi River. Jari didn't know where exactly, but he knew an old trapper, Doug Mitchell, who would. Not only could Doug be trusted to tell no one about his return, but he would help him get the supplies needed for living in the bush. So there it was; spend a month or two in a lonely cabin, and emerge a new man. He was sure of it.

As usual the train was late getting in, which suited Jari because it was now pitch black. Pulling his hat down he strode quickly to the Waverley Hotel, across from the station. Early tomorrow he'd get Mr. Boutin, the town's one-armed taxi driver, to drive him out to Doug's. If Boutin wasn't free, he'd get the other taxi driver. The guy with the one leg.

Having Kerttu so close—one block to the east—kept him awake most of the night. The temptation to throw caution to the wind and bang on her door, was overwhelming, but he forced himself to stay in his hotel room. Best he could hope for would be a glimpse of her as the taxi passed her place in the morning. He hoped no one would witness the scene—him staring out the taxi window, like a big-eyed kid at the candy store. It was sure to be pathetic.

11

Communist Agent

Toronto,
November 1944

S ami felt good. The trip to Canada had gone off without a hitch. Although the route taken—Russia, Iran, North Africa, Spain and finally Halifax—had been a circuitous one, it had been anything but tedious. His cover had him down as a displaced labourer from Estonia, so of course, he was nervous when confronted by the customs agent in Halifax, but so was everyone else in line. After an uneventful train trip to Toronto, he found a rooming house on Pape Avenue, and thanks to the labour shortage, a job with Tippet-Richardson, a moving company that delivered sundry items around the city. "Keep your nose clean and learn the city by heart," his Moscow instructor had ordered. "You'll be contacted, if and when needed."

It was a new start, and a refreshing one. Alvar Sorsakoski was now Sami Aalto, or Agent Sami to the GRU. Should an emergency arise, name, passport, and city could be changed. In that eventuality, he had only to contact his handler. Otherwise, he was on his own, at least for now. Three months on the job and, for all intents and purposes, the transition from training camp to foreign assignment had been seamless. He wondered how Dietrich was doing in China, or if he'd ever see him again. Hardly a day went by that he didn't bless Dietrich for sharing his experience. So far, there had been nothing but minor hurdles. With luck, it would stay that way.

His first major challenge occurred while riding a street car down Gerard Street. He was on his way home when two young boys got on, elbowing and pushing each other like playful bear cubs. They were loud, too, but that didn't bother him because they were conversing in Finn. Instantly, Sami's ears had picked up, although he tried not to show it. Convinced that no one could possibly have any inkling of what they were saying, the boys began making fun of people around them.

"See that guy with the big belly," one lad said, prodding his pal in the ribs, "and that woman two rows over?"

"Which one?"

"The one with the big boobs."

"What about them?"

"They should put them together."

"Put what together?"

"The belly with the tits, stupid. Imagine them dancing."

The second boy looked from one to the other, then exploded in laughter. "Oh, God, they fit together like two pieces in a jigsaw puzzle. I can just see them, gliding across the floor, her boobs ridin' around on top of his big belly."

"And if one of the tits fell off, what then?"

"Gee, with the size of 'em he'd have to use both hands to lift it back up."

This was apparently hilarious. Sami smiled to himself at the irony of the two boys giggling away, assuming no one could possibly understand a word they were saying. Turning his attention away, he noticed that the young woman sitting opposite him was chuckling, too. Moreover, she'd caught the expression on his face and had read it perfectly. "Not often you hear Finnish spoken in Toronto," she announced, in a voice loud enough to carry several rows.

The boys' jaws dropped, and they scrambled to the far end of the car. Sami and the woman struggled not to laugh. A shared moment, but when she got up and moved to the vacant space next to him, he felt a chill wash over him. Air raid sirens began whining in his head. The textbook reaction was clear enough—show courtesy and exit the scene as quickly as prudently possible. For Sami, that meant getting off at the next stop. But the blond curls, wide smile, and smart clothes—a force never before encountered—had him pinned. His backside suddenly grew roots in the hard leather bench, cancelling all possibility of flight. He'd been warned that his situation made him vulnerable, yet he found himself unable to resist. Newfound freedom, a city at peace. It was too much. The car doors opened, the Finn boys scrambled off, Sami stayed put. Other than a teenage sweetheart, he was inexperienced when it came to women. Time at the Front, and the frumpy specimens at the Vorobyevo Training Centre, had done nothing to see him improve on this. He was ill-prepared for the stunningly beautiful woman now sitting beside him.

"Where'd you learn your Finn?" she asked.

Sami relaxed, but only slightly, as he drew upon his stock of prepared answers. "Oregon," he replied. "We spoke it at home. My parents came to America in 1922."

"Ah, right after the Civil War. 'Bout the same time my folks arrived in Canada."

"You born in Finland?" he asked.

She nodded. He'd guessed she was older, and this was proof. Not that it mattered, because he was going to get off at the next stop and would never see her again. But when the bell rang and the doors opened a second time, she was in the middle of explaining something, and how rude it would be to up and leave.

"Can you keep a secret?" she asked. "I tell everybody my name is Carol Walters, but it's actually Carola Waltari."

"Why would you do that?"

"When I left Sturgeon Falls—that's up in Northern Ontario—for Toronto, my parents thought it would be a good idea. Not that Finns are really hated around here, but until recently Finland was fighting alongside the Nazis. When my older brother, Olli, tried to join up he was refused because he was, get this, classified as an enemy alien. People back in Sturgeon found that pretty stupid. Heck, he was just Olli from down the block."

Two more stops came and went. Sami didn't budge. This was no longer a scheming "Mata Hari," but an ordinary Finn girl chatting about her family, and her hometown somewhere up north. He felt himself warming to the conversation, telling her about his upbringing. Only, his were lies. He prayed hers were not. After Carlaw, he knew his stop at Pape would be next. "Where do you get off?" he found himself asking. The question had come out of nowhere and he had to restrain himself from glancing around to ensure no one else had heard. This was in complete breach of protocol. Should the GRU have a tail on him, he'd be on the next boat back to Russia. Somehow the risk seemed worth it.

"Coxwell," she answered.

"If I got off there . . . could I walk you home?"

Her reaction was surprisingly demure. Not for a second did it cross his mind that this might be a ruse. "If you like," she said.

When Sami and Dietrich had said their final goodbyes in Vorobyevo, his friend, ever the exemplary spy, had offered him one final piece of advice. "Don't fall into the comparison trap," he'd warned. "Sometimes, you run into situations where things appear better in the field than at home. Dismiss them. Remember, building socialism takes time. You'll encounter great riches in America, but ask yourself, are they being shared among the proletariat, or hoarded by the capitalists?'"

At the time, Sami recognized this as sound advice, and he still did, but seven months in Toronto had it fraying at the edges. No matter how hard he tried not to make comparisons they were almost impossible to avoid. It was happening to him again this morning, a Saturday, as he approached Eaton's department store on Queen Street. An interesting building he thought, but extremely pedestrian, architecturally, in comparison to the Gum Department Store on Red Square in Moscow. He continued to feel smug as he entered and took in the low-ceilings, and rambling, unimaginative interior. Surely, this department store was poor cousin to its equivalent in Moscow. *One for the socialist side*, he thought, with a smile. But that was before he noticed the shelves bulging with every product imaginable, and the happy faces on the shoppers. How was it possible for so many goods to be available? And where were these people getting their money? Surely, everyone in this store wasn't a capitalist. And what about the war rationing the workers back at Tippet-Richardson railed against? Sugar, they moaned, was scarce, coffee and chocolate hard to come by, and new cars unavailable. Holy cow! What kind of sacrifice was that?

The comparison dilemma had been needling Sami for some time, but today it took on another dimension, because this morning he wasn't alone. Nor had he been by himself on his off hours for several months. Strolling with him, hand in hand, was Carola. GRU protocol was clear—avoid relationships with locals. How would they react to learn that he and Carola had become regulars? That she'd taught him to jitterbug to Glenn Miller, dragged him to the movies to watch Greer Garson outsmart that German airman in *Mrs. Miniver*, and filled his head with Americanisms that would be sure to bamboozle the handlers back in Moscow. He was smitten. Only an idiot would fail to see that.

He'd never been happier, but it was getting complicated. She wanted to bring him to Sturgeon Falls to meet the family. She'd accepted his background story, but would her father? If he'd fought on the White side in the Civil War there would have to be more lies. He was already holding so much back from Carola that adding to the mix was unthinkable. The web was getting tangled. And what kind of a relationship was he building? Certainly nothing like the one his mom and dad had shared. Even Dietrich's wife knew what her husband was all about. Sami considered coming clean, but feared the outcome.

They exited the store and turned north on Yonge St. "Doesn't it bother you," he said, "hearing about all those unemployed men riding around the country in freight trains looking for work?"

She frowned. "What are you talking about?"

"The work camps. The soup kitchens. The starvation wages. All those young guys getting kicked about from one town to the next."

She shot him a puzzled look. "Holy Toledo, where have you been hiding? That was years ago, during the Depression. You know Toronto better than most. Have you seen any line-ups?"

"Not here, maybe, but they say Winnipeg and Regina, and even Oshawa, have them all the time. And Oshawa is not that far away."

"Who's feeding you this stuff? None of that is happening in any of those places."

"How would you know? It's not like you're a big traveller."

She dropped his hand. "I've been to Oshawa and Hamilton and North Bay and can assure you, there's none of that going on. Come home with me to Sturgeon and we'll pop over to Sudbury. Take my word, the mines there are working full blast, and no one's going hungry, or being underpaid, or getting pushed from town to town. The unions wouldn't stand for it."

When his stay in Toronto had hit twelve full months with still no word from his controller, Sami began to think they'd forgotten him. Was it possible he could have a life of his own? Occasionally, Dietrich crept into his thoughts, but his friend's words of wisdom seemed to grow fainter as the days wore on. For the first time in his life he began to think of himself as a free man. He had a half-decent job, knew the city like the back of his hand, and was loved by a woman he adored. So, when she pulled him close one evening, while sitting on a bench in Riverdale Park, and whispered in his ear that she was expecting his child, he was over the moon. As he hugged her close he struggled to hold back the tears. "Guess it's time I met your family," he said.

She gripped him harder. "You're a good man, Sami Aalto. I'm a lucky girl."

A mother pushing a carriage strolled by. Sami and Carol wiggled their fingers at the baby who rewarded them with a grin.

12

Break Out

German POW Bush Camp
(Newago Timber, South of Hearst),
January 1945

Alfred Reiger checked his watch as he peered from his hiding spot near Bush Camp 73. Under other circumstances, he might have marvelled at the orange moon rising over the bunkhouses. He might even have been inspired to sketch the curious way chimney smoke rose up, then flattened and ran parallel to the roofs, turning the buildings into ships at sea and the camp into a flotilla drifting silently through the boreal forest. But Alfred wasn't seeing any of this tonight. Every ounce of his consciousness was focused on the dim outline of the latrines. It was 21:10 hours, and Hans Eimler hadn't shown yet. What was keeping him? You could set your clock by his bladder.

It was a shared love for classical music that had first brought the two men together. Long before going into the army, Alfred had been a devoted listener to Musica Deutschland, hosted by Hans Eimler and broadcast weeknights on Radio Bavaria. Then, during the 1940 invasion of Norway, they met in person. This love of music held them together through France, North Africa, Lapland, and, now, the POW camp in Northern Ontario. While opposites in many ways, they firmly agreed that German music had gone into a tailspin the instant Hitler dictated that Herr Wagner must be played loud and often.

But Hans talked too freely, and Alfred was terrified. Even here in Canada making fun of the Führer was dangerous. It was alright around a few of their Mountain Corps comrades, but lately submariners had been assigned to the bush camp, and some of them were Hitler fanatics. Why these heel-clicking shrimps were in the bush baffled

Alfred; they were too small to cut pulp and only caused trouble. Why couldn't they leave politics behind in Germany? They had spooked the whole camp, including camp leader Feldwebel Eberhardt. Everyone except Hans, who kept shooting his mouth off. Alfred worried for both of them. They had something to hide, and if these Nazi-zealots discovered their secret, neither he nor his friend were going to make it home. Hans had to shut up.

Alfred pressed his hands against the ear-lugs of his woolen peaked cap, as he banged one foot against the other to keep the blood moving. He checked his watch—21:15. He would give Hans ten more minutes, then return to his own bunkhouse. The orchestra in Barrack 9 had ceased playing, a sure sign that the camp was closing down. He was going to miss the music. The stench of war and the nightmares came back less often since he'd started playing again. And Newago, the pulp company which paid them fifty cents a day to cut timber, bent over backwards to keep the players happy. Need a new tuba? French horn? Oboe? No problem, we'll have it for you in a few weeks. And they did. Life was good here. No walls, no barbed wire, no search lights, or parades in the middle of the night, like in the British camps. Not even a curfew. There were a few guards, but they were mostly older veterans from the last war and friendly. Few talked escape, because where would you go? James Bay, to drown in the swamps, or be devoured by mosquitoes? Most were content to wait out the war. Some had even built log cabins in the bush, and made rowboats for fishing. This was against the rules, of course, but nobody cared as long as you cut your cord of wood each day, which was simple once you got the swing of it. The trick was to work like hell and make your week's quota in four days, then take three off.

Alfred liked it in the bush. Life here was light-years ahead of the sprawling prison camp at Monteith. No more war, heel-clicking, *Sieg Heils*, or Third Reich politics. Or so he had thought before the submariners showed up. Why did they have to come now? The end was near, if only these little u-boat runts would accept it.

A door slammed, followed by the sound of feet crunching on snow. In minus fifty temperatures, most men pissed in the snow bank if that was all they had to do, but this prisoner kept coming. Alfred strained to identify him in the yellow light shining from the tiny windows of the tar-paper shacks. As the figure drew closer, he recognized the swaying shoulders and looping gait. "Hans," he said in a stage whisper.

"Alfred?" Hans responded, looking up and down the trail before wading through the snow in the direction of the voice. "What's up?" They shook hands clumsily through thick, leather mitts.

"You alright?" Alfred asked. Hans nodded. "No trouble in your work group? Bunkhouse?"

Hans looked puzzled. "Should there be?" he asked.

"Jesus, Hans! Wake up!" Alfred stared off in disbelief. It would be so easy to escape without him, but they'd protected each other for so long he couldn't abandon him now. "We've got to get away from here."

"Are you crazy?" Hans said. "Leave a prison camp where they pay us to work? I've got a gramophone coming from Eaton's in Toronto."

Alfred held up his hand. "Those new guys in camp—Otto Rust and Willi Stumpt—they're Nazis."

Hans shrugged. "So? You never seen a Nazi before?"

"They're not here to cut pulp. They're here to make sure you and I have an accident. They're in my bunkhouse," he continued. "I'm telling you, they stare at me with sick little smiles. It's only a matter of time. And in the cookhouse today, when you made that joke about Hitler, they didn't laugh. You've got to stop that stuff, Hans."

"*Shissa* Alfred, the war can't last forever. I heard on the radio that the Russians have us on the run and Germany's shrinking every day. Who'd want to hurt us now?"

"Stumpt and Rost, that's who. They actually believe Germany's winning. They've built a short-wave radio to pick up broadcasts from home, and they have a map showing Axis territory expanding. According to them, we're beating the Russians."

Hans stepped closer. "Oh, God! You don't suppose they know about the work we did for the BBC in England?"

Alfred nodded, but said nothing.

Hans stared back at the camp as if seeking confirmation. "But those radio broadcasts weren't anti-Fatherland—just anti-Hitler. And they got us transferred from that horrible prison camp to Canada. Why would anyone want to come after us now?"

"The Führer's adherents are just as fanatical here in Canada. Even in the bush. They carry lists of anyone they think has 'betrayed the cause.'"

A slight quiver crept into Hans's voice. "Maybe Camp Leader Eberhardt could get them transferred."

Alfred shook his head. "Too late. By now they've enlisted others to do their dirty work."

"But who? We have no enemies here."

"Anyone with loved ones in Germany, that's who. Think about it, Hans. Your relatives and mine were killed in the bombings, but most of the men have folks back home. If they don't do what they're told, their families will suffer."

Hans's shoulders drooped. "What'll we do?"

"Escape. There's no other way."

"But that takes preparation."

"I've already started. Got clothes, money, and food stashed in the bush."

"The guards would be onto us in no time. We wouldn't get far."

Alfred shook his head. "Wrong. The way they've got us working in small parties all over the place, it could be days before we're even missed."

Hans windmilled his arms to get his circulation going. "When you figure to do this?"

"First big snowstorm," Alfred replied. "In the meantime, watch your back. I'll talk to Camp Leader Eberhardt. Get him to transfer you to my work group. Safer for us to stick together."

The loaded sleigh glided down the iced road into the clearing where the logs would be transferred to the pulp trucks. To an untrained eye, the horses, a Percheron and a Clydesdale, were indistinguishable under the steam rising from their frost-covered hides. But Alfred had a soft spot for these gentle beasts, and when they halted beside the waiting truck, he jumped off the sleigh and walked up behind them, intending to reward them with a kind word and a pat. Such obedient creatures. A few oats, hay, a warm barn at night and, *voilà*, servants for life.

As he approached, he was aware of movement on the top of the load. Instinct told him to check it out, but at that exact moment the Clydesdale lifted his tail to release a dump. Pinching his nose, in an exaggerated manner to catch the attention of his comrades, Alfred came to an abrupt halt. When he turned to see how his little antic was going down with the others, he saw that their attention was not on him. Rather it was riveted on the top of the sleigh, where Willi Stumpt sat at the controls of the grapple hook. Not only was he manoeuvring the levers, but he had managed to fill the hook with logs, and was swinging it out over top of him. For an instant he mused over why Willi should be sitting there when it was strictly forbidden for prisoners to touch this machine. The musing ended the instant someone screamed his name.

The scream, and the sneer on Willi's face as he pushed forward on the lever, flashed a message to Alfred's legs. He dove under the sleigh with logs falling around. In the commotion, the horses panicked and the sleigh shot ahead, Alfred with it, clinging to a chain dangling from the floor boards. He bumped along for a hundred metres before letting go. Lying still, as he caught his breath, he watched the men frantically swinging away at the logs with their pulp hooks, desperate to rescue the victim at the bottom of the pile. In the panic, instructions were being shouted in a cacophony of English, French, Finn, Slovak, and German. Stumpt climbed down from the sleigh, and ran to join them. Out of all the red circles on all the prisoners' backs, bobbing as they bent to their work, Alfred's eyes were glued on the target on Willi's back. For the first time since northern Finland, he longed for the familiar grip of his Mauser 98K.

It was Camp Leader Eberhardt who finally spotted Alfred lying in the snow. The men turned and ran toward him. Hans locked him in a bear hug, then lunged at Willi. "Nazi pig," he screamed, punching the tiny submariner to the ground and kicking him with his hobnailed boots. Like a boy in the schoolyard trying to get out from under the class bully, Stumpt writhed in the snow. "Accident!" he yelled, over and over. Prisoners and farmers circled the combatants, but no one interfered. Eventually, two veteran guardsmen pushed their way through and rescued Stumpt. When they pulled Willi up, his face a mixture of blood and snow, his black eyes locked onto Hans. *"Tod für alle verräter," he* mumbled. *"Heil Hitler!"* and made a feeble attempt to click his heels.

Back at the camp Hans and Willi were placed under lock and key. When Alfred asked to see Hans he was denied permission, but in compensation the guards assured him that they would keep the two prisoners well separated. Having done all he could, Alfred, deciding it was too dangerous to return to his bunkhouse, opted instead to pace outdoors in full view of the guards. Dinner was coming up shortly and he would have to eat, but after that, he wasn't sure what to do. When the gong sounded he watched from a distance as the others pushed their way in. Entering alone, his eyes flickered about for a welcoming face. Finding none, he sat at an empty table close to the kitchen door, oblivious to the schnitzel, potatoes, and peas piled on platters before him. When the two guards ducked into the kitchen, Rust and a handful of Nazi confederates slid over, glared at him, and drew fingers across their throats. At the other tables men chewed in silence, eyes glued to the plates in front of them.

"You're as dead as the schnitzel on that platter, Reiger," Rust said, in a low voice.

Alfred felt the bile rising in his throat. "The war's almost over," he stammered in reply. "Why are you pursuing this?"

"Because you're a disgrace to the Fatherland. As a soldier, you gave your word to the Führer. Now you mock him. Forgotten the oath, have you?" He jumped to his feet, and with his right hand extended in the Nazi salute, began reciting. Instantly, his coterie of submariners joined in, reciting in unison:

"I swear by God this sacred oath
That I shall render unconditional obedience to Adolf Hitler
Führer of the German Reich and People
Supreme Commander of the Armed Forces
And that I shall at all times
Be ready to give my life to Him."

There was laughter at the door as the guards returned, munching strudel. Rust and company calmly moved away. "Enjoy your dinner, Reiger. It may be your last."

Alfred forced himself to eat. When he had finished, he speared schnitzel from the platter and stuffed it into his pocket. The Nazis laughed.

"Planning on a trip?" Rust sneered. "You won't get far on that."

Alfred forced himself to think like a soldier. That Rust and his confederates had seen him stashing meat was immaterial now. They knew his only alternative was flight, and for that he needed food. What they didn't know was that he had started his cache weeks earlier. He might freeze when he broke out, but he wasn't going to die of hunger. And his escape had to be tonight.

When Camp Leader Eberhardt rose and headed out the cookhouse door, Alfred snatched another handful of schnitzel and followed, three of Rust's minions right behind. "Herr Eberhardt," he called.

Eberhardt slowed for him, hunching his shoulders against the blowing snow. "You alright?" the camp leader asked. "Stumpt won't be back, if that's what you're worried about. As soon as the snow plane arrives from Hearst, he's off to that special camp for Nazi fanatics at Farnham, Quebec."

"Snow plane?" Alfred asked. "Why not the army truck?"

"This storm's going to be a big one. In a few hours, the only thing moving will be snow planes."

Alfred smiled, picturing the abominably noisy machine whisking his would-be killer away. What pleasure it would be to push Rust and Stumpt into its rear propeller and watch fragments of their National Socialist brains splattering into the boreal forest. "What'll happen to Hans?" he asked, remembering his friend.

Eberhardt shrugged. "The usual fifteen days in the POW Detention Camp at the Hearst gravel pit, then he'll be back." With that he turned to go.

Alfred grabbed Eberhardt's arm and turned him around. They stood close, holding their collars to prevent snow from blowing off the roof and down their necks. Rust's men stood a short distance away. "Don't let Hans come back here!" he begged. "He's a marked man. We both are."

The camp leader's eyes bore into Alfred. "Can you prove that?" he asked. Behind them, Rust's men drew closer. Eberhardt turned on them. "*Raus*," he commanded, and they drifted away.

Alfred watched them disappear. "Can we go some place where we can speak in private?" he asked.

At 21:45 the musicians had stopped playing and the camp was settling in. By 22:00 all was still. Alfred lay under the cookhouse as Eberhardt had instructed, his mind a whirlwind. The snow plane had arrived earlier, to take Hans and Willi to Hearst. Cigar-shaped, it was small and cramped, and Alfred smiled as he thought of Hans' regular visit to the outhouse. Would they stop the snow plane for him in this blizzard so he could take his nightly crap? Hans was a treasure; so much musical talent. But he needed a guardian. Alfred felt guilty for abandoning him, but Eberhardt was a good leader who'd knock some sense into him.

At 23:30 hours the silence was punctuated by the slamming of a door followed by shouts. The guards were out. Alfred cursed. Rust must have reported him missing and set off the alarm. He crawled to the edge of the cookhouse and poked a hole through the fresh snow that had accumulated there. To his surprise, the guards were not rushing into the bunkhouses, but had taken up stations around them. *Eberhardt's* doing, he thought, crawling out and quickly replacing the snow covering his exit. He then raced toward the latrines and the logging road that led west to the Algoma Central Railway tracks. For five minutes, he ran at full speed, then slowed to listen. Silence. From that point on, he forced himself to walk briskly, careful not to build up a sweat.

Only when he reached the Obijou River did he stop to pull the civilian trench coat from his bag. In terms of BTUs the coat was next to useless, but it hid the red target on his back, and would help him blend in with civilians. That done, he lit a match for a glimpse at his compass and continued west. So far, his information on the abandoned bush road was accurate; the train tracks couldn't be that far off.

He knew the odds were against him. Surviving the subarctic temperatures wasn't the only hazard he faced. His English was passable, but his accent atrocious. A couple of "w" phrases, such as, "where was Walter when the wagon went west?" would give him away in a flash. Still, in this bush country, with European tongues almost as common as English and French, he felt he could get by—for a while. Eventually, he'd be caught. He knew that, but the challenge was to get as far away as possible, to insure they wouldn't return him to the same camp.

Once he reached the Algoma Central tracks on which the logging trains travelled, he would have two options; south to Sault, Michigan, destination German sympathizers in Bismark, North Dakota, or north to Hearst to catch a westbound freight to Winnipeg. Both presented risks—freezing to death inside a freight car, or numbing up on the roof and falling under the train. Not that Alfred's plan called for travelling atop the cars for anything but short distances, because he'd put together enough money to buy railway tickets once he reached either the Sault or Hearst. Like many of the prisoners, he'd been selling stuff to Newago Timber's local employees—harmonicas and leather goods that arrived in the Red Cross parcels from Germany, via Switzerland; also cigarettes, hair tonic, and other scarce commodities purchased with chits the company gave to the prisoners in lieu of money.

When he finally came to the tracks, it was the wind whipping up from the south that convinced him to head north, destination Hearst. With the snow slamming into his back and swirling around him, progress was slow. Even when the sun rose, visibility hardly extended past his nose. His legs found a rhythm as he ploughed up the line, conscious of the need to keep moving forward and staying between the rails. Occasionally, eyeballs smarting from the icy pellets, he would peer out from under the peak of his cap into the squall. Nothing seemed to change. His pace began to slow.

Several hours later, noticing that the wind had dropped enough to make out trees and forms, he looked up to see what he thought might be the outline of a field and buildings. His first reaction was fear of being spotted, but that thought was quickly overpowered by the urgent need for warmth and sleep.

Could this be Coppell? He wondered, thinking of the village north of Newago's cutting limits. *Or, maybe the farm where prisoners claimed to have bought booze, and been allowed to sleep in the hay?* "Barn," he repeated aloud, plunging down the railway embankment into the waist deep snow, and heading for what he prayed was a not an optical illusion, but a bona fide shelter with hay and warm animals.

Alfred awoke to squawking chickens, a barking dog, and a small man brandishing a pitch fork. *"Qu'est-ce que tu fais là?"* the man demanded. Immediately, Alfred propelled himself backward across the hay, but the man stepped closer, prodding the air with the pitchfork. "Me Alfred Reiger. Work Newago," he said. The farmer barked an order to the dog, who scaled his belligerence back from sabre-toothed tiger to wolf. Carefully, Alfred reached into his pocket and extracted a two-dollar bill. "Beer? Food?" he asked, making eating gestures. A thin smile appeared on the farmer's lips. He lowered the pitch fork, turned, and signalled for Alfred to follow. With the dog switching back and forth from growling, to teeth baring, to barking, Alfred shuffled along behind as fast as his stiff limbs would permit. *"Ta gueule, Croc, ou je pisse dedans!"* the farmer finally screamed to the beast, giving him a swat to the head. Alfred wondered if the name, "Croc," was short for crocodile.

The heat in the house enveloped him the instant he stepped inside. *"Allemand,"* the farmer said to his surprised wife. *"Prépare quelque chose à manger."* She and an older daughter moved to the counter. Six young heads appeared over the stairs. Two older boys came in behind them with wood. Too stiff to bend, Alfred failed to get his boots off as instructed, leaving the farmer to ease him onto a chair and finish the job.

With all those eyes on him, the flush on Alfred's face was not totally due to the heat in the room. He stood and followed the farmer to the table, the blood tingling painfully through his fingers and toes. The host pointed to a chair underneath a crucifix, and a picture of Jesus with a valentine heart. After a moment of silence, he offered his host a cigarette, which the man accepted, lit, and held the flame for his guest. Eggs and blood pudding began making splattering noises on the stove. Alfred's stomach roiled in a growl that echoed off the walls, to the children's amusement. The older boys stood near the door, arms crossed as they examined him with sullen stares. He tried to remember some of the words he'd learned when he'd rolled into France with the Wehrmacht, but gave up when his eyes found those of the older daughter. She reddened and turned away. She was slightly younger than Alfred, with a full figure, and a smile that cut right through him. He longed to talk to her, but in deference to the scolding she was getting from her mother, turned his head.

After several minutes of smiling and nodding, the farmer went to a closet and returned with a bottle of beer which he held out for Alfred, while holding up a dollar bill and two fingers. Even before it touched his lips, the aroma of hops had him back to a time before the war with father treating the family to a meal at the *Ratskeller* in Schwäbische Gmünd. They're all there—moma, papa, his two sisters. The occasion is Alfred's graduation. He's now a full-fledged baker, anxious to take his place in the family business. Father is on his feet, beer in hand, toasting his son. In his mind Alfred hears them, sees them, touches them.

With the farmer's cough, the image began to fade. When he opened his eyes, it was gone. Struggling to regain composure, he turned at the sound of footsteps, and found himself looking up into the warm, concerned face of the young girl approaching with his meal. He swallowed, drinking in the bounty of her youth, prospects and promise. Never had a woman filled a faded, flowered, house dress with such elegance. He longed to touch her hand, but held back, wondering what became of bright young women stuck in the middle of nowhere. But quickly, he realized that even here, she had a future, while he had none. The moment hadn't missed the farmer. "Nicole!" he barked, breaking the spell. *"En haute! Maintenant!"* With that Nicole disappeared.

The farmer, he saw now, was holding up three fingers. Three dollars was piracy, but Alfred was quick to hand over the money. Another two fingers arose when a second beer arrived. Alfred began to panic. Less than twenty-four hours and his cash was melting away, like the snow on his boots. If he didn't leave soon, there wouldn't be enough to get him to Winnipeg. His freedom had cost him an astounding seven dollars so far, but he felt no regrets. If only for those precious seconds with the girl, Nicole, it was money well spent.

With his plate scraped clean, he patted his stomach and stood, hoping to convince his host that he had just slipped away for some home cooking and a forbidden beer, and now, having achieved his goal, he would return to work. "Newago," he said, gesturing to the woods. *"Arbeiten—work."*

Disappointment flashed across the farmer's face. Two beers and a meal was all he had sold. He gestured to the weather. *"Restez ici. Trop dangereux."*

Alfred pointed to the calendar at the door. "Two weeks. Come back. Bring friends." Then he held a finger to his lips and smiled. "Secret, shh, shh." The farmer nodded. A shishing sound filled the room as the children, conspirators to the bootlegging, began mimicking the guest. *"Danke schön,"* Alfred said, climbing into his boots and winter togs and bowing to the lady of the house.

Outside on the steps, he turned to see someone scraping at the hoarfrost on an upstairs window. When a face appeared behind the pane, he saw that it was Nicole. Instinctively, he blew a kiss. To his surprise, she returned it, and waved. Wanting desperately to stay, but knowing better, he forced himself off the stoop, and sprinted for the tracks. "Nicole, Nicole," he repeated over and over.

By Alfred's calculations, only thirty kilometres separated him from Hearst. If not for the stormy conditions he could be there in six hours. He broke off a twig and began recording his progress. In the deep snow, he estimated it took three steps to travel one metre. When he had counted three hundred steps, he marked the twig with his teeth and started counting from zero again. Then, with ten marks on the twig and one kilometre behind him, he broke off a piece of wood and stuffed it into his pocket. "Twenty-nine to go," he announced to no one but himself.

The wind cut through his clothes, but the counting kept his mind off the what-ifs: What if they'd noticed his absence back at camp and put out the alarm? What if Rust and his cohort were in pursuit? What if the farmer had figured out that no sane person braved white-out conditions for beer and food, and had notified the authorities? What if the Canadian Army was waiting for him at the end of the line? He blinked and strained to see through the blowing snow. "Stay focused," he reminded himself, but numbness was setting in. He fumbled in his pocket for his hand-drawn map, and saw that he hadn't even reached the village of Jogues yet, with Hearst a long distance north of that. Next, he counted the pieces of wood he'd broken and put in his pocket. There were only six, meaning he'd hardly a fifth of the thirty-kilometre distance. He dropped his head and continued chaining himself up the line, mumbling like a priest reciting his rosary.

Alfred had just put the seventh twig in his pocket when he found himself face down in the snow. For an instant he lay there stunned, before realizing that he'd walked right into a fallen tree. Carefully, he pushed himself up, but when he tried to stand, a sharp pain ricocheted up his leg. He sank back into the snow and howled. The howl morphed into a curse, followed by hysterical laughter, and finally, quiet acceptance. Having survived bombs, bullets, and Arctic weather in Finland's Winter War, here he was about to die all alone in a Northern Ontario snowstorm. "Hilarious," he mumbled. "Tragic."

Strangely, his thoughts were not on family, now all dead, but on the girl he'd only ever exchanged glances with—Nicole. Foolish to dream of a woman he'd never talked to, and now never would. But he was sure there had been a connection. Hadn't she blown him a kiss from the window.

With every minute on the ground his body temperature dropped closer to the point of shut-down. The temptation to close his eyes and drift away with nothing but the image of Nicole to keep him warm, was overpowering. Freezing to death, they said, was painless. He recalled comrades who'd welcomed hypothermia as a deliverance. Now he understood.

But with the snow swirling around him, a novel sensation began to take root. For several minutes it idled in his consciousness, until at last his sluggish brain found a word for it. Rage! Rage that Hitler had robbed him of his youth. Rage that having come through so much he should fall so close to the end of the war. Rage that he would never see Nicole again. She'd go through life wondering whatever became of that German prisoner who once came to her door.

Summoning energy he never dreamt he had, he pushed himself up, first to his knees, then to his feet, weighing his options, as he sluggishly windmilled his arms. Returning to Newago was out. Ditto getting as far as Hearst. Nicole's barn seemed his only hope. If he could make it back, he could rest up, heal and try again in better conditions. The storm might actually be to his advantage. It would take days for the home-army guards, and the police, to find him. He might even get another opportunity to speak to Nicole. Her parents couldn't keep her locked up forever. In his mind's eye he saw her slipping away to visit him in the barn. He smiled at the foolishness of it, but it was something to hold onto. Using a broken branch as a crutch, he turned around and began retracing his steps.

13

Trapped

Coppell, Northern Ontario,
January 1945

Two full days in the barn had his prospects seemingly on the rise—he hadn't been discovered, and his food stash was holding out. The barn had two levels: a cavernous hayloft with daylight and snow sifting through the cracks, and a main level with stone walls and a low ceiling. Sleeping in the loft seemed safest, but it only took a few hours on the first night to realize that the warmth lay below with the livestock. Night two had him waiting in the hay for the house to shut down before settling into a cozy stall, next to the horses. The danger in this lay in the possibility of not waking before some member of the household came down to do the morning chores.

Shortly after daylight on the third morning, Alfred lay groggy in a manger when someone entered the barn. He lay dead still, buried in the straw. Whoever had come in did their chores quickly, then left. He climbed back into the mow for a peek at who it was, hoping for a glimpse of Nicole. Looking through the cracks he saw one of the boys hustling back to the warmth of the house, and presumably a full breakfast. Croc, he saw, was still chained-up near the front door. When they unleashed him, which was bound to happen, he'd be down to the barn in a flash.

Alfred had stashed the meat pilfered from the cookhouse in a pail, which he kept in the freezing haymow. On this, his third morning, he got out three chops to thaw: one for each meal to be washed down later with handfuls of snow, and a pilfered egg, or two.

He was chewing on half-frozen meat when he heard voices coming from up near the house. Once again he peered through a crack in the barn boards. This time it was to see the younger children pushing and shoving each other, as they made their way to the road. Each had a book pack strapped on their back, just like students back in Germany. Their mother gave them a wave from the open door, but before she could close it, Nicole came rushing out with a basket, and struck a beeline for the barn. Alfred's heart stopped. He knew what he wanted to happen, but one glimpse of him would have her screaming, and fleeing back to the house. Her father would grab that shotgun propped up behind the door and be on him in a flash. Croc, too.

The barn door opened then slammed shut. He held his breath as he listened to her kicking snow off her feet and singing her way towards the chicken coop at the back. She wasn't much of a singer, but he recognized the words from the camp radio—"Chattanooga Choo Choo," Glen Miller, Jazz. *Streng verboten* in the Third Reich, but his POW pals at Newago couldn't get enough of the stuff—at least until the Nazi die-hards had shown up. That he and Nicole should have a song in common, tugged at the cord his imagination was building between them. He longed to join in, but resisted, opting instead to inch his way to the top of the ladder in order to glimpse her as she left. What he hadn't reckoned on was the chaff and dust generated by his movement. It floated down, illuminated in the columns of light slanting in through the cracks in the walls. He noticed it right off. So did Nicole. She stopped and looked up to the source.

For several seconds they stared at each other. Alfred wanted to smile, but couldn't get beyond just taking her in. When she neither screamed, nor beat a panicked retreat, he began to regain his senses. "You blew me a kiss from the window," he said. With no answer forthcoming, it occurred to him that she might not speak English.

At last, she nodded, and cleared her throat. "Only because I never expected to see you again."

"Did you want to? See me that is?"

"You looked so, *dépaysé* . . ."

"What's that?"

"Lost and lonely. From nowhere you popped out of the biggest storm of the year, like it was . . ."

"Meant to be?"

"Don't get carried away," she cautioned. "Took me by surprise, that's all."

He heard the words, but was sure there was a blush in there somewhere. "Since that kiss, I haven't been able think of anything but you."

"*Mais, voyons.* Through a frosty window in a snow storm? Hardly a kiss. And it's not as if we talked or anything."

He hesitated before speaking again. "I guess I haven't been in your head like you've been in mine." Forgetting his injured foot, he moved to get closer to the ladder. A sharp pain shot up his leg, and he dropped to one knee with a groan.

"You're hurt," she said, climbing part way up the ladder. "What have they done to you?"

"Nothing. Hurt my foot, that's all."

"Want me to have a look."

Alfred shifted position until he was sitting on the edge of the loft, his leg and foot dangling down for her to inspect from below. "You a nurse or something?" He asked.

Having climbed the ladder, she pulled his boot off gently and ran her hand up and down his ankle, pressing here and there. He gasped as she gently rotated his foot. "Sprain, I think," she said. "Sometimes hard to tell with a foot, so many bones. And no, I'm not a nurse, but I hope to be one day. That costs money though. For now, I help out at the hospital on weekends. Dr. Chalykoff says that if I . . ."

"Hey, I know him. Comes to the camp. And he fixed my foot when I cut it with an axe. Nice man." They smiled, comforted by the discovery of someone they both knew and admired. Alfred rushed to fill the lull that had fallen. "Chalykoff and Doctor Volkmann at the camp, he's a fellow prisoner, get on really well. They plan to go into practice together when the war's over, or so they say, but who knows if that'll ever happen, what with the fighting dragging on and on." He knew he was talking too much, and too fast, but he worried if he stopped, she would flee.

"Have to go," Nicole finally said. "Maman will be wondering what's taking so long to get the eggs. She's baking a cake." She moved down the ladder a few rungs then stopped. "You can't stay here. Papa comes back day after tomorrow. If he catches you, he'll have to tell the police." When she got to the door, she opened it and turned. "What will you do?"

"Not sure," he replied. "Can't go back to Newago. There are some Nazis there threatening to . . . hurt me."

She frowned. "What do you mean, 'some'? Aren't you all Nazis?"

"Hell, no. Most of us never were."

"So, if you're not all Nazis, how do you explain those Pathé movie reels of people *Seig Heiling* and stuff?"

Alfred's chin dropped. "It's complicated, but I'd love to explain it to you. Think that could ever happen?"

"You can't stay here. As a matter of fact, you should be gone before the boys get back from school. It's their turn to do the chores tonight. They get home just after dark, around five. You'll hear them, because Croc always barks."

"Thank you . . . Nicole. I'll be gone."

Snow blew in through the open door. "You remember my name." She hesitated. "I'll come back with food. Don't go before I do. It'll have to be whatever I can sneak out without Maman seeing, but I'll make sure it's hot. You'll need that."

"Don't get yourself into any trouble on my account."

There was a brief moment of silence. "You have a place to go?" she asked.

He shrugged. "My plan was to get to Hearst and take a train west. Now it's probably best to turn myself in, and pray they don't put me back in with the Nazis."

She looked at him. "Whatever you do, you won't get far on that foot. Not for a few days, at least."

It took an eternity for Nicole to return, or so it seemed to Alfred. While he ate, she sat perched on a hay wagon, swinging her legs like a school girl, and smiling. He sat on a milk can, looking up at her with each bite. "What . . . is . . . this?" he asked, as he wolfed down his first hot meal in three days.

"Pork hock ragout," she replied. "Don't you have that in Germany?"

Alfred shrugged and shook his head as he continued eating.

"With the snow letting up, Mama's gone down the road to Mme. Lapointe's for tea."

"Meaning?" he asked, between mouthfuls.

"That I don't have to rush back to the house, that's all. Still doesn't give us much time, though."

His heart rate quickened. *Doesn't give us much time*, she'd said. Where was she going with that? He noticed that she'd changed her barn coat for a spiffier model, and that her hair was now up off her forehead with big rolls on the sides, just like the women in the Eaton's catalogue the men ogled over back at Newago. He trolled his mind for something witty to say. Five years in the army had done nothing to improve his small talk with girls. "Tell me about yourself, Nicole." He groaned inwardly at how lame that must sound.

"Not much to say. As you can see, I'm a farm girl who'd like someday to be a nurse."

"A wife, too?" he blurted, without thinking.

"Maybe," she blushed, "if the right man ever came along. How about you? What's your story?"

Alfred wiped his lips with the back of a sleeve. "Well, my full name is Alfred Gottfried Reiger and I come from Schwäbisch Gümund, a small city between Stuttgart and Munich. I'm a baker, just like my father. But I had barely joined the family business when I got called up."

"Baking? That what you intend to do when this is over?"

Alfred nodded. "For sure, but not back home. RAF bombs took out our bakery, along with my whole family. We lived behind the shop, you see. So, there's nothing for me in Schwäbisch Gümund any more—or Germany, for that matter."

"How terrible. I'm sorry. They don't talk about ordinary Germans in our papers. Even so, you'd still want to go home, wouldn't you? At least eventually."

Alfred shrugged. "Perhaps . . . some day. For now, just staying here suits me fine. Believe it or not, I love Northern Ontario, black flies and all." He hopped to the wagon and sat beside her, careful to keep a respectable distance between them.

"When the war ends, you'll be changing your mind. You'll see."

"When that day comes, they'll be sending all us prisoners back. I'll have no choice."

"You could always return here as an immigrant," she suggested.

"Ha! Could take years. You'd be an old married woman by then."

"You realize that going home might happen sooner than you think. I keep up on the news. It's just about over. We've taken France, Belgium, and are deep into Holland. Italy's finished, the Finns have quit, and the Russians are on your eastern border."

Alfred frowned. "Which makes me sad. Not because it's going so well for your side," he hastened to add, "but because it puts getting sent home all that much closer."

"You're serious, aren't you? You'd stay if given a choice?"

"Wouldn't hesitate for a second, but I'll have no say in it. Nothing new there. I haven't been allowed to make a decision for myself in five years. Go here, go there, do this, do that. I'm twenty-one and have less control over my life than with my parents."

"You took off from the Newago Camp, didn't you? I'm guessing nobody ordered you to do that."

Alfred smiled. "You're right, I did. And at this moment, in spite of nearly freezing to death and spraining my ankle, I feel pretty good about it."

"Has it occurred to you that you might still have options?"

Alfred wasn't sure whether to smile or frown. "You're kidding me, aren't you?"

"I'm serious. If it's dangerous to go back, why give yourself up? What if you just sat out the rest of the war in the bush? Wouldn't be for long. Then, when it ends, come out and sneak away. If they catch you, all they can do is send you back to Germany, which is what they'd have done anyway. But if they don't catch you, well, you're a free man."

Alfred looked at her like he was seeing her for the first time. "Lovely thought, Nicole, but it's January, I'd be dead before week's end in these conditions. Besides, where would I go, and how would I live?"

"Off the land. Others are doing it."

"Who? Other German prisoners?"

"Don't know. Could be some are prisoners. The ones I know about are conscientious objectors who refuse to fight, or be conscripted.

And as far as surviving goes, of course you'd need help. But that could be arranged."

He looked at her in bewilderment. "In my country, you'd be shot for talking like this. I'm grateful, Nicole, but I would never put you in such a position. Too risky."

"Nobody's going to shoot me. Worst I could expect is a little time behind bars and, frankly, it would be like a holiday from the farm. You seem like a *gentil gars*; I might even know someone who'd be willing to get you started."

"If you got caught the locals would hate you for it."

"Some, for sure, but a lot of farmers, like my father, have worked side by side with the prisoners. They like you guys."

He shifted his weight, inching his way closer to her. She had her palms on the edge of the wagon, and he longed to place his hand on top of hers, but didn't have the courage. "All this stuff about people holing up in the bush. You know this for a fact?"

She dropped her head and smirked. "My uncle was a draft dodger."

"Was?"

"Well, until the RCMP caught him. Took them eleven months, though."

"Sitting here, this all sounds possible, Nicole, but let's be real, where exactly would I go?"

"Not sure, but the guy I have in mind might."

"Someone you can trust?" She nodded. "Boyfriend?" he managed to ask.

"Maybe," she said, "but, only if I was into older, mature gentlemen. He's a retired trapper who worked in the bush in the 1920s and '30s. Came back from the Great War with permanent injuries. Now he hates war."

"And you think he'd be willing to help?"

"Pretty sure. He's a Mennonite, which makes him a pacifist. At least he is now—again. Before the Great War, he broke away from the colony and joined the Canadian Army. Something he's regretted ever since. Now he lives in a log cabin east on Prune Creek, not far from here." She handed Alfred a piece of paper.

"What's this?"

"A map, plus an introduction."

"Look, Nicole, pacifist or not, I can't just show up with a piece of paper and expect him to hide me till the war's over."

"Course not. This is temporary, but he'll have some ideas on safe places. He helped my uncle without blinking an eye. You go to his place for a few days. I'll do my best to get over after my weekend shift at the hospital in town."

"This guy, does he speak English?"

She nodded. "German, too. He'll be delighted with the company."

Alfred placed his hand on Nicole's. For a second neither spoke. "You planned this up at the house, didn't you?" he said, looking directly into her eyes.

Pulling her hand away, she pushed herself off the wagon, and began buttoning her coat. "Let's just say I came prepared, but hadn't made up my mind. Plus, I wasn't sure how you'd react."

"When did you decide to help me?"

She shrugged. "Not sure. Probably when you told me about the mess you're in. They say I'm like a mother hen. Can't stop helping strangers in distress. Maman says it's going to get me into trouble someday."

"There have been others, then?" Alfred asked, hoping he didn't sound jealous. "I mean, there are more . . . guys like me you're helping?" The smile spreading across her face wasn't helping. *Dumb bugger*, he thought, *you're reading too much into her willingness to help get you set up?*

"Best to keep mum about such things, don't you think, Alfred?" she replied, with a wink. "Safer that way. Now button up. Got to get you away from the barn before Maman returns."

"But I can't go far on this foot."

"We're just going to the root cellar. I'll come for you later. Trust me."

14

Sanctuary

Southeast of Jogues, Ontario,
January 1945

ust about there," Nicole said, snapping the reins to get more speed out of the horse. "Giddy up, Charles Eugene."

Alfred knew enough about horses to tell that there was little trot left in swayback Charles Eugene, but Nicole had a gentle way which had the nag doing his best. "What's with the horse's name?" he asked.

"Family joke. *Maman* loved 'Marie Chapdelaine,'" she said, turning to him with a laugh. "It's a book. French Canadian classic. That's what Marie's father calls his horse in the story. You'll have to read it some day."

"I will, but right now I'm kinda worried about this guy you're taking me to. You absolutely sure we can trust him?"

"Known him all my life. Different type. As a kid, most of my friends were afraid of him. Me, never."

"Why afraid?"

"You'll see." A log cabin came into view. Charles Eugene turned towards it with no prompting and, like a milk wagon horse on a familiar route, came to a halt alongside the front door.

"Looks like Charles Eugene has been here before," Alfred said. What he really wanted to know, but didn't dare ask, was if this bushman had helped her with other fugitives, and what her relationship with them might have been, or still was.

Nicole ignored the comment as she handed him a burlap bag, and headed for the door. "Wipe down Charles Eugene while I explain things." She knocked. "And put the blanket on him." The door opened and she entered. Five minutes later she stepped out, and waved him in.

Otto Schneider was shorter than Alfred had imagined, possibly five-foot-seven, but barrel chested, and still powerful for a person his age. While barely a hair grew on the top of his head, the bristles springing from his nose, and brow, made up for that lack. When Nicole had mentioned his war injuries, Alfred had pictured a wooden leg, or hook for a hand. In Otto's case it was his face—most would recoil at the sight of him. Not Alfred. He'd seen it before, and worse.

After the introductions they sat down at the table, with Alfred and Nicole side-by-side facing Otto. For a moment no one spoke. Otto stared at them. "Best I explain," Nicole began.

"Good idea," Otto grunted.

Alfred paid close attention to the old-timer as he frowned at some points and nodded at others. When the kerosene lamp on the table began to smoke the old man drew it closer and trimmed the wick. The lamp came back to life with a deep warm light that cast long shadows on the walls. On the cookstove, the pot of food that Nicole had brought began emitting an aroma that had Alfred close to rapture. Rabbit stew, he thought. When Nicole finished her explanation, Otto went to the stove and began to make tea.

The lull in the conversation that followed gave Alfred a chance to take in the cabin. While it had only three rooms—one small bedroom, a kitchen, and a living area—it was cozy. The opposite to what he considered a shack, as Nicole had originally called it. Although well worn, the couch looked comfortable, as did the twin rocking chairs. On the wall was a scene depicting anglers reeling in fish, as well as a calendar showing a pack of wolves stalking a trapper.

Alfred breathed in deeply. Spartan for sure, but well cared for. It showed in the squared tamarack timbers, the tight chinking between the logs, and the red linoleum on the floor. He envied the old guy and thought that, one day, he'd like to have something similar. But there was an odour he couldn't place—not hospital disinfectant, but close. When he sniffed to identify it, he saw that Otto was watching him.

"Treated chinkum," Otto said. "We stuff it between the logs for insulation. The smell comes from the insecticide in it. Bother you?"

"No. Kinda like it."

Otto turned his attention back to Nicole. "Your parents? They know you're here?"

"They think I'm visiting Rita. It's a lot farther to come here, so I'm going to have to leave pretty soon."

A few minutes later she was at the door, putting on her boots. Alfred stepped forward. "You going to be alright getting home?" he asked. "I mean, this storm is far from over."

She straightened, and turned towards him. "Bah, this is nothing. I'm used it. And I've got Charles Eugene to rely on. I'll be fine." They stood there awkwardly. "Well," she said, finally, placing one hand on the latch, "good luck, Alfred. Hope this works out for you. Otto will do his best, but take care. Maybe we'll run into each other again sometime." She took off her mitt and extended her hand.

Alfred took it gently. "Thank you for everything," he said, holding it more than shaking it. "I won't forget this."

"So long, Otto," she called, breaking her eyes away from Alfred's. "See you."

They were not long into Nicole's stew before Otto put his spoon down and stared at Alfred. "She's a good Catholic girl," he said. "Never misses mass. Obeys her parents. A little too trustful, if you ask me."

"I figured that."

Otto leaned forward. "Well, don't forget it. Understood? Wouldn't want you getting ideas that she could be your horizontal collaborator."

"My what?"

"Your *wurstverstecke.*"

"*Guter himmel nein*! Where'd you get that idea?"

"From the way you were looking at her, that's where." Otto picked up his spoon and resumed eating. "Alright then, just wanted to get that straight. Couldn't stand to see her taken advantage of."

"Me neither," Alfred insisted. "And that look you're referring to was admiration. Nothing more. I assure you. She seems like a lovely, caring, understanding, resourceful woman," he said. "God. I respect that."

Otto looked up at him from his side of the table. "Good. Sorry if I misinterpreted. Kinda had me on edge there for a minute."

After that the talk came easy, although the war as a subject went unbroached. Alfred found his spirits lifting. There was something heart-warming about Otto's little warning. The old guy had taken on the role of surrogate father—a rare opportunity for a life-long bachelor. For him it was serious, and he was giving it all the sternness he could dredge up from deep into his Mennonite past. Alfred felt a sense of belonging, something he realized had been missing for a long, long time.

Three days later a sleigh pulled into the lane. Otto hurriedly directed Alfred to the trap door under the kitchen rug, walked to the window and returned. "False alarm," he yelled down. "You can come out now."

Alfred's head popped up to see Nicole nervously pacing the floor. "Just wanted to see how plans were coming along," she said. "The roads haven't been cleared yet, but it won't be long now, and you know what that means . . ."

"Army, soldiers, police," Otto answered.

She barely had her boots off before Otto had the three of them at the table, thinking caps on. Remembering the old man's words, Alfred concentrated on keeping his eyes anywhere but on her. It was far from easy. His thoughts kept wandering to places they had no business exploring.

"You part of this conversation?" Otto said to him, bringing him back.

Alfred blinked. "Yeah. Sure. Of course."

"As I was saying," Otto continued, turning back to Nicole, "my place is sure to be tops on the RCMP's list for checking. They know I helped out your uncle, which probably puts them at my door no later than twenty-four hours after the roads are passable."

"Got any ideas?" Nicole asked.

"Working on it. Getting him out of the territory is out of the question; they'll have a close eye on the trains and roads. That leaves going into the bush. But it'll have to be in a lot deeper than where we put your uncle."

"Why?" Nicole said. "It took them almost a year to find *mon oncle,* and surely the war'll be long over in that time."

Otto nodded. "Possibly, but that's what they always say about wars, over by Christmas. How else do you think they con the gullible into signing up? I should know, I fell for it in 1914. Cost me dearly."

"*Oui, bien sûr*, Otto, but what about Alfred? No way can he get far on that foot of his."

"It's not that bad," Alfred protested. "Much better now. I'm getting around pretty good."

She looked at him. "Hopping around this tiny cabin is a far cry from bucking deep snow, and climbing over fallen trees."

"Snowshoes will be too tough for him," Otto said. "Which leaves . . ." He smacked his fist into his open hand. "Skis. *Ja*, that's it, skis. No pounding on the feet with every step. A little kick from the knee and push with the arms and you just glide forward. Easy peezey, as the English say."

Nicole looked as if she didn't know whether to laugh or cry. "Really, Otto, doesn't this easy gliding stuff only happen if there's a firm crust? What's out there after six days of heavy snowfall, is soft and deep. Even experienced skiers couldn't buck more than a few kilometres of that stuff. A city boy like Alfred has probably never been up on skis. It'd be a disaster. There must be something else."

Alfred was beginning to feel left out of the planning. "Hold on," he interrupted. "You think I survived the Lapland war without learning how to ski? That was the first thing they taught us. Sneak in and move out fast. And that meant skis. Too slow and you died. How else do you think we were able to kill so many Russians? Piled them up by the hundreds. Poor buggers were never issued quality equipment. We skied rings around them."

Nicole and Otto stared at him. It took but a second for him to understand his gaff. So far, the word "war" had been carefully avoided. Now he'd casually mentioned killing Russians. No wonder they were shocked. They were trying to help, but he was still the enemy, son of a country that had brought misery, and death, to friends and family in these parts.

Alfred cleared his throat. "All that's in the past. Those things were forced on us. There were SS troops making sure we obeyed orders— or else."

Nicole nodded. "We understand," she said, "don't we, Otto?" Otto tugged at the turkey neck under his chin, and looked away. "Don't we, Otto," she repeated.

Otto's eyes snapped back to his German guest. "Oh, God, do I understand. Just like in the Great War. In my nightmares I see a trench mate being shot right in front of me for refusing to go over the top. Why would Alfred's war be any less disgusting?"

"Let's get back to business," Nicole said. "You sure you can handle yourself on skis?"

"Absolutely. No better teachers than the Finns. From them I got it, chapter and verse—hard snow, soft snow, deep snow, wet snow, dry snow, technique, wax—the whole bit."

"Good, because you'll need skis, and I just might have some that'll suit: Papa keeps an old pair in the barn. Hasn't used them for years. He'll never miss them. All I have to do is . . ." She stopped. Otto was shaking his head, Alfred grimacing.

"Old skis? Bad idea," Otto said. "Look, there's a Finn guy, Bert Maki, up in Hearst. Good friend. Skis a lot. He's sure to have what's needed."

"You think he'd help?" Alfred asked. "Considering . . ."

Otto nodded. "Wouldn't worry. When he hears you spent two years in Lapland alongside the Finnish Army, he'll be more than anxious to co-operate."

"*Ja*, but Otto, surely he knows the Finns and Germans have turned on each other, up in Rovaniemi."

"He's a Finn from Karelia. If he has any beefs my guess is they're with the Russians, not you guys. Leave it to me."

Nicole and Otto started planning in earnest. Alfred attempted to join in, but found his thoughts drifting to the danger all this was putting on his two new friends. The RCMP weren't stupid. When they caught up to him, which was certain to happen, they'd know he'd had help. A jail term probably wouldn't phase Otto, but Nicole was another matter. She'd have a police record, and be shunned for the rest of her days. That he couldn't bear.

The discussion around him became a low drone with the odd word penetrating his thoughts. Horses, sleighs, blankets, he understood, but

Bradlo, Glenomo, Val Côté, Fryatt, Mattice, Missinaibi, Mattawitch-ewan? Were they places or people?

"That's it, then," Otto said, slapping the table, and bringing Alfred out of his reverie. "Getting him there will be tricky, but once in, he'll be safe."

Alfred noticed that they'd drawn a crude, but surprisingly detailed, map. His mind skipped to all those pre-attack briefings back at the Front. Some plans worked, some didn't. As for this one, he had a bad feeling. "Listen, I'm grateful for what you're trying to do," he said, "but perhaps we should forget this."

"Forget what, exactly?" Nicole replied.

"The whole thing. Great on paper, but let's be practical."

"What do you mean?"

The touch of disappointment in her voice troubled him, but he pushed on. "It's too risky," he said.

"What have you got to lose?"

Otto, sensing they were talking about more than getting Alfred to a safe place, decided the fire needed attention.

"It's not me I'm worried about. It's you and Otto."

"Do you have a better idea?"

"Go to town when the roads open, and turn myself in."

"Give up completely? Is that it? Let them put you behind bars, and ship you back to Germany when the war's over. You said you wanted to stay here. Or was that just talk?"

"I do, badly, but . . ."

"And where would that leave . . . ?" She broke off and looked away.

Alfred hoped he knew the word she'd almost blurted out. He stared at her, overwhelmed by what was happening. How was it possible to feel this deeply for someone so fast? All they had ever done was touch hands and talk, yet the prospect of never seeing her again had become unbearable.

Otto coughed and returned to the table. "Your decision, Alfred," he said. "If it's to give up, then we can sit back and drink tea until they show up to take you away. But if the decision is to make a run for it, we have to act fast. And that means tonight. What's it going to be?"

Alfred looked from Nicole to Otto, trying to read their faces. Otto obviously understood the odds, and appeared willing to go along with whatever he decided. If anything, saying no to the proposal would relieve him of the responsibility of sending a city boy into an environment so hostile he would have little chance of surviving. The expression on Nicole's face, on the other hand, was more difficult to interpret. He couldn't decide if was anger, disappointment, or disgust. Whatever it was, it cut deep. "Alright," he said. "Let's give the bush a try. But I have one condition. I go alone. Neither of you will accompany me for any part of it. Not one step! Understand? It's my skin."

"Nicole won't for sure," Otto responded. "I'll see to that. But at least let me get you past the roadblocks. After that, I point the way, and you're on your own. Won't be easy, though. You know that, don't you?"

Alfred forced a grin. "I've been dodging bullets for five years," he said. "A little more risk can't be that tough. New challenge. Nobler to succumb to the elements than skulk around camp waiting for a Nazi knife." The bravado was intended to put them at ease. It wasn't working. Neither of them laughed. He dropped it.

"Here's the plan," Otto said, turning the map around so Alfred could get a better look at it. "Right now, the authorities will be figuring you're either in a boxcar and long gone, a frozen cadaver in the bush, or hiding out close to the ACR line. Normally, they don't search more than a few miles out from the rails, which makes it important to get you as far from the tracks as possible. That's why we've picked a spot between the Mattawitchewan and Missinaibi Rivers." He dropped a finger on a point on the map. "Right here."

"Doesn't look that far," Alfred said.

"It's not, at least not the way the crow flies—probably no more than thirty odd miles—but it's dense bush. Problem is getting there without leaving tracks, or being spotted from the air. I propose we take a wide and circuitous route—north to Hearst on the ACR rails, east to Val Côté by sleigh, and south on an old Spruce Falls Pulp and Paper Company road. That gets us to a point close to the junction of the Missinaibi and Mattawitchewan Rivers."

"There's a cabin or something there, I presume?"

"There is, of sorts, but that's where you and I say goodbye. It's a tarpaper shack and good for a night or two only, no more. Too much traffic in the area. The Missinaibi is a preferred route for trappers and hunters. At least once a week someone's bound to come by. So, you need to get away from there as fast as possible." He cleared his throat. "Where you're going is to a cabin, a good fifteen miles straight west into the bush. Here's where the skis come in."

"Geez Otto, me, fifty metres in and I'm already lost. How will I ever find this cabin?"

"Should be a trail."

Alfred sucked air through his teeth. "Should be?"

"Let's say, used to be. Probably a bit filled in since I last travelled it."

"When was that?"

Otto shrugged. "Seven years ago, maybe eight."

"What's to say it hasn't completely grown over."

"Doubt that. Moose maple and saplings will have filled in a bit, but the general outline should be clear enough to follow."

"Let me get this straight. I ski fifteen miles through dense bush and I'm supposed to hit a cabin that's probably no more than twelve feet wide. Needle in a haystack, wouldn't you say?" He took a deep breath and glanced at Nicole. She had her head down.

"Nobody said it would be a walk in the park," Otto replied. "Bear in mind that anyone looking for you will be facing the same conditions. Right Nicole?" She responded with a cautious nod. Otto plowed on. "Look, just before you reach the cabin you'll come to a huge swamp with a high rock face on the far side. Runs right across the trail. You can't miss it. It's a good three miles long. The cabin sits below it. Follow the cliff and you're sure to stumble on it. Easy peezey."

"What's this peezey stuff?"

"Just an expression. Means . . . forget it. Look, granted it'll be hard going, but you'll have a compass. And if you find yourself lost, circle back and start over. Just take your time, and don't panic. You trained for winter in Lapland, so, you know the importance of finding a shelter, and getting a fire going before you run out of daylight. After that you burrow into the snow so as not to freeze. Which you won't. Not with the eiderdown sleeping bag I've got for you."

"What about food?"

"Haul it in."

"Backpack it?"

"Nope. Not with that lame foot of yours. Toboggan. But that's hard work, too."

"And when the food runs out?"

"At that point you're on your own. Lots of game about. And you'll have a rifle. Just make sure to get rid of it if you see any police heading your way. They don't take kindly to escaped prisoners carrying guns."

Alfred sighed and sat back. "No offence, Otto, but I've lost a lot of friends over plans that looked better on paper than this."

"We're not sending you out there to die, son. You've got the training, and the resolve, to pull this off. The alternative, as you said, is recapture, and back to the Nazi fanatics."

"I'm not backing out. But you've got to admit, the odds are long. Just getting to Hearst
undetected would be a miracle."

"That's the easy part," Otto replied. "No trains, no walking, no hitch-hiking required."

"How's that possible?"

"We go by pump car."

Alfred scratched his head. "Pump car?"

"A little vehicle that fits on the rails. The section master at Coppell keeps one in a shed by the tracks. It has a lever you pump for propulsion. Young guy like you should have no problem making that thing go like hell. Keep you warm."

"And this section master? He's going to let you use it to help a POW escape?"

"He goes to bed early. Lots of time for me to *borrow* it, get you to town, and have it back before daylight."

"And all this is 'easy peezey,' I suppose? What about the snow?"

"No worry there," Nicole piped up. "The ACR snow plow cleared the tracks late this afternoon."

Alfred, thoughts going a mile a minute, massaged his forehead. "Fine," he said, with a sigh. "You've got me to Hearst. What then?"

"You hide in the CNR roundhouse until I come and get you."

"Roundhouse?"

"Big shop where they repair the locomotives. I know a warm, safe place to hide there. The work goes on night and day, but stay out of sight and you'll be fine. While you're hiding, I'll be tending to other arrangements."

"How long you figure all this is going to take?"

"Let's see," Otto replied, counting on his fingers, "two nights at the round house for you while I return the pump car, get back to Hearst with the horse and sleigh, borrow skis from Bert Maki, and pick up supplies. After that, one night to Val Côté, and two nights to the drop off point on the Missinaibi. Five nights should do it."

"This cabin you've got me going to, Otto, who owns it? What happens if they show up?"

"Not a problem. It, and a line of other cabins, were built by two American trappers from Connecticut. They haven't been seen in these parts since long before the war. The place will be all yours."

15

Encounter

Near the Mattawitchewan River,
January 1945

ari awoke to the clock ticking in his ears. No need to strike a match to see that it would read 5:00 a.m. "Time to get your ass in gear, Hoivuniemi," he moaned aloud to himself, opening his eyes. It was pitch black, and would stay that way for three more hours. Ample time to get the fire roaring, warm up the cabin, eat, and have the flames extinguished, all before sunup. Timing was essential. As long as no smoke was rising from the chimney come daylight, he'd be clear and safe for another day.

With no radio, he was completely cut off from the world, making him a prisoner to his own thoughts. Top of his mind this morning was his escape from Europe. How disappointed those few Hitler lovers in Lysekil must have been when the *Kriegsmarine* failed to sink the *Gay Viking*. The closest the Germans got to the ship were flares off in the distance. In the end, the only casualties had been Jari and the crew-mate assigned to him, both of whom suffered minor frostbite from the hours riveted to the machine gun. They had arrived in England without firing a shot. Now he was back in Canada, having travelled a circuitous and dangerous route to get close to the woman he feared might no longer be interested in him.

Jari reached over and switched off the alarm before it could go into its cacophonous clanging. Not that it ever got the chance. It was mainly paranoia over the slim possibility he would sleep in, that had him setting it every night. In part it was for the tick-tocking that emanated from it. Strange that after years of deafening warfare in Finland, racket that had permanently damaged his hearing, he should still crave a persistent sound. The clock had become his friend, and the little noise it made a reminder of a world where people invented things, produced gadgets, interacted, and made sounds.

He had little to call his own, other than the clothes on his back, and the down-filled Mountaineer sleeping robe he'd picked up in Sault Ste. Marie. One day, he dreamed, he'd bring Kerttu back here and do nothing but zip it up tight around them and snuggle. Without the bag he might well have frozen to death, but it had its weaknesses, too. The Pioneer Company, in their wisdom, had added a protective flap over the zipper which made rapid exit impossible. Jari often wondered how he would extricate himself if awakened by fire, or a starving bear crashing through the half door. Paranoia was a poor companion.

Swinging his feet to the floor, he struck a match and headed for the stove. The match stayed lit just long enough for him to find his way to the dried birch bark set out the night before. He dropped it, and other kindling, into the firebox. Instantly the coals roared to life, casting a rosy light across the room. Next came progressively larger pieces of wood, which he continued to add until the fire was strong. That done, he replaced the lid on the firebox, adjusted the damper, and scrambled back to bed. Used to the routine, his dog Susi hadn't even moved a muscle.

As usual, Jari's head was too full mulling over daily tasks to go back to sleep. Living here was surprisingly complicated. This particular morning he found himself burdened with a new worry: A week ago he'd heard an airplane. Not that this hadn't happened before, but this plane was flying at a low altitude, and in a pattern. Worrying stuff.

"Who do you think they're after," he said to Susi? "Can't be you, because nobody gives a shit about a stray dog; or me neither, because nobody knows I'm here. However, if they stumble on me they'll check my credentials, and that would spell the end for both of us."

Susi stirred at his feet, but didn't rise. The mammoth mutt released a prodigious number of BTUs, and until the cabin warmed up, was Jari's main source of heat. He had shown up on the trail one day in December, locked onto Jari, and refused to leave. At first sight, Jari mistook him for a *susi*, a wolf, and was about to shoot him. Only at the last moment did he realize it was a dog. He tried to shoo him away, but the stray must have seen him as his last hope and stuck close. Given the sad eyes and lean body, it didn't take long for Jari's conscience to kick in. A bit of moose meat, plus a few affectionate pats, and the two were pals for life.

Only when the cabin began to heat up did he reach over and light a candle. Not that there was much to see: the bunk he was in, a table, two chairs, glazed windows, his boots by the stove, a gun at the door, and a stack of magazines (*Time* and *Life*) addressed to one Donald B. Smith, the man who'd left everything behind a good decade before.

Susi lifted his head. "So, you're awake," Jari said, aware that talking to your animal and obsessing over the past were the primary downfalls of all trappers. "Dreamt of Aunt Toini and Uncle Pentti again last night." Susi's ears picked up. "In it, Auntie is too broken up to speak and Uncle can hardly bring himself to look at me. We're on their back stoop in Kemi, and I'm trying to explain what concussion, hearing loss, and watching your friends blown to pieces does to a man. But Pentti's cutting me no slack. You can see my dilemma, can't you, Susi?" The dog crawled up from the bottom of the bed to get his ears scratched. "Then, when Auntie finally brings herself to speak to me, it's to try to talk me out of killing Sorsakoski. Me, a trained killer with an oath to fulfill. How does a fella switch that off? Sure, I want to, but what am I supposed to do should that son-of-a-bitch ever cross my path? I can't get it out of my head that, as we speak, that traitor's wandering the streets somewhere—Helsinki? Viipuri? Leningrad?"

Susi jumped off the bed and walked to the door. He stood there, waiting. "Oh, for Christ's sake, Susi, I'm coming," Jari mumbled, swinging his legs off the bed. He pulled his felt breeches over the heavy socks and the Penman's 98 wool underwear that he wore day and night. Next came the boots, now warmer thanks to the fire, followed by his parka. The usual procedure was to open the door, at which point they both went to their favourite tree. The door opened out, which meant pushing hard against any snow that might have built up overnight. This would be difficult with a normal door, but in a desire to preserve heat, Donald B. Smith and brother had opted for a low, half door, which meant leaning over to get a shoulder into it. Usually not a problem, but this morning after several days of snow and high winds, the door refused to budge. Anticipating this possibility, the Smith brothers had nailed a piece of lumber on the floor a foot back from the door. Placing one foot against it for purchase, Jari put his weight behind it and pushed. Gradually, the door eased open. Outside, the sky was a kaleidoscope of tinkling stars. "Shit," Jari said, "storm's over; gonna be a clear day. Gotta get the fire out before sunup."

Back in the cabin, Jari carried the candle to the east window, and began scraping at the hoar frost that obscured a thermometer bearing the words, Pellow Hardware, Hearst, New Ontario. "Crap," he said, moving to the stove. "Forty-five below and clear. Looks like another outside working day for sure, Susi." Removing the stove lid, he added more wood, and slid a pail of ice directly over the open firebox. For several minutes he stood watching as the ice began to melt around the edges. Susi sat at his feet, looking up and licking his lips. Absentmindedly, his hand went down to give the dog a pat. Twenty minutes later, he filled the kettle and Susi's bowl. His ears rang in a silence interrupted only by the occasional crackle and pop of the fire, and Susi's slurping. Thirst quenched, Susi began showing his usual impatience for breakfast. "Hang on," Jari said. "I'm warming up what's left of last night's moose stew. No lentils for you and me this morning, old buddy. This weather calls for rib-sticking stuff."

By 8:30, Susi was harnessed to the toboggan and they were heading north, taking turns breaking trail. For a while Jari would lead on his snowshoes, packing the snow slightly for Susi and the toboggan. When he tired, it was Susi's turn. They were partners, a team.

The path had once been maintained, but sight lines had long since been obscured by fallen logs, low hanging branches, and those pesky, bushy, moose maples that got tangled in Susi's harness. Tough sledding on all counts. Still, it was better than fighting their way through the dense bush. Their plan for the day included checking traps in a wide arc, then heading across the swamp and back to the cabin from the east before sunset. Normally, they'd take the easy route and travel on the creek, but that low-flying airplane had spooked him. Leaving tracks in the open was too risky.

All this trapping was illegal, of course. The trapline, and every animal in it, belonged to Smith and Smith, as did the traps, skinning tools, and stretchers. Against their eventual return, the brothers had stocked their cabins with staples—dried food, flour, sugar, noodles, matches, lamps, kerosene, chopped wood. They'd also left a hand-drawn map of their trapline and the locations of the ten cabins, each of which bore a fancy name. Jari currently occupied one euphemistically called Ledgeview, even though it was at the bottom of long, rock ledge that overlooked a swamp. That it was such a dump made him shudder to think what the one called Taj Mahal must be like.

According to Doug Mitchel, the guy who'd shopped his supplies for him in Hearst, the Smiths were Americans who hadn't been back in years. This, of course, did not preclude the possibility of them show-ing up next week, or even tomorrow. Jari was stealing their furs, and in Canada, as in Finland, to trap another man's animals was akin to stealing a cowboy's horse. Poachers got shot doing this very thing. But times were different now. With the war on, markets had dried up, and most trappers had abandoned their lines. But the fighting was going to end sometime, and when it did, luxury items, including fur, would be in hot demand. Or so Jari hoped. Fur, he calculated, would get him out of hiding with enough cash to marry Kerttu, and buy a house. Naturally, none of this was going to happen until he had had overcome his current afflictions. In the meantime, he had to eat, so why not kill two birds with one stone—not much meat on mink and marten, perhaps, but fox was edible and beaver surprisingly delicious.

As they drew closer to the first trap to be checked, Jari's thoughts turned to his dwindling supply of staples. The word crisis popped into his head. After four months, he was down to a box of soda crackers, a few packages of noodles, and a couple of pounds of dried lentils. Worst of all, he'd used up the last of the flour to make the bannock he relied on for lunches on the trail. Although he figured the Smith brothers would have stashed staples in all of their cabins, so far he'd only found two.

"Way I see it, Susi, we've got two options, both risky: go looking for another Smith cabin, or take our chances of being spotted on a trip into town. What do you think?"

Susi didn't seem to have an answer, which made sense, because neither did Jari.

It was mid-morning when they reached their primary objective—the largest beaver lodge Jari had ever set sight on, and one he had great hopes for. It lay buried under a mound of snow with branches and limbs sticking up at odd angles. To the uninitiated it would have seemed abandoned, but Jari knew better. The breathing hole in the ice at one edge was the give-away. However, when he pulled at this snare, it came up empty. Ditto for beaver dams two and three farther upstream. Only at dam four did their luck change. Jari pulled out a huge male, and lay the dripping carcass on the toboggan. In celebration, he pulled out a piece of Bannock for himself, and a bone for Susi. Susi nestled into the snow, maneuvering the bone with his paws to get at the meat. Jari sat on a fallen log, chewing slowly. Consumed by the absolute silence of the forest, he closed his eyes and lifted his face to the bright sun. The moment was interrupted by a low whoosh of wings, as a whiskey jack dipped down from a tamarack and settled at the far end of the log. Jari offered it a piece of bannock. In a flash the bird had picked it up and was off, back to the trees. Emboldened by their friend's good luck, six more whiskey jacks swooped down.

"Sorry, guys," Jari said. "Times are tough. No more to spare." With that he stood, finished the bannock, and squinted into the sun. "Come on, Susi. If we hustle, we can get home with enough light left in the day to skin this beaver."

Forty minutes later, just when they were about to connect with the trail that would take them back to the cabin, Susi came to a full stop. The dog stood still, growling in a low, menacing tone—hackles up, teeth bared.

Jari, taking his cue from the dog, reached for his rifle as he snowshoed carefully past the toboggan. "What is it, fella?" he whispered. Halfway around he began to get a glimpse at what had spooked Susi. Tracks in the snow—someone on skis pulling a toboggan had passed this way. Sidestepping carefully, he maneuvered himself to a tree, rested his gun on a branch, removed a mitt to free up his trigger finger, inhaled deeply, and listened. The air was still. Nothing moved. Minutes passed. His exposed hand began to go numb. Still, he didn't budge. An old feeling came flooding back. It was the Winter War all over again—watch, wait, listen.

Observing the tracks, Jari began to see the picture. This was no professional bushman, nor the Smith brothers suddenly back, and certainly not the RCMP who would never venture this deep into the bush alone. Whoever this was, was not having a good day. He'd fallen several times, leaving a trajectory that was more corkscrew that straight line.

"Come on, boy," Jari said, motioning Susi forward with his arm. "Let's get to the bottom of this." They moved cautiously, until they reached the swamp with its unimpeded sight line. "Jesus Christ Almighty," Jari muttered. "Shit! Shit! Shit!" Ahead, he could see an abandoned toboggan, and holes in the snow where the man had fallen and struggled to get up. But that's not what was fueling his rage; rather it was the distant smoke, rising high into the clear, late afternoon sky.

Jari took off at a run. After a kilometre, the initial rage began to give way to his war training, with sergeant Keltamaki's ripsaw voice echoing in his head: "Never move into a situation without a clear plan." Jari unzipped the top half of his parka to prevent overheating and slowed his pace, his mind exploring the options. With a full hour of light left in the day, extinguishing the fire was paramount. This idiot was going to sabotage his future and had to be stopped. But that meant overpowering him. Barging in might catch the intruder off guard, but moving from bright daylight to a dark cabin would have Jari blind. The other option was to lure him out. A few shots in the air, and shouts announcing the RCMP, might work.

Jari opted for surprise. On arrival, he worked his way to the door, yanked it open, and plunged inside, shrieking every English swearword he knew. For good measure, he fired two rounds into the floor and aimed his rifle in the direction of the stove.

"*Nicht schieBen!*" the man pleaded. "Don't shoot. I'm not armed."

Jari stood silent with his gun pointed in the direction of the voice, while he eyes adjusted to the gloom. Gradually, he was able to make out the form of a man seated, with his hands in the air, and his feet pressed against the oven. They stared at each other. Susi came through the door, still dragging the toboggan.

"I've no weapon. I mean no harm. My feet are frozen."

"Move away from the fire!" Jari ordered." The man hesitated. "Now! Get your feet off my stove."

The intruder sat hunched over in the cabin's only chair, looking up at Jari. "I mean no harm," he said.

Jari glanced about for a gun, before remembering that he'd seen an unzipped rifle case on the abandoned toboggan. Once he was satisfied that this guy was in no condition to do him any damage, he approached the stove. To his surprise, there was little heat coming from it. Removing the lid he saw why. In his haste to get a fire going, the intruder had stuffed the firebox so full he had cut off the oxygen. The result was no flame, but enough smoke to broadcast to anyone within a hundred miles that someone was living out here. Cursing, he carted the smoldering sticks of wood to the door and threw them out into the snow.

The man looked like he was about to cry. "Why?" he said. "Why would you do that? I told you, my feet . . ."

"Fucking idiot!"

"*Ich verstehe nicht!*"

"I don't give a shit whether you understand or not. You've got no right coming in here helping yourself to my stuff. And a German to boot. Well, you're one Kraut who won't be free for long. With all that smoke, the law'll be here in a flash."

"My toes. Without a fire I could lose them."

Jari shrugged. "Another hour isn't going to make any difference. After dark you can have a fire. A real one." Jari turned to unharness Susi and dragged the toboggan back outside. He returned with the beaver, and slapped it on the end of the table. "Tomorrow we move on."

The German sat staring at the dead stove. "I'm going nowhere. Can't. Not on these feet."

Jari stepped closer, standing over him and raising his voice. "I said 'we' and meant it. I'm moving, and you're coming with me. No way are you staying behind."

The German looked up at him. "Why? I'd only slow you up. Who are you, anyway?"

"None of your business. There was a plane in the area a few days back, and now I know why. With the clear skies today they'd have seen the smoke if they were up. We got two days, max, to get clear of here."

"So, you're a fugitive."

"Could be. But if I was, the last thing I'd want is some desperate POW left behind to put the finger on me."

"Why would I do that?"

"Because you're a German. I've seen what you people are capable of when your backs are to the wall. So, get this into in your Aryan skull: You're coming with me tomorrow, even if I have to tie you to the toboggan and drag you out myself."

"You're that desperate?"

Jari felt his fists tightening. "What I am is none of your business. Now. That toboggan you left back there on the trail? What's on it?"

"Food, blankets, kerosene, survival equipment. A rifle, too."

"Food for how long?"

The German shrugged. "Two months. Three, if the hunting's good."

"So, if I shot you, I'd be set 'til spring."

"You'd kill an unarmed man with frozen feet?"

"Don't give me that shocked-look shit. I've seen you Krauts at work. Killing's your specialty. All for the greater good of the Third Reich, and *der Fuhrer,* of course."

"Not every German."

"Right," Jari smirked. "Once caught, no German's ever been a Nazi."

"I don't have the energy to argue. And even if I did, you don't strike me as the listening type."

Jari dismissed this with a wave of the hand. "How about you shut up and listen. Here's what's happening right now. I'm going back for your toboggan. Let's hope I beat some lynx or wolverine to it. Before I go, though, I'm tying your hands with snare wire. That stuff cuts right into the vein if pulled on. You'd bleed to death." Jari paused to let that information sink in. "See that dog over there?" he continued. "Big isn't he? He's got the teeth to match. One move and he'll be on you in a flash. I shudder to think of the mess I'd have to clean up." With that he put on his ski boots, tied the snowshoes on his back with a harness, grabbed his gun, and was out the door. The last thing he saw was the German glaring at him. The guy looked so beaten up Jari almost felt sorry for him, but pity was one sentiment he couldn't afford at the moment.

16

Frozen Feet

Trapper's Shack (Ledgeview),
January 1945

There was only a faint glow in the west when Jari got back to the cabin with the toboggan. He could see why the German had had so much trouble; it was a heavy load to pull on snowshoes, let alone skis. Thankfully, the trek back and forth had packed the trail enough to make for tolerable progress. On arriving he scraped away the snow that had packed in around the ski bindings. He considered rewaxing, in order to be prepared for a fast get away should it prove necessary, but decided it could wait until morning. The day's adventures had left him exhausted.

Opening the door, he found the German still slouched in the chair in front of the cold stove. Susi, on the other hand, was on the bed sound asleep. Jari smiled. *So much for assigning him to guard duty*, he thought. He turned, intending to fetch supplies from the toboggan, but opted instead to light a candle and start the fire. That done he removed the wire that bound the intruder.

The German watched him unload the supplies, tightening his arms across his chest each time the door opened. Not a word was exchanged. Job done, Jari banged the snow off his boots and began rummaging through the new supplies. The intruder hadn't been lying, there was a lot here. A real bonanza.

"I'm Alfred Reiger," the German said. He proffered his hand for a shake, but let it drop when Jari showed no sign of accepting it.

Jari grunted, but that was as far as he was willing to go. Certainly, he had no intention of giving the intruder his name.

Reiger was watching him intently now. "Looking for anything in particular?" he asked sarcastically after several minutes.

"Aspirin. Got any?"

"Don't know."

Jari looked at him. "So, who packed this stuff?"

"No idea."

"Bullshit."

"If you say so. Why aspirin? Got a headache or something?"

Ignoring the question, Jari moved to the stove, put another log into the firebox, then slid the frozen water pail directly over the open flame.

"You're heating water?" Alfred said. "I don't get it."

"It's for you," Jari replied, wondering how long it would take the German to figure out what lay in store for him. "So, about that aspirin?"

"My foot has gone numb, why the need for . . . oh, shit." He slumped back in his chair as he realized what was coming.

"At last, he gets it," Jari said, removing a liquor bottle from the cabin's only shelf.

"Never occurred to me that the frost bite might be that far along, so, yeah, I get it now. Seen it too."

"And where might that have been? Russian Front, I'm guessing?"

"Something like that," Alfred replied, enigmatically.

"You know what has to be done then?" The German nodded. "It's gonna hurt like hell. This will help," Jari said, removing the cap from the bottle and taking a deep breath, as if having second thoughts. "It's vodka, and it's my last, damn it. I'm only wasting it on you because I can't stand screaming, and that's what you're about to be doing." With that he poured several fingers into the dipper, and thrust it at the intruder. "Drink!"

The German did as ordered, and handed the dipper back. With that, Jari removed a bag of flour from the intruder's supplies, picked up a large Ogden's Tobacco tin, and returned to the stove.

The German had been watching his movements intently. "I don't believe what I'm seeing," he said. "Tobacco? A man's got frozen feet, could possibly lose them, and you're about to roll a cigarette?"

"No, I'm getting ready to cook. But we can get going on your feet right away if you'd rather not wait for the vodka to kick in." With that, he dropped hunks of meat, flour and salt into the tobacco tin and shook vigorously, before dumping the final product into a frying pan.

"Hope you like moose," he said, "although I'm guessing your appetite's about to take a serious dip. So, about that aspirin? Got any or not?"

"My napsack," Alfred replied, pointing to the bag by the door. "Left side, bottom pocket."

"Okay then," Jari said, adding lard to the frying pan and sliding it to the edge of the stove. "We'll let the meat thaw while we get busy." With that, he retrieved the aspirin, rolled up a sleeve, and tested the water with his elbow. "Not ready yet," he announced. "Gotta be body temperature. Ten more minutes should do it." They waited in silence, which suited Jari because he had no intention of trying to fill the dead air with soothing chatter. When the second elbow test proved more satisfactory, he plunked the pail in front of Alfred, got down on his knees, and began unlacing the German's boots.

Alfred looked at him, fear flashing across his face. "Please tell me you know what you're doing," he said, in a voice that was beginning to slur.

Jari shrugged. "Like you, I've seen it before. Even helped a guy through it, once. No fun. Here, take these," he said, holding out a half dozen aspirin tablets in one hand and a small piece of wood in the other. "The pills and the vodka should numb the pain. With luck you might even pass out. But if it gets to be too much, bite down on the wood. It's poplar, nice and soft."

The intruder looked from the aspirin to Jari and struggled to speak with his thickening tongue. "Pills. Can't jus' chew 'em. Need somethin' to wash 'em down."

"Oh, for chrissake!" Jari said, reaching for the vodka bottle. He took a slug, wiped his lips with a sleeve, and poured the remainder into the dipper. "Don't spill any," he ordered. "That's the end of it. I was saving it for a special occasion. Shit!"

"Please . . . get at it."

Jari was peeling dead skin off the intruder's swollen big toe when he came to. "You conked out so fast I thought I'd killed you," he said.

The response was garbled, but Jari got most of it. "Not used to drugs and alcohol," he said. "How long was I out?"

Jari looked over at Big Ben. "Hour and a half. I've been peeling off the dead skin for a good forty-five minutes. You don't remember?"

"All I recall is my feet hitting the water, and pain shooting up my legs. You held my feet in the pail, didn't you?"

Jari nodded. "Took all my strength. You let go with a few nasty words in German."

"My toes? Did I lose any?"

"Don't be stupid. Too soon to tell. For that to happen, they go black first then gangrene sets in and rots them. They don't just fall off you know."

Jari started rummaging under the bunk bed and came up with a cobweb-ridden, canvass cot that looked like something left over from the Great War. It was bound to be uncomfortable, but no way was he going to give up the bottom bunk for this unwelcomed intruder, and sure as hell the guy was in no condition to climb to the top. He brushed off the dust bunnies and began setting it up. "Jesus Christ, man!" Alfred said, at last. "Do I have to pry it out of you? Tell me, is gangrene liable to set in or what? I mean, look at my feet. They're all pocked and red and doubled in size. What does that mean?"

Jari cocked his head and stared at the stranger's feet. "Good sign, I think. When I took your socks off, your toes were as white as skimmed milk. They're swollen now, which is to be expected." He finished putting the cot together and pointed. "Lie down and get your feet up."

Although he tried to ease his way over to the cot, the minute Alfred put any weight on his feet, he gasped in pain. Jari didn't budge, determined not to help. Serious decisions had to be made, and getting friendly with the enemy was not going to make the task any easier. He had no intention of killing the German, but he hadn't ruled out abandoning him, which in itself was probably a death sentence.

With the German finally on the cot, Jari used magazines to elevate his feet, then placed twigs between his toes. "Three things," he said. "Keep your feet up, toes separated and drink lots of warm liquids."

"You're the doctor," Alfred moaned.

"I'm not your fucking doctor," Jari snapped. He returned to the stove and slid the frying pan over the fire box. Within minutes the log cabin was alive with the sound of hissing lard, and the aroma of cooking meat. Susi lifted his head from the bed, and looked hopefully at his master.

Jari was having a bad night—the tossing, turning, moans, and mumbled curses coming from the German made sure of that. He bit his tongue, determined not to feel sorry for the guy. Only with the bullet going off in a thunderous bang, and the German screaming, *Schüsse in Deckung gehen,* did he finally speak up. "Calm down, for crying out loud. Nobody's shooting, and there's no need to take cover. What you're hearing are nails contracting in the walls. Happens when the temperature dips below minus fifty."

Jari wasn't sure of the time when he finally gave up trying to get back to sleep. Judging from the frigid temperature in the cabin, he'd guess 03:00. Normally, after a full day on the trail, he'd be dead to the world for the entire night. The German's sudden appearance had put paid to that. It was more than what to do with the guy that had him in a sweat. Shoot, shovel, and shut up had worked well with burdensome prisoners at the Front. And in this instance, even in the unlikely event that the German's body was discovered, who'd care? Simple case of an escaped POW getting what he deserved. End of story. But could his conscience take another hit? How would it affect the life he dreamed of with Kerttu? For sure, he'd mumble in his sleep some night, or lapse into one of those ten-mile stares he was prone to. And each time she'd know something was wrong and start asking questions. So why, after four months of solitude in the bush, was this tug-of-war still going on in his head? In his mind's eye, he could see Aunt Toini's finger wagging at him, and her saying, "told you so."

Somewhere around 04:30 Jari finally gave up on sleep and lit one of the candles from the intruder's supplies. He'd come to a decision, and was determined to follow it through. The German's fidgeting suggested he was awake, too. Jari dressed and set about stoking the fire, preparing breakfast, and stuffing clothes into his packsack. Only when he began to divide up the supplies did the German speak.

"Hey! What are you doing? That's my stuff."

"Call it a trade," Jari replied. "I get half your supplies, and you get a cabin, a bed, cut wood, and snares. Fair deal in my books."

Alfred put a foot on the floor, winced, and plopped back onto the cot. "I had you figured for a cold-hearted son-of-a-bitch, but not one who'd just up and desert a man in my condition."

Jari continued stuffing staples into a box. "No choice. You won't be able to walk for several days, and I've got to get away from here."

"Bastard."

Jari let it go with a shrug, and set the box by the door. That done, he moved to the stove and began making porridge. This was going to be a treat because in addition to oatmeal, he'd found brown sugar and raisins in the German's pack. When it was ready, he ladled it into two bowls, plus a lard pail for Susi. The three of them ate in silence.

Alfred hardly touched his. "You don't say much, do you?" he said. Eyes closed, Jari continued savouring his meal. The German tried again. "Okay, don't speak then. Doesn't matter, because I've got you figured out."

"Really? Care to share, Herr Master Race?"

"Your English is better than mine, but you're no Canadian. You were swearing in your sleep—in Finn. That, and the puukko knife on your belt, confirms my suspicions. Nobody but a Finlander would carry one of those."

"Got a problem with that?"

"Nothing like you seem to have for us Germans."

"Maybe, I have good reason."

"What puzzles me is why you're on the run? Bush company I worked for as a POW had Finns on the payroll. They seemed a pretty happy bunch. What's that make you? Thief? Murderer? Conscientious objector? Coward, perhaps?"

"Maybe, you should be worried."

"Or, thankful. You're the one heading out in the cold to who knows what, and where. Me? I'm left with a warm cabin, and enough food to tide me over until I get back on my feet."

"Ha! I wouldn't be too smug. You haven't the faintest idea how to survive out here. Your food will run out fast enough. After that, you die, cuz you don't know the first thing about hunting and trapping."

"So, why not just shoot me and get it over with? Would solve both our problems."

"Believe me, the bullet idea has crossed my mind. But that would make me a murderer."

"And robbing me of my supplies, and leaving me to starve to death doesn't?"

Out on the trail, Jari cursed his luck. Just when he had settled in, and was beginning to feel safe, new dangers had popped up. Foremost, was the appearance of the German. Sure as hell the guy would get himself caught, and blab to the authorities. Then there was the fifty below weather he was heading into, with no certain destination in sight. What if this Taj Mahal place didn't exist? Sure, the map the Smith brothers had left behind showed a trapline stretching all the way from the Missinaibi River to the Kabinakagami River, but what if it existed on paper only? Was it possible they'd never gotten around to building any more than the two cabins he'd already found? Taj was supposedly well northwest of Ledgeview, the one he'd left behind for the German, but was it really out there? And even if it was, what were the odds of finding it? He could die in the search. A few nights in the open would be okay, but beyond that?

In spite of the polar temperatures, his first night under the stars had gone well. Experience saw him through. Survival in the open called for stopping with enough light left in the day to prepare. When Jari came upon a fallen spruce tree sitting up on its branches a metre off the ground, he knew he'd found the ideal shelter. Unharnessing Susi, he retrieved the axe from the toboggan, and set to chopping. Thirty minutes later, he had enough birch bark, kindling, and wood to start and keep a fire going all night. For shelter, he cut slender poles from poplar saplings, which he leaned against either side of the downed spruce. Next step was to prop spruce branches against the poles for a windbreak, and lay more inside on the floor for bedding. That done, he used a snowshoe to bank snow against the spruce bows. Jari smiled with satisfaction at the finished product—an abode large enough to house Susi, himself, the toboggan, and a small fire. He crawled in. By the time darkness had fallen he had the tea pot boiling and a rabbit cooking on a spit.

Navigating on Day One had been relatively simple. The Smith brothers' map had him following the Mattewitchewan River in a northeasterly direction. Day Two called for cutting north along a creek to an unnamed lake on which Taj was supposedly located. But which creek? With his destination little more than a spot on the map, it was a crap shoot. His best hope lay in the word pine, printed in a little circle around the word, Taj, on the Smith map. This was predominately spruce country, so if he picked the creek that led to a lake that happened to have a grove of pine trees, he'd have hit the target. Four hours later, the odds against this happening began to sink in. Having sighted neither a lake nor a pine grove up the creek he'd selected, he realized he'd erred and returned to the camp site abandoned in the morning.

"Well, that was a waste," he said to Susi, when they'd settled in. "Two days out and nothing to show."

Day Three had him heading up a different creek. This time he had the feeling they weren't alone. From Susi's periodic growls, he thought so, too. Only when he saw tracks did he know what it was: a pack of wolves had picked up their scent, and was following them in a huge circle. Gradually, as the morning wore on, they grew bolder, exposing themselves on his flank. Jari got the gun off the toboggan, and slung it on his shoulder.

Close to noon, just as he was beginning to think he'd erred again, the creek opened onto a lake. Trekking a few hundred metres out onto the ice, he stopped to scan the trees on the south side. Visibility was blurred by the strong wind that was picking up loose snow and blasting it in undulating waves against the frozen shoreline. "Yes!" he said aloud, reaching down and patting Susi. "See those trees over there, big fella? They're pine. Taj Mahal's gotta be around here someplace—if it exists. But if it does, don't be expecting anything more than another shithole. Nothing could live up to the grandeur of name like that." Susi nuzzled his head against Jari's leg. "Come on, boy, let's go look. Those dark clouds tell me we're in for another blow."

It took an hour, but there it was, Taj Mahal, nestled in the pines, just like the Smith map suggested. The cabin he'd left to the German had a roof of moss and mud, a dirt floor, a bunk bed with spruce bows under bear skin, and a small stove. By comparison, this place was indeed a palace—definitely not the dump he'd been fearing. It boasted a tin roof, a wood floor, three windows, a separate bedroom complete with a bunk bed and mattresses, a cook stove with a large oven, tins of dried food, animal traps, and an outhouse. All it lacked was a sauna, which Jari swore to rectify in short order.

Even before the snowstorm had a chance to build up steam, he had unloaded the toboggan, cleared the stovepipe of leaves and nests, and got the fire roaring. The heat brought the cluster flies out of the woodwork, and a mouse appeared, but that was alright. Kind of gave the place a cozy and lived in air. He sat at the table with a mug of tea, looking out the window at the snow swirling off the roof in the fading light. "Tracks just about erased, Susi," he announced, as he sipped. "Nobody's going to find us now. We're home, safe and sound." He couldn't remember when tea had tasted this good.

It only took a few days for Jari to fall into a routine similar to the one that had proven productive at Ledgeview. To his delight, with Taj Mahal's tight-fitting door, and squared-log construction, this cabin held its heat much longer. He still had to restrict his fires to nighttime, and bad weather, but no longer did he have to hit the trail quite so early each morning, or sleep with half his clothes on.

He was busy, but it wasn't just day to day stuff that occupied his thoughts. In fleeing here he'd abandoned his stash of furs at Ledgeview. Months of hard work. As the days wore into a week, with no signs of an aerial search, he began to consider the possibility of returning for them.

There was more—guilt; he'd abandoned a helpless kid. Maybe the guy was a just another battle-scared soldier, sickened by his past, and longing to set a new course. Jari tried to convince himself that charting his own path was hazardous enough without taking on a stranger, but his conscience wouldn't let it go. Finally, after three weeks of dithering, he decided the furs were worth the risk. Caution was called for, of course. He'd nip in, take what he came for, and leave.

With minimum supplies to carry, and travelling on skis, Jari was closing in on Ledgeview by mid afternoon of the second day. He had no idea if the German would still be there, or if he'd been discovered and carted away. What he did know was that the guy had a high-calibre rifle, knew how to use it, and was bound to be anything but friendly. Once again, his military training kicked in; he tied Susi to a tree down the trail, manoeuvred himself into position on the cliff behind the cabin, and waited. The only thing differing this from the Russian Front was the absence of a machine gun to set up, and the line of fire to contemplate. Everything else was identical—reconnoitre, plan, establish an escape route. Today the elements were in his favour—dull weather, dark bush, no shadows. He settled in and watched. One hour stretched to two, still no movement below, nor smoke, nor trip to the pee tree. Daylight began to fade.

He was considering what to do next, when he spotted movement in the swamp to the east. Alone, and on snow shoes, head down and hood up, someone was approaching. From the exhausted gait, and noticeable limp, it had to be the German. Jari moved to intercept.

Alfred was bent over unfastening his snowshoes when Jari approached from behind, rifle at the ready. "*Wei geht es dir?*" he said.

Alfred straightened so quickly he nearly fell over. Instinctively, he reached for the gun strapped to his back, but staring at Jari's rifle, reconsidered. "What the hell do you want?" he snapped.

"Heat. Bed for the night."

"Piss off. You abandoned this place. It's mine now."

Jari lowered his weapon in appeasement. "Understood. Not a problem. I'm here to collect my furs. Nothing more."

"Let me guess," Alfred said. "Things aren't going well, so if it's the rest of my food you're after you can *lech mich im Arsch.* You'll have to kill me first."

Jari shook his head. "I'm not interested in your food, so I will not be kissing your ass. Got plenty of my own back at my new place."

"What then?"

"I told you. The furs in the back shed. So, come on, it's freezing out here. How about we go inside and get a fire going. We can talk."

"Talk? Really? Three weeks ago I couldn't get a word out of you. But now that you want something from me, you want to talk. *Fich dich.*"

"*Haista paska,*" Jari snapped back. For a second they stopped and stared at each other, realizing that they had both told each other to piss off in two different languages, neither of which was English, and understood each other perfectly. Obviously, they shared a past. Jari saw an opening. "Where did you serve?" he asked.

Alfred took his time responding. "France, Norway, North Africa, Lapland, Karelia, Italy." he replied, cautiously. "I was with the XXXVI Mountain Corps. You?"

"Karelia mostly, but Lapland, too. With the Finn VII Corps all the way through the Winter War and the Continuation War. I remember your unit."

"I suppose you think that makes us comrades, or something?"

Jari shrugged. "You mountain guys were good soldiers. Not monsters, like those SS assholes alongside you. Always puzzled me how they had so much influence over regular troopers like you."

"I try not to think about that stuff," Alfred replied.

Jari nodded. "Understood. Turns my stomach, too."

"So, okay, let's go inside. Maybe, we can find something else to talk about. My feet, for example. Or why you've really come back."

"How are they? Your feet that is?"

"Sore as hell, but I've still got all my toes."

"I'll fetch Susi," Jari said.

Alfred nodded. "By the way, my name's Alfred Reiger. You going to tell yours this time, or is that still off limits?"

Jari pulled off his mitt. "Jari Hoivuniemi," he said, extending his hand. There was a bark in the distance. "Back in a minute."

Jari left Alfred to tend to the food while he worked on the fire. He had it going in a flash, but when he turned around nothing much appeared to be happening in the grub department. Taking in the room he began to understood why: there were no signs of fresh meat, anywhere. "Had any luck with the hunting?" he asked, trying to make it sound casual.

Alfred took his time replying. "Hasn't been great. They seem to know when I'm coming, and scatter."

"Been surviving on the staples, have you?" Alfred gave him an embarrassed nod. "Maybe, I could teach you a few things before heading back to Taj."

"What, for instance?"

"Basic survival—hunting, trapping, stuff like that." Alfred nodded, but wasn't committing. Jari watched him light a second candle, which was a wasteful extravagance given the circumstances, but he said nothing. The candlelight gave him an opportunity to study Alfred's features. Taller, larger framed, and a good ten years younger than himself, the German was far from the blue-eyed, blond Aryan, poster-boy so fondly extolled by Herr Hitler. Which didn't mean this dark-haired guy wasn't good looking. Jari guessed he'd been a hit with the *Fräuleins*, and felt an unexpected twinge of jealousy.

"Does that mean you're intending to hang around a while?" Alfred asked, suspiciously.

"Hadn't planned on it, but could. A few days, maybe."

"Three weeks ago you couldn't get away from me fast enough."

"Can you blame me? You showing up out of nowhere could have got me shipped back to Finland."

"You in trouble over there, or something?"

"Let's get a couple of things clear, Alfred. I'll stick around long enough to give you a few hunting tips, provided you respect two no-go subjects. One is the war, or anything to do with it. The other is who, or what, may be waiting for me in Finland. You alright with that?" He waited for Alfred to nod before continuing. "Good, how about we get busy cooking the partridges I shot this morning?"

"How many you got?"

"Four," Jari replied, pulling them from his bird bag, and handing them over.

Holding them by the feet Alfred looked from the birds to Jari. "What's the first step?" he asked.

Jari sighed. "We dunk them in boiling water then pluck them. Normally, I'd do it on the trail, while they're still warm, but today I couldn't afford the time."

"Don't roll your eyes at me," Alfred said. "I'm a baker, not a butcher."

"Fine. I'll handle the meat. You get busy with the bannock. And pound a few raisins into it, will you. That is, if you've got any left."

The meal went well, even though there was little talk. Which was fine with Jari. Fact was, he was anxious to get back to Taj, and with the German suspicious of his every move, perhaps it would be best for both of them if he cleared out in the morning. But somewhere in the black of night a new wrinkle entered the scene when he awakened to tossing, turning and mumbled groans from the bunk above. He listened respectfully, mindful of the nightmares common to a soldiers' sleep. "Alfred," he said, gently, when he figured the German had nightmared himself awake, "we all get them."

"I never wanted to be anything but a baker," Alfred responded. "Instead, they thrust a gun in my hands and set me to murdering. First, I killed Poles, then Frenchmen, Norwegians, Englishmen in North Africa, and, finally, Russians. Five devastating, wasteful years. And what have I got to show for it? Family dead, home destroyed, bakery burned, police on my tail, Nazi fanatics out to kill me right here in Canada, and endless nightmares."

Jari could have told him how close this came to his own situation, but wasn't prepared to go there; not now, and probably never—too private.

"Five years, lurching from disaster to disaster. Rotten luck, every step of the way."

"There must have been some happy moments along the way, Alfred. Try concentrating on them. What about your comrades, or special leaves you took, or food at the pulp camp you talked about? And that girl you mentioned last night, the one who got you out here?"

"Nicole. Yeah, she's in my head alright, but the more I think about it, the more I realize she probably just felt sorry for me."

"Come on. Her helping you says a lot. Something to hang on to. Lots of guys never get that much."

Judging by the deep breathing that followed their conversation, Alfred had managed to suppress his horrors and get back to sleep. Not so Jari. His head was too full. Three weeks had passed since the German had showed up, and, so far, the expected catastrophe from the outside world hadn't happened. For now, he was still in the clear. But what to do with Reiger? Deserting him a second time could spell the end of the guy. Call it whatever you like—shell shock, depression, combat fatigue—he needed help. The options scrolling through Jari's head were far from appealing. Alfred was still too shaky on his feet to abandon, and a couple of days of bush training wasn't going to achieve much. Bringing him to Taj was probably best, but then he'd be stuck with him. *"Never work,"* he kept repeating to himself. *"For starters, I hate meaningless chatter, and I get the feeling that once started this kid never shuts up. We'd kill each other."*

Towards morning he noticed that the German's breathing had changed. "Alfred," he whispered, "you awake?"

"Yeah."

"I've got a proposition for you."

"What's a proposition?"

"A proposal."

"Go on."

"How would you like to come work for me?"

"You crazy? How's that even possible? We're two fugitives in the bush."

"No different here than in the outside world. I teach you how to do some things, and if you catch on quick, I put you on the payroll. That way we both survive, and build up capital while we're at it."

"I'm a baker, for chrissakes."

"You're young, strong."

"Yeah, and hobbling around like a friggin' old man."

"That'll heal."

Alfred rolled onto his back and linked his hands behind his head. "Continue. I'm listening."

"Here's the deal. From every animal I kill I get food and fur. Fur has no value right now, but that's going to change. Once the war is over, I'm guessing prices will be going off the charts."

"What's my role? You said yourself that I'm helpless in the bush. And I sure as hell know nothing about trapping."

"You seem smart enough to learn. How about coming back with me to the Taj Mahal and I'll teach you?"

"Where?

"Taj Mahal. That's what the guys who built these cabins called my new place. It's a big improvement over Ledgeview."

"So, what would I be doing?"

"Helping out. Look, nobody is running traplines these days, so animal populations have soared. There's more furs than I could ever handle by myself."

"What about pay?"

Jari hesitated. "To be determined, I guess."

"No way. What do you take me for?"

"Okay, obviously, I've no money now. But, when it's safe to come out of the bush, we cash in our furs. You'll get paid same time as me."

"How much?"

"Jari thought for a moment. "How about twenty-five percent?"

"Thirty-five."

"What? You know squat about bush life. Plus, I'm going to have to feed, house, and train you, like a friggin' apprentice."

"Correct, but for all I know you're higher on the RCMP wanted list than me. Maybe, as high as 'shoot to kill', even. I could be collateral damage."

Jari sighed. "You do recognize that I'm the one saving your ass here, don't you?"

"How do I know you won't work the hell out of me, then walk away in the end. No, gotta be thirty-five percent to make it worth the risk."

"*Jumalauta*! Fine then, you hard-headed son-of-a-bitch, make it thirty-five percent. But I'm going to work your butt off. Just remember, I'm the boss, and if it doesn't work out you come back to Ledgeview."

"Deal."

"Deal," Jari repeated, with a chuckle, which quickly morphed to a full laugh."

"What's so funny?" Alfred asked. "You think you screwed me, or something?"

"No. You're just too German to see the humour. Hard to believe that a *Suomalainen* like me actually gets it. Here we are, two enemy aliens, both fugitives in the bush, planning a business venture in a foreign country. How crazy is that?"

17

Truce

Taj Mahal,
February 1945

Two hours into the trek to Taj had Alfred regretting his decision. Skiing was something his tender feet could barely tolerate, yet here he was forced to snowshoe, which was proving much worse. Factoring in the heavy cargo they were pulling—packsacks, loaded toboggans—plus the deep snow, had this trip turning into a painful ordeal. Regardless, it was fear of showing the Finn any weakness that had him biting his lip, and pressing on.

Jari rarely spoke, and when he did it was to give instructions. The man was anything but a patient teacher. Alfred quickly learned to get it right the first time, or suffer the verbal abuse. Such was the case when he was scolded for not using the tumpline. "Use your goddamn head," Jari barked, as he pointed to the strap that stretched across his own forehead. "You're relying too much on your shoulders to do the pulling."

After two days of heavy slogging they reached Taj Mahal with enough light left to unload the toboggans, and get the stove going. The chores done, Alfred plopped down on the bed and was almost asleep when Jari dropped the bomb: "In the morning we go back to Ledgeview for the rest of the goods," he said.

"You can't be serious?"

"No choice. Gotta take advantage of the packed trail before the next storm blows in."

"My feet won't take it. For the love of God, give me a day, at least."

Jari hesitated before answering. "Okay. One day, but no more."

Determined to show the Finn that he had what it took to be a bush-man, Alfred stuck with him on the way back to Ledgeview. Travelling light, and on skis, they flew, managing the trip in a ripping seventeen skiing hours. Jari appeared to be content, as they settled in for what was to be their last night at the camp they both despised. He even complimented Alfred on his skiing. "Pretty damn good for a German," he said. "Wonder what other skills you've got hiding under your hat?"

Long before daylight the next morning, Jari was up and had the fire going. "Got a treat in store for us this morning," he announced, startling Alfred.

"Really?" Alfred replied, yawning.

"Bannock and mouth-watering beaver."

Alfred moaned. "Right now, at the Newago bush camp, they'll be eating *Bröetchen*, *Eier*, *Schwarzwäelder Schinken*, *Emmentaler* cheese and marmalade."

"You can always go back."

Alfred slid out of bed and peed in a tin can—to be emptied later; something he'd started doing in deference to his feet. His movements were slow as he dressed, like a man recovering from a marathon for which he had not trained. "All this time on skis with two more days ahead, and that's all you've got to offer?"

"Welcome to living off the land," Jari replied.

Breakfast down, they got to work chopping wood. "Why the hell are we doing this?" Alfred asked. "We are leaving Ledgeview for good, aren't we?"

"Same reason we're not taking all the food: tomorrow we return to Taj, but we'll probably be back. Possible, too, that some cold, hungry, stranger might stagger in. It's an unwritten trapper law: always leave your cabin stocked and ready."

"Sort of a brotherhood of the bush," Alfred said.

"Yeah, you could call it that," Jari replied.

Snowshoeing in tandem made conversation difficult. Nevertheless, with two days of hard trekking ahead, Alfred was determined to try. "Having seen Taj Mahal," he said, "I never want to see, or sleep, at Ledgeview again. You?" He cocked his head for an answer, but no response was forthcoming.

Five minutes later Jari finally spoke up, but on a completely different subject. "Remember those Smith brothers I told you about? Well, I got to thinking about them. According to the map they left behind, their trapline stretched for seventy kilometres. Our little enterprise will never get that big, but we could make it to three, possibly four cabins. Depends on how much work I can get out of you."

"Maybe you'll be needing a whip."

Alfred thought he'd heard a chuckle, but couldn't be sure. They lapsed into silence again. Alfred found his movements becoming automatic. "Amazing how you can get yourself into a rhythm," he shouted, "even on snowshoes." No reaction from up front. Well, he decided, if the Finn wasn't going to show him the courtesy of conversing, he'd talk to himself. "Alfred Reiger, you're as regular as a metronome—step one-two, step one-two—just like the one grandfather had on the piano back in Schwäbisch Gmünd. Same cadence. Kinda pleasing, wouldn't you say? Know what else feels good? Sweat and aching muscles. Know why? Because they're mine. Haven't worked this hard since harvest days on Uncle Karl's farm."

It had been a long time since he'd thought about those happy harvest days. Work had been hard, but he had a place, was respected, even needed. Could he ever feel that again? Could it happen right here in the bush?

Hour after hour they trudged on, Alfred doing his best to keep up. Head down, and pushing into the tumpline, oblivious of his surroundings. Periodically, he would look up, only to see that he had fallen even farther behind the Finn. The remedy was to speed up and close the gap, which left him out of breath, and prone to falling back all over again. At one point, he raised his head to see that Jari had stopped dead on the trail, and was motioning him to come forward, cautiously and quietly.

"Too late," Jari said, when Alfred caught up.

"Too late for what?" Alfred puffed.

"There was a cow moose and a calf, fifty metres down the trail. You scared them off."

"Impossible! I was quiet as a mouse."

Jari shook his head. "You're a human noise machine."

"Bullshit!"

"It's that canvass jacket you're wearing. To the animals, every move you make is like a siren going off. We gotta remedy that. There's an old wool coat back at Taj that might fit. From now on you wear that."

"But this is warm."

"Warm or not, we'll never get moose with the noise it makes. And another thing about that jacket; I don't fancy walking close to a guy with a red-circle target painted on his back. Gives me the jitters."

When they got going again, Alfred listened carefully to his movement. "Christ, Jari, aside from a little rubbing, there's hardly any sound."

"You may not be able to hear it, but the moose sure as hell can. It's the canvas on the sleeves rubbing against the sides. A moose can pick that up a hundred metres off. That's why when you tried hunting on your own, you kept seeing tracks, but never any game. Their eyesight may be piss poor, but there's nothing wrong with their ears and noses. To bag one, you've gotta be downwind, and as quiet as a sniper."

"Shit," Alfred said. "Sorry if I screwed up a chance for food back there."

Jari shrugged. "Wouldn't have made sense to kill that moose anyway; not with the toboggans already loaded down."

"*Shit*," Alfred thought. *"Four days on the job and I've already cost us in meat. How long's this partnership going to last?"*

The first few weeks at Taj Mahal were difficult. Alfred felt like a klutz as he continued to stumble about. Jari's reaction to his every move seemed to confirm it. But as they got used to each other, and as Alfred's feet improved, so did their relationship. Jari's criticisms grew less frequent as Alfred proved he could learn, if not quite toe the line. It wasn't long before he was handling the traps—setting, baiting, scenting, camouflaging. It was going so well he got after Jari to teach him how to gut, skin, stretch, and cure.

"Will the furs spoil if we don't do something with them soon?" Alfred asked one day. They had just returned from checking traps, and were unloading a beaver and two muskrats. Both frozen solid. "Who knows when we'll ever get to sell them."

"I have a theory on that," Jari said.

"Theory? That's it? I thought you knew all this stuff?"

"Before the war it was seldom a problem," Jari shrugged. "Trap a few furs and sell them to the Hudson's Bay. Little need for long-range storage."

Alfred slumped. "But now?"

"A trapper told me once that if you gut, skin, scrape, cure, and dry your furs, then press them out flat, they'll keep for a long time," Jari said. "The exception is beaver, it spoils, so you gotta roll them tight as you can, fat in, fur out. Trick is to keep them cold, too. Make sense?"

"How the hell would I know? You're supposed to be the expert."

"Our problem is going to be summer. We got a lake full of ice out there, but nothing to cut it with, nor place to store it in. If we could put a half-decent shed together, we could turn it into an icehouse."

"Ah, like the one at Otto's place."

"Otto? Who the hell's he?"

"Nicole's friend. The guy who got me in here. He cuts ice and sells it to the locals for their iceboxes in summer."

Weeks went by, with Jari talking up the trapping. Privately, Alfred had begun to lose faith in the fur-bonanza dream, but kept it to himself, not wanting to upset his Finn boss. Despite this, and their personal differences, they fell into working the trapline like their lives depended on it. On the trail they seldom conversed, leaving Alfred longing for a good old-fashioned chin wag come evening. It seldom happened. So far, all he'd gotten was crickets from the taciturn Finn.

"Worst storm in a while," Alfred muttered, early one morning, coming in with the wood. "Be stupid to go out in that."

Jari went to the window and nodded. "Got a feeling this one will last days. Gives us a chance to get a little scraping and stretching done." Turning around, after what was for him a long speech, he caught Alfred pouring flour into a jam jar, and mixing it with water. "What the hell do you think you're up to? That stuff's precious. Without flour there can be no bannock."

"I'm making yeast. Wild yeast."

"Jesus wept!"

"Relax. I'm a baker. If this works, we'll have sourdough bread. Hell of a lot better than bannock. All it takes is seven or eight days of continuous heat and, whammo, I'll have the starter I need."

"Don't be stupid. The storm will break in three or four days and we'll have to put the fire out. Then what will we have? Paste, that's what. Useless paste and wasted flour."

Alfred sloughed off the scolding and continued stirring, before setting the mixture carefully at the back of the stove. That done, he picked up a sock and darning needle, and moved to the bench. He'd just threaded the needle when he looked up to see Jari laying out knives and the emery stone. "Hey," he said, "it's my turn to do that job."

Jari didn't bother looking up.

Alfred threw the sock on his bunk. "You're to chop wood, and clean the guns. We agreed on it."

"No, you just assumed it."

"You nodded. That's agreement. Why do you always get to do what you want? Yesterday you had me curing gut to mend the snowshoes. I hate that job, but I did it, didn't I? So, it's only fair that I get to do what I like once in a while."

"The last time you sharpened the knives they were so bloody dull I had to redo them halfway through skinning a muskrat pelt."

"That's crap."

"*Jumalauta*," Jari mumbled, biting his lip and reaching for the emery stone.

Alfred slipped into his boots and reached for his parka. "You really do have to be the boss, don't you?" he said, slamming the door on his way out.

Days passed, with the storm swirling snow about them. Alfred checked his wild yeast every morning, and on the eighth day they sat down to the results.

"Well?" he said, watching Jari take his first bite of the sourdough bread. "What's the verdict?"

Jari had his eyes closed as he chewed. "Pretty good," he said, noncommittally.

"Pretty good? Is that the best you can do?"

Jari opened his eyes, a faint smile tugging at the sides of his mouth. "Alright, damn good. Possibly the tastiest, crustiest, sourdough bread ever."

They continued eating in their usual silence, but meal over, Jari went into a long story about his aunt Toini's coffee bread, the Chelsea buns he had tasted for the first time in England, and how great it was to have a bit of culinary sophistication introduced right here at Taj. Encouraged by what was turning out to be their first ever, real conversation, Alfred launched into his dream of one day setting up a bakery here in Canada. It was a project he mulled over most nights after they turned in. To his surprise, Jari showed genuine interest, even proffered a few words of encouragement.

Other than grunts and nods, it wasn't until after supper the next evening that they finally spoke again—really spoke. They were at the table, each flipping through an old magazine from the stack the Smith brothers had left behind. Both men had been through them several times. As usual, it was Alfred who opened the conversation. "How come we manage to get along okay out on the trail, but fall apart back here at Taj?"

"Because you keep getting in my way, here. And you're always going on and on about nothing."

Alfred, happy to get a response even if he didn't like what he was hearing, was determined to keep the conversation going, and civil. "We come home wackered every day to a tiny cabin. So, yes, we get in each other's way. Would a duty roster be a solution?"

"Like in the army?"

"Kinda. Just a list of who does what, and when. One we *stick* to."

"I could live with that," Jari grunted.

Alfred put his July 1932 copy of *Saturday Evening Post* down. "Honestly?" He got up and came back with a pencil and paper. For half an hour they worked on it, bickering here and there, but never letting it get out of hand.

When it was done, Jari picked up the list and read it through. "Christ your spelling's awful," he said.

"I'm a fucking German writing in English, and how the hell would you know anyway?" Only when he saw the smile on Jari's face, did he realize that the Finn's sense of humour was making a rare appearance.

"Just pulling your leg. Hell, I can't even spell in Finn."

As far as witticisms went it was weak, but tonight it was a thigh slapper. They were soon making so much noise that Susi got up from his burlap bag next to the stove, to come over to investigate. "What's this on the back of the paper?" Jari asked, turning the paper over.

"Don't read that! Please."

"Looks like a letter."

"Not a letter. Just a note. Nicole gave it to me last time I saw her. Instructions and stuff." To his relief Jari handed it over without further examination.

"Jesus, Alfred, we can't nail that to the wall. You've been carrying it with you, haven't you?"

"Had to use it. It's the only paper in the place."

Jari sat back and looked at him. "You know," he said, "I never thought we'd make it this far. Living with a garrulous German has its drawbacks, but this partnership's turning out pretty good. We got the traps going full tilt at Taj, Ledgeview, and now at the next place, Grinnin."

"Grinnin's a shithole. Smiths should have named it Grin and Bear It—fits better."

"Righto, but the trapping's good around there. With three camps going, the furs are rolling in—marten, mink, fisher, lynx, beaver, even the occasional otter. How about I stick close to Taj, scraping, stretching, and curing, and you do the setting, baiting, fetching and delivering."

"You still believe these furs are going to be worth something, someday?" Alfred asked. "Not that it matters much. Way I see it, we'd be going nuts if not for the trapping; probably wind up killing each other. And we have to eat."

"Listen, young man, when the soldiers come marching home, their women will be demanding luxuries. And that includes fur. You'll see. We'll do just fine."

Conversation was flowing freely. Another rare moment. Alfred hadn't enjoyed himself this much in months. Which is why he was taking a risk when he asked the question that had preyed on his mind for some time. They both had nightmares and talked in their sleep, but never had it been a topic. For the first few months, Jari's nocturnal shouts had revolved around the war. Lately, though, Alfred detected a new subject creeping in.

"Can I ask you something? It has to do with things you sometimes say in your sleep."

Jari's smile began to fade. "Careful," he growled.

"I know. I know. It's just that, the word 'Kerttu,' keeps coming up. That a person or a place?"

Jari stroked his chin and looked away. "Woman in Hearst," he said.

"A special one?" Alfred prodded. "The kind you might want to marry, or just . . . you know?"

"Marry."

Alfred relaxed. "You son-of-a-gun. You've had a woman up there all this time, and haven't said boo."

"It's private."

"How can you stand it? Eight months in the bush without seeing her. And she's so close."

"You know damn well I can't risk a trip to town."

"She must be going nuts with you stuck here in the bush. Couldn't you at least arrange to meet somewhere? Matter of fact, I know just the place." He stopped when Jari began patting the dog, and looking off. "Oh, shit! She doesn't know you're here, does she? Jesus Christ, Jari, how come?"

Jari shrugged. "Waiting for the nerves to settle, I guess."

"Hey, ask me and I'd say you're well on the way. There's been nothing about Mica, or Korpi, or Sorsakoski for a long time. Just this Kerttu. She must be some woman. Come on, tell me about her. How'd you meet?"

The smile returned to Jari's face, as he scratched Susi behind the ears. "At an *iltamat* at the Finn Hall on the lake road, north of Hearst. It was in 38. When I first laid eyes on her, she was twirling and laughing on the dance floor, with me watching from the corner. It was three or more dances before the band played something slow. I screwed up my courage, and she accepted. But after a few bars the music switched from a waltz to a polka. Disaster. My two left feet couldn't handle it. When it was over, she squeezed my hand and thanked me."

"What did you do?"

"Slunk back to the bar. That's the end of that, I thought, except she had other ideas. When Albert Lahde, young local guy, picked up his accordion and began playing a waltz, she came up to me, pulled the drink out of my hand, and led me onto the floor. I shuffled my way through it like a clod, wondering if this was a cruel joke on her part. But a tango followed, and it turned out nobody knew the steps but me, thanks to Aunt Toini. Believe it or not, the tango is a big thing in Finland."

Alfred nodded. "Don't I know it. Got to a few dances over there myself. All those gloomy Finns sliding around the floor, like zombies at the undertaker's ball."

"Anyway, I was a big hit. The girls were lining up in front of me, but I only had eyes for Kerttu. She was everything I wasn't—personable, outgoing, assertive, good looking. Soon we were walking out. I got a job cutting pulp, and began working on my English. A year passed. Things were going well. Her family accepted me. We became regulars at the Finn Hall. People would ask, 'When are you two going to tie the knot?' Then Russia attacked Finland, and a whole bunch of us Finns shipped out for home."

"She promise to wait?"

"Yeah, but that was 1939, a lifetime ago."

The following morning, Alfred left to check on the Grinnin end of the trapline. Four days later he returned, face beaming. "Guess what I discovered at Grinnin," he said, all smiles.

"No idea," Jari replied, as he continued scraping a mink pelt.

"A new pile of magazines."

"Dates?"

"Late twenties, mostly," Alfred replied.

"Swell, that'll get us up to date."

"There's one with an article that kinda applies to us. Stop what you're doing and I'll read it to you."

Jari put the pelt down, went to the stove and pulled the kettle towards the front. "Let me make tea first."

Alfred rolled his eyes. "Jesus! You're just as bad as my father; always making us wait for good things."

When Jari had the tea made and had finally settled in, he turned to Alfred. "Shoot," he said. "Better be worth all the excitement."

"It's an article in the *Toronto Star Weekly*, September 1928. It's about the Canadian government's treatment of the Great War vets." Jari gestured for Alfred to get going. "Written by a woman. Here's what she says:

> *Well, dear reader, as you've undoubtedly noticed, our govern-
> ment is sparing no expense in prepping us for the upcoming tenth
> anniversary of the November 11, 1918, armistice. A day of free
> beer, bunting, and rally round the flag may go down well with the
> soldiers who came back healthy, but, for once, could Ottawa not
> pay some attention to those returnees who came home emotion-
> ally damaged?*
>
> *Professor Hazel Shuttleworth, in her recent publication, "Of
> Shell Shock and Government Shame," broadsides the government
> with questions yet to be answered. When, she asks,will Ottawa
> acknowledge that 20% of our boys came home suffering from
> shell-shock—not "soldier's heart," as they euphemistically refer to
> it. These men were neither shirkers nor malingering cowards, and
> as such deserve the same attention and respect as their physically
> wounded comrades. So far, the best the government has been able
> to do is introduce them to electric shock therapy.*

Alfred looked up from the magazine. "Now here's the interesting part." Jari raised his eyebrows.

> *When the war ended the government promised to get the troops
> home in short order.Eleven months later they were still dribbling
> in. The veterans were furious; ditto their families. But, for many
> shell-shocked victims this turned out to be a blessing in disguise.
> The long wait may have left them stranded in England, but
> because of the care shown them over there, many found them-
> selves launched on the long road to recovery.*

Alfred stopped reading. "There's more, but that's the part that got to me," he said. "It's us in a nutshell, Jari. The Shuttleworth woman was saying it's a slow process."

"Come on Alfred, you can't compare us with those fellows. I mean, we never had the shakes, or ran screaming into the night."

"Maybe not, but what about the nightmares, and sudden fits of anger? We get those, don't we? Or used to."

"You don't actually believe the Canadian government would ever provide two enemy aliens like us the kind of understanding she's talking about?"

"Course not. But our women might."

"They're not 'our women', Alfred. Get it through your head. They've probably already moved on. Both of them."

"What if you're wrong? What if they'd be dying to help. Why else would Nicole have taken me on the way she did? Who knows, maybe Kerttu would feel the same. I say we both get our asses in gear and find out. What's the alternative? Spend the rest of our lives holed up here in the bush?"

"I've no intention of passing my problems onto Kerttu. When my ghosts have been completely vanquished, that's when I'll go to her."

"That's nuts. They're never going to go completely away. Suppose you're with her one day, and something happens that freaks you out? Wouldn't it be best if she was prepared? It can happen. Take that time two months ago at the campfire, when the rabbit fell into the flames. I had a seizure. It was the smell of burning flesh. Right away you knew what was going on, and what to do. Soon's you threw spruce needles into the fire to kill the stench, I came out of it. Burning flesh. That's what triggers me. For you, it's the screams of men drowning. Right? That's what I hear in your nightmares."

Jari stared at the candle so long that Alfred figured his question had just killed another conversation. To his surprise, Jari responded. "I try not to think about it, but it's night on Lake Ladoga and we've lured the Russians onto the ice. When we blow the dynamite, not all of them die. They're in the water, screaming, pleading, calling for their mothers. A few manage to crawl up onto the ice, but soaking wet they don't have a chance. Gradually the shrieking gives way to moans, and whimpers. Then all goes silent." He looked at Alfred. "How does a Kerttu, or a Nicole, handle stuff like that?"

18

Trapline

Taj Mahal,
April 1945

It was April before Alfred finally shot his first moose. He was alone when a young bull sauntered into view, not twenty metres away. Like a seasoned professional, he raised the 30-30, took a deep breath, and fired. The moose tumbled onto his side, legs flailing, and died.

"What's up?" Jari said, watching as a grinning Alfred raced into the yard, wheezing like he was being chased by a wolverine.

"Moose! I got a moose!"

"So I see," Jari replied, approaching the toboggan and examining the carcass. "Good timing, too; we're low on meat." He walked around the toboggan nodding approval. "My god, man, you've done everything right—gutting, a bit of butchering, the whole shebang. Must have had a good teacher."

"Yeah, a hard-boiled Finlander who would have tanned my hide if I'd wasted more than one bullet."

"And rightly so," Jari said, walking over to pump Alfred's hand. "You, my German friend, are turning into a real bushman."

Alfred was a bit overwhelmed by the gushy praise, but wasn't going to question it. "Haven't felt this healthy since I was a kid," he laughed. "No nightmares for a long time, either. When I went out to take a leak last night, I even caught myself examining the stars. What's that tell you?"

"Jari slapped him on the back with a grin so huge it took Alfred by surprise. "Don't look so shocked," Jari said. "I do know how to smile you know."

"Try it more often. Looks good on you. Glad the moose is such a spirit lifter."

"Yeah, well, that and . . ."

"What?" Alfred asked.

"Well, bringing in that moose means we have ample meat, but can't say that for the staples."

"Where you heading with this?"

Jari bent to give Susi a pat. "Town," he replied, straightening and facing Alfred square on. "Gotta go. Can't put it off any longer."

It took a second for this to sink in, and when it did, Alfred broke into a jig. "Town? We're going to town? Yippee! Been dreaming about this for months." He stopped. "Why the long face?"

"Because we can't both go. Too soon, and too risky; especially, for you."

"Get off it! It's been six months. They'll have forgotten all about me."

"You think so? With nothing better for the OPP to do in these parts, other than flush out the odd bootlegger, an escaped POW is big game."

"I'd be careful. Promise."

"Aren't you forgetting something? The traplines. We can't just up and abandon them. Besides, Hearst is a small town. People talk. You're a stranger. Word would get out, and bingo, both our gooses would be cooked."

"Ah, but that's where you're wrong, my friend. You're going to Hearst. Me, I won't be stepping one metre past Coppell. That's where Nicole lives, and you'll find few busybodies there." He waited. "Come on, Jari, just for a couple of days? What's the harm in it?"

"But the traps. They need constant checking, and time's running out on the season. You saw how poor the fur was on that last mink we brought in?" Alfred nodded. "Come spring, mink furs go first, but in a month with the warm weather, most furs will be like that. By the time the dandelions are up, even muskrat will be worthless. No furrier's going to take them in that state. We've only a few weeks left in the season. Can't waste them."

"So, you get to go to town and I stay behind, is that it?"

"It's what makes sense, Alfred. One of us has to be here. I meant it when I said you've turned into a real trapper. You caught on quick. You take as few steps as possible approaching the traps, and are careful to never touch them with your bare hands. You're good at setting them, too, especially the way you give the bait just the right amount of beaver musk, not to mention . . ."

"Cut the crap, Hoivuniemi! Stop trying to butter me up!"

"Look, it's just that I have a better chance of getting into town and back undetected, that's all. We're onto a good thing here. Wouldn't want to spoil it."

"And you're the boss, and I'm the hired hand. That it?"

"Oh, for Christ's sake. We're partners. And I want to keep it that way. Hell, we have no idea what's going on out there in the world. We don't even know if the war is still on. But even if it's over, that doesn't mean we can just go walking about. Get deported and we kiss goodbye the new start we've got riding on the furs. They're our ace in the hole."

Alfred plunked himself down atop the frozen carcass on the toboggan. "Fucking pipe dream," he said. "All of it. Admit it."

"What are you talking about?"

"This fur shit stuff. We've been dreaming in colour. You said yourself that come warm weather they start deteriorating. Including the ones we've got put away. Even if you go to town, you can't just walk into some butcher shop and say, hey, we're enemy aliens hiding out in the bush, would you mind storing these in your walk-in cooler until the war's over."

"Okay, you've got a point, but I've had an idea. A couple of months ago, didn't you say something about that old guy, Nicole's friend, cutting ice in the winter?"

"Otto, you mean?"

"Yeah, him. Did you say he had an icehouse? Any chance he'd agree to let us store our furs there?"

Alfred was on his feet again, the smile returning. "Geez, I don't know, Jari. That'd be putting him at risk, wouldn't it? I mean, anybody snooping around would be sure to know he's too old to trap. There'd be questions."

"He took a risk for you once, didn't he? Just tell me how to get to his place and I'll talk to him. Try to convince him."

"You, a complete stranger, convince him? Not a chance." Alfred began to pace. "But . . . maybe, with Nicole's help, I might just be able to pull it off. Course I'd have to be there to do it in person."

Jari stared at him for a long second. "*Perkele!*" he said. "You scheming, Kraut son-of-a-bitch."

Alfred gave him an exaggerated shrug. "Just trying to help, partner," he said. "Besides, both of us going means two toboggan loads of furs delivered to Otto's. Fewer to haul out later."

"And if he turns you down?"

"Well, with the right approach, and given my winning ways, I'm pretty sure I can bring him around. Now that I recall the shed, it's a good size. Big enough for all our furs. What's our count up to, anyway?"

"Including the ones I trapped before you showed up—ninety-nine pelts."

"Holy Hannah! Never dreamt we'd ever get the count that high."

"Easy on the 'we', Reiger. You're forgetting, I was at this months before you showed up."

"Oops. So, what was the count before I arrived?"

"Twenty-five."

Alfred did the numbers in his head. "That makes me a thirty-five percent owner of seventy-four pelts, right?" Getting no response, he added: "That was the agreement, wasn't it?"

"*Joo*, but don't forget that with your frozen feet, and complete ignorance of the bush, you were useless for the first few months, while I . . ."

"What the hell? You trying to cheat me outta my share? Charge me room and board, or something? Maybe doctor's fees, too? Trust a goddamn Finlander to pull a stunt like that. And you think it's funny to boot. I've a mind to wipe that smile off your face."

"Hey! Let a guy finish? I'm laughing, because I was about to suggest upping your cut to half—fifty-fifty." He let this sink in before continuing. "Still want to pound the piss outta me?"

Alfred stared at him. "You having me on, or just trying to save yourself from a shit-kicking?"

"I'm serious. Just on the furs we brought in together, though."

"I don't know what to say."

"*Jumalauta*, motor-mouth Reiger at a loss for words."

"So, that's it then," Alfred replied, rubbing his hands, fifty-fifty split. And I get to go to Otto's, too. Wow!"

"But only for as long as it takes to convince Otto to let us rent his icehouse," Jari stressed.

"Agreed. But that'll take some doing. He's a tough bargainer. Won't be easy to win over."

"Well, make it fast, and you're not to take one step beyond his place. Understood?"

"Wouldn't think of it."

"Something else you should consider. You hardly know that girl. You saw her for, what, little snatches over four days? You might have been right when you said it's possible she was just being nice. Think about it: a young, pretty, girl, stuck in a farmhouse in the middle of nowhere, when out of the night pops this half-frozen, handsome stranger. So, what happens? Her heart does a flippety-flop. Then he disappears. Very romantic—for a couple of days. But not something to plan a life on."

"Jesus, man. You were the guy who convinced me to hope for the best. For God's sake, don't take it away from me now. And Jari, her name is Nicole. Use it."

"Have it your way," Jari shrugged, "but when we get to Otto Schneider's place, you're to arrange for the icehouse, see her, and get back, pronto. Two days ought to take care of it. There's work needs doing here."

"Two days! What about you? How long you figure taking in Hearst?"

"Longer, but I've gotta get to town, find a place to hide, line up supplies, and figure out how to get them here—a week, more or less."

"So now who's the sly son-of-a-bitch? Rounding up supplies, my ass. You'll be shacked up most of the time."

Jari smiled. "Pleasant thought, but might be awkward with mom and dad around."

"Good God, man, you're both what, mid-thirties? Are you Finns so stuffy that even a middle-aged woman needs chaperoning?"

"Can't risk her parents knowing I'm even in the territory, let alone getting caught sneaking into their daughter's bedroom."

"Well, if you need a hiding place try the round house. That's where Otto put me. As a matter of fact, I'm sure he'd be only too happy to get you to town. We could pay him from fur sales to come. Can't wait to go. When we leaving?"

"Day after tomorrow. We'll head northwest through Newago's old cutting limits, as far as the ACR tracks. Lots of abandoned logging roads that way. I figure two days, tops, to make the trip."

"Just keep me clear of those Nazis."

"We'll keep an eye."

"Wonder if the war is over?" Alfred said. "Nicole and Otto thought it wouldn't be long, but the Hitler freaks at Newago, with their short-wave radios, kept going on about secret weapons. What do you think?"

Jari shrugged, and wandered away, over to the woodpile. Which suited Alfred fine, because he'd begun to fret. What if Jari was right about Nicole? Or, conversely, what if Kerttu slammed the door on Jari's dreams. Living with him was already next to impossible. He couldn't imagine how difficult it would be having him return crushed and broken-hearted.

Three days later, shortly after dark, Alfred was banging on Otto Schneider's door. As a precaution, Jari remained out of sight in the spruce grove down the lane. They had arrived earlier in the day, but at Jari's insistence, had reconnoitred to ensure Otto was alone. In that time the old timer had taken one trip to the outhouse and let his aging cocker spaniel out twice. No one else appeared to be on the premises.

Remembering that Otto was hard of hearing, Alfred banged harder. "Otto, it's me, Alfred Reiger."

The door opened a crack. Otto stared at the big smile behind the frost-rimmed, bushy beard. It took a second before he got it: "Alfred? *Gott im Himmel*! You survived. When I watched you limp off down that trail, I figured . . . never mind what I figured, come in, come in. With that scraggly beard I hardly recognized you."

Alfred didn't budge. "I've got a friend with me," he said.

Otto glanced over Alfred's shoulder and frowned. "In the middle of nowhere you managed to find a friend?"

"Yeah, and good thing, too. His name is Jari Hoivuniemi, and he saved my life."

Otto reacted with a laugh that echoed off the trees. "Oh, a male friend," he said, clasping his hands, and bobbing his head like he'd won the jackpot at the bingo. "Where is he?"

Alfred waved Jari in from trees, and turned back to Otto. "What's so funny?" he asked.

"Well, guess I, sorta, leapt to the conclusion that you had found female company, say an Indian girl from one of the Missinaibi bands. That would've been awkward. Somebody we both know would have been mighty disappointed to hear that."

When Jari reached the doorstep, his business partner completely ignored him. "Really?" Alfred was saying. "You're not having me on, are you? Have you seen her? Is she alright?"

"Oh, yeah. She's fine. Comes around every once in a while. Your name usually comes up."

Behind them Jari cleared his throat. "Sorry," Alfred said, motioning him forward. "Otto, meet Jari Hoivuniemi."

"Do I take it you just gave Alfred happy news," Jari said.

"He's told you about her, has he?" Otto responded, as they moved into the house.

Jari nodded. "Won't shut up."

"Can't say for sure, but I think our friend is in for a warm reception."

"Not too warm I hope," Jari replied. "He's got work waiting for him back in the bush."

Alfred blinked. "My God," he said, walking into the room. "I'd forgotten how bright a kerosene lamp can be. We ran out of fuel months ago."

"Is that what brings you back?" Otto asked "Supplies?"

"That and information," Alfred replied. "Plus, a business proposition we hope you might be interested in."

Otto looked from one face to the other. "Interesting. Let me put the kettle on."

The two guests clasped the mugs of steaming coffee, and inhaled the rich aroma. Jari closed his eyes as he sipped. "Eight months, no Java," he sighed.

"Before we get to this proposition of yours," Otto began, all business, "let me bring you up to date. I've no idea who or what you are, Jari, but Alfred, you're still a hunted man. They blow hot and cold, but they come nosing around here every so often. I reckon they're due again any day now. Best you make your stay a short one."

Alfred drummed his fingers on the table and nodded, but made no comment.

"Warning taken," Jari said. "What about the war?"

"Dragging on, but the Wehrmacht is reeling and the Allies are now deep into Germany. Won't be long now."

"And my homeland, Suomi? Any news there?"

"All quiet. Crazy thing is, the new Russo-Finn border isn't much different from what it was three years ago. Kinda makes you wonder what it was all about."

19

Hearst by Night

Hearst,
April 1945

ari waited for nightfall before venturing from his hidey-hole at the roundhouse. To Alfred, this tiny room in the train yards had been a doorway to freedom. Jari saw it for what it was—a disgusting little storage bin, shellacked under decades of coal dust and burnt cinders. It didn't help that all he had to occupy himself with were thoughts of Kerttu, and what kind of reception awaited him.

Leaving his safe place, he scooted around the railway station and followed the tracks east, past the Imperial Oil depot, the CNR freight shed, and Mercier and Shirley, the town's one and only food wholesale establishment. His destination was the British American oil depot, where the tall tanks would provide an ideal observation point. Here he waited, breathing in the aroma coming from the lumber piles across the tracks behind him. It was a curious scent, kind of a mix of cat urine and puppy-dog poo, but he liked it for the way it smelled of honest work and new beginnings. Behind him a locomotive snorted as it shunted boxcars into a line that would comprise the morning train. In other circumstances, Jari might have found comfort in the hissing, chuffing, and clanging, as the locomotive coupled the freight cars together. But, tonight, his attention was on the building across the road, where the Ontario Department of Lands and Forests office sat nestled among the poplar trees. The workers would soon be leaving. Head secretary Kerttu Nurmi among them. Or, so he hoped.

Jari stomped his feet. It was April, but spring had yet to make an appearance. The sleet bit into his cheeks like porcupine needles. Out on Front Street a car went by, its lights boring tunnels through the darkness. The few pedestrians on the sidewalk tilted into the wind, as they hustled home. *Workers from Fontaine's sawmill,* he thought. Windows began darkening at the Forestry Branch. The front door opened. Jari straightened. A handful of employees exited. Kerttu was not among them. They stood about for a moment, lighting cigarettes and listening to a tall man who held one hand on his fedora to keep it from blowing away. He must have been telling a joke, because they suddenly erupted in laughter, before heading off. The door opened again. This time a woman stepped out. Jari's heart quickened. Even with the dim light and pelting sleet, there was no mistaking the squared shoulders and erect posture—Kerttu. She stopped, pulled her fur collar up snugly around her neck, and set off at a fast clip, heading west on Front Street. Jari tightened the hood on his parka, and set out after her.

The easy thing would have been to angle across the street and intercept her, but he hung back. *Close the gap slowly he told himself. Don't want to scare her. There are people about, can't afford making a scene. It's three blocks to her place. Loads of time. Can't have tongues wagging about some stranger popping out of the dark, and making a move on Kerttu Nurmi.*

By the second block he realized that short of running, another attention grabber, she'd be home before he caught up. Ahead, at the corner, a logging truck, chains flapping noisily, turned in front of her. She stopped to let it pass, then crossed. He was close enough now to make contact without drawing attention, but as he glanced over his shoulder to confirm that no one was within hearing distance, she stopped again. This time to talk to a woman standing on her front stoop, brushing the snow off a young boy. They conversed in Finn. Again Jari slowed and was relieved to hear Kerttu say, "Good night, Mrs. Luoma," and continue on her way. Three doors from her destination, a drunk staggered out of the alley, forcing her to step aside. Jari tensed, as he watched the man stumble on past. "Excuse me!" she exclaimed, turning around and glaring at the drunk. When she did, she found herself looking directly at the stranger following behind. Her mouth dropped open, recognition slowly sinking in. They stared at each other. "Jari?" she asked hesitantly, advancing a step.

He lowered his hood, and nodded. *"Hei, kultaseni,"* he said, immediately regretting having addressed her as sweetheart. "I made it. I'm back."

She stood, taking him in, not sure what to say, or do. Jari felt his chest tighten. *I'm too late*, he thought. *She's moved on.*

Kerttu looked up at him. "What am I supposed to do?" she said. "Pound you or kiss you."

"Kiss would be nice," he replied.

She hesitated. "I'll go as far as a hug," she replied, stepping into his arms. He rocked her gently and nuzzled her hair, but when he bent to kiss her, she turned her head away, and stepped out of his embrace.

Clearly, this was not the welcome that had fuelled his will to survive on the Karelian Front. Afraid that she was about to shake his hand and leave, he cleared his throat. "Could we walk a while?" he asked. "There's so much I need to explain, Kerttu. Please, just for a few minutes. I know it's been a while but . . ."

"A while!" she interrupted. "Five damned years you've been gone, with no word for the last two. I'd given you up for dead. And, yes we can, *talk*, but don't count on anything more. A walk, though, is out. Not in this crappy weather. We'll go upstairs to the apartment."

"The apartment? Is that a good idea? I mean . . ."

She tipped her head back into the streetlight. "If it's *Äiti* and *Isä* you're worried about, relax. My parents left on the train for Sudbury, yesterday. Aunt Aini's sick."

Heart in his throat, he followed her down the narrow alleyway, and up the stairs to the apartment above the family store. That her folks were away was a relief, but might there be another man waiting for her? He held his breath as they entered, only letting it go when it was clear no one was coming forth to greet her. Coats and boots off, she led him into the kitchen, where she placed two glasses and a bottle of her father's vodka on the table. She poured, but did not sit down. Neither did he.

"I'm expected downstairs," she said, downing her drink. "With *Isä* away, I close up the store." She looked at the kitchen clock. "Best you stay seated. Wouldn't want the clerks hearing footsteps and asking questions. Hell, they might get the idea that Kerttu Nurmi isn't the prim spinster they've got me down for. I'll be half an hour. We'll talk then. Pour yourself another drink if you like. Might help you open up for a change."

Jari did have another drink, but recognizing the need for a clear head, only one. When at last she returned, she headed to the fridge. "When did you last eat?" she asked.

"Lunch. Baloney sandwich."

"Well, you're in luck. *Äiti* left me a big crock of *lohikeitto*. How's that sound?"

"*Hyvänen aika*! Creamy salmon soup. The dish of my dreams."

"Good," she said, "because that's what's being served." She placed the crock on the counter and opened the pantry door. A familiar aroma filled the room.

Jari closed his eyes. "Cardamon," he said. "Coffee bread. Maybe some of that, too?"

"I see the war hasn't damaged your smeller, Mr. Hoivuniemi."

He watched her ladle *lohikeitto* from the crock into a smaller pot, and place it on the stove. She stood with her back to him, stirring. He sat, struggling with how, and when, to start on all the things that needed telling.

She turned, ladle in hand. "With Finland out of the war, things have changed around here. Finns are now allowed to join the Canadian army. You must remember, Wayne Halme, and Eino Hillman, and Tauno Suni?" Jari nodded. "Well they've all joined up."

"Not sure I envy them," Jari said. "I'm out of it, and happy for it."

She frowned. "Come to think of it . . . how'd you get from Finland to here with the war still going strong?"

"Long story," he replied. "Not a pleasant one. I'll say that much."

"Well, getting back there isn't going to be any easier."

"Suits me. Got no intention of going back. Can't. Truth be told, I'm AWOL. They'll be looking for me over there."

"Doubt that," she responded. "You really think that with all their problems the Finns have time to worry about one rogue soldier?"

Jari shrugged. "Not now, perhaps, but later they might. People have long memories. Nobody loves a deserter."

"Well, being AWOL from the Finn army won't hurt you on this side of the ocean. Just tell people you couldn't stomach fighting for Hitler any longer."

Jari stiffened. "Who was ever fighting for him? Not me. Not any of us."

She turned back to the pot. "Unfortunately, that's not how it looked from here. Not with the papers full of pictures of bodies piled up in the streets of Leningrad. And like it or not, Jari, the Finnish army played a role in that."

"We only wanted to push the Russians off the land they stole from us in 1939."

"Agreed. But you didn't exactly stop at the old border, did you?"

"Only because those damn Nazis . . ." He stopped. "Look, I didn't come to argue the war."

"Why did you come?"

He sighed, the long-rehearsed words gone from his mind. "To explain things. Talk things over. To see if . . ." he stammered.

Still clutching the ladle, she sat down opposite him and stared. "Go on."

"I came, hoping we could . . . "

"What? Pick up where we left off?"

"Kinda. Yeah."

"When we parted, I thought we had an understanding. The last twenty-four months of silence put paid to that. Not even a postcard let alone a letter. And don't tell me it was because there's no mail delivery between Canada and Finland. Hell, families right here in town get letters to their sons in German POW camps. The Red Cross sees to that."

"It was never my intention to let things slide. It's just that, it all seemed so . . . impossible. In my whole platoon only two of us made it through—me and one other guy, who's probably dead now, too. Look, all I'm asking for is a chance to make it up to you."

The *lohikeitto* began to boil over. Kerttu jumped up, ladled out two bowls and plunked them down. "I'll listen if it makes you feel better," she said, "but that's as far as it goes."

The conversation continued over dinner and late into the evening. It was painful, but in his own stumbling way, Jari managed to get it all out—the ambush, running into Korpi, Mr. Vatanen, the oath, the gun, the killing and dumping of the body in Helsinki Harbour, Kemi, Sweden, England, New Jersey, and finally Canada.

Occasionally, Kerttu interrupted for clarification, but mostly she listened. When he described the final scene with aunt Toini, he fought back the tears. "A lot about me has changed, Kerttu, but not my feelings for you. And regardless of how it sounds, the war hasn't turned me into a monster."

"Yet, you killed a man in Helsinki. In cold blood."

"Not a man. A traitor. And when it happened, I was still in war mode. But I promise, that's all done with. Believe me. Things I did then, I could never do again."

"You say that, Jari, but supposing you came face-to-face with Korpi's partner, Sorsakoski? How would you react to that?"

"Put the thought out of your head, Kerttu. I'm in complete control. I mean it when I say I don't have it in me to kill again. Besides, for that to happen, I'd have to go to Finland—now out of the question—drive into Russian Karelia, which is all but impossible, and try to find a guy who more likely than not had been operating on a fake name."

"So, you're saying you'd walk away from your oath, then?" He nodded. She stared at him for a long moment. "I want to believe you, Jari. Deep down you're a good man."

"Does this mean . . . ?"

"It means I'm happy for you. That's all. Nothing more." She glanced at the clock on the china cabinet. "Good, God, it's midnight, and we haven't touched the dishes."

Kerttu washed, he dried. "You are in a pickle, aren't you," she said. "The Finnish army's after you for desertion, the Helsinki police want you for murder, and your passport identifies you as Olaf Anderson from Sweden. Quite a dossier you've wracked up. How do you expect to survive in this country with credentials like that?"

"Hiding in the bush seems to have worked so far."

Kerttu frowned. "So, it's jail in Canada if you're caught, jail in Finland if they deport you, or a lifetime in the bush? Dim prospects, I'd say."

He studied his stocking feet. Said in such blunt terms, it hurt, but from her point of view, it made sense. *Why would any sane woman ever want to tie herself to this?* he thought. "I'll figure something out," he managed to say.

"The man you, um, disposed of, what was his name again?"

"Korpi. Tuomas Korpi."

"Was his friend with him in Helsinki? Might he have seen the two of you together?"

Jari shook his head. "While I was trailing him, he left the hotel with another soldier, but it wasn't Sorsakoski. If so, I would have killed him, too."

"And you're sure no one saw you frog-marching him to the pier? Or got a good enough look at you to tie you to the . . . murder?"

"Pretty sure, but it's possible I was noticed lurking about the hotel. Someone might have remembered and described me to the police."

"Do you know anyone in Helsinki you trust enough to find out?"

"Nobody really, except for Mr. Vatanen, Teemu, and Kimi's dad. It's possible he read about Korpi's death in the paper and made the connection."

"That's it then," Kerttu said. "Write to him. It's a start."

"And what would I use for a return address? J. Hoivuniemi, somewhere in the bush south of Hearst, Ontario, Canada? Anybody else's address would only drag them into it. Wouldn't want to do that to anyone; especially not you."

She stood with her hands in the dishwater, staring straight ahead. "Not mine, maybe, that would trace you back to Hearst. I could ask my friend, Katri in Timmins. She'd be up for it. Wouldn't ask questions, either."

"Wouldn't be fair to her."

"I think you're exaggerating the risk."

"Besides," he replied, "with the war on, a reply would take forever."

"Worth a try," she said.

He straightened his shoulders, as a ray of hope fluttered through his chest. Not because he saw anything coming from a letter to Mr. Vatanen, but because of the manner in which she had responded. Here was the vintage, take-charge Kerttu, getting straight to the heart of the matter. It wasn't acceptance, far from it, but the warmth creeping into her voice was, at least, an encouraging sign.

Dishes done, Jari hung the tea towel under the sink, and turned to her. For a moment they stood looking at each other. Not surprisingly, it was Kerttu who spoke first. "Why don't you have a bath while I make up your bed in the spare bedroom," she said.

It was getting light when he heard her moving in the kitchen. Reaching for his clothes he hurried to join her, but by the time he got there, she was gone. Dejected, he was about to sit down, when he noticed that the stairway door down to the store was open. He took it, and found her wrapped in a heavy, mauve housecoat, feeding wood into the potbellied stove.

"Got to get the temperature up for staff and customers when they begin coming in at 8:30," she said. She adjusted the damper, then headed back upstairs. "Saturdays are always busy," she continued, "right through until closing at 9:00 p.m. If you like, you're free to stay here for a while, but you'll have to move about on tiptoes. And another thing: If you use the sink, be sure to turn the taps off gently to avoid clanging pipes."

"What about the toilet?"

"Use it, but don't flush. You can do that at mealtimes when the store is closed." She showed him the stack of magazines and newspapers her parents subscribed to, all more recent than anything left behind by the Smith brothers.

"Super," he said. "It'll give me a chance to catch up on the outside world."

"You mentioned that you needed supplies to take back with you. Make a list and give it to me when I come up for lunch."

Breakfast was Shredded Wheat, brown sugar, and milk. A treat for him, but the usual for her. They ate in silence. "I'll clean up," he said, when they finished. Kerttu nodded, and went to dress for work.

Jari got little out of the magazines. He'd finish a paragraph only to realize that nothing had sunk in. It didn't help that Kerttu remained cool when she joined him for lunch and supper. He understood her well enough to know that she wasn't consciously freezing him out. She was struggling, and there was nothing he could say, or do, to advance his cause. Through the day, he busied himself—making the beds, sandwiches for lunch, dishes after the meals.

When she mounted the stairs at 9:15 that night, she flopped onto the sofa and kicked off her shoes. "Didn't have the energy to do up the cash," she announced. "It'll have to wait until morning."

He went to the fridge and came back with two filled cocktail glasses. She stared at him as he handed one to her, and held his own out at arm's length. There was hesitation on her part before she clinked. "To the future," he said.

She took a sip and smiled. "Salty dog," she said. "You haven't forgotten."

"How could I forget your favourite. We've got the vodka, and when I spied the can of grapefruit juice, I couldn't resist." He sat down beside her.

"Nice," she said.

The silence that followed was broken by Jari clearing his throat. "I'll be out of your hair Tuesday—soon's you're able to get the supplies I need. After that, I won't bother you again. Promise. Just know that it was thoughts of you that got me through hell over there." He paused. "I loved you then, and I still do."

She placed her salty dog on the floor. "You're an asshole, Jari Hoi-vuniemi," she said, taking his hand. "What am I to think? No word for an eternity, now I find out you've been back for months without as much as letting me know."

"I'm sorry," he replied, "but I was terrified of you seeing me in the state I was in. That would have sunk my chances, for sure. And it wouldn't have been fair to you. I had to work it out, myself."

"Hold me, you silly bugger."

They were still curled up together when the clock on the china cabinet struck eight the next morning. Kerttu lay facing him with her fingers weaving their way through the hair on his chest. "Your stomach sounds like Mom's washing machine. I'll fix us something to eat," she said, kissing him on the head. He followed her to the kitchen. "How's toast, coffee and some of Mom's blueberry jam sound?" she asked.

Over breakfast they discussed the supplies he was going to need. "The food we can get from downstairs," she said, "but me buying snare wire and all that ammunition, is sure to raise eyebrows. If it was hunting season no one would bat an eye, but right now, whew, there'll be questions."

"How about splitting the order between the two hardware stores— half at Pellow's, half at Dehaitre's."

"Why do you need so much stuff, anyway?" she asked.

Jari took a deep breath. "Because, I have a partner."

"Continue," she pressed.

"He's a young German."

"Meaning what, exactly? His parents were German?"

"He's an escaped POW."

She lurched, spilling her coffee. "Good God, Jari! Are you nuts?" She jumped up, and began dabbing at the stain on her housecoat with a tea towel. "Do you have any idea what will happen if this ever got out? Jail, and after that, deportation, faster than you can say Jack Robinson. What on earth possessed you?"

"I know it sounds bad, but the guy showed up on my doorstep half frozen. I only intended to patch him up and send him packing, and would have, except he hadn't a clue how to survive in the bush. So, I figured I'd teach him a few skills, then drop him. Finally seemed easier to let him have my place and move on myself. And that's what I did. Found a good place of my own, another cabin, two days away."

"So, how does that make him your partner?"

"Well, when I returned for my furs, I found him with no fresh meat, and not much else. So, rather than leave him alone to die, I brought him to my new place."

"And this happened . . . ?"

Jari shrugged. "About five months ago, I guess."

"Wait a minute! What's this guy's name?"

"Reiger, Alfred Reiger."

"*Jumalauta*! That's the guy who triggered the big manhunt. Hearst was crawling with cops for weeks. You're dead meat if they catch you with him. Don't you realize, with the war still on they have the right to shoot people. On sight."

"He's a nice kid, Kerttu. Really. Needed a break, that's all. Goddamn Krauts scooped him up at seventeen and forced a rifle on him. The boy has been through some terrible, terrible times."

"So, how does this make you two partners?"

"Because of the trapping I was telling you about last night. It just seemed more efficient to divvy up the work."

"My God. Two entrepreneur fugitives. I suppose it makes sense. Beats sitting around twiddling your thumbs, I guess."

Jari got up and refilled their cups. "Kerttu, do you know a girl called Nicole Fontaine? She works weekends at the hospital."

"I might. What's she look like?"

"No idea. Never met her. Alfred's got it in his head that she's his girlfriend."

"Good lord! How does an escaped POW come up with an idea like that?"

Jari shrugged. "Anyway, because her farm is down at Coppell, she sleeps at the nurses' residence when she's on duty in town. I was wondering if you might invite her over here? To meet her."

"Check her out you mean?" Kerttu replied, shaking her head. "Stupid idea! She'd blab for sure. Besides, if this Reiger made it through the war, he can survive a broken heart."

"Just a thought," he said.

The town custom was for the stores to close Wednesday afternoons— Kerttu's parent's grocery store included. That Wednesday, shortly after closing, Kerttu had Jari on the back seat floor of her father's car, under a blanket. Confident that he was well hidden, she headed the car south through town, towards the wooden bridge over the Mattawishkwia River. With her parents coming back the following night, it was important that Jari vacate. They had packed the staples in the trunk the night before, plus a few treats for Otto, whom she knew by reputation, but had never had occasion to meet.

"Yikes," Jari said, as the car rattled over the wooden planks that constituted the bridge deck. "Wouldn't want to take a loaded truck over this thing."

"Nip and tuck every spring whether the bridge goes out with the ice," Kerttu said. "People place bets on it, but the old thing keeps hanging on."

The car bounced off the bridge onto the road heading south. Snow began slushing up in the wheel wells and rocker panels as they picked up speed.

Forty minutes later, they turned onto Otto's side road. Kerttu gasped, her knuckles going white on the steering wheel. Ahead was a single line of tire tracks in the snow leading around a bend and out of sight. A hundred yards in they came to a spot where a car had been pulled out of the ditch. "This is crazy," she said, slowing down. "Why don't we park and walk the rest of the way?"

"No, no, you're doing fine. It's not far now. Keep the wheels in the tracks. Don't slow down, just power through. If we get stuck, Otto's got a horse."

"Here goes," she replied, tromping on the gas. Snow began flying up around them Twice, the wheels veered out of the ruts heading for the ditch, but she kept her foot on the accelerator and managed to steer them back on the track. The grimace on her face became a smile, followed by squeals of delight.

"You're getting the hang of it," Jari yelled. He began singing a song from when they'd first met, "Saw You Last Night and Got That Old Feeling." Kerttu joined in. By the time they reached Otto's they'd gone through "A-Tisket, A-Tasket," "Jeepers Creepers," "Harbour Lights," and "I've Got My Love to Keep Me Warm."

When they piled out of the car they were singing, "Bei Mir Bist Du Schön," at the top of their lungs. Otto came out, and Jari made the introductions. "Where's Alfred?" Jari asked, when they were taking off their coats. "You got him working outdoors or something?"

Otto cocked his head towards the back window. "Check for yourself."

They peered out. Kerttu looked at Jari and burst out laughing. "I see what you meant when you said they were just a couple of kids. I think I'm going to like these two."

Otto joined them at the window. "Gotta envy them, right?" he said.

For several minutes, they watched in silence as Alfred aimed a snowball at Nicole. Missing, he rushed her, knocked her down and threatened to wash her face with snow. She screamed, but stopped struggling, opting for a kiss instead.

"Think you can squeeze us in tonight?" Jari asked. "We brought our own bedrolls."

"No problem," Otto replied. "You can sleep out here with the boys, Jari. That leaves the bedroom for Kerttu and Nicole."

Kerttu caught the look of disappointment on Jari's face and snickered. "Suits us to a T. Doesn't it, Mr. Hoivuniemi?" she said, poking him in the ribs.

20

Otto's Place

East of Coppell,
February 1946

"Y ou awake, Alfred?" Jari whispered. Ten months had gone by since he'd gathered up his courage and made contact with Kerttu. In all that time he'd only seen her twice. Now, he and Alfred were back at Otto's place dying to see their girls. As usual, Jari had been given the couch, and Alfred the floor beside him. It was getting light, but judging by the snoring coming from the bedroom, Otto was still fast asleep.

"What?" Alfred replied.

"These furs we're storing here at Otto's?"

"What about them?"

"Are we asking too much of the old man? They're worth a lot. If word ever got out, it would be sure to bring thieves, and probably cops, down on him. Just the thought's gotta be stressful for the poor guy."

"How would anybody find out? Hell, we're the only ones who ever visit him."

"What if he goes to town, and lets something slip?"

"Come on, Jari. Otto's no youngster, but he's sharp as a tack."

When Otto got up he was surprised to find Jari and Alfred already halfway through breakfast. It didn't take a genius to guess why. "As much as it pains me," he began, after clearing his throat for attention, "three things need to happen before either of you set foot outside this cabin: Beards get trimmed, baths taken and underwear changed." With that he put two pails of water on the stove and dragged out the zinc washtub.

Jari winced. "Are we that bad?" he asked, sniffing at his armpit.

"You've no idea," Otto replied, shaking his head. "Acrid says it best.

Animals could smell you, miles off. How you ever get close enough to shoot moose is a mystery."

"Oh, shit!" Alfred groaned. "Underwear. I've only got what I'm wearing."

"Then wash it," Otto said.

Alfred looked at the clock on the shelf. "But, it's Penman's 98. Wool that thick takes forever to dry."

"You've got scads of time, Reiger. You're in no hurry."

Alfred got to his feet. "Course I'm in a hurry. And what do you mean, 'scads of time?'"

"If you'd bothered to look at a calendar," Otto replied, "you'd see that you've come on a Friday. You know what that means, don't you?"

Alfred slumped back into his chair. "Shit! She's working at the hospital, and won't be home until late Sunday. Earliest I'll get to see her will be Monday."

"As if that's not bad enough," Otto continued, "it gets worse. The police keep tabs on me and they're long overdue. They could show up any day. Best you leave and come back at another time."

"Screw that, Otto. Cops or not, I'm not going anywhere til I see her."

With Alfred moping, Otto and Jari tried their best to steer clear of him for the next couple of hours. "Snap out of it, Reiger," Otto said finally, when Jari was nearly ready to leave for town. "Get dressed, and come help me harness the horse. You can survive outside without long johns for a bit."

"Lucky me," Alfred moaned. "Not only do I get to stay behind, but I get to work, too. Whoopee." Behind him, Jari suppressed a snicker.

Outside, they headed straight for the barn. "Sitting around brooding isn't going to help pass the time," Otto said, as they harnessed the horse to the cutter. "Besides, there's things that need doing around here. First, the furs you brought yesterday have to be spread out and covered with sawdust; horse blankets, too, if you want to hide them from prying eyes. When you've finished that, get the toboggans and skis out of sight in the barn. And Susi's a problem. Best tie him up outside, so it looks like I've taken on a new dog."

"Anything else?" Alfred asked, scarcely bothering to hide the sarcasm in the tone. It didn't help to see Jari emerge from the cabin all fresh, clean, and anxious to get going.

"Yeah," Otto said with a smirk, "how about splitting and piling some wood for me?" Jari climbed into the sleigh, not daring to look at Alfred's scowl for fear of laughing. Otto grabbed the reins, "I'm serious about the police," he said. "Keep your ears open and eyes peeled."

Alfred waited for the cutter to disappear before heading back into the cabin. "Screw this," he said to Susi. "Work can wait. Couple of magazines need flipping through first."

Well into the second magazine, and having noticed the temperature dropping, he was about to add another log in the stove when he reconsidered. Daytime fires in clear weather at Taj were a no-no, yet Otto hadn't said a word about letting the fire go out. He went to the front window and scanned the yard. Nothing was moving except the trees. "Damn Otto got me all jumpy," he said to Susi. "Best forget the fire." With that, he set about hiding evidence of visitors—dirty coffee cups, blanket on the couch, makeshift bed on the floor. That done, he put on his boots and parka. "Come on, boy, let's get it over with."

It might have been the strange yard, or because he was missing Jari, but Susi was sticking so close to Alfred that he kept getting in the way. When he stumbled over him a third time, Alfred had had enough, and went in search of a rope. "Sorry," he said, tying Susi to the hitching pole outside the barn door. "You can see me from here. And it's not for long, so stop with the sad face."

He'd picked that spot for Susi for a reason. In the unlikely case that someone did come around, his best bet was to slip into the barn. A vicious-looking dog tied outside the door, might be just enough to keep snoopers at bay.

Moving the furs into the icehouse went smoothly. In no time he had them spread out under the tarp, and covered as instructed. He saw that ice was running low, and made a mental note to cut more from the creek, before leaving. Closing up, he wondered where Otto had put the lock, but gave up looking when he noticed Susi on his feet, ears up. Alfred stood still, listening. It was unmistakably a vehicle, and getting closer, but when he caught the sound of slapping chains, he relaxed. "Pulp truck," he said, to Susi. "Not cops. Go back to sleep."

Susi lay back down in the snow, paw over his nose, eyes already closed. Alfred chuckled at the sight of him. He considered slipping back inside for a nap himself, but the truck was a reminder that the outside world was but a hair's breadth away. Cursing himself for not starting sooner, he hauled the toboggans and skis to the barn, and began raking snow over the tracks they left. In the process, he decided that should he have to hide, the outhouse might be his best bet. No one would question tracks going down to the privy. If they did decide to inspect, there was always plan B—dropping through the shit hole.

He was splitting wood, when the silence was interrupted a second time. This time no chains, only the unmistakable sound of a car picking its way carefully down a snow-covered road—gas on, gas off. It grew louder. He propped the axe against the chopping block, and ran for the outhouse.

A minute later a car pulled into the yard. Two men got out, one dressed in RCMP winter issue, the other wearing what Alfred assumed had to be the OPP equivalent. Susi was on his feet, back arched and teeth bared.

"Dog's new," the mountie said.

"His old mutt must have died," the OPP officer remarked. "Judging by the sleigh tracks, it looks like Otto is not here. I'll try the door just in case." He knocked, and when no one came, turned the knob and opened the door a crack, then closed it again.

"Aren't you going in?"

"Not without him here."

"Why not? He's harboured fugitives in the past, hasn't he? Nobody's going to complain, and if they do, we just say we were worried about the old codger being sick and wanted to check on him."

Five minutes later they came out, and sauntered over to the ice-house. "No place to hide in there," the mountie observed from the open door, "but what about these tracks in the snow? Been a lot of activity."

"Otto, sells ice to the locals," the OPP constable replied. "Cuts and stores it off and on all winter."

They approached the barn, slowing at the sight of Susi crouched and ready to spring. The mountie unbuckled his holster and pulled out his revolver.

"Don't!" the OPP constable said. "You go home to Timmins tonight, but I gotta live with these people. Killing their dogs doesn't make it any easier."

The mountie lowered his revolver. "Fine, but if he lunges he's done for."

"I'll check the outhouse," the OPP constable said, when they exited the barn.

Horrified at the sight of the constable heading down the path, Alfred realized he now had to go to plan B. Only when he turned, did he discover that the shit hole was too small. In full panic he strained to pull the top off the bench, but Otto had it nailed down tight.

"Tom," the mountie called, "there's something fishy here."

The OPP stopped. "What?"

"The barn. Just struck me. Those skis in the mow? There's snow caked on the bindings."

"So? Maybe Otto . . ."

"He's too old for skis. And the toboggans? Doubt he could still pull one of those heavy things. There's more, too. In the house. Did you notice the size of the underwear hanging over the stove? Must be a size forty-four. Hell, the Otto you introduced me to would swim in it."

The OPP walked back to confer with his colleague. "How 'bout we take another look?"

The mountie looked at his watch. "It'll have to wait. We got other places to check, and I'd like to get home early for the weekend. I'm back in ten days. We can do a thorough search then. Time we shook old man Schneider up again."

21

Ultimatum

Near Jogues,
March 1946

*A*nother spring had arrived, and once again the two couples had come together at Otto's. Two months had passed since their last gathering, and almost twelve since V-E Day. The night was cold, but with the fire crackling in the giant cooking stove, Otto's cabin was cozy warm. Dinner had turned into a Finn/French-Canadian cook-off, with Kerttu putting her *myocka*, a fish stew, against Nicole's *ragout de pattes de cochon*, pork hocks. After the cleanup, the cards had come out, and they were playing poker for pennies, financed by Otto's penny jar. Jari had just won another hand, with Alfred getting ready to deal, when Otto leaned over and stopped him.

"Hold on," he said. "We have to talk. No putting this off any longer. You guys got decisions to make. Big ones."

Under normal conditions, Alfred, always keen to party on, might have dismissed Otto's concern with a smart-aleck remark, but Otto's tone advised caution.

"It's about the furs, isn't it?" said Jari. "They're making you nervous, and I don't blame you. You've been risking your neck for too long. We'll make other arrangements."

"Yes, it's about the furs, and, yes, I'm nervous. But for you guys, not me. Have you any idea how much those fur bales out there are worth? Prices are going nuts. Canadian pelts are like gold on the world market."

"I don't understand," Nicole said. "That's a good thing, isn't it?"

"Normally, yes," Otto replied, "but there's a dangerous side to it, too." With that he held up two newspapers, the *Timmins Press* and the

Sault Ste Marie Star. They gasped at the headlines: "Fur Wars Erupt," and "Trapper Murdered North of Chapleau."

"Where's Chapleau?" Alfred asked, breaking the silence.

"Near the south end of the Missinaibi River," Otto replied. "Two week's paddle from Taj." He sat back. "You can see why this worries me. I'm happy you had the sense to stockpile furs, but scared as hell, too. That murder took place a week ago."

"They get the guy who did it?" Alfred asked.

Otto shook his head. "Still out there. Possibly close to your trapline. And they figure it's not one guy but two."

"So, thanks for the warning," Jari responded, rolling his hand at Alfred. "We'll be sure to keep our eyes open. Deal the cards, buddy."

Otto leaned forward. "You're not getting it, Jari. The bush around here will soon be swarming with cops, not to mention fur rustlers. You guys are in no position to handle that kinda stuff."

"Well," Kerttu said with a smile, "this brings things to a head, doesn't it? Going back into the bush is definitely out now. Frankly I'm delighted, and I suspect Nicole is, too. How much longer did you guys think we were going to sit around waiting for you to screw up your courage, and break free?"

Nicole nodded. Jari rose and began pacing. "Look, I get it. But there's a stack of furs back at Taj Mahal all scraped, stretched, and ready to go. Some at Ledgeview and Grinnin, too. No way are we abandoning them. There's a good ten thousand square miles of bush out there, and we're not about to be spooked just because someone *might* show up in our little patch. And that's final." He sat back down and motioned again for Alfred to start dealing.

"Not so fast!" Kerttu responded, slapping the table. "Alfred put those cards down." She waited for him to comply before continuing. "We all heard Otto. Now's the time to cash in and walk away."

Jari sat down and began rubbing his hands. "Be reasonable, those furs represent a good four months' hard work. Look, we get it, it's time for us to come out, but five days is all we need to fetch them and return, six tops. We'll be careful, keep out of sight, but if some goddamned fur rustler shows up, well, they'll get their asses burned." He looked at Alfred for confirmation. When none came, he shook his head in disgust. "Shit! Leave it to a Goddamn German to bail out when the going gets tough. If it wasn't for . . ."

"Jari!" Kerttu interrupted. "That's not fair. Apologize to Alfred. Shooting somebody will only get you two into a hole deeper than you ever imagined. Do that and you kiss everything goodbye."

Jari had regretted the "bailing out" insult the instant it had crossed his lips. From the look on Alfred's face, it had cut deep. Nicole must have noticed it too, because she took his hand and whispered something in his ear. "Sorry, Alfred," Jari said. "You know me, say things I don't mean sometimes."

Alfred nodded and cleared his throat. "I've had enough shooting to last me a lifetime. But Jari's got a point." Nicole dropped his hand and looked at Kerttu, who sat shaking her head. "Think about it," he continued, "all that work. What's a few more days? Can't be that dangerous."

Kerttu glared at him. "Money? Is that what it comes down to? Or is it male ego? I gave you credit for more smarts than that, Alfred Reiger."

Alfred reached for Nicole's hand, but she pulled it away. "Put yourself in my shoes," he said. I'm an illegal alien, which means no one will, or can, hire me. My only option is to start my own business, and that takes cash. For years I've dreamt of having my own bakery, and I'm this close," he said, holding up his thumb and index finger. "Nobody's taking that away from me. Not now. If it calls for defending what's mine, so be it."

Kerttu sighed. "You don't have to prove your manhood to us."

"He's just being realistic, Kerttu," Jari said. "We're not kids who run and hide."

"Don't you dare talk about hiding," Kerttu snapped. "What the hell do you think you two have been doing for the last two bloody years?"

"That's different."

Nicole cleared her throat. "Can I get a word in here?" she said. Heads turned her way. "Kerttu's right. The police are bound to show up. They may not find the murderer in Otto's newspaper, but sure as heck they'll find you two, and if they don't, the poachers will. I hate to think what will happen then."

An awkward silence settled in around the table. Alfred and Nicole stared at the wall. Jari brooded. Kerttu slouched with her arms crossed. Otto escaped to the kitchen.

"Look," Otto said, returning to his seat, "might as well get it all out. There's more." He took a deep breath. "Apparently, the government's about to implement a big crackdown on trapping. It's in all the papers. With the looming fur bonanza, there's concern that the animals could wind up getting trapped out."

"So what?" Alfred responded. "If we're quitting anyway, who cares?"

Otto grimaced, but continued. "In addition to poachers and police crashing around in the bush, there'll be game wardens, too; scads of them; guys with bush smarts."

"He's right," Kerttu added. "The big news at work last week was that Lands and Forests is getting an airplane. I assumed it would be to spot forest fires, but now that I think of it, the game wardens will have access to it, too. They're out to clamp down on unlicensed trappers." She looked from Jari to Alfred. "You two sure fit that bill."

Nicole pulled Alfred over to the stove, and began talking to him in hushed tones. It looked to Jari that his partner was getting an earful. When they came back to the table, Alfred turned to Jari. "This game warden thing puts a new light on it. Sure, it's a gigantic forest, but airplanes? They'll spot us for sure. No strafing or bombing maybe, but right now jail and deportation sounds even worse."

"Hallelujah," Kerttu said. "At last, common sense. Listen to him, Jari. Forget the Taj furs. We'll get by without them."

"Jesus, Kerttu. I already agreed to quit, didn't I? All I'm asking for is six more days. I'll go alone if I have to, but no way am I abandoning those furs." He turned to Alfred. "You do what you have to, now start dealing the cards."

"Don't you dare, Afred Reiger," Kerttu ordered. "We're not done here. Alright, so you get the last furs out. What then? How do we sell them without getting caught? You don't have a license."

The kettle began to scream. Otto made tea, and returned. "There could be a way," he said. "I read an article in MacLean's magazine claiming that while Ontario is tightening up, things are still pretty loose in Quebec. Apparently, 'fur bootleggers' have been buying illegal furs at discount prices here, and selling them to dealers in Val-d'Or; guys who don't ask questions."

"Do they say what kind of discount they take?" Jari asked. "I mean, twenty, fifty, seventy-five percent? Hell, they could take us to cleaners."

Otto shrugged. "No mention. My guess is that it's negotiable, but not negligible. It would hurt. Best to think of it as the cost of doing business, like a tax. Regardless, I've done the math, and I think you're in for a surprise." He looked directly at the girls. "I see Jari with his house and truck, and Alfred in his own bakery."

"Not bad for two foreigners with no papers," Alfred said, with a grin. "But it's still a big step. Maybe best to wait and see if they catch those guys."

Kerttu stared at him. "That's pathetic. Haven't you had enough hiding? Nicole's invested a lot in you. Don't you start getting cold feet on her now with more of that 'wait and see' nonsense. Decisions must be made. Now. If you're having trouble getting started then let me help you. Two questions. Are you Catholic? And are you going to marry Nicole?"

"Kerttu!" Jari cut in. "That's none of your business."

"Isn't it?" she shot back, tapping the table hard with her finger. "Applies to you, too, Jari Hoivuniemi. The sooner you two crawl out from your hidey-holes, the sooner we all get our lives in gear. Isn't it obvious? Having a Canadian wife will be a bonus for both of you." She crossed her arms, her head pivoting from Jari to Alfred. "Just how long do you think Nicole and I plan to wait for you two bushwhackers to get your asses in gear?"

"Jesus, Kerttu," Jari said. "You're pushing Alfred into impossible territory; he hasn't even properly met her father yet."

"So, do it. Now. Hightail it over to her place tomorrow."

"To do what, exactly?"

"Present himself. Have it out with her folks. Apparently, the priest in Jogues is a family friend. Great. He can marry them, quiet and fast. That out of the way, they can skedaddle to some town with lots of foreigners—Timmins, say, or Kirkland Lake, or, if it's blending with other Germans he wants, south to Kitchener. I'll bet there are scads of illegal aliens doing this very thing right now; making hard decisions, and getting their lives in order."

"Stay out of it, Kerttu," Jari snapped. "It's their future you're toying with."

"But I agree," Nicole interrupted, grabbing Alfred's hand. "I've had it with living a lie, and fearing the future. Whatever has to happen will happen. Let's face it. Now."

Her resolve shocked Jari. He had seen her as a nice, quiet girl, but a bit of a lightweight, meek even. One look at Otto told him that the old guy knew better. "What have you got in mind?" Jari asked.

"Talk to my parents. Then go and see the priest. Alfred and I have already decided to get married. We just hadn't figured out how or when. The money from the furs would be a nice, but we can get by without it, if we have to. Everybody else starts with nothing, why not us?"

Kerttu nodded. "Good girl," she said. "But don't dismiss the furs too soon. There's still that shed full of them out back here."

"How about the priest?" Otto asked. "Is it the one I figure you've got in mind?"

Nicole's smile broadened. "Yup. Father Letourneau, and believe me, he won't be saying no." The others looked puzzled. "Letourneau's a nice man. So nice, he couldn't turn his nephew away when he showed up on the run from the RCMP, and the conscription board."

Kerttu slapped the table. "Don't tell me your kindly parish priest actually . . ."

"Yup. He put his nephew up in a cabin on the Kabinakagami River, west of the ACR tracks, and lied like heck when the police came nosing around. Wasn't long before there were three fugitives under his wing. Sometimes, they'd show up at the rectory for a visit. You'd know they were there when the curtains stayed shut. *Maman* cleans house there from time to time. She used to drag me along."

"You actually saw these guys?" Jari asked.

Nicole shook her head. "Not quite, but there were rumours, and we'd hear laughing behind closed doors. Then one day I stumbled on this, and figured it might come in handy some day." She rummaged through her purse for a photograph of a priest and two young men, smiling. One was pointing to a headline in a newspaper that read, "Dragnet Ends: Northern Ontario Cleared of Zombies."

Jari exchanged glances with Alfred. "Think we just found out who the brains are at this table," he said. "And it's not you or me."

"Love it." Kerttu added, rubbing her hands. "So, you got the priest where you want him, what about *maman* and *papa*?"

"They'll just have to get used to the idea, that's all. What will be harder is explaining why we need *Papa's* truck."

"You need your Dad's truck?" Kerttu asked.

"For the furs. It's old and rickety, but it moves."

"My, God," Kerttu said. "Jari and I could go to Quebec to hunt down one of these fur bootleggers, while you guys pack the bales in steamer trunks. Then, arrangements made, you drive them to Hearst and ship them by train. Sound good?"

"Hold on." Jari said. "What about Alfred and me. We get a say in this, or what?"

"If we leave it to you two, it'd be 1950 before anything gets sold," Kerttu said, looking back to Nicole. "What do you think?"

Nicole shook her head. "Don't like the train idea. Part of my hospital job has me ferrying patients to and from the station. The CNR cop is always there, nosing around. Showing up with a bunch of trunks would be sure to prompt questions. Best skip the CNR freight, and take the truck to Quebec."

"I'll go for that," Kerttu responded, slapping the table. "We can hide the furs in among the furniture for the newlyweds. We can even decorate the truck a bit. You know, 'Just Married' kinda stuff. If stopped along the way, you can flash your wedding certificate and look bashful. And Jari and I can follow in my Dad's car. Once done, you two drive off for wherever."

"Let's not get our hopes up," Jari said. "What if Nicole's Dad throws Alfred out on his ass? Or, worse, turns him in?"

Nicole smiled. "Got that covered, too. Dad did pretty well bootleg-ging to the POWs. Last thing he wants is that getting out. I'd never do it, but he doesn't need to know that."

Kerttu was on a role, and when she fixed her gaze on Jari every-one at the table knew where she was headed next. "What?" he said, beginning to redden. No one spoke. They waited. "Okay, Miss Lone-lyheart," he continued, "now that you've got Alfred and Nicole driving off into the sunset in an old truck, I'm guessing your advice to the lovelorn has another chapter."

She nodded, smile growing. "You got that right, Buster. I see one Jari Hoivuniemi tying the knot, and settling down in Hearst."

"How many times have we been over this, Kerttu. You know my answer, the marriage bit suits me to a T, but settling down in Hearst gives me the willies. I'm too well known in town. People are bound to ask questions, and put two and two together."

She shook her head. "A year ago, yes, but no longer. Remember Bikko Lampi and Vaino Kivikangas, the two Hearst boys who left with you to fight in Finland? They got back a week ago. More are arriving every day. Things are returning to normal."

"Okay, we'll give Hearst a try."

"Shake on it," she said, extending her hand.

He looked at it. "A handshake? That's all I get? Alfred got a hug."

"You get your hug when we settle this fur problem."

"Come on Kerttu, with the fur scalpers in Quebec cutting into our profits we need them now more than ever. And stop fretting. We'll be in and out of the bush in a flash. Promise."

22

Coming Out

The Bush,
March 1946

Alfred wouldn't shut up on their way back to Taj. Desperate to get away from hearing once again how Nicole had stood up to her father, Jari skied on ahead. The Reiger-Fontaine showdown had taken place in front of the whole family. Mr. Fontaine adamantly opposed having a German POW for a son-in-law, until his daughter reminded him how he'd had no problem selling to them. Next it was off to the priest, with similar results. The wedding would take place in the vestry attended by family, Nicole's friend Rita, plus the fur adventure crew. Jari would be best man. The date was set for twelve days hence; enough time to slip back to Taj Mahal, fetch the remaining furs, bring in the traps, and get back to Otto's.

Getting Kerttu's and Nicole's blessing to return to Taj had taken some effort. Certainly, the fact that Father Letourneau had to be away for ten days played a role, but mostly it was Jari and Alfred's promise to proceed with speed and caution, and be back in six days, that brought them around.

There had been a mild spell, and with the wet snow, skiing was slow, even pulling empty toboggans. Late in the afternoon of the second day, they picked up the faint sound of an airplane. "Ignore it and keep going," Jari said. "As long as we're in the trees, they won't be able to see us."

"I hate that goddamn noise," Alfred replied.

"Relax, they're not Russian. Just a plane, probably heading down to Hawk Junction, or Chapleau."

"Getting closer," Alfred said, a minute later.

They stopped. Jari pulled his ear lugs up, and like a lynx listening for rabbit movement in the snow, began rotating his head. "Coming in from the west," he said, grabbing Susi by the collar. "Buggers are following the bush trail we're on. Don't move."

"Thought you said this trail was too overgrown for them to see our tracks from the air?"

"They can't, but it's an old path; one they can make out because the trees are younger and shorter."

Suddenly, the roar of pulsating pistons fell silent. "*Scheisse!*" Alfred swore. "They've cut the engine." Each man hugged his tree, and stared up through the branches. Jari had Susi lying flat in the snow. A huge shadow passed over them, then the motor roared back to life. "Think they saw us?" Alfred asked.

"We'll know if he banks and comes back," Jari replied.

They waited. The plane lumbered on. "Missed us, you bastards," Alfred screamed shaking his fist.

"We're not out of the woods yet," Jari replied. "This trail leads straight to Taj. Let's hope last week's snowfall was enough to cover our tracks around the cabin. If not, those guys in the plane will be back."

There wasn't much conversation after that. The sun was beginning to set when they closed in on Taj. Earlier, they had joked about how they'd handle the murderer should he/they be holed up in their camp. But now, as they drew closer, there was no joking. Automatically they spread out, drew their rifles, and moved in lurches from tree to tree. "Well that was stupid," Jari said, as they surveyed the grounds from a distance. "There're no tracks or nothin'. Why'd you pull your gun?"

"You pulled yours first," Alfred chuckled.

"Did not. You were the one who . . . Oh, for Christ's sake, look at that." Ahead, Susi was scratching on the cabin door, and looking back at them impatiently.

Big Ben had them up at 5:00 a.m. the next morning, with Jari outlining the schedule. "I figure nine days to bring in the traps and make it back to Otto's," he said, ladling out the porridge.

"Hold on a sec, that's far longer than we promised the girls."

"Sure, and they'll be pissed off, but nothing we can do about that now. Today, I'll start with the south end of the Taj line, you take the north. Two days should do it. Then it's over to Grinnin. After that, Ledgeview, and then back to Otto's for good. Nine days, max."

"That's cutting it pretty close, Jari. Geez, I'm getting married in eleven. What if we run into problems?"

"Come on."

"Don't give me that, 'come on,' stuff. Lots of things can happen—weather, broken equipment, intruders."

"*Kein sweat*, my friend," Jari replied. "Put your faith in your best man. I'll have you back in scads of time."

The pace was frenzied—up early, home late, bed, sleep, repeat—but productive. The airplane had not returned, and they were ahead of schedule. Four days had Jari dripping confidence, in spite of Alfred's constant fretting. "Will you just relax," Jari kept repeating. "We've got two lines done, haven't we? Tomorrow we head for Ledgeview, and after that it's bye, bye bush, and hello girls."

"Ledgeview," Alfred groaned. "Place still gives me the spooks."

"How come?"

"Do you really have to ask? Aside from memories of my feet, and your asshole reception, it's too close to the Missinaibi for comfort."

"What have you got against the Missinaibi?"

"It's the only place we've ever encountered signs of people."

"Told you before, Alfred. Probably just Indians from up near Mattice."

"Yeah, well, Otto calls that river a highway; one fur rustlers are bound to be using."

"For Godsakes, get that article out of your head. Newspapers always blow things out of proportion. If they didn't nobody would read them."

"Still."

"Still what?" Jari replied, reaching for his parka.

"Still, it's a possibility."

"And that's what's got you tied up in knots? Getting jumped?"

"It's not that, it's what we'd be forced to do about it. Say we did run into rustlers who pulled a gun or something. Wouldn't that leave us with no option but to . . . you know?"

Jari dismissed the question with a wave of the hand, and moved outside to hitch Susi to the toboggan. Hot on his heals, Alfred followed, hoping to continue the conversation. "Ski conditions look good today," was all he got.

"Come on, Jari. What if . . . ?"

"Cut the crap and get your skis on. If we're going to make Ledgeview before dark we gotta get moving."

Sleeping at Ledgeview once again had been a tosser and turner for Alfred. He awoke in the morning, nerves on edge and grumpy. Little was said at breakfast, which made for an extra-early start. By their calculations this was to be the easiest line to bring in. That being the case, the plan was to split up, with each starting at the opposite end of the line, then meeting in the middle for lunch. Alfred's end had slightly more traps, so he took the dog, to whom he talked incessantly, with absolutely no reaction. "You're just as bad as Jari," he grumbled. Susi didn't appear insulted. Only after leaving the point closest to the Missinaibi, with no sign of human activity, nor spotters in the sky, did he begin to relax. The feeling intensified when, last trap on the toboggan, he headed back to the rendezvous point. He arrived first. "What took you so long, old timer?" he said, when Jari finally showed up.

"Up yours."

They brushed the snow off a log, and dug into their lunch. "Let's see if the whisky jacks are about," Jari said, placing raisins in a line on the log. They waited. No birds showed.

"Strange." Alfred said. "They're usually here in a flash. Wonder if somebody else is feeding them."

"Oh, for God's sake, get off it, Reiger. We're home free."

As they drew near to Ledgeview Alfred's thoughts were on that first time, two years earlier, when he'd stumbled down this same trail, frozen of foot and out of hope. He was toying with mentioning this to Jari, and might have, if not for Susi stopping dead in his tracks. The bared teeth, and low, ominous growl had both men on instant alert. No words were spoken. None were needed. Acting on Jari's signal, they unfastened their skis, grabbed their rifles, and moved to opposite sides of the clearing as they approached the shack.

Ledgewood came into view. So did the fur shed and the wide-open door. Two men came out, one in an army greatcoat that looked like something out of the Spanish Civil War, the other in a mackinaw parka with a fur collar. They were carrying fur bales to a half-loaded toboggan, and engaging in idle banter. Alfred was terrified. Not by the rustlers, but by the look in Jari's eyes. He'd seen it often on the faces of soldiers before an attack. Worse, he recognized it in himself; familiar, suppressed, pre-battle sensations were flooding back—tightness in the chest, sharpening of the heartbeat, surreal calm. Here in the wilderness, just like at the Front, they were on their own before the enemy, with absolute freedom to use whatever means they saw fit to defend what was theirs. There would be no witnesses, nor limits. Who would miss two thieves deep in the bush?

Alfred watched Jari raise his rifle. It was his moment to stop him, but he stood mute, awaiting the gun-blast to come. One thief farted, as he bent to place his furs on the pile. They both laughed, and returned for more, each step taking them farther from the guns left propped against their toboggan.

When the solitude was broken, it wasn't by a gun-blast, but by an unrecognizable, high-pitched voice that came from Jari. "Halt!" he screamed, as the rustlers reappeared from the shed, arms full. Fur Collar froze. Great Coat dropped his load and broke for his gun. Jari fired, the explosion echoing off the trees. Great Coat fell, landing halfway to the toboggan.

"Don't shoot! Don't shoot!" Fur Collar screeched, hands pumping the air.

The ringing in his ears brought Alfred back to his senses, but Jari's voice was still up an octave. "On the ground," he ordered, at first in Finn, then in English. Fur Collar went down instantly. Jari pumped another shell into the chamber, and moved closer.

"Jesus, Jari, take it easy," Alfred said. "We don't have to kill them."

He stared at Great Coat, looking for signs of blood. Suddenly, the downed man was on his knees scrambling for his rifle. Jari fired again, dropping the man a second time. "*Gott im Himmel!*" Alfred screamed. "Jari. What have you done?"

Still shouldering his rifle, Jari stepped into the clearing. "*Ei, ei, älätapa häntä, älä tapa häntä,*" he repeated. "*Lopputtava.*"

Alfred had no idea what he was saying. Nor did Fur Collar, who lay whimpering, head in his hands. Great Coat was the concern. Alfred approached, slipped a foot under the body and flipped him on his back. The man's eyes popped open, then blinked. "Sweet Jesus," Alfred sighed, "I was sure you'd killed him."

"I still might."

"Don't be crazy," Alfred replied, switching to German. "Think of Kerttu. Think of our plans. These guys are scared shitless. We take their guns, and send them packing. That'll be enough."

It took a moment for Jari to respond, and when he did, the high pitch had slipped a notch. "Not this guy," he said, taking a kick at Great Coat. "He's dangerous."

"Jari, listen to me," Alfred said, "lower your gun, and go get the fire going in the cabin. I'll lock these two in the shed. Then we can decide what's to be done. Okay?"

Surprisingly, Jari did as he was told. Alfred waited for the door of the cabin to close, before herding the prisoners into the shed and barricading the door. That done, he unharnessed Susi from the toboggan, and tied him to a tree. "This dog's a killer," he shouted. "And he's on a long leash. I wouldn't even think about trying to break out." Then, turning to Susi: "Rip 'em apart if they come through that door, fella." The dog licked his hand and panted.

Even when they had the stove roaring Alfred held his tongue. In time they might address what had just happened, but there was a lot of coming down to get through before that could happen. Thankfully, the intruders where still alive, in spite of the killer instincts that had come roaring back.

Jari watched his German friend take down two mugs, and uncork the last of the schnapps. "When I fired," he said, "it was only for show.

I aimed away. No way would I have missed If I'd intended to kill them. You know that, eh?"

Alfred was far from sure, but was comforted by the near return of the familiar voice. "No explaining needed, Jari. You weren't alone out there. I felt it, too. I just happened to come out of it faster. Question is, what do we do now?"

Jari downed his schnapps, and refilled his glass. "There's an easy solution, and a hard one."

"Meaning?"

"Let these guys go and they'll only come after us."

"So what? We've got their guns. What could they do?"

"They're desperate. Those furs are a goldmine. Set them free and they'll find a way, especially, Great Coat. Sure as hell he's a war vet."

"For God's sake, we can't leave them to freeze to death in the shed."

Jari gulped down his schnapps, and poured a third glass, his hand still shaking, but less so now. "Yeah, you're probably right," he replied, after a moment, "but they don't know that. Best keep it that way. For now, anyway."

"Suppose we give them half the furs if they agree to go east, to the Missinaibi?" Alfred suggested.

"You actually believe those assholes would settle for that?"

"They can't haul any more than that. They only have one toboggan."

"What's to prevent them caching them, and coming after us for the remainder?"

"We'll have their guns."

Outside, they could hear their prisoners shouting, and banging for release. Jari grabbed his rifle, opened the door, and fired. Instantly, the noise ceased. He returned to the table, put the top back on the bottle, and paced. "Okay," he said, "maybe what you say is not so stupid. If any cops were looking for them, a trail going east is the one they'd follow."

Alfred nodded. "Agreed," he said. "How be we let them cool off a bit while we eat. After that we'll bring them in for the night, and take turns standing guard."

They were on the trail before daylight the next morning, but not before tying each prisoner to a chair, and topping up the stove. "How long you figure before they break out?" Alfred asked, when they were well under way.

"I give them an hour. After that they'll be wanting to cook and eat. I doubt they'll come after us, but even if they do, we'll have a good two-hour head start. My guess is they'll grab what we've left, and figure they've gotten away Scot-free."

"Hated to leave those furs behind."

"Don't worry about it," Jari replied, moving ahead and upping the pace. "We took the best ones."

The hours passed, with Alfred keeping pace, and trying to come up with a way to broach what happened yesterday without setting his friend off. About mid-morning he couldn't hold it any longer. "Know what Otto asked me to do?" he said. Not unexpectedly there was no response, but he pressed on. "Keep an eye on you. He's worried you're not quite ready for town living—too many people, too many chances for . . ."

"Otto's an old man!"

"Yeah. But a smart one. He's seen a lot."

"So?"

"So, after yesterday with those guys, and as a friend, I got to wondering what your thoughts might be, that's all." Silence. "Come on Jari, we're just talking here. I ask a question and you answer. It's called conversation."

"It's called prying," Jari shot back, upping the pace and increasing the gap. Alfred let him go, but twenty minutes later when he rounded a bend in the trail, there he was up ahead, sitting atop the fur load, snowshoes off, face buried in his hands. Susi lay at his feet. Alfred slowed as he approached, not sure what to do, other than shut up and wait.

"Convalescing in Helsinki," Jari began, without looking up, "the staff did their best to buck us up. Figuring we were terrified of going back to the Front, the doctors preached the gospel of good cheer. The nurses were into it too, prancing about with their phony smiles, fluffing up pillows, applying ointment to our bed sores. The harder they tried, the flatter it fell—for me at least. But it wasn't fear of dying that had me by the balls, it was the rush that comes from the killing. I was addicted to it. I mean, shit, with a gun in your hands, and licence to shoot your problems into oblivion, you're God. It's the ultimate solution, and it had a hold on me. So right there in that convalescent home, I vowed to overcome it. Twelve hours later I'd killed again. Why? Because, when Korpi walked back into my life, the easy solution took hold. I didn't even mull it over, it just came naturally."

"Jari," Alfred said, "I won't lie to you. Yesterday I felt the same urge as you. It was tempting. We could have done anything we wanted, but we didn't, did we? Even with the adrenaline pumping we held on. Know what that says? That Otto's wrong. About you and about me. We're both ready to face the world."

"But I wanted to. If you hadn't been there . . . What do I do next time, when you're not around?"

"Why would there be a next time? Your war's over. Mine, too."

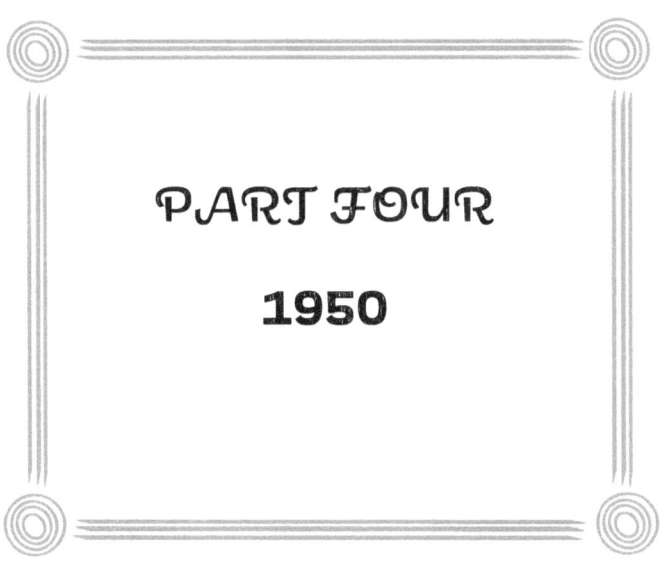

PART FOUR

1950

23

Strike

Toronto,
April 1950

Where'd you put the mail?" Sami shouted from the living room. He'd been reading a bedtime story to Sami Junior, but the boy had fallen asleep before he was halfway through.

"On the hall table," Carola answered from the kitchen. She put the last of the dinner dishes in the cupboard, and ambled in to join him. Eight months into her second pregnancy and movement was slow. "Oh, you found it," she said, looking at her husband, who stood frowning at one of the letters. "Something wrong?"

"What? No. Nothing. Bills, mostly."

She eased herself into the armchair. "There was one there that piqued my curiosity," she said. "Strange envelope. Square and large, like you seldom see these days. Kinda old worldish. And no stamp; like someone delivered it by hand. What's that one all about?"

Sami felt his stomach roll. Ignoring Carola, he fled to the bathroom. It was happening. Contact. After five years of silence, the agency that had smuggled him into the country, and set him up, now wanted their quid pro quo. Hard-suppressed memories of what he'd done behind enemy lines, ones that surfaced usually in the wee small hours, began scrolling through his head. He cursed the oath he'd made to the GRU. Why were they doing this? The war was long over, the Germans vanquished. What was the point? He knew of course. There was a new war raging. Something the newspapers were calling a cold war.

When he hadn't reappeared after several minutes she rose and knocked on the bathroom door. "What is it, Sami?" She pressed. "It's that letter, isn't it?"

He opened the door and rushed past her. "I have to go out," he said.

The park where Sami junior played was a half block up the street. Dark and deserted at this time of day, Sami had it to himself. Running to a tree as far from the sidewalk as he could get, he puked, swabbed his chin with a handkerchief, and moved to the swing close to the street lamp, where he sat down, and reread the letter. Only a Vorobyevo graduate would fully get the implications of the message: "Toronto Union Station, Front Street, 2:00 p.m., Saturday. Wear green shirt and red tie. Carry teddy bear. Contact will ask, who's the lucky child? Reply, my sister's boy in Sturgeon Falls."

He began to sob. The reference to Sturgeon Falls said it all: while he'd been settling in, forgetting his past, and growing a family, they'd been monitoring his every move, right down to the in-laws. The taste of vomit that remained in his mouth had him puking again. When the heaving finally stopped, he walked to the fountain and splashed water on his face. The taste lingered. "Life Savers," he mumbled to himself. "Spearmint. They'll do the trick." He headed for Gerrard Street and the nearest corner store.

"You've been a busy boy, Agent Sami," the contact said the next afternoon, as they walked west on Front Street. "Goodness: wife, in-laws, one baby, and another on the way. All unapproved, and counter to policy, of course."

"Others have married."

"Correct, but invariably within the agency. We're a family. You've strayed. They're not happy about this in Moscow. You could be recalled. Unless . . ."

"What do you want?" Sami interrupted.

"You're being offered a chance to redeem yourself. Pass this test and you stay. Mess it up and you go home."

"Spell it out."

"Seems there's a call for someone with your specialty."

"My specialty?" Sami replied, struggling to hang on. "What's that?"

"Come, come, Agent Sami, don't pretend you have no idea. Or, have you gone so native it's slipped your mind? Why do you think you were stationed here?"

A cold chill swept over him. They'd never come out and told him explicitly what they expected when he joined, but he'd had his suspicions. Now he knew for sure. He took a deep breath and straightened his shoulders. "Get to the point," he said.

"There's labour unrest in Northern Ontario."

"I read the papers. I thought that was to our advantage."

"Normally, yes, but this time there's a problem."

"You're saying the puck's not rolling our way."

"Puck?"

It was a small victory, but it felt good to score one over on this asshole. The agent was obviously new to Canada. Sami resolved to throw him off with a few more Canadian expressions he'd picked up from his co-workers at Tippet and Richardson. "Never mind," he said, "just get it out. Be specific."

"Truckers refusing to haul wood unless they get a raise from the lumber companies. They're trying to form a union."

"I'm still baffled. How's that not good for our side?"

"The capitalist lumber barons have hired a union basher."

Sami felt the sweat ticking down from his armpits and wished he hadn't worn such a heavy jacket. Although he saw where this was going, he asked, "Where do you see me fitting in? I know nothing about unions."

"Don't need to. Your assignment is to take care of the union basher. His name is Paavo Kekkonen, and he's from Sudbury. Heard of him?" Sami shook his head. "He's a White Finn bent on blunting our progress. We've been subtly trying to nudge people to our way of thinking; get more pro-communists elected to government positions. Sometimes trouble makers like Kekkonen get in the way, and have to be taken care of."

"They'll just replace him."

"We hope so. Fact is, we're counting on it. And we've just the man ready to step in. Another Finn, of course, but Red like us. Before the war, we had a good thing going in Northern Ontario, but this guy Kekkonen's so popular we're losing converts up there. He has to be stopped and fast."

Sami spied a bench and made a beeline for it. The handler caught up and sat down. "You don't seem quite up to this."

"Couldn't you get somebody else this time? I've got a wife and kids."

"If you're turning down the assignment, I'll let Moscow know right away." The agent let the implication set in. "Well?"

"Gimme the details," Sami groaned."

"What? I didn't hear you."

"I said give me the GODDAMN details." It was a mistake to react this way, and Sami knew it. He took a moment to calm himself. "You want me to go to Sudbury. What else?" he said, in a level voice.

The agent shook his head. "Not Sudbury, Hearst. That's where it's hot at the moment, and that's where you'll find him. They're planning a rally up there which Kekkonen is apparently intending to interrupt, probably with the help of a gang of OPP goons."

"And I'm to get to him first, I suppose." The agent nodded. "Why not just buy him off? Maybe, Kekkonen has a price. Give me the money and I'll talk to him."

The agent gave him a blank stare. "What a fucked-up idea! Pay the guy once and he'd be blackmailing us forever. That's if he didn't run to the police about Soviets interfering in Canadian affairs. Do that and the RCMP would have our embassy shut down, and you in jail, in a flash. Stupid. I warned the agency about you, but they were all for giving you a chance."

"What do mean warned them? What is it you think you know about me?"

"Everything, it's all in your file. If you want that cozy little family of yours to bloom and prosper, you'd better not mess this up. Do we understand each other?"

Sami nodded. The agent began to rhyme off the instructions. "We're giving you a car so you can get around without drawing attention to yourself. You're to find Kekkonen, take care of him, then get out. It's that simple. Get caught, and you're on your own. There'll be some extra cash in the glove compartment to cover expenses, plus a revolver."

"You want me to shoot him?"

"Not necessarily. Think of the gun as a last resort; in case of emergency. Making Kekkonen's death look like an accident would be best. Do a good job and there will be a bonus waiting for you back here.

Mess up and . . . well, you get the picture. And one more thing. Your chequing account at the Imperial Bank. The one the GRU set up for you and has been depositing your salary in for six years. You've never touched it. Why's that?"

"I have my own income from work."

"Fine," he shrugged. "Just remember, trying to be independent doesn't release you from your oath. You're a GRU sleeper. You're one of us, and that's the way it's going to stay. Got it?"

A street car squealed to a stop and a number of people got off. Sami used the opportunity to collect himself. "When do you expect this to happen?" he mumbled, when the street car pulled away.

"You leave tomorrow."

"What? I can't possibly . . ."

The agent shook his head as he continued. "You'll find a black Ford sedan in front of that park you puked in last night." With that he handed Sami the keys, and walked away.

Thanks to his job at Tippet & Richardson Sami had a driver's licence, and knew his way around the city. He also knew a bit about Ontario highways. Not so difficult considering there were only a handful worthy of the name. Getting to Hearst would be easy; all he had to do was head north on Yonge Street, follow it up through Hog's Hollow, where it turned into King's Highway No. 11, and keep going—six-hundred miles. The journey would require two days, taking into account the slowdown for villages and the gravel surface on the road north of New Liskeard, the halfway point. All-in-all, he was expecting the highway to be a darn sight better than anything he'd travelled on in Russian Karelia.

The excuse he'd given Carola had gone over like the proverbial lead balloon. He longed to lay everything out, but feared the consequences for her and the kids should he fail. Deciding it was best that she knew nothing, he had concocted a story about Tippet and Richardson sending him north to meet with prospective clients. He'd be gone ten days.

The prospect of living the lie in perpetuity haunted him as he drove. His mind went down several avenues of possible outcomes, and their repercussions. Maybe he could appeal to the RCMP, like that guy, Igor

Gouzenko, who defected from the Russian Embassy back in Ottawa, in 1945. They'd given him a new identity, replete with a whole new life. Problem was, that would require giving them his real name. How long would it take before they linked him back to atrocities committed behind the lines in Finland? On paper, the Canadians shouldn't really care what he'd done in that war because Russia had been the ally, and Finland the enemy. But already that was reversing itself—countries, like lovers, seemed prone to changing partners in new situations. Besides, shooting soldiers in the back, regardless of whose side you were on, was never going to win any sympathy. In all likelihood he'd be shipped back to Finland to face a firing squad.

No matter how hard he banged the steering wheel, he couldn't come up with a plausible, long-term solution. In the end he decided to concentrate on completing the task at hand as expeditiously as possible. For justification he reminded himself that Kekkonen was out to make life tough for the working man, and even though he no longer considered himself a communist, he was still a socialist. Problem was, it didn't seem to carry the weight it once had.

His Toronto handler had been firm that he should execute his task in the shadows. Was that possible? He had only a blurred photograph of Mr. Kekkonen. How would he recognize the man, let alone corner and snuff him out? Just to find his whereabouts and timetable, called for some exposure. It was a logistical nightmare. The more he thought about it, the more he got the feeling that he was being set up. Maybe Moscow had concluded that having gone rogue, they wanted him gone, and were sending him up north where some White Finn, maybe even Kekkonen himself, was waiting to assassinate him. One thing was certain: this was not going to end well. But whatever lay ahead, his family came first. Somehow, he had to come up with a way to see to that.

By the time he was driving through Powassen he'd narrowed his course of action to three possibilities. The first was see the mission through, go home, lie to Carola, and try to pick up where he'd left off. But the downside to a "successful" mission would surely result in continuous calls for repeat performances, not to mention never-ending guilt. Option two saw him, and his family, going off the grid.

According to the papers there was lots of this taking place—displaced persons sneaking into the country and disappearing. This, too, called for life-altering changes—relocating every few months, and severing ties with family and friends. Then there was option three—suicide. Dead, and out of the way, what would the Russians gain by retaliating against his family? Reasonable assumption, but when did the GRU ever act reasonably? In all probability they'd go ahead anyway, if only as a deterrent to other agents.

The common denominator in all three options was provision for Carola and the kids. Slowly, a plan began to form in his mind. The chequing account at the Imperial Bank, the one the contact agent had referred to, was foremost in his thoughts. By now, it was bound to show a substantial balance to which he had full rights. He assumed that some bank employee was being paid to keep an eye on it for the GRU, so he would have to plan carefully, in order for Carola to be able to access it, should anything happen to him.

By the time he reached Ferris, on the outskirts of North Bay, he had decided on a course of action. Step one called for immediately withdrawing the GRU money from the bank. But, checking his watch, he saw that it was late in the day, meaning he would have to stay over and wait for the banks to reopen at 10 in the morning. Scanning the road for a suitable place to spend the night, he spied a chip wagon under a sign with an arrow pointing to Little Joe's Cabins, across the street. Rolling down the window, he signalled, and pulled in. A little person with a broad smile and an outstretched hand, came out of the office. "Just call me Joe," he welcomed.

Both the money withdrawal, and departure from North Bay, went swimmingly, as Carola might say. Changing into third gear as he climbed the big hill north of the city, he was quite pleased with himself. Realizing that withdrawing all the money would set off alarm bells, he had opted to leave a little in. But now, as he drove through the Temagami Forest, he began to sweat over the large amount of cash stowed in his suitcase. It was essential to find a place for the money where Carola could access it, without being detected. Haileybury and New Liskeard offered banking possibilities, but he still hadn't worked out the logistics, so kept on driving. Ditto, Kirkland Lake and Cochrane. By the time he was crossing over the hydro dam at Smooth Rock Falls, he realized his options were petering out. Hearst was a bad idea, because the Russians would be sure to search there first. That left Kapuskasing, but when he got there he discovered that, once again, he was too late and the bank had closed—this time for the weekend. Having no option, he continued on to Hearst.

24

Retribution Interrupted

Hearst,
April 1950

Kerttu stuck her head out the front door. She and Jari had owned their house for four years now, but there was still a ton of improvements to be made. "Time to clean up and get ready," she called. "That culvert can wait."

Jari leaned on the shovel and sighed. His objective had been to get the culvert in today, but the wet weather had worked against him. Still, unfinished or not, he was pleased with the way things were turning out. With money from the furs, plus Kerttu's savings, they had managed to buy a used, ten-ton truck, and a tiny house on Prince Street. Lacking access to the driveway—deep ditches being the town's answer to storm sewers—he'd been parking the truck on the street. This, of course, was far from popular with the neighbours, who viewed his big rig as an eyesore, not to mention a potential hazard. Swiping his wet face with his sleeve, he headed in. Kerttu held the door open for him.

"I'm still not convinced that going to this meeting is wise," he said.

"For crying out loud, Jari, you don't have to skulk around town any more. People know you. You're accepted. This meeting's as important to you as to the other drivers. They're counting on solidarity. And that includes you."

"Yeah, yeah," he answered, taking off his boots and wet togs.

The strike was now into its third week and the truckers had called a meeting for 4:00 o'clock at the Finn Hall, out on the lake road. Word was, they had a feisty speaker coming up from Sudbury.

She followed him into the bathroom and sat on the edge of the tub, watching him as he shaved. "Ran into Mr. Ranta at the grocery store yesterday," she said. "We talked."

"Good to see a farmer still willing to talk to a striker's wife," he answered, tipping his head back and scraping at his chin. "What's his take on the situation?"

"Getting desperate, but who can fault him. Like most settlers, he's worked his backside off all winter cutting spruce on his land, and now can't get it hauled to the mill. With the clay roads, and frost coming out of the ground in a few weeks, they'll soon be impassable. Feel sorry for him. Could be a long time before guys like Ranta get their logs delivered and get paid."

"So, he's bitter?"

"Surprisingly, no. He's sees our side, too. What bugs him is the way the mill owners are using the farmers to force the drivers to back down; as if you guys are supposed to show pity on the farmers and give up, or something."

Jari washed the last of the shaving cream off his face and reached for the towel. "Old tactic," he said. "Drive a wedge between your adversaries and claim the day."

"Well, Mr. Ranta is pretty unhappy. He plans to attend today's meeting. A lot of the farmers do."

"Hmm," Jari said. "Could get ugly. Hope the organizers showed enough sense to have a police presence."

"Oh, yeah," Kerttu replied. "Word in the store yesterday was that the OPP were pulling in reinforcements from Kapuskasing and Long Lac."

"You sure you want to come to the meeting, Kerttu? It could get out of control."

"Damn right I do. And I'm sitting right up there in the cab with you in the haulers parade through Hearst after, too. It's Saturday night, with the stores open and the town packed. I want them to see us together."

"Let's hope the parade comes off."

"Promise me this, Jari: things get ugly, you stay out of it. You can't afford to get arrested."

Jari smiled. "How could I do anything but, with you riding herd on me."

"*Jumalouta,*" Jari exclaimed, as he parked the truck down the road from the hall. "Hell of a turnout." He jumped down from the cab, opened the umbrella, and walked around to Kerttu's side. Ahead of them, truckers and farmers, men and women, were hurrying for the warmth of the Finn Hall. The truckers had arrived in their big ten-wheelers, the farmers in a mix of cars and horse-drawn wagons. Jari nodded to Armand Cloutier and Yvon Morrissette, two guys he'd shared hauling contracts with in the past. Ahead of them, Oskar Multamaki, a White Finn, was having words with Eero Suvi, a Red. Jari steered Kerttu across the road to avoid them. "You suppose they're talking the strike, or having one more go at the Civil War?" he joked.

"Who knows," Kerttu replied, shaking her head. "Could be either, or both. This is a political meeting after all."

"No! It's not. I wouldn't be here if it was. It's about economics. The farmers want to get their wood hauled, and we'll only do it if the mill owners give us a raise. Christ, with the price of lumber soaring they can afford it. Our costs—gas, maintenance, insurance—have sure as hell gone up."

"Easy boy," she said. "You don't have to convince me."

The mix of smells on entering the hall—wet wool, stale beer, old smoke—had Kerttu hesitating at the door. "What's wrong?" he asked, taking her aside.

"It's the memories—drinking, yelling, fighting; sometimes with the puukkos out. I just realized how much I don't miss this place."

"Want to wait in the truck?"

She shook her head. "Not on your life."

The quality of the air wasn't bothering Jari. His attention had gone to the faces and languages in the packed hall. To his delight, he took in a mix of French, Finn, Ukrainian, and English. Homesteaders sat with straight backs, their faces a blend of determination to promote their cause, in spite of having the least leverage in this fight. Two policemen stood inside the door, and two more on either side, halfway up the room. Arms crossed, they scanned the crowd for troublemakers. Two truck leaders were seated at the table up front, one on each side of the man Jari assumed to be tonight's star attraction, Kekkonen.

Kekkonen was introduced, and took the floor. "We're all working men here," he began, "so let's clear the air right away. I was once a communist, but now support the CCF party of Canada. This quarrel should not be between farmers and haulers. Both sides are getting a raw deal at the hands of the mill owners. What I recommend is that the truckers get the farmers' wood out to the all-season roads right away. Pile it there for hauling to the mills when, and only when, the mill owners come around. Don't haul anybody else's wood, and don't allow any of your brothers to do so, either. Let me detail what I have in mind."

The speech that followed was a barn burner. Jari was impressed. The police relaxed. A new perspective had been added to the mix, one that saw farmers and truckers united in common cause. Jari had put his arm around Kerttu's shoulder and had turned to survey the reaction of the crowd behind, when his eyes fell on a face from the past. He froze, his hand squeezing Kerttu's shoulder so tightly, she squirmed, and when that didn't work, elbowed him in the ribs. Jari had gone stiff. He began to curse.

"Shush," she said. "What the heck's gotten into you?"

"Impossible!" he mumbled. "It can't be."

Turning to push his hand away, she couldn't miss the pain, confusion, and rage on his face. "Talk to me, Jari," she said, in a hushed voice.

"That . . . man," he said, between short breaths, "the one standing beside Nelson Hatch. It's him."

"Him who?"

"Sorsakoski! Alvar Sorsakoski!"

Kekkonen must have said something sensational because suddenly the audience was on its feet, clapping and shouting. Seconds later, the meeting was over, and they were heading out to their trucks to get the parade going. Jari jumped to his feet, but by the time he'd made it outside, Sorsakoski was nowhere in sight. Trucks were firing up. He raced back and forth looking in windows, wiping the rain from his eyes, but no sign of Sorsakoski. Several people spoke to him. He breezed past, ignoring them.

When Kerttu got to their truck, she found him slumped forward with his head on the steering wheel. She opened the passenger door, climbed up and took a deep breath. "It's been seven years, Jari. I'm sure you're wrong. It's probably just someone who resembles Sorsakoski. Happens all the time."

He raised his head. "No way. That face is etched in my brain like a Robert Capa war photograph. A hundred years couldn't erase it."

"What are you going to do?"

"My duty."

"Which is?"

"You know damn well; fulfill my oath to the Vatanens for the murder of their sons. Avenge Teemu and Kimi."

Kerttu sagged in her seat. "That's crazy. You can't be serious? How much are you willing to risk, to keep a seven-year-old promise made in a lost cause?"

"That's not in the equation."

"Isn't it? You do realize this could spell the end. For you. For us. For everything we're trying to build. They still hang people for murder in this country."

"They'd have to catch me first."

"Oh, great! Run for the rest of your life? Go back to Taj Mahal? Is that it? Be reasonable, darling, you did everything right: went home to Finland in their hour of need, stayed on for the sequel to the Winter War, came back to Canada, beat off the demons, and got yourself straightened around. Do you really want to throw it all away?"

"I'll make it look like an accident."

Kerttu took a deep breath. "This is nuts. Think. If it really was Sorsakoski, he's probably here with Kekkonen. They'll be eating together and sharing a room at the Queen's Hotel, or wherever. What are you going to do? Rush in and kill them both? And what about burying the past and turning another page? Or was that just talk?"

The last truck pulled out around them, eager to catch up to the cavalcade. It was Ben Cloutier and his wife. They honked, but Jari and Kerttu ignored them. After a few minutes, Jari started the engine. "An oath is an oath," he said. "Right now, I'm taking you home"

"Then what?" she sighed.

"Find him."

"What about the parade?"

"Screw it!"

"Oh, I see, promise made to new life and friends, not to mention your wife, takes second place to some ridiculous oath 'sealed in blood.' How primitive is that?" When he failed to respond, Kerttu threw herself back in her seat, and crossed her arms. "Fine. Take me home. Throw our lives away."

She was gripping the phone so tightly her fingers had gone white. "Kerttu," Alfred said, at his end of the line. "Good to hear your voice. It's been too long."

"Forgive me," she said in a weak voice. "I shouldn't be bothering you this late at night. Did I get you out of bed?"

He checked his watch—9:30 p.m. "Pyjamas on, but not in bed yet. Folks in the bakery business go down early, even on a Saturday night. What's up?"

"It's Jari. I'm . . ." she stopped, to get herself under control.

Alfred straightened. Across the room Nicole watched him, concern spreading across her face. "Take your time, Kerttu," he said, cupping the phone and whispering to Nicole.

"Something dreadful has happened. Jari hasn't come home. I don't know what to do. I'm terrified."

"Terrified? About what? What's going on?"

"Does the name Sorsakoski mean anything to you? Jari ever mention him?"

Alfred plunked himself down on the chesterfield and took a deep breath. "Yes," he replied, "at length. Never voluntarily, until the end of our time at Taj, but in the early days, when he still raved in his sleep, that name came out often. When I'd ask him about it, he'd clam up. Get real furious, too. Only after the nightmares stopped would he talk about it. Don't tell me those dreams are back?"

"Worse. Sorsakoski showed up . . . here. In person."

"In Hearst? Impossible! The guy was a soldier in the Russian Army. Gotta be a mistake."

"Jari's positive. We were at the Finn Hall to hear a speaker from Sudbury, and Jari swears he saw him standing at the back. Fortunately, the room was packed, and by the time Jari got outside he was gone.

That was five hours ago. He's been out looking for him ever since."

"Surely, you don't think he's going to . . . ?"

"Yes! He is! Says he's honour-bound. Has no choice. Won't listen to reason."

"What about your father? Maybe he can talk him out of it."

"Not a chance! Dad's so goddamned White he'd kill Sorsakoski himself if he knew the full story."

"How about the police? Go to them. Explain everything to that OPP guy, Griffin."

"Can't, and you know why. One look at Jari's papers and they'll have him on a boat back to Finland."

"Griffin's a good guy, he'd understand. Maybe even put Sorsakoski behind bars. Or Jari too, for that matter, before he does something really stupid." He stopped to listen to something Nicole was saying. "Hold on a second, Kerttu."

Kerttu could make little out of the muffled conversation. When he finally came back on she said, "Sorry to drag you into this, Alfred."

"We'd be upset if you hadn't," he replied. "Listen, Nicole and I just had a quick family conference. I'm coming up. Don't argue. Hearst's not that far from Kirkland. I should pull in no later than five tomorrow morning. Meanwhile, it's important to contact Otto. Nicole will phone her dad to go fetch him and bring him to your place. Otto's a rock. Jari trusts him."

"This isn't fair to you two. What about the bakery?"

"Not to worry. Nicole'll stay behind to work with the young lad I've been training. She can bring the baby to the shop. He loves it there."

It was still dark when Alfred pulled in. As he entered, he could see Jari and Otto staring into their coffee mugs at the kitchen table. "Thank God he showed up," he whispered to Kerttu at the door. "Please tell me he hasn't done anything stupid."

She shook her head. "Couldn't find Sorsakoski."

Alfred moved to the table and sat down. Otto greeted him with a handshake, Jari nodded. Kerttu handed him a coffee.

"We're just working out a plan," Otto said. "Come sunup, I'm going to make the rounds of the hotels. I know the night clerks at the Queen's and the Palace. Considering the dodgy credentials you two are carrying, best I go alone."

"And if you find him?" Alfred asked.

Otto shrugged. "To be decided, but I'm guessing I won't. Jari spent half the night on lookout at the Waverley where Kekkonen is staying, but no sign of Sorsakoski."

Jari looked over at Otto. "Don't you dare come back here saying you haven't found him if you have," he snapped.

Otto put his mug down and leaned forward. "I wouldn't do that, even if I think what you've got in mind is crazy. To me it's just more of that old-world nonsense you and Alfred spent months struggling to get out of your systems. Makes me sick. Every bit of it."

Two hours later Otto returned. "It appears nobody has laid eyes on anyone answering the name Sorsakoski, or the description. And that includes Kekkonen."

"You talked to him?" Jari asked.

"We had coffee at the Waverley. He's an early riser. Doesn't know a Sorsakoski, but was interested. Not that I told him much. Said he'd keep an eye out, just in case. By the way, did you know there's to be a second meeting this afternoon at the Orange Hall in town? Seems yesterday's was such a success they want Kekkonen to do a repeat. To hear him tell it, sounds like he bridged a real gap between farmers and haulers."

Jari raised his head at the news. "Is it possible that Sorsakoski's stalking Kekkonen? If so, he's sure to come nosing around the meeting."

"Give it up, Jari," Kerttu said, moving to the sink.

Alfred followed her with his empty cup. "Otto and I won't let him out of our sight," he whispered.

"And if Sorsakoski shows up? What then?"

"Nothing's going to happen, Kerttu. We won't let it."

"Huh!"

"You don't sound convinced."

"If you really think you two can stop him, you don't know my Jari."

They parked across from the Orange Hall long before the doors opened. Aside from churchgoers on the way home for Sunday dinner, there wasn't much traffic on the street. The three men sat in silence on the front bench of Alfred's delivery van, Jari wedged in the middle. It took several minutes for Alfred to notice the sign on the building in front of them. "Holy crow," he said. "That's Chalykoff's office. He's the doctor who treated me at the Newago camp, that time I put an axe in my foot. What if he recognizes me? I'm just as illegal as Jari."

"Shut up," Jari said. People were beginning to drift into the hall. A few yards ahead a black Ford sedan had stopped to let a group of men cross the street. "*Perkele*, it's him. Sorsakoski."

"You sure?" Otto asked.

They watched as the car eased ahead and parked. Jari nudged Otto to open the door and let him out. "Move, goddamn it!" he ordered.

Otto didn't budge. Alfred grabbed Jari's arm in a firm grip. "Listen to me," he said. "Back at Taj you used to brag about a sergeant Keltamaki. What was it he used to say? 'Take stock before you commit, then go with a plan,' was it? Well, that's what's about to happen right now. You and I are going to sit tight while Otto approaches Sorsakoski."

"To do what? Warn him off?"

"To talk him up. Friendly local, welcoming him to town, sort of thing. Then, when Otto waves to us, you stroll up and slide into the back seat. Got it? Good. Now give Otto a cigarette."

"He doesn't smoke."

"Just do it!"

Alfred and Jari watched Otto stroll past the car, the unlit cigarette in his mouth. He stopped, fumbled in his pocket for a match. Finding none, he approached the car and tapped on the window. The window came down, and a small packet of matches was handed out. Otto lit the cigarette and puffed hard. At the exact instant he handed the matches back, he waved to the others, and reached in and unlocked the back door. Before Sorsakoski realized what was happening, Alfred was in the back seat and had him by the neck. The others piled in, Otto in the passenger seat, Jari in the rear.

"Listen carefully," Otto said. "When my big friend behind you lets go of your neck, you take a deep breath and start the car. Move out slowly. I'll tell you where to go. Got it?"

Sorsakoski gasped, coughed and followed instructions. The first left turn had them passing the high school, the second, the hospital. The last turn, right, had them heading south on 9th Street, over the wooden bridge and out of town. Otto craned his neck to check through the rear window. "No commotion behind," he said. "Nobody noticed."

"Why are you doing this?" Sorsakoski rasped. "You said I could do it in my own way and time."

"Shut up!" Jari ordered, from the back, as they passed the cemetery. "We'll do the talking."

But Sorsakoski wasn't giving up. "It doesn't make sense," he stammered. "Why would you send me all the way up here, just to stop me before I even had a chance to prove myself? If it's about the bank withdrawal, I can explain."

Alfred was concentrating on Jari, ready to grab him should he attempt something stupid. Jari sat ramrod still, glaring at Sorsakoski. No one spoke. Loose gravel pinged off the rocker panels. Puzzling to Alfred, was how in the short while it took to reach the Bradlo cutoff, Sorsakoski's state of mind had altered from confusion to terror, and finally to resignation.

Jari was having trouble with this, too. "This asshole has no idea what's going on," he said.

Otto motioned Jari to be quiet. "What exactly did you mean by, 'bank withdrawal, and a chance to prove yourself?'" he asked.

Sorsakoski relaxed. "Oh, I get it now," he said. "This is a test of my resolve. Whew, you had me going there for a while."

"Just answer the damn question," Otto pressed. "Get what done? And how?"

Sorsakoski frowned. His face paled again. "Just what our people told me back in Toronto. As for the how, that was supposed to be my decision. Your instructions were clear: get it done, however I saw fit, and there'd be no questions. After that, I get to go home to my family."

"What is this shit?" Jari demanded. "We got the guy. We know what we have to do. The less he talks, the easier it's going to be."

"Easy on the 'we,'" Otto replied. "Alfred and I never agreed to back you on this. Block your ears if you don't like what you're hearing, but I need answers, beginning with who he is."

Alfred tapped Sorsakoski on the shoulder. "You heard the man, he wants to know your name?"

"Sami Aalto."

Jari exploded. "Fucking, lying, Russian bastard. Your name's Alvar Sorsakoski and everyone in this car knows it. Personally, I don't give a shit what brings you to Hearst. All I know is that you're the asshole who infiltrated my unit in Finland, and wiped out my whole platoon. You and that Tuomas Korpi prick. Woulda killed me and Mika, too, if we hadn't lagged behind to take a piss."

"No! This is all a mistake. You got the wrong person. I was born in Oregon. Now I live in Toronto. Sure, I speak Finn, but it's my parents who come from Finland, not me. I've never even been there." He looked at Otto. "You, older guy, surely, can see I'm telling the truth?"

"You'll have to do better than that," Otto replied.

The rain had started again, running across the road and collecting in the potholes. The windshield wipers made a strange whining sound with each swipe. Sami, oblivious to the road conditions, didn't bother trying to avoid the potholes. His full attention was now focused on the rear-view mirror, and Jari.

"Say something in Finn," Jari demanded.

"What? Say what?"

"I don't give a shit what. Anything. Just talk."

He hadn't completed his first sentence when Jari cackled. "Nice try with the Helsinki accent, but not good enough to hide the Karelian." Jari reached over the seat and slapped him hard on the side of the head. "Your name's Alvar Sorsakoski, and your past just caught up with you. My vow of retribution is about to be fulfilled."

Sami gasped. "It was you," he said in a low voice.

"Me what?"

"You killed Korpi?"

"You got that right."

"You did the world a favour."

"I think so, but the job's only half done my friend," Jari said.

Coming into Jogues, Otto ordered Sami to pull in at the general store. "Gotta get word to Kerttu," he said. "They let me use the phone here, as long as I leave a dime. You should speak to her, too, Jari. Come on."

"No! She'll only try to talk me out of it."

Kerttu picked up the phone on the first ring. With other customers in the store within hearing distance, Otto kept the details to a minimum.

"And you're certain it's Sorsakoski?" she asked.

"No doubt about it. He even asked about that other guy, Korpi"

"Holy cow, Otto, you gotta put a stop to this."

"I'm not sure I can."

"Well, stall him at least. I've got Dad's car. I'll be at your place in forty minutes. Distract him, threaten him, insist on hearing Sorsakoski's full story, tie him up, anything. Just make sure nothing happens."

"That was fast," Alfred called to Kerttu from the open door. He'd heard the car pulling into Otto's yard. Without a word she sprinted up the steps and into the cabin, stopping only long enough to slip off her boots and lock eyes on the stranger in the corner. "Where's my husband?" she asked.

"Out back," Alfred replied. "Cooling off. He hasn't laid a finger on him. Yet."

"Thank God," she said, moving closer to examine Sorsakoski. He was lying in the corner, knees pulled up into his chest and hands covering his face. "Have you . . . ? Is he . . . ?"

Alfred shook his head. They moved to the far corner of the room. "I told you. None of us have touched him."

"Does he talk?"

"Took some doing but, yes. He's got a good line, actually. Rehearsed for sure, but some might believe it."

"Not Jari I'm guessing. What about you?" Alfred shrugged.

"What's he saying?"

"Kinda what you'd expect: Russian gun to his head, threat to his family for non-compliance, that sort of thing. He claims to be haunted by the memories and feigns remorse, but it could be no more than crocodile tears. Says he's been contemplating suicide."

"Why do I get the impression you believe him?"

"Because I've seen it; because there are parts of my war history that only my maker is ever going to hear; because he willingly fessed up to everything. Jeez, it just poured out of him like he'd been dying for someone to come along and listen."

"So, what's he up to in Hearst?"

"No good, probably, but from what I can piece together, nothing to do with any of us."

The door opened and Jari entered. Alfred and Otto stood back while Kerttu rocked him in her arms. The sobs could have come from either or both of them. No one spoke. As usual, Otto found refuge at the stove, adding a stick to the fire and getting the coffee going. They sat down at the table, Kerttu clinging to Jari's arm. Sorsakoski remained in the corner. He hadn't budged.

"Alright," Kerttu said, "where do we go from here?" All eyes went to Jari who stared into his mug, which, judging from her expression, she took for a good sign. "Why do you think he's here, Jari?"

"Ask him yourself," Jari snapped. "Hey! Sorakoski! You got ears. The lady has a question."

Otto took a mug of coffee over to Sorsakoski. He sat up, giving Kerttu a chance to see his face for the first time. Expecting a monster, like those on trial in Nuremberg, she instead saw nothing more than a frightened young man. Like most Finns, he was thin with high cheekbones, similar to many of their Finn neighbours in Hearst. Only the weariness in his eyes gave credence to a history of betrayal and disillusionment.

Sorsakoski took a sip of coffee and cleared his throat. "What I'm doing in Hearst has nothing to do with any of you." He spoke in such a low voice, the others had to strain to hear him. "Truth is, the Russians sent me to put Mr. Kekkonen 'out of business.' They told me that he was an anti-communist out to crush the truckers on behalf of the lumber bosses. One minute into his speech at the Finn Hall and I knew . . ."

"Baloney," Jari interjected, cutting him off.

Kerttu put a hand on Jari's shoulder. "Let's hear him out, honey," she said.

Sorsakoski wrapped his hands around his mug. "I knew instantly that the guy was no more a capitalist goon than anyone in this room. What I saw was a lapsed communist which, in Soviet eyes, is about as low as you can get. They hate apostates. I knew right away I'd been fed another lie. It's what saved him."

"Something wrong here," Jari said. "If you were so convinced last night that Kekkonen was on the side of labour, why show up for this afternoon's meeting?"

"Would you believe, to warn him?"

"This is bullshit. Surely you can see that, Kerttu? And it doesn't cancel what he did in Finland."

"You may be right, Jari," she replied, in a soft voice, "but at the moment were hearing him out. When he's done, we can decide whether he's lying or not."

She looked at Sorsakoski. "Pretty far-fetched, don't you think, that a minor labour dispute away up here would interest the Russians. Doesn't make sense."

"Oh, but it does," Sorsakoski said, his voice stronger now. "The Russian Comintern exists to spread communism. Hard sell here in Canada, but they were counting on the Red Finns to help them establish a base. Kekkonen's turned White, you see, and too popular for the Reds."

"So, you didn't fulfill orders," Kerttu asked. "Where does that leave you now?"

"Jesus Christ, Kerttu," Jari said. "Stop trying to make him out to be some kind of martyr. He's a hired killer and admits it. I say Alfred and I drag him out to Taj and put an end to this horseshit. He's a Soviet agent who sneaked into town to execute a socialist organizer. Who'd miss him? The RCMP would thank us." He turned to Alfred. "You with me?"

Alfred swirled the remaining coffee in his cup as he fished for an answer. Kerttu came to his rescue. "You're not going to do that, Jari, and you and I both know it. Because if you were, he'd be dead already. In Finland, back when you'd just come off the Front, yes. But that's not you anymore. Is it? Is it?" she repeated, this time louder.

Jari jumped to his feet and stepped away from the table. Alfred was about to speak, but Otto placed a hand on his arm and shook his head. Kerttu rose and hugged Jari from behind.

Jari dropped his chin to his chest. "I gave my oath to Mr. Vatanen. If I don't fulfil it, what does that make me?"

"A changed man, Jari. A better one. Healed. Look, what if I wrote to him? When you made your vow, he'd just lost his two boys. What father wouldn't want revenge? But so much has passed, I'm sure he'd release you." She rubbed the top of his shoulders. "Come back to the table, darling. Let's hear Sorsakoski out, then we can decide what's to be done."

"Better make this good, Sorsakoski," Jari snapped. "Your life depends on it."

Sorsakoski nodded. "If I tell you my story, will you grant me one favour?"

"Jesus Christ Almighty!" Jari snapped. "You're in no place to bargain."

"All I want is for you to call me Sami—Sami Aalto. That's who I am now. I buried Alvar Sorsakoski a long time ago. Please don't make me go back."

25

Suicide or Murder?

Hearst,
April 1950

When mealtime came, Otto and Kerttu saw to it that Sami was given a place at the table. They listened as he explained how his Finn communist parents had found refuge in Russia in 1921 after the Civil War, only to be treated like scum by the government. How he'd been conscripted in 1941, then given the option of infiltrating the Finn lines, or seeing his family harassed, possibly executed. This he explained had put him to working alongside Korpi, a man he both loathed and feared. He told how, after eluding the Helsinki police, the GRU recruited him for training as a Russian spy at Borobyevo, and then posted him to Canada. He pulled out his wallet, and showed them a picture of a beaming pregnant Carola with her arm around their young son. He finished by addressing Jari directly. "Thank you for ridding the world of Tuomas Korpi."

From the moment she had set foot in the door, it was clear that Kerttu had assumed control. When Sami finished his story, all eyes turned to her. "There are several roads we can take on this," she said. "One is to hand Sami over to the Finns. But that's a no-go, because it would dredge up Korpi's murder and Jari's role in it. In no time the Finns would be clamouring for extradition."

"Really?" Alfred broke in. "Even with his service in the Winter and Continuation wars?"

"'Fraid so," Otto replied, shaking his head. "All they'll see is a guy who went AWOL."

"Then there's the RCMP," Kerttu suggested.

"Please, not them," Sami pleaded. "The Russians will blame me for getting caught, and take it out on my family."

Kerttu nodded. "Course we could just let him go back to Toronto. That way we break no laws and draw no attention to either Jari, or Alfred. Plus, we come out of it with a clear conscience. Seems to me it's the only way."

She said this to everyone, but it was clearly directed at her husband. Jari knew it, but wasn't ready to give in. "Let him off?" he said. "Where's the justice in that? That son-of-a-bitch murdered half my platoon. And you," he said, turning to Alfred, "I expected a hell of a lot more backing from a comrade in arms."

"How about helping us out here," Kerttu said, turning to Sami. "Any ideas?"

"Shoot me. It's the only solution. Nobody need ever know who did it. Least of all the Russians."

"*Herran tähden*," Kerttu responded, "that's not going to happen. Is it, Jari?"

Sami leaned into the table. "My dead body would be proof to the GRU that, even if I was dumb enough to get myself killed, I hadn't turned my back on them. That way Carola and the kids would be safe."

The last log in the stove must have been spruce because suddenly it exploded in a series of loud pops, startling the lot of them. Kerttu rubbed her eyes. "I can't believe we're having this conversation," she said. "What a horrid thing to even imagine. There's got to be some way out of this situation."

"Doc Smith," Otto suggested from the stove. "We could lay it all out to him. Maybe he'd have a few ideas."

Alfred frowned. "Who the hell's Doc Smith?"

Otto returned to the table. "New minister at the United Church. Ex-army chaplain. Served with the troops all the way from Normandy to Berlin. If anyone understands this kind of thing, it's him. He's army, through and through. Still drives a Jeep."

It was early evening by the time they pulled into the driveway at the manse. The unflappable Mrs. Smith answered the door, and ushered the five of them into the living room. Tea was served. Smith turned out to be oversized and gruff, but also a good listener. "There's a solution out there somewhere," he boomed, when he'd heard them through, "even if I don't see it at the moment. One thing for sure, you're going to have to come to a consensus, because you'll be living with it for the rest of your lives. In the meantime, how about spending time at the church camp, north of town on Pivabiska Lake? It's secluded. You'd have it to yourselves. I'd come up every day, or so, to see what you need, and help in any way possible. That's the best I can do right now, other than think about it, and pray."

"Pardon me," Alfred asked, "but how do we know you won't go to the police?"

Smith shrugged. "You don't. You'll just have to take my word as a Christian."

Doc Smith had been correct about the need for consensus, but it kept eluding them. Sami never again mentioned his death as a solution, but to Alfred's eye it was there, written indelibly on his face. The rest of them could chase their tails all they liked, but only the Russian knew where the final solution ultimately lay.

It wasn't until Wednesday morning that Sami finally laid it all out. "This has gone on long enough," he announced. "Kekkonen is supposed to be dead by now, and I'm overdue in Toronto. My handlers will be getting suspicious. They probably have someone nosing around Hearst as we speak. And for sure the house in Toronto will be under surveillance. Face it, we've reached a dead end here. There's only one way out. I have no choice but to take it."

"What are you saying?" Alfred asked.

"You know darn well what I'm saying."

Alfred threw up his hands. "You can't just give up. At least try the RCMP. They could set you up with new identity and stuff, just like they did for that guy Gouzenko from the Russian Embassy."

Sami shook his head. "Gouzenko had something to trade. His information set the GRU's global spy network back a decade. No way is the RCMP going to let a hired Russian killer go because he's seen the light. And even if they did, what kind of a life would it be—constantly on the move, never knowing who's in the car behind, terrified for the kids. I couldn't do that to Carola."

"And ending your life is a solution?" Otto said.

Sami got up from the couch and stared out the window. "I need an accident. One that somebody else, other than any of you, discovers, and one that gets my dead face in the papers."

"This is pathetic." Otto responded. "Young guy with a family wants to kill himself, and we're to help him? Count me out." He got to his feet and headed for the deck. Alfred followed.

Sami turned from the window. "Guess that leaves you and me, Jari. Few days ago, you were all for killing me on the spot."

"If you'd hung around the Finn Hall after Kekkonen's speech, you'd be cold in your grave right now."

"It's not too late. You promised Mr. Vatanen. An honourable man doesn't walk away from an oath. Now's your chance. You wouldn't have to pull a trigger, or anything like that. All you have to do is help me set the scene, and get things in motion. You walk away with a clear conscience, while saving my family and honouring your oath at the same time."

"Everything's changed, Sami. In war it would be easy. Everyone on the other side is a bad guy. That's how it was on the Karelian Front, and that's how I felt when I laid eyes on you last Saturday. It all came rushing back, making you the worst piece of shit this side of Helsinki. Now you're just another poor bastard caught in circumstances beyond his control. That was my story back in '44. I had a Kerttu in my corner. You've got a Carola. Contact her for God's sake. Give her a chance to help you work something out."

"You're not going to help me, are you? In the end, you're just as gutless as the others."

"I see the trap you're in, Sami, but no way am I doing what you're asking. Call it selfish, but I've clawed myself out of a black hole and have no intention of falling back in." He headed out to the deck to join the others.

"Don't think of it that way," Sami said to his back. "Think of it as clearing up loose ends."

Jari joined the others at the railing. Noting his state of mind, Alfred and Otto gave him a minute to collect his thoughts. The day was turning out to be unseasonably warm. Signs of rebirth were everywhere, from the budding trees to the cedar waxwings flitting about. Out on the lake, a male goldeneye duck was struggling to keep competitors away from his harem. It was a day to savour, because in two weeks the black flies and mosquitos would have everyone, and everything, seeking cover—moose to the windy clearings, people indoors.

The noise of a car engine shattered the idyll. It grew louder. "Sounds like the Jeep," Otto said, "and coming fast."

Alfred looked at his watch. "Doc Smith making up for lost time, I guess. He's late today."

Suddenly, they realized that more than one vehicle was driving in. Doc Smith was the first to pop out of the trees. He goosed the engine to gain some ground, then came to a halt in a cloud of dust.

"Sorry, sorry," he apologized, sprinting up the steps to the deck. "I had a funeral this morning, and couldn't get here to warn you about the Grade VIII school picnic. It's an annual event catered by the church ladies. There's no fixed date, just the first good day before the bugs arrive. They try to make it a Wednesday, when the stores are closed for the afternoon so families can join in."

There was no time to hide, but to Jari's relief, the cavalcade of packed sedans and two trucks did not contain one police car. In an instant, screaming kids were piling off the back of the trucks and running in all directions. The ladies began gathering up the food as they glanced suspiciously at the sight of strangers fleeing into the church cottage.

Once inside, Doc Smith took charge. "Put on something decent," he ordered. "I'll go out and get the ball game going."

"Put on what?" Jari asked. "All we've got are these old grubs and the suits we had on for last Sunday's meeting at the Orange Hall. Either way, we're going to stick out like wolves amongst the lambs."

Smith hesitated. "Go with the ties and jackets," he advised.

"We gotta get away from here," Jari said.

Smith shook his head. "Too late. Best you mingle."

"This is bad," Jari said, "Otto and I are locals, but Sami and Alfred . . . there will be questions."

I'll pass you off as friends from Toronto," Smith said. "Now quick, get changed."

"Mingle?" Jari said. "I'm crappy at that even when things are going good."

"Do your best," Smith replied.

The stress took its tole. Several hours had Jari and the others exhausted. Clearly, the adults were dismayed to discover four non-parishoners, two of them complete strangers, using their church camp. In spite of the 'mingle' suggestion, the four suits had stuck close together. There had been a few questions, the odd raised eyebrow, and the occasional overheard comment about DPs taking over, but Doc Smith's presence managed to keep curiosity to a minimum. In the main, with boating, a ball game, tons of food, and Smith's blessing of the soon-to-graduate grade-eighters, there was enough to divert attention.

At one point during the ball game, Alfred sidled up to Jari and whispered, "Have you been watching Sami?"

Jari nodded. "Scary. Looks like he could break down any second."

"The kids are getting to him."

"How come? He's a father. Why would a little noise affect him like this?"

"It's not the noise that's getting to him, Jari, it's the joy in it. If he goes through with his plan, he'll never get to see his kids romping around like this."

"Then let's get him out of here and fast," Jari said, signalling to Doc Smith.

"What's up?" Smith asked.

Jari pulled him aside. "We've got to get Sami away from here. Being around happy kids is too much. He's going downhill, fast. State he's in, who knows what he might do, or say."

"I've been watching," Smith replied.

"Something else is bothering me, too, Doc," Jari said. "People have been taking photographs. Not good. In our suits we'll stick out like crazy. Especially, that group shot taken down at the water with the church cabin and the bush in the background."

Smith shrugged. "I can't confiscate their film if that's what you're suggesting."

"I know. Too late. We just need to get away."

Smith nodded. "I'll announce it's time for a last swim. What about Sami?"

"We're taking him to a Finn rooming house. Probably Koski's. Olga'll keep him fed and out of sight."

That night, lying in bed, Jari shared the day's events with Kerttu. "The more the kids ran about and shrieked," he said, "the more depressed Sami became. In the end he was a total wreck."

She shook her head. "Poor man. Wondering if he'd ever see his own again. What about you? You've never been around kids much. They bother you?"

"Truth be told, had me kinda wishing I had one or two of my own out there, running with the horde."

She smiled and pressed in closer. "And Alfred?"

"Fine, mostly. The picture taking got to him, though. Last thing he wanted was people staring at his face and wondering who he was, and what a strange delivery van might be up to at a church camp north of Hearst."

"Goes for you, too, Jari. You and Alfred may have settled in pretty good, but you're still illegals. You don't want your face flashed about in photographs for some government official to take notice of."

Jari reached over and switched off the bedside light. He lay on his back with his hands behind his head, and his eyes wide open. Beside him, Kerttu relaxed as she began to drift off. "Did I tell you Sami took off on us earlier in the week?" he asked.

She jerked awake. "What? No."

"Tuesday morning I got up, and he was gone. Had us worried as hell. Didn't come back until mid-afternoon."

"What was he up to?"

"Something about making arrangements to sell his car. We didn't press him on it. Pretty vague."

"Without the car, how will he get back to Toronto?"

"That's the worrying part."

"Holy mackerel! He wouldn't . . . oh, no."

"He might. That's why he needs watching. I'll go over to Olga's first thing in the morning."

"Funny how things turn out," she said. "A week ago we hated the guy, now we're conniving to keep him alive. Putting him up at Olga's was a good idea. Aino will keep an eye on him."

"Odd, though, how Sami jumped at the idea of the rooming house. Otto wanted him to go to his place, but he turned him down. Then, when we dropped him off at Koski's, he gave us a knapsack to keep for him, shook hands, and went inside."

"Where's the knapsack now?"

"Otto took it home with him."

"Any idea what's in it?"

"None whatsoever. He just said he felt safer with one of us holding onto it; rooming house you know."

"Must be important," Kerttu said.

It was getting on seven o'clock when Jari awoke to footsteps in the driveway. Whoever it was, was wasting no time. Jari had barely reached the back door when the pounding started. He opened it to discover Aino, short of breath. "Your friend," he said between pants, "you said to keep an eye on him. He's gone. I got up to take a pee and his door was wide open, and his bed untouched."

"Did he take the car?"

Aino shook his head. "Still locked in the garage."

"Good, he won't have gone far. I'll dress. You and I can look for him with the truck." When he closed the door Kerttu was standing behind him. "You heard?" he asked. She nodded. He brushed by her, and was pulling on his pants when there was a second knock.

It was Constable Costello. "Come," was all he said, summoning Jari with his finger.

Half-way to the police car, Jari stopped. "Forgot my rain jacket," he said. "Be right with you." Back in the house he whispered to Kerttu. "Go with Aino to Sami's room. Search for stuff that may be incriminating to any of us. And make sure nobody sees you."

In the car, Jari's first thoughts were on Sami. But he hadn't forgotten the danger he and Alfred could be in, too. Other than Alfred and Otto, had anyone else heard him threaten to kill Sami? And all those snapshots taken at the school picnic? Horrible possibilities swirled in his head, each one worse than the last. And if it got out, the town would be awash in speculation. He wished Kerttu was with him. She was so much better at answering questions.

"Where we going?" Jari asked, more calmly than he felt.

"This man Sami Aalto, what do you know about him?" Costello asked, ignoring Jari's question.

"Not much. Showed up at last week at the Finn Hall. That's about it. Why do you ask?"

"Then why were you and him at the church camp?"

"Jesus, Costello, small-town hospitality. He's a Finn from out of town. We hit it off. The guy likes to fish. That's all. What's he done, anyway? And why have you got me out in the pelting rain at this hour of the morning?"

"To identify a body."

It wasn't until after they had driven past the Catholic Church, and were approaching the wooden bridge, that Jari knew exactly what was coming. Sure enough, Costello pulled the car over and led Jari down the steep embankment to the river. Another constable stood by a body under a tarp.

"Recognize this man?" Costello said, pulling back the edge.

"We both know who it is," Jari replied, turning away from the bloated face and bulging eyes. "Sami Aalto."

Costello cocked his head as he gazed at the body. "The man is too well groomed for the usual deadbeats we find hanging from the bridge. Why do you think he'd do this? Or, did he have help?"

"What the hell are you getting at?"

"You tell me"

"Listen. I knew the guy briefly. He seemed kinda lonely, but who can tell what's in people's heads, eh? And if you're thinking I may have helped him over the edge, then think again. I was home in bed with Kerttu."

"Well, you can explain it all at the inquiry."

Jari felt the blood drain from his face. "What makes you think he had help?"

"Two things: first, his apparent healthy state, and second, the footprints under the bridge." He pointed. "I see three sets here, a bit of a crowd for a suicide. So already we have an Exhibit A and an Exhibit B."

Jari winced. Once a cop with promise, Costello had never had an opportunity to prove himself. At last, here was a case to bolster his reputation. "So, who do you figure the other prints belong to?"

"Besides you? That's easy, you're old-geezer friend, Otto Schneider. Apparently, he was at the church camp along with you and some other guy whom I've been unable to identify. I'm sure you'll fill me in on that score."

Not on your life, Jari thought, following Costello back up the embankment. "Where are you going?" he asked, when they were in the car.

"To notify the OPP."

Jari took a deep breath. "Is that really necessary? This is a town affair, and you're head cop. You got the authority here, solve it yourself."

"That's not how the system works, Hoivuniemi."

Jari bit his tongue. It was bad enough to have the OPP crawling all over this, but the instant they failed to come up with Sami's true identity the mounties would have to be brought in. The investigation was bound to go deep. He wanted Kerttu close by. "Take me home," he said.

"All in good time," Costello replied.

PART FIVE

Northern Ontario, 1955

26

Reconciliation

Sturgeon Falls,
June 1955

Finding the store proved to be the easy part. A quick drive down King Street and there it was, Higgins Men's and Ladies Wear, exactly as the friendly local had directed when they arrived in Sturgeon Falls. Kerttu entered first, spotted the Ladies' section, and headed for it. Jari strolled in several feet behind, playing the role of the reluctant husband coerced into joining his wife on a shopping expedition. He noted the distinctive clothing-store aroma, and wondered what caused it. Mothballs he thought.

A clerk approached. "May I help you?" she asked, quickly adding, "*puis-je vous aidez*?" in case the shopper turned out to be French.

"Just looking," Kerttu replied, approaching a rack of dresses and sliding hangers for closer inspection.

"Let me know if I can," the clerk said, returning to the counter.

Kerttu motioned Jari in closer. "Gotta be her," she said. "She's the right age; early thirties, I'd say." Jari nodded and stepped back. Kerttu lifted a dress from the rack, held it against her body, and summoned the clerk.

"Very nice," the clerk said. "That colour works well on you."

Kerttu looked at the price tag and raised her eyebrows. "Little more than my budget, but what the heck," she grinned. "Would you have this in a size fourteen?"

The clerk left and returned all smiles, holding the dress up as she escorted Kerttu to the fitting room area. "Visiting friends in Sturgeon?" she asked.

"Actually, we're looking for someone."

"Maybe I can help. Except for a few years in Toronto, I've lived here my whole life."

It was the cue Kerttu was hoping for. She switched to Finn. "We're trying to track down a Carola Aalto."

The clerk pivoted abruptly, turning her back. She placed the dress on the hook behind the door, and began smoothing out imaginary wrinkles with her hand. "No one in town by that name," she said.

"Strange that you speak Finn, but wouldn't know her."

"This is a mill town," she replied, all signs of friendliness evaporating. "People come and go. I was away for several years."

Kerttu placed a hand on the woman's shoulder and gently turned her around. "My husband I were friends with Sami, and there are things you have a right to know. Believe me, Carola, we're not with the government—any government. Far from it."

Carola backed off a foot, glaring at Kerttu. "What makes you think I'd want to talk about Sami with anyone, let alone two complete strangers? My husband killed himself, leaving me pregnant with our second child and no explanation whatsoever. End of story. That was five years ago, and now you come waltzing in here wanting to stir up things that are none of your business."

"Can't begin to imagine what you've gone through," Kerttu answered, sympathetically.

"I returned to Sturgeon and took back my maiden name. But people don't forget, do they? I'm still the woman whose husband up and did himself in. My oldest boy has just started school. It won't be long before the kids will be asking what happened to his father. But they'll know something's amiss because they'll have picked it up at home."

"I'm sorry, Carola, but we have information we think may be vital. Is there somewhere we can talk? Even, if only for a few minutes? Please, it's important to us, especially to my husband," she said, motioning to Jari.

Carola stared at the floor, then at her watch. "Mrs. Higgins takes over in half an hour—at three o'clock. I'll meet you at the Riviera Restaurant. It's down the street. Pick a back booth. But if there's anyone nearby, I won't be joining you."

Kerttu reached around behind Carola, and lifted the dress off the hook. "I'll take it," she said.

"You haven't tried it on."

"I sew. I'll make it fit. And you're right, the colours do suit me."

At ten past three, the front door of the Riviera opened, and a wedge of strong afternoon sunlight penetrated the length of the restaurant. Kerttu looked up to see Carola standing inside the door, waiting for her eyes to adjust. After a minute she checked the room for locals, then headed to the back booth.

Jari rose to greet her, and held out his hand. She hesitated before shaking it, while Kerttu introduced her husband and herself. To Jari's surprise her grip was firm, in stark contrast to the rest of her. Her bright blue eyes, he thought, must once have been a joy to behold, but the sparkle appeared to have disappeared.

She dropped his hand, and sat down next to Kerttu. "I haven't got much time," she said, waiving away the waitress. "Kids, you know."

Jari got right to it. "There are things about Sami that I've been hanging onto. Kinda like loose ends."

"Loose ends? What the hell! It's been five years." She swung her knees out from under the table, ready to bolt.

Kerttu placed a hand on Carola's arm. "That was clumsy of my husband. Please don't go. Give us a few minutes. After that we'll never trouble you again." Carola sat at the edge of the bench, half in, half out, hesitating. Behind them came the faint hum of the wall fan, as it laboured to clear the room of a thin haze of smoke and the smell of frying onions.

"I'll get to the point," Jari began. "What did the police tell you about how Sami died?"

"Not much," she said, after a long hesitation. "Several days after his death, two policemen showed up on my doorstep in Toronto to tell me he'd committed suicide, up in a small town I'd hardly ever heard of, and asking what I wanted to do with the body. When I told them it couldn't possibly be my Sami, they suggested I go to Hearst to see for myself."

"But you didn't go?"

She shook her head. "I was pregnant, and too far along to travel."

"Did they ask any questions about Sami?"

"Oh, yeah. Wanted to know about his state of mind, our marriage, what kind of father he was, that sort of thing. They also had me try to identify people from some snapshots."

Jari tensed. "Was I in any of them?"

Carola looked at him quizzically. "I don't know. It was five years ago, and I was in no condition to take anything in." She sat back. "I think you better tell me what gives you the right to be asking me questions about Sami. What were you to him?"

"We're not the enemy," Kerttu said, reassuringly.

"Prove it."

Kerttu nodded and continued. "We will, Carola. Promise. A couple more questions, so we know we're on the right track, then we'll get to the point." She cleared her throat. "Did they hand anything over? A note, say?"

"Wouldn't that have been nice. All I got was his body, and a battered suitcase with some personal effects."

"Did that include his pearl-handled shaving brush, his puukko, and the picture of you and your son?" Jari asked.

She looked at him, hard. "How do you know about those things?"

"Because I lived with him the days leading up to his . . . passing."

Carola stiffened. "Enough questions. Why are you here?"

"Because he left you a letter," Jari said, "and we have it." Kerttu reached into her purse and pulled out a large, creased, manilla envelope, which she handed to Carola.

Carola turned it over several times, unsure what to do with it. "What's in it?" she asked.

"No idea," Kerttu responded, "it's addressed to you. We only got it a week ago."

"How's that possible? It's been five years."

"There were three of us with him the week before he died," Jari said. "Sami passed the envelope to an older guy named Otto, who was supposed to give it to me."

"And it took him five years to hand it over?"

"I've been . . . away," Jari said. "Seems that after talking to you, the police got it in their heads that it mightn't be suicide after all, and that I may have had something to do with his death. They couldn't find proof, but by then they'd discovered that I was an illegal alien and had me deported to Finland. Took me all this time to get back to Canada, and Kerttu. Got home last month."

"Did you . . . kill him?"

"No. But we did know who may have wanted him dead, and tried to prevent it."

Carola placed the envelope on the table and closed her eyes. "I'm so confused," she said, fighting back tears. "Why was Sami so troubled he'd want to kill himself? We were happy. He was a good husband and father. Believe me, I've searched my mind for warning signs I might have missed, but could never find anything."

"We'll take you through what we know," Kerttu said, "but first, how about opening the envelope?"

Two elderly women in hats came in, and sat at the booth opposite. They nodded to Carola and got a nod in return. Carola switched to Finn. "Let's continue this at my place. I live with my dad on Parker Street, a few blocks over. Big veranda. I'll walk. You follow behind. Give me a few minutes to fill dad in. And come to the back door."

"How's half an hour sound?" Kerttu asked.

Carola answered the door, then introduced her father and the two boys. Mr. Waltari stood back, polite, but far from welcoming. After the introductions he gathered the boys, and announced they were going for a walk. Jari hoped it would be a long one.

Seated on the couch, and taking in the living room, Jari felt instantly at home. For an instant, he was back in Finland. From the furniture down to the decorations it was all here—hardwood floor, braided rugs, rocking chair, photograph of Olavinlinna Castle at Savonlinna. Kerttu sat beside him, with Carola in a maroon easy chair, facing them. The hint of cardamon wafting in from the kitchen had Jari wondering if coffee bread might be coming. He hoped so, but realized it would depend on the contents of Sami's letter.

"Love your home," Jari said. "Reminds me of my Aunt Toini and

Uncle Pentti's place in Kemi."

Carola, eyes red and swollen, opened the envelope and extracted the letter. Jari and Kerttu waited in silence as she read. Going through it a second time, she began to cry. When she finished, she folded the letter and looked up. "This is Sami's letter to me," she stressed. "I've read his version of what happened those last few days. Now I would like to hear yours."

"It might be easier if we knew what was in his letter," Jari said.

Carola shook her head. "No, you first. I don't want to give you a chance to doctor your story." She caught Kerttu's furtive glance at Jari. "Do I take it there's more? Possibly stuff you hadn't planned on telling me?"

Jari was about to deny they'd ever do this, when Kerttu stepped in.

"You're right. My husband should tell you everything. Obviously, you're strong enough to handle the truth."

"Jesu Marie!" Carola responded. "Surely, you didn't think I'd rather spend the rest of my life guessing?"

Jari nodded. "Good. No half truths, and no holding back. Let's start with this: I hated Sami from the first day we met."

"And would that have been back in Oregon?"

"Carola," Jari said, leaning forward, "Sami never set foot in Oregon. I'm betting he would have had trouble placing it on a map. The man you knew as Sami Aalto was really Alvar Sorsakoski, born and raised in Russian Karelia, not in the States. He was a corporal in the Red Army. We fought on opposite sides." He stopped to let this sink in. "I take it Sami didn't mention any of this in his note, did he?"

"If you were on opposite sides, how could you have possibly met? She asked, through clenched teeth."

Jari took a deep breath and began recounting how Alvar Sorsakoski had infiltrated the lines in Finn-army uniform, how he had helped organize the ambush and murder of Jari's comrades, and how he, Jari, had sworn to avenge their deaths. When he got to the part about killing Korpi in Helsinki, he could feel Kerttu's hand squeezing his in warning, but he plowed on. Carola deserved to know the whole story. He then explained why Sami had wound up in Hearst, the circumstances that brought them together again, and how he would have killed him on the spot if not for Kerttu.

"How could I have been taken in by such a deceitful man?" she sobbed. "If this is true, I'd want to kill him myself."

Jari shook his head. "But you'd have been wrong, Carola. Just like I was. When Kerttu, Alfred, and Otto convinced me not to kill him, and we talked, I began to see things through his eyes. The guy was under unimaginable pressure from the Russians. In similar circumstances, I'm sure all of us would have done exactly the same thing. He had no choice."

"He didn't do these terrible things voluntarily, then?"

"Hell, no. At first it was the army who threatened to wipe out his whole family if he refused to follow orders. Then they kept thrusting more and more jobs on him, each more nauseating than the last. Finally, he came to the notice of the GRU, whose main intention was to spread communism worldwide. They're the ones who sent him to Canada."

"Are you telling me . . . ?"

"Yes, he was a Russian agent—what they call a 'sleeper.' But it took them so long to make contact, he honestly believed they had forgotten him. Turns out they hadn't. Hearst was his first active assignment in Canada. He balked, but with threats now directed at you and the children, had no choice but to comply. When we met him, he was struggling for a solution that would keep you safe, and the man he was sent to assassinate alive. The last thing on his mind was his own safety"

Carola dropped her head into her hands and cried openly. Jari and Kerttu looked away. Then, as quickly as the tears had started, they stopped, as if, after five years, the well had gone dry. Handkerchief in hand, she dabbed at her eyes and cleared her throat. "Those last days with him," she said, "tell me about them."

"For five days, Otto, Alfred, me, and the church minister kept throwing around ideas. But Sami kiboshed all of them, because they endangered you. Then, on the fifth day, the police came to our place to tell us he'd been found hanging from the bridge."

"Suicide?"

"I don't know, Carola. Honest. That's what the police finally concluded, but there were three sets of footprints in the mud, Sami's and two others. Tell me, in his letter, are there any hints about taking his own life?"

She shook her head. "Only that if something should happen to him, I was to get in touch with Otto Schneider. Why not you?"

"That son-of-a-gun," Jari said. "To save me. He knew that I'd killed Korpi, and was an illegal alien. It's obvious now that he didn't want to leave any trails that could lead the police to me."

She smiled for the first time since their initial meeting in the store. "That was the Sami I knew, alright. In the end he was trying to save you, too."

"Kinda," Kerttu said. "But Jari still had to return to Finland, do time for desertion, and wait for proper papers. Fortunately, they never associated him with the Korpi . . . thing. Took five years. Now he's here legally, under his own name."

"All that time wasted," Carola said, "must have been difficult."

Jari nodded. "Only been back a month, so I'm still adjusting. Otto died while I was gone, and left me a box of papers. That's where I found Sami's letter, addressed to you."

Carola sank back in her chair. "Thank you," she said. "These are the happiest thoughts I've had of him since he died. I feel guilty now for ever doubting him."

Jari leaned forward. "Something else. Otto's box also contained a letter for me. Does he mention anything about money in yours?" She shook her head. "Well, he does in mine. It appears he opened a bank account in your name."

"Bank account. Where? Hearst?"

"Not sure, but I suspect Kapuskasing."

"I don't get it," she responded. "His pay cheque from Tippet Richardson barely covered food and rent."

"Turns out that all the time he was in Canada, the GRU was paying him a monthly salary and depositing it in his name with the Imperial Bank. He never touched it, hoping that if he didn't, they'd forget about him. Then there was that brand new Ford he drove up to Hearst."

"Car?"

"Yeah. They gave it to him just before he left. Registered it in his name, too. Which is why he was able to sell it just before he died. Whatever is in the account probably includes what he got for the car, plus six years salary, not to mention whatever interest may have accumulated since 1944. It won't be a fortune, but whatever is there is rightfully yours."

Carola's eyes widened. "Holy moley. Enough for a new start, maybe. I love my dad, but living under his roof and being dependent on him . . . you know, it's hard. How would I go about getting hold of this money?"

"You'd have to move carefully," Jari warned, not wanting to dampen her hopes. "It's possible the GRU has been keeping an eye on the account."

"How can they do that if it's in a Canadian bank?"

"If they can infiltrate half the governments in the western world, keeping tabs on an account in a bank shouldn't be too hard."

She sat back in the chair and sighed. "Not worth it then, is it? Touching the money might have them coming for me, and the kids."

"It's your call, Carola," Jari said, "but in your shoes, I wouldn't walk away too fast. There's got to be some way of accessing it, safely."

"You got something in mind?'

He looked to Kerttu. "Not really, but we're happy to work on it with you, if you're willing to take the risk. What do you think?"

Carola's eyes went to the picture of the fortress at Savonlinna on the wall. "*Isä* would be furious. But I have to think of the boys."

"Hold on," Kerttu interrupted, "aren't you two getting ahead of yourselves? You're guessing that there may be a small fortune in an account somewhere. Pretty vague. And Sami gives no specifics in your letter either, Carola?"

"Just that he'd put some money in safe keeping, but no mention of where." She scanned the letter again, and shook her head. "It looks like he wrote this in a hurry."

Kerttu turned to Jari. "Where did you get the idea he might have redeposited it in the Imperial Bank in Kapuskasing?"

"We were at the church camp from Sunday to Wednesday. On the Tuesday morning, we woke up to find Sami gone. It was mid-afternoon before he returned. Then, when Doc Smith came around, he'd claimed he'd seen Sami's car going to beat fifty, and coming into town from the east. When we pressed Sami on it, he admitted sneaking off to Kapuskasing to clear up some business. Well, there's only one bank in Kap, and it's an Imperial. Makes sense that's what he could have been up to."

Kerttu frowned. "He could have done it in any number of towns on the way up from Toronto."

"Possibly, but Kap makes sense. I'm thinking Sami decided that the best way to save you from harm, Carola, was to have the Russians kill him, so he needed something to lure them to Hearst. What better than to drain the account the GRU had set up for him. That was sure to have them on him in a flash."

"And the car?" Carola asked. "You say you were with him for most of those last days. How could he ever have arranged to sell it without you knowing?"

"Maybe with someone in the rooming house, that last night. I know there were two Finn brothers there, and both flush—steady work, no women, nothing to spend their money on. And right after the war, cars were hard to get." He looked from Carola to Kerttu. "It's a stretch, but he could have taken cash from the sale and mailed it to Kap."

Carola left the room to make coffee. She returned with cups, hard-rock sugar, and coffee bread. "*Isä* will be back in a few minutes with the kids," she said, "so I've had to come to a decision fast." She took a deep breath and turned to Kerttu. "You probably think it's a wild goose chase, and possibly dangerous, too, but it's my boys' future, so I'm willing to risk it."

"We're going up that way tomorrow," Jari said. "If you like, you can come with us to Kap and take the train back."

"You sure?"

"Positive. We'll book in at the hotel up on the highway, and get an early start in the morning. Right Kerttu?"

"Better still," Carola said, "stay here at our place. That way you can fill *Isä* in on the possibility of a bank account. But no more. I don't want him knowing about Sami's past. I'll leave the kids with him for a few days."

"And if there's nothing there," Kerttu asked. "What then?"

"Then it's over, and I continue living as before. However, money or not, I walk in peace with Sami, knowing he wasn't a monster, and that it wasn't me who pushed him to suicide. Thank you for that. Someday I'll tell the boys about their dad. They'll need to know. What they do with the information will be up to them. With luck, that's as far as it will ever go."

The drizzling rain since New Liskeard suited Jari to a T. By eliminating dust on the gravel highway, it made for a more relaxing drive. The downpour that came after Cochrane was another matter. Little rivulets formed on the road, coalescing into larger streams which eroded the gravel surface down to washboard and potholes. What had been smooth motoring, became a mix of speed ups, slow downs, and swerves. None of this seemed to phase Kerttu and Carola, who chattered on like two long-lost pals. Jari, never one for small talk, was content with contributing the occasional nod and "yup." He focused on the road. The highway had turned into a soupy mush that swished up from the wheels in a steady hiss. There was little traffic, but when they did meet another vehicle, he slowed and held his breath in anticipation of the coming wash. These were windshield-destroying conditions, and regardless of how much he slowed down, or hugged the shoulder, rocks were sure to fly. They'd borrowed his father-in-law's prized Packard, and it would be a disaster to return it pockmarked with stone bites, or worse, a cracked windshield.

With relief, they finally pulled onto Kapuskasing's paved streets. "Company town," Kerttu sniffed. "Most towns up here don't have a big international corporation to pay for luxuries like pavement. The rest of us have to settle for gravel and dust."

"And mud," Jari added. "Kinda makes you feel guilty dripping all this muck onto Kap's clean streets."

Carola didn't respond. From Smooth Rock Falls on she had hardly uttered a word.

Jari turned off the highway onto Mcpherson Avenue. Several blocks ahead was the circle, the town's main business area and the location of the Imperial Bank of Canada. He angle-parked the car a few buildings away from the bank, placed his arm on top of the front seat, and turned to Carola. "Do it just as we rehearsed," he said. "Ask to speak to the manager. Show him your identification and tell him you have reason to believe your late husband opened an account at this branch in the late 1940s. Kerttu will go with you. Best to keep me out of it."

Carola didn't budge. "Maybe, it would have been better to go through this at the Imperial in North Bay," she said. "They could have inquired for me."

"We went over that, Carola, but we decided that would create paperwork at head office, and draw more eyes to the account. Going in at the branch in question keeps it local. Less risk that way."

"What if the Russians have prying eyes here in Kapuskasing?"

Jari raised his eyebrows. "A possibility, I guess, but slim. If this were Toronto, or even North Bay, maybe, but not here, in the middle of nowhere."

With Kerttu at her side, Carola approached the teller's cage, and was directed to the accountant's office, a Mr. E.A. Mills. "How can I be of help," he asked pleasantly, in a slight Irish accent. He listened attentively, and left with Carola's identification in hand. Two minutes later he was back. "Sorry," he said, with a frown, "but we have no record of an account in the name of Carola Aalto."

"Might he have put it in his own name?" Carola asked.

He shook his head. "That occurred to me, but we have no Aaltos registered here. Could your late husband have opened it at some other branch? I could ask head office in Toronto to do a search if you like?"

"No! That won't be necessary," she responded, and quickly rose and left.

The sudden departure seemed to surprise Mr. Mills. Kerttu leaned forward and spoke, as if in defence. "Truth is, her husband might not have been as thoughtful a person as we've been led to believe. The war, you know. Carola was left alone with two small children, and little income."

"Sorry to hear that," Mr. Mills replied, sympathetically. "She seems like a nice young lady."

"She is, and strong, too."

To Kerttu's surprise, upon returning to the car, Carola was not devastated. "Something that Mr. Mills said," she was telling Jari, "got me thinking. Sami was a socialist, and even if he couldn't vote, he thought the world of the CCF Party. One time, when we were visiting Sturgeon Falls, he cut an article out of the *North Bay Nugget*. It was about a new kind of bank called Caisse Populaire, which was opening branches in Northern Ontario. He liked the idea that it was a place for the little guy to deposit his hard-earned money, without worrying about the big banks making large profits on it."

Jari and Kerttu looked puzzled. "When Mr. Mills suggested that Sami might have opened an account elsewhere," Carola continued, "that's what jumped into my head."

Without a further word, Kerttu was out the door and back into the bank. Glancing about she saw Mr. Mills talking to one of the tellers. "Mr. Mills," she interrupted, "is there a Caisse Populaire in Kapuskasing?"

"There is," he smiled, "and it's giving us a bit of a run for our money, pardon the pun." He walked her to the door and pointed her in the right direction.

Jari sat in the car and waited, fingers crossed. The instant Kerttu and Carola walked out the front door, he had his answer. Still, when they got into the car, he couldn't resist asking. "Any luck?"

All tears and smiles, Carola held up a manilla envelope and wagged it at him.

"You took it in cash?" he said.

"No paper trail," she answered. "Money extracted. Account closed. End of story." She looked from Jari to Kerttu. "There's more money here than I ever dreamed of. The boys will have a life." Arms open, she leaned over the front seat and hugged them both.

To Jari's surprise he found himself tearing up. He thought about how close he'd come to killing Sami. A mixture of emotions flooded through him, including one he had never felt before. He couldn't quite put his finger on it, but he wondered if it was what Doc Smith might have called fulfillment. In a strange way he'd given life, rather than taking it. But there was guilt, too. Was it possible that Tuomas Korpi had also been propelled by the same forces and threats as Sami? He'd never know Korpi's story. Just like he'd never know the stories of those mysterious bush-recluses, trappers and prospectors, who came into his in-law's grocery store. For now, the squeals of delight from the girls were enough to buoy his spirits. They were getting on famously. Here was a friendship that would last. Jari and Kerttu would see her children, Sami's children, grow, maybe become Uncle Jari and Aunt Kertu. In time, Carola would have to tell them about Sami. He prayed they would come to see their father as a hero, a man who had sacrificed dignity and life for those dear to him.

"I'd like to do something for you two," Carola said, interrupting Jari's thoughts.

"Well," Kerttu replied, "there's the Kapuskasing Inn. Queen Elizabeth stayed there with her husband, Prince Phillip, when she visited Canada as princess. They say the chef there is fantastic. How about treating us to a steak dinner?"

"You're on. What's more, I'm booking you into the royal suite."

"No way," Kerttu protested. "Waste of money. We'll eat and drive on. Hearst is only an hour and a half away. You can stay with us. Tomorrow, we'll visit my parents. They'll be delighted to see me bringing home a *Suomalainen. Äiti* will stuff you with coffee bread. And *Isä*, well you'll love him; he's the spitting image of your father."

Jari slapped his forehead with his hand. "Oh, my God, the car! *Isä*. He'll be furious. I'll have to get it washed before he lays eyes on it."

"That," Carola said, "is something I definitely will pay for."

PART SIX

Hearst,
Northern Ontario,
2022

27

Hearst, 2022

Foyer des Pionniers,
Hearst, Ontario,
March 2022

We'd been going at it all day. Sonny, big eyed and full of questions, me talking a mile a minute, with the Hoivuniemi-Aalto-Reiger-Schneider saga pouring out. I could hardly remember leaving his room for lunch, let alone how we wound up on a couch in the retirement home's pub, waiting for the five o'clock Happy Hour to get started. The photograph that had triggered the telling of the story, the one taken at the picnic on the lake seventy years earlier, now sat on the coffee table staring up at us. Eight hours earlier he'd forced the picture on me, and when I'd reluctantly agreed to look at it my head had exploded with memories coming at me like rush-hour traffic on the 401. Naturally, having witnessed my reaction to the photograph, Sonny would settle for nothing less than a full explanation. Out of politeness I'd agreed, intending to touch on a few highlights, and let it go at that. But, once rolling, I couldn't stop. The story had first grabbed my attention as a kid, and had such a hold on me that I kept digging at periodically over the decades. As a journalist, I should have been able to put it to bed in short order, but with so many jagged edges, cul-de-sacs and phony leads, I could never quite wrestle it to the ground; until today, when Sonny's photograph had decades of missing pieces falling into place. Surprising was Sonny's rapt attention to the saga, and how good it felt to share what had lain in the back of my head for so many years.

The bar had just opened and around us the regulars were lining up for their usual libation. "Holy Toledo, R.J.," Sonny said, "this is dynamite. Who knows this story, anyway?"

"My wife got snatches here and there, but would you believe you're the first to get the entire package?"

"Geez, I'm honoured. But how come you never wrote it up? And you a reporter for the *Timmins Press* for all those years. Crikey, with so many Finns around these parts, the paper sure as hell would have run it."

"Always meant to, but until today could never quite get it into focus. Even if I had though, I probably wouldn't have. Got too close to the characters. You don't air family laundry in public. People stood to get hurt."

"Why not do it now? It's not too late. Be better time spent than rambling around in that moose yard up the river you're always going on about. And who's left to get hurt, anyway? They've all gotta be dead by now."

I shook my head. "Not Sami and Carola's boys. The oldest has enough on his plate without me adding to the load. He didn't turn out too good. During the Cold War, it couldn't have been easy knowing that your father had been a Russian spy who ended up dangling from a rope. The boy wound up living on the streets in Toronto. Other lad did better, though—made it all the way to Deputy Mayor of North Bay."

"What about the Hoivuniemis and the Reigers?" Sonny asked.

"The Hoivuniemis had no children. As for Alfred and Nicole, their kids all moved away from Kirkland Lake, except for one who became a miner. With no baker to carry on the family business, they sold out to Canada Bread and moved to Kitchener."

"And Jari and Alfred? What became of them?"

"Both died early."

"The girls remarry?"

"Nope, but Kerttu and Carola kept in close touch. They finished their days living together at that Finlandia Village retirement complex, in Sudbury. Finland heaven, that place."

For a few minutes we didn't talk. The silence was a welcomed respite after the marathon story telling. "R.J.," Sonny said at last, "you can't just let this story die. For God sakes, put it to paper. People are bound to get a lot out of it. There's a lesson here."

I looked at him closely. Here was a side of Sonny I'd never seen before, a serious side. It occurred to me that maybe we could be good friends after all. "What, lesson's that?" I asked.

Sonny rubbed his hands and looked off. "You know me," he said, "I'm not good at this analysis kinda stuff, but a couple of things come to mind. For starters, 'DPs' and bush hermits. Your story kinda gives them context. Gotta admit, I'll probably be looking at them through new eyes. Could be, they aren't all rubbydubs after all. That good enough?"

"Just might be, my friend," I replied, "just might be."

Glossary of Finnish and German Words and Idioms

Finnish

Äiti — Mother
Ei, ei, älä tapa häntä, älä tapa häntä — No, no, no killing, no killing
Herran tähden! — Oh my God!
Haista paska! — Shove it!
Hei kultaseni — Hey sweetheart
Hyvänen aika! — Oh my goodness!
Iltamat — Soiree, party
Isä — Father
Isoisä — Grandfather
Jumalauta! — Oh, God!, Holy shit!
Lohikeitto — Salmon Soup
Mummo — Grandmother
Perkele! — Vile swearword meaning, Shit, fuck, damn it!
Puukko — Small general purpose belt knife with a curved cutting edge
Susi — Wolf
Ymmärsi — Understood, as in, understood?

German

Bröetchen — Bread bun
Eier — Eggs
Emmentaler — A type of German cheese
Fick dich! — Fuck you!
Gott im himmel — God in heaven
Kein problem — No problem
Lech mich im Arsch! — Kiss my ass
Scheisse! — Shit!
Schwarzwälder schinken — Blackforest ham
Wie geht? — How are you?
Wei ghet es dir? — How is it going?

About the Author

Terrence Rundle West is a former teacher and school administrator. Born in Hearst, Northern Ontario, he studied at Carleton University, Ottawa, and at the University of British Columbia in Vancouver. He lives with his wife, Peggy, in Old Ottawa East, close to the Rideau River and Rideau Canal.

West is the author of four historical novels and a book of short stories. Other writings include op-ed pieces in major newspapers: the *Toronto Star, Winnipeg Free Press, Edmonton Journal,* and the *Ottawa Citizen.*

West is a past winner of the Northern 'Lit' Award.

For further information go to: www.terrencerundlewest.com. Comments and queries are handled at: pivpub@gmail.com.